August Faul

A Short Treatise on Leveling by Vertical Angles

and the method of measuring distances by telescopie and rod, with table

of heights for all angles from zero to 22 1/2 degrees

August Faul

A Short Treatise on Leveling by Vertical Angles
*and the method of measuring distances by telescopie and rod, with table of heights
for all angles from zero to 22 1/2 degrees*

ISBN/EAN: 9783337392949

Printed in Europe, USA, Canada, Australia, Japan

Cover: Foto ©Andreas Hilbeck / pixelio.de

More available books at **www.hansebooks.com**

August Faul

A Short Treatise on Leveling by Vertical Angles
and the method of measuring distances by telescopie and rod, with table of heights for all angles from zero to 22 1/2 degrees

ISBN/EAN: 9783337392949

Printed in Europe, USA, Canada, Australia, Japan

Cover: Foto ©Andreas Hilbeck / pixelio.de

More available books at **www.hansebooks.com**

A SHORT TREATISE

ON

LEVELING BY VERTICAL ANGLES

AND

THE METHOD OF MEASURING DISTANCES

BY TELESCOPE AND ROD,

WITH

TABLES OF HEIGHTS

FOR

ALL ANGLES FROM ZERO TO 22¼ DEGREES (IN MINUTES) AND
FOR ANY DISTANCE REQUIRED.

BY

AUGUST FAUL,

CIVIL ENGINEER, GENERAL SUPERINTENDENT DRUID HILL PARK, &C., BALTIMORE.

BALTIMORE:
CUSHINGS & BAILEY,
NO. 262 WEST BALTIMORE STREET.
1878.

DEDICATED

TO

HIS HIGHLY ESTEEMED FRIEND

BENJAMIN H. LATROBE, ESQ.,

BY

THE AUTHOR.

CONTENTS.

I. LEVELLING BY VERTICAL ANGLES.

§ 1.—The annexed tables have been computed to save labor in the tedious calculations for *Levelling by vertical angles* (by Engineers called Trigonometrical Levelling) as performed in connection with *Geodetic operations* and *Topographical Surveying*, &c.

The angles of elevation or depression (*Ascent* or *Descent*), together with the horizontal distances between Stations, are the data used in trigonometrical calculations. To save labor in reaching these results is the purpose of these tables. The heights are given to hundredths of feet for all angles (one to each minute between 0 and 22½ degrees, and for all distances from 1 foot to 1000, from which any other figures within and above may readily be composed as the following examples will show in the next paragraph.

§ 2.—APPLICATION OF THE TABLES.

1. Given the angle of inclination, 5° 44′ and horizontal distance 785 feet, the height may be found as follows:

On p. 12, headed 5 Deg., find in the column of 44 min.

$$
\begin{array}{rl}
700 \text{ ft.} =& 70.28 \\
80 \text{ “} =& 8.03 \\
5 \text{ “} =& 0.50 \\
\hline
785 \text{ “} =& 78.81 \text{ ft.}
\end{array}
$$

2. Given angle 12° 30′ distance 150 ft. Find on p. 26, headed 12 Deg., in the column of 30 min.

$$
\begin{array}{rl}
100 \text{ ft.} =& 22.17 \\
50 \text{ “} =& 11.09 \\
\hline
150 \text{ “} =& 33.26 \text{ ft.}
\end{array}
$$

3. Given angle 3° 15′, distance 530 ft. Find on p. 9, headed 3 Deg., in the column of 15 min.

$$
\begin{array}{rl}
500 \text{ ft.} =& 28.39 \\
30 \text{ “} =& 1.70 \\
\hline
530 \text{ “} =& 30.09 \text{ ft.}
\end{array}
$$

4. Given, same angle, distance 2600 ft. Find in the same column: 1000 ft. = 56.78 (× 2)

$$
\begin{array}{rl}
2000 \text{ ft.} =& 113.56 \\
600 \text{ “} =& 34.25 \\
\hline
2600 \text{ “} =& 147.81 \text{ ft.}
\end{array}
$$

5. Same angle, distance 5280 ft. (or 1 mile) Find in the same column: 1000 = 56.78 (× 5)

$$
\begin{array}{rl}
5000 \text{ ft.} =& 283.90 \\
200 \text{ “} =& 11.36 \\
80 \text{ “} =& 4.54 \\
\hline
5280 \text{ “} =& 299.80 \text{ ft.}
\end{array}
$$

6. Given the same angle (3° 15′), distance 20.650 ft. Find on p. 9, headed 3 Deg., in the column of 15 minutes:

$$
\begin{array}{rl}
1000 \text{ ft.} = 56.78 \; (\times 20) \ldots\ldots 20.000 \text{ ft.} =& 1.135.60 \\
600 \text{ “} =& 34.07 \\
50 \text{ “} =& 2.48 \\
\hline
20.650 \text{ “} =& 1.172.12 \text{ ft.}
\end{array}
$$

These few examples show sufficiently that these tables will be of use even for the longest distances occuring in Geodesy. They are calculated only to *single minutes*, but it is evident that proportional of these, fractions may be taken for any required number of seconds.

For Geodetic operations a correction of heights taken from these tables may be required for the difference between the *apparent* and *true* level (curvature of the earth and refraction of light) for which tables can be found in some books on Surveying. This difference, however, is so small for ordinary distances as to be seldom taken into account by the Engineers for whom these tables are calculated. Their principal design is to bring *levelling by vertical angles* into more general use, and save the many stations required in the ordinary way of levelling. Horizontal sights and the vertical rod, in constant repetition, are very tedious in hilly localities where great accuracy ($\frac{1}{100}$th of a foot) is immaterial, especially so in all *preliminary surveys*. Here the principal object is: *Approximate results in the shortest possible time.*

§ 3.—How to take Levels by Vertical Angles.

We first suppose that the line to be levelled be marked out on the ground by stakes set 100 feet apart, the usual distance in all branches of engineering.

The sights of elevation (Ascent) or depression (Descent) should be made parallel to the line showing the inclination of the ground, that is to say, instrument and signal point on the rod should be of equal heights, to accomplish which, the centre of the target is to be set even with the eye-glass of the telescope. The sight to the target being thus parallel with the line of rise or fall in the ground, gives its true angle of inclination, and that angle will show, at once, the vertical height of Ascent or Descent in our tables.

Note.—In marking out points for levelling generally, every stake should be accompanied by a peg driven to the surface of the ground on which to hold the rod for observations, the projecting stake standing up and showing the position of the solid point whose level is sought. Any of the points thus secured, may serve as a bench-mark from which to start future levels on the work of grading.

§ 4.—In consideration of parallel sighting with the general inclination of the ground (§ 3) for measuring vertical angles, at every change of station the rodman would have to set the target to the new height of the instrument before other angles of inclination could be taken. This delay may be avoided by taking notice of the height of target, on the arrival of the rodman at the new station from his last position. The observed angle between the preceding station and the new one would be affected in proportion to the difference between the previous height of the target and the new height of the instrument. The difference of *one minute* in 100 ft. distance amounting always (practically) to 0.03 ft. or about ⅓ of an inch, the angular equivalent of one inch in 100 ft. must be equal to *three minutes*. This simple observation constitutes the rule of reducing such angles, as are under consideration, to their true value.

The difference between heights of target and instrument being usually only a few inches, their equivalent in minutes can easily be added to or subtracted from, the observed angle of Ascent or Descent.

Suppose the angle of Descent, on a back sight of 100 ft., is found to be 8° 24′, and the target when brought up to the new station shows the instrument to be 2 inches higher, the observed angle is 2×3 = 6 minutes too great, and must be reduced from 8° 24′ to 8° 18′: or if the target is found 2 inches higher than the instrument, the angle is to be increased to 8° 30′. In an ascending angle the correction must be added in the first case, and subtracted in the second.

The target once set to an average height of the instrument, say 4.4 ft., may thus be used for a number of observations, without changing its original height; and the survey may be so arranged that for uniform distances, on a line of profile, the rodman may pass the engineer, and the engineer the rodman, alternately without comparing heights, thus saving much time.

§ 5.—The method of keeping notes for levelling by angles, should be as simple as possible. The direction of sighting, whether fore- or backward, can be marked by the words "From" (Sta.) and "To" (No. of stake) with the distance in feet following, after which the angle of *Ascent* or *Descent* (in degrees and minutes) should follow.

To insure the proper reading of *elevation* or *depression* of the telescope against errors, it is advisable to have the words "Asc." and "Desc." engraved on the arc of the instrument to the left and right of zero. If this (zero) be on the perpendicular line of the instrument, the vernier coinciding, and the sight, therefore, describing a horizontal line, the divergence from this line on the *left* will appear as Ascent, on the *right* as Descent. Without this precaution, there is much liability to mistakes, especially in angles diverging but little from zero (level).

From the above remarks it appears that the entries in the field-book will necessarily occupy only 5 columns, viz:

1. Name or number of station (From);
2. Direction or number of stake (To);
3. Distance in feet;
4. Inclination of ground (Asc. or Desc.);
5. Number of degrees and minutes.

These 5 columns will constitute all data required for calculations in the office, although extra notes and rough sketches may sometimes be required in particular and uncommon features of the ground.

For office-work, these columns must be increased by two more to complete the results in tabular shape, i. e. one for the *single* heights (to be taken from the tables) and one (the last) for the *total* heights, simply computed by adding or subtracting the former ones which should be prepared by affixing the signs $+$ or $-$ as the case may require.

Though, generally, Ascent will carry $+$, and Descent $-$, these signs have to be reversed when backsights occur in an opposite direction to the course of the survey.

To illustrate these remarks the following example of a number of observed points of regular distance of 100 ft. may be given:

The starting point (0) of a certain height being known or supposed to be 200 ft. above tide-water, and the measurement of distances and vertical angles recorded in the manner above indicated, the results will appear thus:

	Single height in ft.	*Plus* or *Min.*	No.	Total heig't in ft.
			0	200.00
From Sta. 1 To No. 0 100 ft. Desc. ($-$) 9° 45′	17.18	$+$	1	217.18
" " 1 " " 2 100 " Asc. ($+$) 7° 15′	12.72	$+$	2	229.90
" " 3 " " 2 100 " Desc. ($-$) 9° 30′	16.73	$+$	3	246.63
" " 3 " " 4 100 " Asc. ($+$)10° 15′	18.08	$+$	4	264.71
" " 5 " " 4 100 " Asc. ($+$) 3° 30′	6.12	$-$	5	258.59
" " 5 " " 6 100 " Asc. ($+$) 8° 45′	15.39	$+$	6	273.98
" " 7 " " 6 100 " Desc. ($-$) 8° 30′	14.95	$+$	7	288.93
" " 7 " " 8 100 " Asc. ($+$)10° 0′	17.63	$+$	8	306.56
" " 8 " " 8 100 " Desc. ($-$)11° 15′	19.89	$+$	9	326.45
" " 9 " " 10 100 " Asc. ($+$)12° 30′	22.17	$+$	10	348.62
" " 11 " " 10 100 " Asc. ($+$) 1° 45′	3.06	$-$	11	345.56

NOTE.—The proof of correspondence of *single* and *total* heights can easily be made by adding the single heights of equal signs together which will give in this case

Single.   Total.

$+$ 154.74
$-$ 9.18

$+$ 145.56 $= 345.56 - 200.$

In glancing over these notes and results it appears that, in 6 stations, we have ascended an elevation of 145 ft., in equal distances of 100 ft., sighting *for-* and backward. Applying the common method of levelling with a 12 ft. rod, the number of stations would necessarily have to be doubled, at least, to reach that elevation, with much more labor and exertion too, whilst the measurement of *vertical angles* will shorten the work even more than shown in the above example, if the sights were chosen to be longer, so that perhaps two or three stations might have been sufficient to arrive at the same results.

II. MEASURING DISTANCES BY TELESCOPE AND ROD.

§ 6.— The foregoing examples are given on the supposition that the line of profile was marked by stakes set at certain distances as customary in the various branches of engineering. But on all *preliminary* or *experimental* surveys, as on locations of railroads, canals, &c., or where profiles are required for other purposes, as in Topography, the usual staking out and chaining of distances, in advance, can be dispensed with, if the same instrument used in measuring vertical angles, carries the means of *reading* distances from a graduated rod held on the points of elevation or depression required in the profile. The angle of Ascent or Descent being read from the rod at the height of the instrument (§ 3) the distance can be read simultaneously, on the same rod; and the elements of height are ascertained in the shortest possible time. If, besides the arrangement for reading distances, the instrument is furnished with a compass, the experimenting engineer has all the means for rough ground-*plans* as well as for *profiles*.

§ 7.— The reading of distances by the telescope, from a graduated rod, being little known and only appreciated, here and there, by a few who have had ample experience of its great usefulness, the writer will give a short description of it as follows:

Two essential parts constitute the contrivance for reading distances: the telescope and the rod (telemeter).

1. The telescope contains an additional horizontal wire at the cross-hair which is adjusted so that both horizontal hairs when directed to the rod (telemeter) will cut off or include a certain space on the rod, the painted divisions of which are made to correspond with the distance measured on level ground. The accuracy of reading depends on the magnifying power of the telescope and the rectangular position of the rod to the sight of the telescope, which latter object is accomplished by a small sight connected with the rod,

by which the rodman is enabled to hold the rod in proper position to the observer's eye.

2. The telemeter, as used in the U. S. Coast Survey is described in the excellent "Treatise on the Plane-Table and its use in Topographical Survey-ing" published with the U. S. Coast Survey Report for 1865 in which is said: "The telemeter is simply a scale of equal parts painted upon a wooden rod about 10 feet long, 5 inches wide, and 1¼ inch thick, so graduated that the number of divisions as seen between the horizontal wires of the telescope is equal to the number of metres in the distance between the observer's eye and the rod held at right angles to the line of sight."

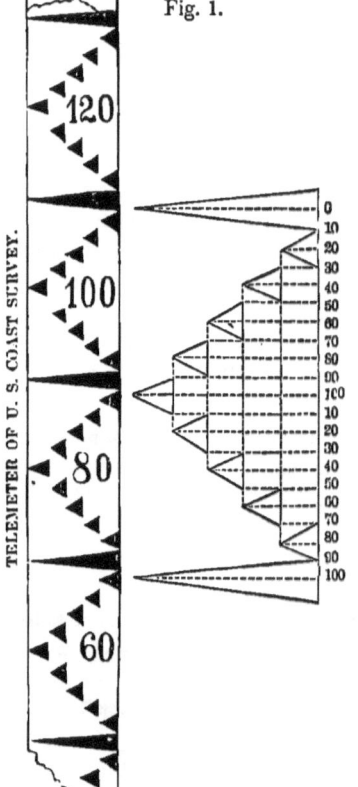

Fig. 1.

The treatise quoted above, gives the rule that in all cases the telemeter should be graduated experimentally for the particular instrument and eye of the observer who has it in use, and further states that in reading there is no sensible error at any distance greater than 20 metres *) and less than 260, and that it would be safe to rely upon the telemeter for any distance from 15 to 300 metres. The diagram (Fig. 1) is given to show the mode of dividing and painting the telemeter in use by the U. S. Coast Survey.

§ 8.—From the experience of the author of this little work has resulted another rod differing little from the common levelling rod and answering the two purposes of *levelling*, and *reading distances*, at the same time. The target in this new rod which he has used for many years is dispensed with, and its divisions in feet, tenths

* Shorter distances are easier and more reliably measured by a rod or tape-line.—*Note of the Author.*

and hundredths, painted as shown in diagram (Fig. 2) are read with any telescope of moderate power. In taking levels, *reading* generally should be preferred to using a sliding target which causes loss of time and even uncertainty of result, as the engineer depends on the correctness of his rodman. This may be avoided and an easy and reliable reading effected if the rod be painted in the following manner. On a rod painted white lay off the division lines of feet, tenths and half tenths, with a lead-pencil, add a short line about $\frac{1}{2}$ inch long, at a distance of $\frac{1}{100}$ ft. above each division line. This space when painted will show black marks of $\frac{1}{100}$ ft. thickness, leaving white spaces of $\frac{4}{100}$ ft. width. The dimensions of $\frac{1}{100}$ and $\frac{4}{100}$, before the eye of the observer, will enable him to read the single hundredth of a foot at any point the cross-hair may strike the rod. The centre of the white space as well as the bottom and top of the black marks, can plainly be discerned by almost any telescope of ordinary surveying instruments. If the horizontal wire of the cross-hair strikes the bottom of any black mark, it will read 0 or 5 or 10 hundredths, on the top it will read 1 or 6; in the centre of the white space, 3 or 8; at the thickness of one mark, *above* (in the white) 2 or 7; *below*, 9 or 4 hundredths. In short distances frequently occuring in common levelling, even fractions of hundredths can be read if desired, although hundredths may be considered sufficient for all practical purposes.

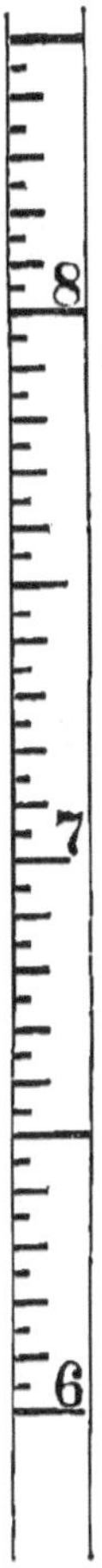

§ 9.—The same *levelling rod* may be used as a telemeter, and distances within 1000 ft. can be read from it to the closeness of *one foot*, or with the same accuracy as hundredths of a foot can be read with a good level instrument. For still easier reading, with less powerful telescopes, the writer has experienced great advantage from doubling the thickness of the black marks, but leaving out those of the half tenths and also the numbers of feet in place of which he substitutes painted squares of half inch size to serve as little targets their bottom of which may be considered a zero for one of the horizontal wires from which to count the feet, tenths and hundredths to the other parallel wire, thus reading off 100 ft. distance for every foot-mark of the rod.

Though by this graduation of the rod the reading of a single foot is not so directly given as on the former rod, the means of close estimation are not wanting—and the stronger marks, well separated by open spaces, afford great

FIG. 2.—THE AUTHOR'S LEVELLING ROD AND TELEMETER.

facilities in reading long distances without the necessity of very powerful and inconvenient telescopes.

§ 10.—REDUCTION OF HYPOTHENUSE.

The distances obtained by reading, representing the hypothenuse of a rectangular triangle, instead of the required horizontal base, have to be reduced to their proper length according to the different slopes on which they have been measured. To do this in an easy and practical way, the writer has arranged, on the principle of percentage, the following little table for the slopes from 1° to 40° and for the distance of 100 ft. from which the value of any other distance can easily be deduced.

Slope in Degrees $\angle a$	Subtr. from 100 ft.	Slope in Degrees $\angle a$	Subtr. from 100 ft.
1	0.02	21	6.6
2	0.06	22	7.3
3	0.14	23	7.9
4	0.24	24	8.6
5	0.38	25	9.4
6	0.55	26	10.1
7	0.75	27	10.9
8	0.98	28	11.7
9	1.23	29	12.5
10	1.52	30	13.4
11	1.8	31	14.3
12	2.2	32	15.2
13	2.6	33	16.1
14	3.0	34	17.1
15	3.4	35	18.1
16	3.9	36	19.1
17	4.4	37	20.1
18	4.9	38	21.2
19	5.4	39	22.3
20	6.0	40	23.4

$$(\log. 100 + \log. \cos \angle a)$$

EXAMPLES.

1. On a slope of 3°, a distance of 700 ft. was found—what is the horizontal?

Answer. Subtract 0.14 (7 times)=0.98 or nearly 1 ft. from 700 = 699 ft. horiz. distance.

2. On a slope of 10° the measured distance of 1000 ft. will be reduced by subtracting 1.52×10=15.2 ft. from 1000, leaving 985 ft. (fractions neglected).

3. On a slope of 14° the measured distance being 600 ft. 3.0 × 6 = 18 ft. subtracted from 600, leaves 582 ft. horiz. distance.

4. On a slope of 20° (6.0) the distance of 100 ft. has to be reduced to 94 ft. horizontal distance.

From the foregoing table it appears that the difference in length between a horizontal and an inclined line, amounts,

in 100 ft., about
1 ft. on a slope of 8 degrees,
2 " " 11—12 degrees,
3 " " 14 "
4 " " 16—17 "
5 " " 18—19 "
6 " " 20 "

and so on, and that within the first 8 degrees, an inaccuracy of 1 per cent. will be the effect of neglecting the strict measurement of slope-angles for ascertaining true horizontal distances. Bearing in mind these few facts the engineer has to judge himself of the degree of care required in observations under various local circumstances.

§ 11.—The length of slope-lines as obtained from reading, is effected too, in a small degree, by the perpendicular position of the instrument at the point from which the slope-angle is to be taken. Though of no great consequence to the general results of reading, the engineer should be aware of this source of slight error.

If $a\,b$ (Fig. 3) is to represent the perpendicular instrument, $a\,d$ the distance of slope read on $b\,e$, this distance would be too long by $a\,c$ when on Ascent, or too short when on Descent.

Fig. 3.

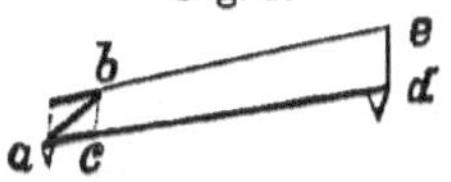

Assuming the height of the instrument to average 4.4 ft., the following little table will show how much should be added to or subtracted from, the distance read on slopes of different angles.

Angles of slope in degrees.	Differ. in feet.
2	0.15
4	0.31
6	0.46
8	0.62
10	0.78
12	0.94
14	1.10
16	1.26
18	1.43
20	1.60
22	1.78
24	1.96
26	2.15
28	2.34
30	2.54
32	2.75
34	2.97
36	3.20

From this little table it appears that the error of distance read on a slope of 12° does not amount to quite one foot; 22° to 1¾ ft.; 30° to 2½ ft.; 36 to 3⅕ ft.; and as reading to the accuracy of a foot is all that can be required practically, it may be judged *how far* and *when* to take notice of this effect on distances found by reading.

As distances read from a rod will count from the eye-point, the eye-glass should, theoretically, stand perpendicular over the ground-point on which the observation is to be made; or if the instrument is set so that its centre corresponds with that point, allowance should be made for the space differing from the centre of the telescope to the eye-glass. But as this difference will not amount to feet, and the reading of inches can reasonably not be pretended by telescope and telemeter, it might be left out of consideration altogether.

§ 12.—ON THE MAGNIFYING POWER OF INSTRUMENTS.

In § 7 it has been stated that the correctness of reading distances from a rod depends in a great measure, on the magnifying power of the telescope. As this object is of great importance to the reader, the writer of these pages feels induced, before closing this treatise, to devote a paragraph to the construction of telescopes, in view of obtaining the greatest power with the least sacrifice of space or length of tube.

The two principal telescopes in use with surveying instruments are the *astronomical* and the *terrestrial*, the first one containing only two glasses and being, therefore, the simplest of the two, though not as popular as the latter which shows the image in an upright position by the help of additional glasses counteracting the originally reversed appearance of the image created in the simple astronomical telescope. This apparent advantage, however, is more imaginary than real, as for surveying purposes it is immaterial whether *points* on *vertical* or *horizontal* sights appear in *upright* or *reversed* position. To secure uprightness in the image a sacrifice of about 4 inches is to be made in the length of the terrestrial telescope. If this were, for instance, 10 inches long, the focus of the object-glass could only be about 6 inches, and the instrument would magnify perhaps 5 or 6 times, whilst, on the principle of the astronomical construction, the same length of telescope (10 inches) would admit of about double that power.

As the magnifying power of an astronomical telescope is, according to optical laws, in the proportion of the focus of the eye-glass to that of the object-glass, a tube of 10 inches length containing an object-glass of 9 inches focus, and an eye-glass of $\frac{3}{4}$ inch focus; an astronomical telescope magnifying $(9 : \frac{3}{4} = 12)$ about 12 times should be chosen instead of a terrestrial one of half that power. Unnecessarily long telescopes as often met with on levelling instruments can easily be shortened 3 or 4 inches in length, without impairing their reading power, by throwing out several of the compound glasses and using but one of them as eye-glass, or introducing an object-glass of longer focus, and a single eye-glass of short focal length, thus increasing the magnifying power without increasing the length of tube.

Before closing this paragraph it may be stated that wherever the method of reading distances by telescope has been adopted, no positive rule for extent of distance and power of instrument is given. In the U. S. Coast Survey Report (cited in § 7) the limit of reliable reading is mentioned to be 300 metres with no extra large reading power. In Europe where reading distances by telescope has been practiced for more than 30 years, the telescopes are made to magnify about 15 times, sometimes 20 and even 25 times, and almost in all instances on the *astronomical* plan. Much less reading power, however, will be sufficient, if the marks on the *telemeter* are made in the distinct way (proposed in § 8) which will materially assist in convenient and correct reading, within 1000 ft. distance, with the application of an astronomical telescope of from 10 to 12 inches length. Greater distances may easily be divided and read in parts, by sighting back- and forward and adding up the single distances.

TABLES OF HEIGHTS

FOR

ALL ANGLES FROM ZERO TO 22½ DEGREES AND FOR ANY DISTANCE
REQUIRED.

O Degree.

Minutes	0	1	2	3	4	5	6	7	8	9	10	11	12	13	14
Dis. in ft.															
1	0.00	0.00	0.00	0.00	0.00	0.00	0.00	0.00	0.00	0.01	0.00	0.00	0.00	0.00	0.00
2	0.00	0.00	0.00	0.00	0.00	0.00	0.00	0.00	0.00	0.01	0.01	0.01	0.01	0.01	0.01
3	0.00	0.00	0.00	0.00	0.00	0.00	0.01	0.01	0.01	0.01	0.01	0.01	0.01	0.01	0.01
4	0.00	0.00	0.00	0.00	0.00	0.01	0.01	0.01	0.01	0.01	0.01	0.01	0.01	0.02	0.02
5	0.00	0.00	0.00	0.00	0.01	0.01	0.01	0.01	0.01	0.01	0.01	0.02	0.02	0.02	0.02
6	0.00	0.00	0.00	0.01	0.01	0.01	0.01	0.01	0.01	0.02	0.02	0.02	0.02	0.02	0.02
7	0.00	0.00	0.00	0.01	0.01	0.01	0.01	0.01	0.02	0.02	0.02	0.02	0.02	0.03	0.03
8	0.00	0.00	0.00	0.01	0.01	0.01	0.01	0.02	0.02	0.02	0.02	0.02	0.03	0.03	0.03
9	0.00	0.00	0.01	0.01	0.01	0.01	0.02	0.02	0.02	0.02	0.02	0.03	0.03	0.03	0.04
10	0.00	0.00	0.01	0.01	0.01	0.01	0.02	0.02	0.02	0.03	0.03	0.03	0.03	0.04	0.04
20	0.00	0.01	0.01	0.02	0.02	0.03	0.04	0.04	0.05	0.05	0.06	0.06	0.07	0.08	0.08
30	0.00	0.01	0.02	0.03	0.03	0.04	0.05	0.06	0.07	0.08	0.09	0.10	0.10	0.11	0.12
40	0.00	0.01	0.02	0.03	0.05	0.06	0.07	0.08	0.09	0.10	0.12	0.13	0.14	0.15	0.16
50	0.00	0.01	0.03	0.04	0.06	0.07	0.09	0.10	0.12	0.13	0.15	0.16	0.17	0.19	0.20
60	0.00	0.02	0.03	0.05	0.07	0.09	0.11	0.12	0.14	0.16	0.17	0.19	0.21	0.23	0.24
70	0.00	0.02	0.04	0.06	0.08	0.10	0.12	0.14	0.16	0.18	0.20	0.22	0.24	0.26	0.28
80	0.00	0.02	0.05	0.07	0.09	0.12	0.14	0.16	0.19	0.21	0.23	0.26	0.28	0.30	0.33
90	0.00	0.03	0.05	0.08	0.10	0.13	0.16	0.18	0.21	0.24	0.26	0.29	0.31	0.34	0.37
100	0.00	0.03	0.06	0.09	0.12	0.15	0.18	0.20	0.23	0.26	0.29	0.32	0.35	0.38	0.41
200	0.00	0.06	0.12	0.17	0.23	0.29	0.35	0.41	0.47	0.52	0.58	0.64	0.70	0.76	0.81
300	0.00	0.09	0.17	0.26	0.35	0.44	0.53	0.61	0.70	.79	.87	.96	1.05	1.13	1.22
400	0.00	0.12	0.23	0.35	0.46	0.58	0.70	0.82	0.93	1.05	1.16	1.28	1.40	1.51	1.63
500	0.00	0.15	0.29	0.44	0.58	0.73	0.88	1.02	1.17	1.31	1.46	1.60	1.75	1.89	2.04
600	0.00	0.17	0.35	0.52	0.70	0.87	1.05	1.22	1.40	1.57	1.75	1.92	2.09	2.27	2.44
700	0.00	0.20	0.41	0.61	0.81	1.02	1.23	1.43	1.63	1.83	2.04	2.24	2.44	2.65	2.85
800	0.00	0.23	0.46	0.70	0.93	1.16	1.40	1.63	1.86	2.10	2.33	2.56	2.79	3.02	3.26
900	0.00	0.26	0.52	0.78	1.04	1.31	1.58	1.84	2.10	2.36	2.62	2.88	3.14	3.40	3.66
1000	0.00	0.29	0.58	0.87	1.16	1.45	1.75	2.04	2.33	2.62	2.91	3.20	3.49	3.78	4.07

O Degree.

Minutes	30	31	32	33	34	35	36	37	38	39	40	41	42	43	44
Dis. in ft.															
1	0.01	0.01	0.01	0.01	0.01	0.01	0.01	0.01	0.01	0.01	0.01	0.01	0.01	0.01	0.01
2	0.02	0.02	0.02	0.02	0.02	0.02	0.02	0.02	0.02	0.02	0.02	0.02	0.02	0.03	0.03
3	0.03	0.03	0.03	0.03	0.03	0.03	0.03	0.03	0.03	0.03	0.03	0.04	0.04	0.04	0.04
4	0.03	0.04	0.04	0.04	0.04	0.04	0.04	0.04	0.04	0.05	0.05	0.05	0.05	0.05	0.05
5	0.04	0.05	0.05	0.05	0.05	0.05	0.05	0.05	0.06	0.06	0.06	0.06	0.06	0.06	0.06
6	0.05	0.05	0.06	0.06	0.06	0.06	0.06	0.07	0.07	0.07	0.07	0.07	0.07	0.08	0.08
7	0.06	0.06	0.07	0.07	0.07	0.07	0.07	0.08	0.08	0.08	0.08	0.08	0.09	0.09	0.09
8	0.07	0.07	0.07	0.08	0.08	0.08	0.08	0.09	0.09	0.09	0.09	0.10	0.10	0.10	0.10
9	0.08	0.08	0.08	0.09	0.09	0.09	0.09	0.10	0.10	0.10	0.10	0.11	0.11	0.11	0.11
10	0.09	0.09	0.09	0.10	0.10	0.10	0.10	0.11	0.11	0.11	0.12	0.12	0.12	0.13	0.13
20	0.17	0.18	0.19	0.19	0.20	0.20	0.21	0.22	0.22	0.23	0.23	0.21	0.24	0.25	0.26
30	0.26	0.27	0.28	0.29	0.30	0.31	0.31	0.32	0.33	0.34	0.35	0.36	0.37	0.38	0.38
40	0.35	0.36	0.37	0.38	0.40	0.41	0.42	0.43	0.44	0.45	0.47	0.48	0.49	0.50	0.51
50	0.44	0.45	0.47	0.48	0.49	0.51	0.52	0.54	0.55	0.57	0.58	0.60	0.61	0.63	0.64
60	0.52	0.54	0.56	0.58	0.59	0.61	0.63	0.65	0.66	0.68	0.70	0.72	0.73	0.75	0.77
70	0.61	0.63	0.65	0.67	0.69	0.71	0.73	0.75	0.77	0.79	0.81	0.84	0.86	0.88	0.90
80	0.70	0.72	0.74	0.77	0.79	0.81	0.84	0.86	0.88	0.91	0.93	0.95	0.98	1.00	1.02
90	0.79	0.81	0.84	0.86	0.89	0.92	0.94	0.97	0.99	1.02	1.05	1.07	1.10	1.13	1.15
100	0.87	0.90	0.93	0.96	0.99	1.02	1.05	1.08	1.11	1.14	1.16	1.19	1.22	1.25	1.28
200	1.75	1.80	1.86	1.92	1.98	2.04	2.09	2.15	2.21	2.27	2.33	2.39	2.44	2.50	2.56
300	2.62	2.71	2.79	2.88	2.97	3.05	3.14	3.23	3.32	3.41	3.49	3.58	3.67	3.75	3.84
400	3.49	3.61	3.72	3.84	3.96	4.07	4.19	4.30	4.42	4.54	4.66	4.77	4.89	5.00	5.12
500	4.37	4.51	4.66	4.80	4.95	5.09	5.24	5.38	5.53	5.68	5.82	5.97	6.11	6.26	6.40
600	5.24	5.41	5.59	5.76	5.93	6.11	6.28	6.46	6.63	6.81	6.98	7.16	7.33	7.51	7.68
700	6.11	6.31	6.52	6.72	6.92	7.13	7.33	7.53	7.74	7.95	8.15	8.35	8.55	8.76	8.96
800	6.98	7.22	7.45	7.68	7.91	8.14	8.38	8.61	8.84	9.08	9.31	9.54	9.78	10.01	10.24
900	7.86	8.12	8.38	8.64	8.90	9.16	9.42	9.68	9.95	10.22	10.48	10.74	11.00	11.26	11.52
1000	8.73	9.02	9.31	9.60	9.89	10.18	10.47	10.76	11.05	11.35	11.64	11.93	12.22	12.51	12.80

0 Degree.

Minutes	15	16	17	18	19	20	21	22	23	24	25	26	27	28	29	30
Dis. in ft.																
1	0.00	0.00	0.00	0.01	0.01	0.01	0.01	0.01	0.01	0.01	0.01	0.01	0.01	0.01	0.01	0.01
2	0.01	0.01	0.01	0.01	0.01	0.01	0.01	0.01	0.01	0.01	0.01	0.02	0.02	0.02	0.02	0.02
3	0.01	0.01	0.01	0.02	0.02	0.02	0.02	0.02	0.02	0.02	0.02	0.02	0.02	0.02	0.03	0.03
4	0.02	0.02	0.02	0.02	0.02	0.02	0.02	0.03	0.03	0.03	0.03	0.03	0.03	0.03	0.03	0.03
5	0.02	0.02	0.02	0.03	0.03	0.03	0.03	0.03	0.03	0.03	0.04	0.04	0.04	0.04	0.04	0.04
6	0.03	0.03	0.03	0.03	0.03	0.03	0.04	0.04	0.04	0.04	0.04	0.05	0.05	0.05	0.05	0.05
7	0.03	0.03	0.03	0.04	0.04	0.04	0.04	0.04	0.05	0.05	0.05	0.05	0.05	0.06	0.06	0.06
8	0.03	0.04	0.04	0.04	0.04	0.05	0.05	0.05	0.05	0.06	0.06	0.06	0.06	0.07	0.07	0.07
9	0.04	0.04	0.04	0.05	0.05	0.05	0.05	0.06	0.06	0.06	0.07	0.07	0.07	0.07	0.08	0.08
10	0.04	0.05	0.05	0.05	0.06	0.06	0.06	0.06	0.07	0.07	0.07	0.08	0.08	0.08	0.08	0.09
20	0.09	0.09	0.10	0.10	0.11	0.12	0.12	0.13	0.13	0.14	0.15	0.15	0.16	0.16	0.17	0.17
30	0.13	0.14	0.15	0.16	0.17	0.17	0.18	0.19	0.20	0.21	0.22	0.23	0.24	0.24	0.25	0.26
40	0.17	0.19	0.20	0.21	0.22	0.23	0.24	0.26	0.27	0.28	0.29	0.30	0.31	0.33	0.34	0.35
50	0.22	0.23	0.25	0.26	0.28	0.29	0.31	0.32	0.33	0.35	0.36	0.38	0.39	0.41	0.42	0.44
60	0.26	0.28	0.30	0.31	0.33	0.35	0.37	0.38	0.40	0.42	0.44	0.45	0.47	0.49	0.51	0.52
70	0.31	0.33	0.35	0.37	0.39	0.41	0.43	0.45	0.47	0.49	0.51	0.53	0.55	0.57	0.59	0.61
80	0.35	0.37	0.40	0.42	0.44	0.47	0.49	0.51	0.54	0.56	0.58	0.60	0.63	0.65	0.68	0.70
90	0.39	0.42	0.45	0.47	0.50	0.52	0.55	0.58	0.60	0.63	0.65	0.68	0.71	0.73	0.76	0.79
100	0.44	0.47	0.50	0.52	0.55	0.58	0.61	0.64	0.67	0.70	0.73	0.76	0.79	0.82	0.84	0.87
200	0.87	0.93	0.99	1.05	1.11	1.16	1.22	1.28	1.34	1.40	1.45	1.51	1.57	1.63	1.69	1.75
300	1.31	1.40	1.49	1.57	1.66	1.75	1.83	1.92	2.01	2.09	2.18	2.27	2.36	2.45	2.58	2.62
400	1.74	1.86	1.98	2.10	2.21	2.33	2.44	2.56	2.68	2.79	2.91	3.02	3.14	3.26	3.38	3.49
500	2.18	2.33	2.48	2.62	2.77	2.91	3.06	3.20	3.35	3.49	3.64	3.78	3.93	4.08	4.22	4.37
600	2.62	2.79	2.97	3.14	3.32	3.49	3.67	3.84	4.01	4.19	4.36	4.54	4.71	4.89	5.06	5.24
700	3.05	3.26	3.47	3.67	3.87	4.07	4.28	4.48	4.68	4.89	5.09	5.29	5.50	5.71	5.91	6.11
800	3.49	3.72	3.96	4.19	4.42	4.66	4.89	5.12	5.35	5.58	5.82	6.05	6.28	6.52	6.75	6.98
900	3.92	4.19	4.46	4.72	4.98	5.24	5.50	5.76	6.02	6.28	6.54	6.80	7.07	7.34	7.60	7.86
1000	4.36	4.65	4.95	5.24	5.53	5.82	6.11	6.40	6.69	6.98	7.27	7.56	7.85	8.15	8.44	8.73

0 Degree.

Minutes	45	46	47	48	49	50	51	52	53	54	55	56	57	58	59	60
Dis. in ft.																
1	0.01	0.01	0.01	0.01	0.01	0.01	0.01	0.02	0.02	0.02	0.02	0.02	0.02	0.02	0.02	0.02
2	0.03	0.03	0.03	0.03	0.03	0.03	0.03	0.03	0.03	0.03	0.03	0.03	0.03	0.03	0.03	0.03
3	0.04	0.04	0.04	0.04	0.04	0.04	0.04	0.05	0.05	0.05	0.05	0.05	0.05	0.05	0.05	0.05
4	0.05	0.05	0.05	0.06	0.06	0.06	0.06	0.06	0.06	0.06	0.06	0.07	0.07	0.07	0.07	0.07
5	0.07	0.07	0.07	0.07	0.07	0.07	0.07	0.08	0.08	0.08	0.08	0.08	0.08	0.08	0.08	0.09
6	0.08	0.08	0.08	0.08	0.09	0.09	0.09	0.09	0.09	0.09	0.10	0.10	0.10	0.10	0.10	0.10
7	0.09	0.09	0.10	0.10	0.10	0.10	0.10	0.11	0.11	0.11	0.11	0.11	0.12	0.12	0.12	0.12
8	0.10	0.11	0.11	0.11	0.11	0.12	0.12	0.12	0.12	0.13	0.13	0.13	0.13	0.13	0.14	0.14
9	0.12	0.12	0.12	0.13	0.13	0.13	0.13	0.14	0.14	0.14	0.14	0.15	0.15	0.15	0.15	0.16
10	0.13	0.13	0.14	0.14	0.14	0.15	0.15	0.15	0.15	0.16	0.16	0.16	0.17	0.17	0.17	0.17
20	0.26	0.27	0.27	0.28	0.29	0.29	0.30	0.30	0.31	0.31	0.32	0.33	0.33	0.34	0.34	0.35
30	0.39	0.40	0.41	0.42	0.43	0.44	0.45	0.45	0.46	0.47	0.48	0.49	0.50	0.51	0.51	0.52
40	0.52	0.54	0.55	0.56	0.57	0.58	0.59	0.61	0.62	0.63	0.64	0.65	0.66	0.67	0.69	0.70
50	0.65	0.67	0.68	0.70	0.71	0.73	0.74	0.76	0.77	0.79	0.80	0.81	0.83	0.84	0.86	0.87
60	0.79	0.80	0.82	0.84	0.86	0.87	0.89	0.91	0.93	0.94	0.96	0.98	0.99	1.01	1.03	1.05
70	0.92	0.94	0.96	0.98	1.00	1.02	1.04	1.06	1.08	1.10	1.12	1.14	1.16	1.18	1.20	1.22
80	1.05	1.07	1.09	1.12	1.14	1.16	1.19	1.21	1.23	1.26	1.28	1.30	1.33	1.35	1.37	1.40
90	1.18	1.20	1.23	1.26	1.28	1.31	1.34	1.36	1.39	1.41	1.44	1.47	1.49	1.52	1.54	1.57
100	1.31	1.34	1.37	1.40	1.43	1.45	1.48	1.51	1.54	1.57	1.60	1.63	1.66	1.69	1.72	1.75
200	2.62	2.68	2.73	2.79	2.85	2.91	2.97	3.03	3.08	3.14	3.20	3.26	3.32	3.37	3.43	3.49
300	3.93	4.01	4.10	4.19	4.28	4.36	4.45	4.54	4.63	4.71	4.80	4.89	4.97	5.06	5.15	5.24
400	5.24	5.35	5.47	5.58	5.70	5.82	5.94	6.05	6.17	6.28	6.40	6.52	6.63	6.75	6.86	6.98
500	6.55	6.69	6.84	6.98	7.13	7.27	7.42	7.57	7.71	7.86	8.00	8.15	8.29	8.44	8.58	8.73
600	7.85	8.03	8.20	8.38	8.55	8.72	8.90	9.08	9.25	9.43	9.60	9.77	9.95	10.12	10.30	10.47
700	9.16	9.37	9.57	9.77	9.98	10.18	10.39	10.59	10.79	11.00	11.20	11.40	11.61	11.81	12.01	12.22
800	10.47	10.70	10.94	11.17	11.40	11.63	11.87	12.10	12.34	12.57	12.80	13.03	13.26	13.50	13.73	13.96
900	11.78	12.04	12.30	12.56	12.83	13.09	13.36	13.62	13.88	14.14	14.40	14.66	14.92	15.18	15.44	15.71
1000	13.09	13.38	13.67	13.96	14.25	14.54	14.84	15.13	15.42	15.71	16.00	16.29	16.58	16.87	17.16	17.45

1 Degree.

Minutes	0	1	2	3	4	5	6	7	8	9	10	11	12	13	14
Dis. in ft.															
1	0.02	0.02	0.02	0.02	0.02	0.02	0.02	0.02	0.02	0.02	0.02	0.02	0.02	0.02	0.02
2	0.03	0.04	0.04	0.04	0.04	0.04	0.04	0.04	0.04	0.04	0.04	0.04	0.04	0.04	0.04
3	0.05	0.05	0.05	0.05	0.06	0.05	0.06	0.06	0.06	0.06	0.06	0.06	0.06	0.06	0.06
4	0.07	0.07	0.07	0.07	0.07	0.08	0.08	0.08	0.08	0.08	0.08	0.08	0.08	0.08	0.09
5	0.09	0.09	0.09	0.09	0.09	0.09	0.10	0.10	0.10	0.10	0.10	0.10	0.10	0.11	0.11
6	0.10	0.11	0.11	0.11	0.11	0.11	0.12	0.12	0.12	0.12	0.12	0.12	0.13	0.13	0.13
7	0.12	0.12	0.13	0.13	0.13	0.13	0.13	0.14	0.14	0.14	0.14	0.14	0.15	0.15	0.15
8	0.14	0.14	0.14	0.15	0.15	0.15	0.15	0.16	0.16	0.16	0.16	0.16	0.17	0.17	0.17
9	0.16	0.16	0.16	0.16	0.17	0.17	0.17	0.18	0.18	0.18	0.18	0.18	0.19	0.19	0.19
10	0.18	0.18	0.18	0.18	0.19	0.19	0.19	0.19	0.20	0.20	0.20	0.21	0.21	0.21	0.22
20	0.35	0.36	0.36	0.37	0.37	0.38	0.38	0.39	0.40	0.40	0.41	0.41	0.42	0.42	0.43
30	0.52	0.53	0.54	0.55	0.56	0.57	0.58	0.58	0.59	0.60	0.60	0.62	0.63	0.64	0.65
40	0.70	0.71	0.72	0.73	0.74	0.76	0.77	0.78	0.79	0.80	0.81	0.83	0.84	0.85	0.86
50	0.87	0.89	0.90	0.92	0.93	0.95	0.96	0.97	0.99	1.00	1.02	1.03	1.05	1.06	1.08
60	1.05	1.07	1.08	1.10	1.12	1.13	1.15	1.17	1.19	1.20	1.22	1.24	1.26	1.27	1.29
70	1.22	1.24	1.26	1.28	1.30	1.32	1.34	1.36	1.38	1.40	1.43	1.45	1.47	1.49	1.51
80	1.40	1.42	1.44	1.47	1.49	1.51	1.54	1.56	1.58	1.61	1.63	1.65	1.68	1.70	1.72
90	1.57	1.60	1.62	1.65	1.68	1.70	1.73	1.75	1.78	1.81	1.83	1.86	1.89	1.91	1.94
100	1.75	1.78	1.80	1.83	1.86	1.89	1.92	1.95	1.98	2.01	2.04	2.07	2.10	2.12	2.15
200	3.49	3.55	3.61	3.67	3.72	3.78	3.84	3.90	3.96	4.01	4.07	4.13	4.19	4.25	4.31
300	5.24	5.33	5.41	5.50	5.59	5.67	5.76	5.85	5.93	6.02	6.11	6.20	6.29	6.37	6.46
400	6.98	7.10	7.22	7.33	7.45	7.56	7.68	7.80	7.91	8.03	8.14	8.26	8.38	8.50	8.61
500	8.73	8.88	9.02	9.17	9.31	9.46	9.60	9.75	9.89	10.04	10.18	10.33	10.48	10.62	10.77
600	10.47	10.65	10.82	11.00	11.17	11.35	11.52	11.69	11.87	12.04	12.22	12.40	12.57	12.74	12.92
700	12.22	12.43	12.63	12.83	13.03	13.24	13.44	13.64	13.85	14.05	14.25	14.46	14.67	14.87	15.07
800	13.96	14.20	14.43	14.66	14.90	15.13	15.36	15.59	15.82	16.06	16.29	16.53	16.76	16.99	17.22
900	15.71	15.98	16.24	16.50	16.76	17.02	17.28	17.54	17.80	18.06	18.32	18.59	18.86	19.12	19.38
1000	17.45	17.75	18.04	18.33	18.62	18.91	19.20	19.49	19.78	20.07	20.36	20.66	20.95	21.24	21.53

1 Degree.

Minutes	30	31	32	33	34	35	36	37	38	39	40	41	42	43	44
Dis. in ft.															
1	0.03	0.03	0.03	0.03	0.03	0.03	0.03	0.03	0.03	0.03	0.03	0.03	0.03	0.03	0.03
2	0.05	0.05	0.05	0.05	0.05	0.06	0.06	0.06	0.06	0.06	0.06	0.06	0.06	0.06	0.06
3	0.08	0.08	0.08	0.08	0.08	0.08	0.08	0.08	0.09	0.09	0.09	0.09	0.09	0.09	0.09
4	0.10	0.11	0.11	0.11	0.11	0.11	0.11	0.11	0.11	0.11	0.12	0.12	0.12	0.12	0.12
5	0.13	0.13	0.13	0.14	0.14	0.14	0.14	0.14	0.14	0.14	0.14	0.15	0.15	0.15	0.15
6	0.16	0.16	0.16	0.16	0.16	0.17	0.17	0.17	0.17	0.17	0.17	0.18	0.18	0.18	0.18
7	0.18	0.19	0.19	0.19	0.19	0.19	0.20	0.20	0.20	0.20	0.20	0.21	0.21	0.21	0.21
8	0.21	0.21	0.21	0.22	0.22	0.22	0.22	0.23	0.23	0.23	0.23	0.23	0.24	0.24	0.24
9	0.24	0.24	0.24	0.24	0.25	0.25	0.25	0.25	0.26	0.26	0.26	0.26	0.27	0.27	0.27
10	0.26	0.26	0.27	0.27	0.27	0.28	0.28	0.28	0.29	0.29	0.29	0.29	0.30	0.30	0.30
20	0.52	0.53	0.54	0.54	0.55	0.55	0.56	0.56	0.57	0.58	0.58	0.59	0.59	0.60	0.61
30	0.79	0.79	0.80	0.81	0.82	0.83	0.84	0.85	0.86	0.86	0.87	0.88	0.89	0.90	0.91
40	1.05	1.06	1.07	1.08	1.09	1.11	1.12	1.13	1.14	1.15	1.16	1.18	1.19	1.20	1.21
50	1.31	1.32	1.34	1.35	1.37	1.38	1.40	1.41	1.43	1.44	1.46	1.47	1.48	1.50	1.51
60	1.57	1.59	1.61	1.62	1.64	1.66	1.68	1.69	1.71	1.73	1.75	1.76	1.78	1.80	1.82
70	1.83	1.85	1.87	1.89	1.91	1.93	1.96	1.98	2.00	2.02	2.04	2.06	2.08	2.10	2.12
80	2.10	2.12	2.14	2.16	2.19	2.21	2.23	2.26	2.28	2.30	2.33	2.35	2.37	2.40	2.42
90	2.36	2.38	2.41	2.44	2.46	2.49	2.51	2.54	2.57	2.59	2.62	2.65	2.67	2.70	2.72
100	2.62	2.65	2.68	2.71	2.74	2.76	2.79	2.82	2.85	2.88	2.91	2.94	2.97	3.00	3.03
200	5.24	5.30	5.35	5.41	5.47	5.53	5.59	5.64	5.70	5.76	5.82	5.88	5.94	5.99	6.05
300	7.86	7.94	8.03	8.12	8.21	8.29	8.38	8.47	8.55	8.64	8.73	8.82	8.90	8.99	9.08
400	10.48	10.59	10.71	10.82	10.94	11.06	11.17	11.29	11.40	11.52	11.64	11.76	11.87	12.00	12.10
500	13.10	13.24	13.39	13.53	13.68	13.82	13.97	14.11	14.26	14.40	14.55	14.70	14.84	14.99	15.13
600	15.71	15.89	16.06	16.24	16.41	16.58	16.76	16.93	17.11	17.28	17.46	17.63	17.81	17.98	18.16
700	18.33	18.54	18.74	18.94	19.15	19.35	19.55	19.75	19.96	20.16	20.37	20.57	20.78	20.98	21.18
800	20.95	21.18	21.42	21.65	21.88	22.11	22.34	22.58	22.81	23.04	23.28	23.51	23.74	23.98	24.21
900	23.57	23.83	24.09	24.35	24.62	24.88	25.14	25.40	25.66	25.92	26.19	26.45	26.71	26.97	27.23
1000	26.19	26.48	26.77	27.06	27.35	27.64	27.93	28.22	28.51	28.80	29.10	29.39	29.68	29.97	30.26

1 Degree.

Minutes	15	16	17	18	19	20	21	22	23	24	25	26	27	28	29	30
Dis. in ft.																
1	0.02	0.02	0.02	0.02	0.02	0.02	0.02	0.02	0.02	0.02	0.02	0.03	0.03	0.03	0.03	0.03
2	0.04	0.04	0.04	0.05	0.05	0.05	0.05	0.05	0.05	0.05	0.05	0.05	0.05	0.05	0.05	0.05
3	0.07	0.07	0.07	0.07	0.07	0.07	0.07	0.07	0.07	0.07	0.07	0.08	0.08	0.08	0.08	0.08
4	0.09	0.09	0.09	0.09	0.09	0.09	0.10	0.10	0.10	0.10	0.10	0.10	0.10	0.10	0.10	0.10
5	0.11	0.11	0.11	0.11	0.11	0.12	0.12	0.12	0.12	0.12	0.12	0.13	0.13	0.13	0.13	0.13
6	0.13	0.13	0.13	0.14	0.14	0.14	0.14	0.14	0.15	0.15	0.15	0.15	0.15	0.15	0.16	0.16
7	0.15	0.15	0.16	0.16	0.16	0.16	0.16	0.17	0.17	0.17	0.17	0.18	0.18	0.18	0.18	0.18
8	0.17	0.18	0.18	0.18	0.18	0.19	0.19	0.19	0.19	0.20	0.20	0.20	0.20	0.20	0.21	0.21
9	0.20	0.20	0.20	0.20	0.21	0.21	0.21	0.21	0.22	0.22	0.22	0.23	0.23	0.23	0.23	0.24
10	0.22	0.22	0.22	0.23	0.23	0.23	0.24	0.24	0.24	0.24	0.25	0.25	0.25	0.26	0.26	0.26
20	0.44	0.44	0.45	0.45	0.46	0.47	0.47	0.48	0.48	0.49	0.49	0.50	0.51	0.51	0.52	0.52
30	0.65	0.66	0.67	0.68	0.69	0.70	0.71	0.72	0.72	0.73	0.74	0.75	0.76	0.77	0.78	0.79
40	0.87	0.88	0.90	0.91	0.92	0.93	0.94	0.95	0.97	0.98	0.99	1.00	1.01	1.02	1.04	1.05
50	1.09	1.11	1.12	1.13	1.15	1.16	1.18	1.19	1.21	1.22	1.24	1.25	1.27	1.28	1.29	1.31
60	1.31	1.33	1.34	1.36	1.38	1.40	1.41	1.43	1.45	1.47	1.48	1.50	1.52	1.54	1.55	1.57
70	1.53	1.55	1.57	1.59	1.61	1.63	1.65	1.67	1.69	1.71	1.73	1.75	1.77	1.79	1.81	1.83
80	1.75	1.77	1.79	1.82	1.84	1.86	1.89	1.91	1.93	1.96	1.98	2.00	2.02	2.05	2.07	2.10
90	1.96	1.99	2.02	2.04	2.07	2.10	2.12	2.15	2.17	2.20	2.23	2.25	2.28	2.30	2.33	2.36
100	2.18	2.21	2.24	2.27	2.30	2.33	2.36	2.39	2.42	2.44	2.47	2.50	2.53	2.56	2.59	2.62
200	4.36	4.42	4.48	4.54	4.60	4.66	4.71	4.77	4.83	4.89	4.95	5.00	5.06	5.12	5.18	5.24
300	6.55	6.63	6.72	6.81	6.89	6.98	7.07	7.16	7.25	7.33	7.42	7.51	7.59	7.68	7.77	7.86
400	8.73	8.84	8.96	9.08	9.19	9.31	9.43	9.54	9.66	9.78	9.89	10.01	10.12	10.24	10.36	10.48
500	10.91	11.06	11.20	11.35	11.49	11.64	11.79	11.93	12.08	12.22	12.37	12.51	12.66	12.80	12.95	13.10
600	13.09	13.27	13.44	13.61	13.79	13.97	14.14	14.32	14.49	14.66	14.84	15.01	15.19	15.36	15.53	15.71
700	15.27	15.48	15.68	15.88	16.09	16.30	16.50	16.70	16.91	17.11	17.31	17.51	17.72	17.92	18.12	18.33
800	17.46	17.69	17.92	18.15	18.38	18.62	18.86	19.09	19.32	19.55	19.78	20.02	20.25	20.48	20.71	20.95
900	19.64	19.90	20.16	20.42	20.68	20.95	21.21	21.47	21.74	22.00	22.26	22.52	22.78	23.04	23.30	23.57
1000	21.82	22.11	22.40	22.69	22.98	23.28	23.57	23.86	24.15	24.44	24.73	25.02	25.31	25.60	25.89	26.19

1 Degree.

Minutes	45	46	47	48	49	50	51	52	53	54	55	56	57	58	59	60
Dis. in ft.																
1	0.03	0.03	0.03	0.03	0.03	0.03	0.03	0.03	0.03	0.03	0.03	0.03	0.03	0.03	0.03	0.03
2	0.06	0.06	0.06	0.06	0.06	0.06	0.06	0.07	0.07	0.07	0.07	0.07	0.07	0.07	0.07	0.07
3	0.09	0.09	0.09	0.09	0.10	0.10	0.10	0.10	0.10	0.10	0.10	0.10	0.10	0.10	0.10	0.10
4	0.12	0.12	0.12	0.13	0.13	0.13	0.13	0.13	0.13	0.13	0.14	0.14	0.14	0.14	0.14	0.14
5	0.15	0.15	0.16	0.16	0.16	0.16	0.16	0.16	0.16	0.17	0.17	0.17	0.17	0.17	0.17	0.17
6	0.18	0.19	0.19	0.19	0.19	0.19	0.19	0.20	0.20	0.20	0.20	0.20	0.20	0.21	0.21	0.21
7	0.21	0.22	0.22	0.22	0.22	0.22	0.23	0.23	0.23	0.23	0.23	0.24	0.24	0.24	0.24	0.24
8	0.24	0.25	0.25	0.25	0.25	0.26	0.26	0.26	0.26	0.27	0.27	0.27	0.27	0.27	0.28	0.28
9	0.27	0.28	0.28	0.28	0.29	0.29	0.29	0.29	0.30	0.30	0.30	0.30	0.31	0.31	0.31	0.31
10	0.31	0.31	0.31	0.31	0.32	0.32	0.32	0.33	0.33	0.33	0.33	0.34	0.34	0.34	0.35	0.35
20	0.61	0.62	0.62	0.63	0.63	0.64	0.65	0.65	0.66	0.66	0.67	0.68	0.68	0.69	0.69	0.70
30	0.92	0.93	0.93	0.94	0.95	0.96	0.97	0.98	0.99	1.00	1.00	1.01	1.02	1.03	1.04	1.05
40	1.22	1.23	1.25	1.26	1.27	1.28	1.29	1.30	1.32	1.33	1.34	1.35	1.36	1.37	1.39	1.40
50	1.53	1.54	1.56	1.57	1.59	1.60	1.62	1.63	1.64	1.66	1.67	1.69	1.70	1.72	1.73	1.75
60	1.83	1.85	1.87	1.89	1.90	1.92	1.94	1.96	1.97	1.99	2.01	2.03	2.04	2.06	2.08	2.10
70	2.14	2.16	2.18	2.20	2.22	2.24	2.26	2.28	2.30	2.32	2.34	2.36	2.38	2.40	2.42	2.44
80	2.44	2.47	2.49	2.51	2.54	2.56	2.58	2.61	2.63	2.65	2.68	2.70	2.72	2.75	2.77	2.79
90	2.75	2.78	2.80	2.83	2.85	2.88	2.91	2.93	2.96	2.99	3.01	3.04	3.06	3.09	3.12	3.14
100	3.06	3.08	3.11	3.14	3.17	3.20	3.23	3.26	3.29	3.32	3.35	3.38	3.41	3.43	3.46	3.49
200	6.11	6.17	6.23	6.29	6.34	6.40	6.46	6.52	6.58	6.63	6.69	6.75	6.81	6.87	6.93	6.98
300	9.17	9.25	9.34	9.43	9.52	9.60	9.69	9.78	9.86	9.95	10.04	10.13	10.22	10.30	10.39	10.48
400	12.22	12.34	12.45	12.57	12.69	12.80	12.92	13.04	13.15	13.27	13.38	13.50	13.62	13.74	13.85	13.97
500	15.28	15.42	15.57	15.72	15.86	16.01	16.15	16.30	16.44	16.59	16.73	16.88	17.03	17.17	17.32	17.46
600	18.33	18.50	18.68	18.86	19.03	19.21	19.38	19.55	19.73	19.90	20.08	20.26	20.43	20.60	20.78	20.95
700	21.39	21.59	21.79	22.00	22.20	22.41	22.61	22.81	23.02	23.22	23.42	23.63	23.84	24.04	24.24	24.44
800	24.44	24.67	24.90	25.14	25.38	25.61	25.84	26.07	26.30	26.54	26.77	27.01	27.24	27.47	27.70	27.94
900	27.50	27.76	28.02	28.29	28.55	28.81	29.07	29.33	29.59	29.85	30.11	30.38	30.65	30.91	31.17	31.43
1000	30.55	30.84	31.13	31.43	31.72	32.01	32.30	32.59	32.88	33.17	33.46	33.76	34.05	34.34	34.63	34.92

2 Degrees.

Minutes	0	1	2	3	4	5	6	7	8	9	10	11	12	13	14
Dis. in ft.															
1	0.03	0.04	0.04	0.04	0.04	0.04	0.04	0.04	0.04	0.04	0.04	0.04	0.04	0.04	0.04
2	0.07	0.07	0.07	0.07	0.07	0.07	0.07	0.07	0.07	0.08	0.08	0.08	0.08	0.08	0.08
3	0.10	0.11	0.11	0.11	0.11	0.11	0.11	0.11	0.11	0.11	0.11	0.11	0.12	0.12	0.12
4	0.14	0.14	0.14	0.14	0.14	0.15	0.15	0.15	0.15	0.15	0.15	0.15	0.15	0.15	0.16
5	0.17	0.18	0.18	0.18	0.18	0.18	0.18	0.18	0.19	0.19	0.19	0.19	0.19	0.19	0.20
6	0.21	0.21	0.21	0.21	0.22	0.22	0.22	0.22	0.22	0.23	0.23	0.23	0.23	0.23	0.23
7	0.24	0.25	0.25	0.25	0.25	0.25	0.26	0.26	0.26	0.26	0.26	0.27	0.27	0.27	0.27
8	0.28	0.28	0.28	0.29	0.29	0.29	0.29	0.30	0.30	0.30	0.30	0.30	0.31	0.31	0.31
9	0.31	0.32	0.32	0.32	0.32	0.33	0.33	0.33	0.33	0.34	0.34	0.34	0.34	0.35	0.35
10	0.35	0.35	0.36	0.36	0.36	0.36	0.37	0.37	0.37	0.38	0.38	0.38	0.38	0.39	0.39
20	0.70	0.70	0.71	0.72	0.72	0.73	0.73	0.74	0.75	0.75	0.76	0.76	0.77	0.77	0.78
30	1.05	1.06	1.07	1.07	1.08	1.09	1.10	1.11	1.12	1.13	1.13	1.14	1.15	1.16	1.17
40	1.40	1.41	1.42	1.43	1.44	1.46	1.47	1.48	1.49	1.50	1.51	1.52	1.54	1.55	1.56
50	1.75	1.76	1.78	1.79	1.80	1.82	1.83	1.85	1.86	1.88	1.89	1.91	1.92	1.94	1.95
60	2.10	2.11	2.13	2.15	2.17	2.18	2.20	2.22	2.24	2.25	2.27	2.29	2.31	2.32	2.34
70	2.44	2.46	2.49	2.51	2.53	2.55	2.57	2.59	2.61	2.63	2.65	2.67	2.69	2.71	2.73
80	2.79	2.82	2.84	2.86	2.89	2.91	2.93	2.96	2.98	3.00	3.03	3.05	3.07	3.10	3.12
90	3.14	3.17	3.20	3.22	3.25	3.27	3.30	3.33	3.35	3.38	3.41	3.43	3.46	3.48	3.51
100	3.49	3.52	3.55	3.58	3.61	3.64	3.67	3.70	3.73	3.75	3.78	3.81	3.84	3.87	3.90
200	6.98	7.04	7.10	7.16	7.22	7.28	7.33	7.39	7.45	7.51	7.57	7.62	7.68	7.74	7.80
300	10.48	10.56	10.65	10.74	10.83	10.91	11.00	11.09	11.18	11.26	11.35	11.44	11.53	11.61	11.70
400	13.97	14.08	14.20	14.32	14.44	14.55	14.67	14.78	14.90	15.02	15.13	15.25	15.37	15.48	15.60
500	17.46	17.61	17.75	17.90	18.05	18.19	18.34	18.48	18.63	18.77	18.92	19.06	19.21	19.36	19.50
600	20.95	21.13	21.30	21.48	21.65	21.83	22.00	22.18	22.35	22.52	22.70	22.87	23.05	23.23	23.40
700	24.44	24.65	24.85	25.06	25.26	25.47	25.67	25.87	26.08	26.28	26.48	26.68	26.89	27.10	27.30
800	27.94	28.17	28.40	28.64	28.87	29.10	29.34	29.57	29.80	30.03	30.26	30.50	30.74	30.97	31.20
900	31.43	31.69	31.95	32.22	32.48	32.74	33.00	33.26	33.53	33.79	34.05	34.31	34.58	34.84	35.10
1000	34.92	35.21	35.50	35.80	36.09	36.38	36.67	36.96	37.25	37.54	37.83	38.12	38.42	38.71	39.00

2 Degrees.

Minutes	30	31	32	33	34	35	36	37	38	39	40	41	42	43	44
Dis. in ft.															
1	0.04	0.04	0.04	0.04	0.04	0.04	0.05	0.05	0.05	0.05	0.05	0.05	0.05	0.05	0.05
2	0.09	0.09	0.09	0.09	0.09	0.09	0.09	0.09	0.09	0.09	0.09	0.09	0.09	0.09	0.10
3	0.13	0.13	0.13	0.13	0.13	0.14	0.14	0.14	0.14	0.14	0.14	0.14	0.14	0.14	0.14
4	0.18	0.18	0.18	0.18	0.18	0.18	0.18	0.18	0.18	0.19	0.19	0.19	0.19	0.19	0.19
5	0.22	0.22	0.22	0.22	0.22	0.23	0.23	0.23	0.23	0.23	0.23	0.23	0.24	0.24	0.24
6	0.26	0.26	0.27	0.27	0.27	0.27	0.27	0.27	0.28	0.28	0.28	0.28	0.28	0.28	0.29
7	0.31	0.31	0.31	0.31	0.31	0.32	0.32	0.32	0.32	0.32	0.33	0.33	0.33	0.33	0.33
8	0.35	0.35	0.35	0.36	0.36	0.36	0.36	0.37	0.37	0.37	0.37	0.37	0.37	0.38	0.38
9	0.39	0.40	0.40	0.40	0.40	0.41	0.41	0.41	0.41	0.42	0.42	0.42	0.42	0.43	0.43
10	0.44	0.44	0.44	0.45	0.45	0.45	0.45	0.46	0.46	0.46	0.47	0.47	0.47	0.47	0.48
20	0.87	0.88	0.88	0.89	0.90	0.90	0.91	0.91	0.92	0.93	0.93	0.94	0.94	0.95	0.95
30	1.31	1.32	1.33	1.34	1.34	1.35	1.36	1.37	1.38	1.39	1.40	1.41	1.41	1.42	1.43
40	1.75	1.76	1.77	1.78	1.79	1.80	1.82	1.83	1.84	1.85	1.86	1.87	1.89	1.90	1.91
50	2.18	2.20	2.21	2.23	2.24	2.26	2.27	2.29	2.30	2.31	2.33	2.34	2.36	2.37	2.39
60	2.62	2.64	2.65	2.67	2.69	2.71	2.72	2.74	2.76	2.78	2.79	2.81	2.83	2.85	2.86
70	3.06	3.08	3.10	3.12	3.14	3.16	3.18	3.20	3.22	3.24	3.26	3.28	3.30	3.32	3.34
80	3.49	3.52	3.54	3.56	3.59	3.61	3.63	3.66	3.68	3.70	3.73	3.75	3.77	3.80	3.82
90	3.92	3.96	3.98	4.01	4.03	4.06	4.09	4.11	4.14	4.17	4.19	4.22	4.24	4.27	4.30
100	4.37	4.40	4.42	4.45	4.48	4.51	4.54	4.57	4.60	4.63	4.66	4.69	4.72	4.75	4.77
200	8.73	8.79	8.85	8.91	8.97	9.02	9.08	9.14	9.20	9.26	9.31	9.37	9.43	9.49	9.55
300	13.10	13.19	13.27	13.36	13.45	13.54	13.62	13.71	13.80	13.88	13.97	14.06	14.15	14.24	14.32
400	17.46	17.58	17.70	17.82	17.93	18.05	18.16	18.28	18.40	18.51	18.63	18.75	18.86	18.98	19.10
500	21.83	21.98	22.12	22.27	22.42	22.56	22.71	22.85	23.00	23.14	23.29	23.44	23.58	23.73	23.87
600	26.20	26.37	26.54	26.72	26.90	27.07	27.25	27.42	27.59	27.77	27.94	28.12	28.30	28.47	28.64
700	30.56	30.77	30.97	31.18	31.38	31.58	31.79	31.99	32.19	32.40	32.60	32.81	33.01	33.22	33.42
800	34.93	35.16	35.39	35.63	35.86	36.10	36.33	36.56	36.79	37.02	37.26	37.50	37.73	37.96	38.19
900	39.29	39.56	39.82	40.09	40.35	40.61	40.87	41.13	41.39	41.65	41.91	42.18	42.44	42.71	42.97
1000	43.66	43.95	44.24	44.54	44.83	45.12	45.41	45.70	45.99	46.28	46.57	46.87	47.16	47.45	47.74

2 Degrees.

Minutes	15	16	17	18	19	20	21	22	23	24	25	26	27	28	29	30
Dis. in ft																
1	0.04	0.04	0.04	0.04	0.04	0.04	0.04	0.04	0.04	0.04	0.04	0.04	0.04	0.04	0.04	0.04
2	0.08	0.08	0.08	0.08	0.08	0.08	0.08	0.08	0.08	0.08	0.08	0.09	0.09	0.09	0.09	0.09
3	0.12	0.12	0.12	0.12	0.12	0.12	0.12	0.12	0.12	0.13	0.13	0.13	0.13	0.13	0.13	0.13
4	0.16	0.16	0.16	0.16	0.16	0.16	0.16	0.17	0.17	0.17	0.17	0.17	0.17	0.17	0.17	0.17
5	0.20	0.20	0.20	0.20	0.20	0.20	0.21	0.21	0.21	0.21	0.21	0.21	0.21	0.22	0.22	0.22
6	0.24	0.24	0.24	0.24	0.24	0.24	0.25	0.25	0.25	0.25	0.25	0.26	0.26	0.26	0.26	0.26
7	0.28	0.28	0.28	0.28	0.28	0.29	0.29	0.29	0.29	0.29	0.30	0.30	0.30	0.30	0.30	0.31
8	0.31	0.32	0.32	0.32	0.32	0.33	0.33	0.33	0.33	0.34	0.34	0.34	0.34	0.34	0.35	0.35
9	0.35	0.36	0.36	0.36	0.36	0.37	0.37	0.37	0.37	0.38	0.38	0.38	0.39	0.39	0.39	0.39
10	0.39	0.40	0.40	0.40	0.40	0.41	0.41	0.41	0.42	0.42	0.42	0.43	0.43	0.43	0.43	0.44
20	0.79	0.79	0.80	0.80	0.81	0.82	0.82	0.83	1.83	0.84	0.84	0.85	0.86	0.86	0.87	0.87
30	1.18	1.19	1.20	1.20	1.21	1.22	1.23	1.24	1.25	1.26	1.27	1.28	1.28	1.29	1.30	1.31
40	1.57	1.58	1.59	1.61	1.62	1.63	1.64	1.65	1.66	1.68	1.69	1.70	1.71	1.72	1.73	1.75
50	1.96	1.98	1.99	2.01	2.02	2.04	2.05	2.07	2.08	2.10	2.11	2.13	2.14	2.15	2.17	2.18
60	2.36	2.37	2.39	2.41	2.43	2.45	2.46	2.48	2.50	2.51	2.53	2.55	2.57	2.58	2.60	2.62
70	2.75	2.77	2.79	2.81	2.83	2.85	2.87	2.89	2.91	2.93	2.95	2.98	3.00	3.02	3.04	3.06
80	3.14	3.17	3.19	3.21	3.24	3.26	3.28	3.31	3.33	3.35	3.38	3.40	3.42	3.45	3.47	3.49
90	3.54	3.56	3.59	3.61	3.64	3.67	3.69	3.72	3.75	3.77	3.80	3.83	3.85	3.88	3.90	3.93
100	3.93	3.96	3.99	4.02	4.05	4.08	4.10	4.13	4.16	4.19	4.22	4.25	4.28	4.31	4.34	4.37
200	7.86	7.92	7.97	8.03	8.09	8.15	8.21	8.27	8.32	8.38	8.44	8.50	8.56	8.62	8.67	8.73
300	11.79	11.87	11.96	12.05	12.14	12.23	12.31	12.40	12.49	12.57	12.66	12.75	12.84	12.92	13.01	13.10
400	15.72	15.83	15.95	16.06	16.18	16.30	16.42	16.53	16.65	16.76	16.88	17.00	17.11	17.23	17.35	17.46
500	19.65	19.79	19.94	20.08	20.23	20.38	20.52	20.67	20.81	20.96	21.10	21.25	21.40	21.54	21.69	21.83
600	23.57	23.75	23.92	24.10	24.28	24.45	24.62	24.80	24.97	25.15	25.32	25.50	25.67	25.85	26.02	26.20
700	27.50	27.71	27.91	28.11	28.32	28.53	28.73	28.93	29.13	29.34	29.54	29.75	29.95	30.16	30.36	30.56
800	31.43	31.66	31.90	32.13	32.37	32.60	32.83	33.06	33.30	33.53	33.76	34.00	34.23	34.46	34.70	34.93
900	35.36	35.62	35.88	36.14	36.41	36.68	36.94	37.20	37.46	37.72	37.98	38.25	38.51	38.77	39.03	39.29
1000	39.29	39.58	39.87	40.16	40.46	40.75	41.04	41.33	41.62	41.91	42.20	42.50	42.79	43.08	43.37	43.66

2 Degrees.

Minutes	45	46	47	48	49	50	51	52	53	54	55	56	57	58	59	60
Dis. in ft.																
1	0.05	0.05	0.05	0.05	0.05	0.05	0.05	0.05	0.05	0.05	0.05	0.05	0.05	0.05	0.05	0.05
2	0.10	0.10	0.10	0.10	0.10	0.10	0.10	0.10	0.10	0.10	0.10	0.10	0.10	0.10	0.10	0.10
3	0.14	0.14	0.15	0.15	0.15	0.15	0.15	0.15	0.15	0.15	0.15	0.15	0.15	0.16	0.16	0.16
4	0.19	0.19	0.19	0.20	0.20	0.20	0.20	0.20	0.20	0.20	0.20	0.20	0.21	0.21	0.21	0.21
5	0.24	0.24	0.24	0.24	0.25	0.25	0.25	0.25	0.25	0.25	0.25	0.26	0.26	0.26	0.26	0.26
6	0.29	0.29	0.29	0.29	0.30	0.30	0.30	0.30	0.30	0.30	0.31	0.31	0.31	0.31	0.31	0.31
7	0.34	0.34	0.34	0.34	0.34	0.35	0.35	0.35	0.35	0.35	0.36	0.36	0.36	0.36	0.36	0.37
8	0.38	0.39	0.39	0.39	0.39	0.40	0.40	0.40	0.40	0.41	0.41	0.41	0.41	0.41	0.42	0.42
9	0.43	0.43	0.44	0.44	0.44	0.45	0.45	0.45	0.45	0.46	0.46	0.46	0.46	0.47	0.47	0.47
10	0.48	0.48	0.49	0.49	0.49	0.49	0.50	0.50	0.50	0.51	0.51	0.51	0.52	0.52	0.52	0.52
20	0.96	0.97	0.97	0.98	0.98	0.99	1.00	1.00	1.01	1.01	1.02	1.02	1.03	1.04	1.04	1.05
30	1.44	1.45	1.46	1.47	1.48	1.48	1.49	1.50	1.51	1.52	1.53	1.54	1.55	1.55	1.56	1.57
40	1.92	1.93	1.94	1.96	1.97	1.98	1.99	2.00	2.01	2.03	2.04	2.05	2.06	2.07	2.08	2.10
50	2.40	2.42	2.43	2.45	2.46	2.47	2.49	2.50	2.52	2.53	2.55	2.56	2.58	2.59	2.61	2.62
60	2.88	2.90	2.92	2.93	2.95	2.97	2.99	3.00	3.02	3.04	3.06	3.07	3.09	3.11	3.13	3.14
70	3.36	3.38	3.40	3.42	3.44	3.46	3.48	3.51	3.53	3.55	3.57	3.59	3.61	3.63	3.65	3.67
80	3.84	3.87	3.89	3.91	3.94	3.96	3.98	4.01	4.03	4.05	4.08	4.10	4.12	4.15	4.17	4.19
90	4.32	4.35	4.38	4.40	4.43	4.45	4.48	4.51	4.53	4.56	4.59	4.61	4.64	4.66	4.69	4.72
100	4.80	4.83	4.86	4.89	4.92	4.95	4.98	5.01	5.04	5.07	5.10	5.12	5.15	5.18	5.21	5.24
200	9.61	9.66	9.72	9.78	9.84	9.90	9.96	10.02	10.07	10.13	10.19	10.25	10.31	10.36	10.42	10.48
300	14.41	14.50	14.59	14.67	14.76	14.85	14.93	15.02	15.11	15.20	15.29	15.37	15.46	15.55	15.64	15.72
400	19.21	19.33	19.45	19.56	19.68	19.80	19.91	20.03	20.15	20.26	20.38	20.50	20.61	20.73	20.85	20.96
500	24.02	24.16	24.31	24.46	24.60	24.75	24.89	25.04	25.19	25.33	25.48	25.62	25.77	25.91	26.06	26.21
600	28.82	28.99	29.17	29.35	29.52	29.69	29.87	30.05	30.22	30.40	30.57	30.74	30.92	31.09	31.27	31.45
700	33.62	33.82	34.03	34.24	34.44	34.64	34.85	35.06	35.26	35.46	35.67	35.87	36.07	36.27	36.48	36.69
800	38.42	38.66	38.90	39.13	39.36	39.59	39.82	40.06	40.30	40.53	40.76	40.99	41.22	41.46	41.70	41.93
900	43.23	43.49	43.76	44.02	44.28	44.54	44.80	45.07	45.33	45.59	45.86	46.12	46.38	46.64	46.91	47.17
1000	48.03	48.32	48.62	48.91	49.20	49.49	49.78	50.08	50.37	50.66	50.95	51.24	51.53	51.82	52.12	52.41

3 Degrees.

Minutes	0	1	2	3	4	5	6	7	8	9	10	11	12	13	14
Dis. in ft.															
1	0.05	0.05	0.05	0.05	0.05	0.05	0.05	0.05	0.05	0.06	0.06	0.06	0.06	0.06	0.06
2	0.11	0.11	0.11	0.11	0.11	0.11	0.11	0.11	0.11	0.11	0.11	0.11	0.11	0.11	0.11
3	0.16	0.16	0.16	0.16	0.16	0.16	0.16	0.16	0.16	0.17	0.17	0.17	0.17	0.17	0.17
4	0.21	0.21	0.21	0.21	0.21	0.22	0.22	0.22	0.22	0.22	0.22	0.22	0.22	0.22	0.23
5	0.26	0.26	0.26	0.27	0.27	0.27	0.27	0.27	0.27	0.28	0.28	0.28	0.28	0.28	0.28
6	0.31	0.32	0.32	0.32	0.32	0.32	0.33	0.33	0.33	0.33	0.33	0.34	0.34	0.34	0.34
7	0.37	0.37	0.37	0.37	0.37	0.38	0.38	0.38	0.38	0.39	0.39	0.39	0.39	0.39	0.40
8	0.42	0.42	0.42	0.43	0.43	0.43	0.43	0.44	0.44	0.44	0.44	0.44	0.45	0.45	0.45
9	0.47	0.47	0.48	0.48	0.48	0.48	0.49	0.49	0.49	0.50	0.50	0.50	0.50	0.51	0.51
10	0.52	0.53	0.53	0.53	0.54	0.54	0.54	0.54	0.55	0.55	0.55	0.56	0.56	0.56	0.56
20	1.05	1.05	1.06	1.07	1.07	1.08	1.08	1.09	1.09	1.10	1.11	1.11	1.12	1.12	1.13
30	1.57	1.58	1.59	1.60	1.61	1.62	1.63	1.63	1.64	1.65	1.66	1.67	1.68	1.69	1.69
40	2.10	2.11	2.12	2.13	2.14	2.15	2.17	2.18	2.19	2.20	2.21	2.22	2.24	2.25	2.26
50	2.62	2.64	2.65	2.66	2.68	2.69	2.71	2.72	2.74	2.75	2.77	2.78	2.80	2.81	2.82
60	3.14	3.16	3.18	3.20	3.21	3.23	3.25	3.27	3.28	3.30	3.32	3.34	3.35	3.37	3.39
70	3.67	3.69	3.71	3.73	3.75	3.77	3.79	3.81	3.83	3.85	3.87	3.89	3.91	3.93	3.95
80	4.19	4.22	4.24	4.26	4.29	4.31	4.33	4.36	4.38	4.40	4.43	4.45	4.47	4.50	4.52
90	4.72	4.74	4.77	4.80	4.82	4.85	4.87	4.90	4.93	4.95	4.98	5.01	5.03	5.06	5.08
100	5.24	5.27	5.30	5.33	5.36	5.39	5.42	5.45	5.47	5.50	5.53	5.56	5.59	5.62	5.65
200	10.48	10.54	10.60	10.66	10.71	10.77	10.83	10.89	10.95	11.01	11.07	11.12	11.18	11.24	11.30
300	15.72	15.81	15.90	15.98	16.07	16.16	16.25	16.34	16.42	16.51	16.60	16.69	16.77	16.85	16.95
400	20.96	21.08	21.20	21.31	21.43	21.55	21.66	21.78	21.90	22.01	22.13	22.25	22.36	22.48	22.60
500	26.21	26.35	26.50	26.64	26.79	26.93	27.08	27.23	27.37	27.52	27.67	27.81	27.96	28.10	28.25
600	31.45	31.62	31.79	31.97	32.14	32.32	32.50	32.67	32.84	33.02	33.20	33.37	33.55	33.72	33.89
700	36.69	36.89	37.09	37.30	37.50	37.71	37.91	38.12	38.32	38.52	38.73	38.93	39.14	39.34	39.54
800	41.93	42.16	42.39	42.62	42.86	43.10	43.33	43.56	43.79	44.03	44.26	44.50	44.73	44.96	45.19
900	47.17	47.43	47.69	47.95	48.21	48.48	48.74	49.01	49.27	49.53	49.80	50.06	50.32	50.58	50.84
1000	52.41	52.70	52.99	53.28	53.57	53.87	54.16	54.45	54.74	55.03	55.33	55.62	55.91	56.20	56.49

3 Degrees.

Minutes	30	31	32	33	34	35	36	37	38	39	40	41	42	43	44
Dis. in ft.															
1	0.06	0.06	0.06	0.06	0.06	0.06	0.06	0.06	0.06	0.06	0.06	0.06	0.06	0.06	0.07
2	0.12	0.12	0.12	0.12	0.13	0.13	0.13	0.13	0.13	0.13	0.13	0.13	0.13	0.13	0.13
3	0.18	0.18	0.19	0.19	0.19	0.19	0.19	0.19	0.19	0.19	0.19	0.19	0.19	0.20	0.20
4	0.25	0.25	0.25	0.25	0.25	0.25	0.25	0.25	0.25	0.25	0.26	0.26	0.26	0.26	0.26
5	0.31	0.31	0.31	0.31	0.31	0.31	0.32	0.32	0.32	0.32	0.32	0.32	0.32	0.33	0.33
6	0.37	0.37	0.37	0.37	0.37	0.38	0.38	0.38	0.38	0.38	0.38	0.39	0.39	0.39	0.39
7	0.43	0.43	0.43	0.43	0.44	0.44	0.44	0.44	0.44	0.45	0.45	0.45	0.45	0.46	0.46
8	0.49	0.49	0.49	0.50	0.50	0.50	0.50	0.51	0.51	0.51	0.51	0.52	0.52	0.52	0.52
9	0.55	0.55	0.56	0.56	0.56	0.56	0.57	0.57	0.57	0.57	0.58	0.58	0.58	0.59	0.59
10	0.61	0.61	0.62	0.62	0.62	0.63	0.63	0.63	0.64	0.64	0.64	0.64	0.65	0.65	0.65
20	1.22	1.23	1.24	1.24	1.25	1.25	1.26	1.26	1.27	1.28	1.28	1.29	1.30	1.30	1.31
30	1.83	1.84	1.85	1.86	1.87	1.88	1.89	1.90	1.91	1.91	1.92	1.93	1.94	1.95	1.96
40	2.45	2.46	2.47	2.48	2.49	2.50	2.52	2.53	2.54	2.55	2.56	2.58	2.59	2.60	2.61
50	3.06	3.07	3.09	3.10	3.12	3.13	3.15	3.16	3.18	3.19	3.20	3.22	3.23	3.25	3.26
60	3.67	3.69	3.71	3.72	3.74	3.76	3.77	3.79	3.81	3.83	3.84	3.86	3.88	3.90	3.92
70	4.28	4.30	4.32	4.34	4.36	4.38	4.40	4.42	4.44	4.47	4.49	4.51	4.53	4.55	4.57
80	4.89	4.92	4.94	4.96	4.99	5.01	5.03	5.06	5.08	5.10	5.13	5.15	5.17	5.20	5.22
90	5.50	5.53	5.56	5.58	5.61	5.64	5.66	5.69	5.72	5.74	5.77	5.79	5.82	5.85	5.87
100	6.12	6.15	6.18	6.20	6.23	6.26	6.29	6.32	6.35	6.38	6.41	6.44	6.47	6.50	6.53
200	12.23	12.29	12.35	12.41	12.47	12.52	12.58	12.64	12.70	12.76	12.82	12.88	12.93	12.99	13.05
300	18.35	18.44	18.53	18.61	18.70	18.79	18.87	18.96	19.05	19.14	19.22	19.31	19.40	19.49	19.58
400	24.46	24.58	24.70	24.82	24.93	25.05	25.16	25.28	25.40	25.52	25.63	25.75	25.87	25.98	26.10
500	30.58	30.73	30.88	31.02	31.17	31.31	31.46	31.61	31.75	31.90	32.04	32.19	32.34	32.48	32.63
600	36.70	36.87	37.05	37.22	37.40	37.57	37.75	37.93	38.10	38.27	38.45	38.63	38.80	38.98	39.15
700	42.81	43.02	43.23	43.43	43.63	43.83	44.04	44.25	44.45	44.65	44.86	45.07	45.27	45.47	45.68
800	48.93	49.16	49.40	49.63	49.86	50.10	50.33	50.57	50.80	51.03	51.26	51.50	51.74	51.97	52.20
900	55.04	55.31	55.58	55.84	56.10	56.36	56.62	56.89	57.15	57.41	57.67	57.94	58.20	58.46	58.73
1000	61.16	61.45	61.75	62.04	62.33	62.62	62.91	63.21	63.50	63.79	64.08	64.38	64.67	64.96	65.25

3 Degrees.

Minutes	15	16	17	18	19	20	21	22	23	24	25	26	27	28	29	30
Dis. in ft.																
1	0.06	0.06	0.06	0.06	0.06	0.06	0.06	0.06	0.06	0.06	0.06	0.06	0.06	0.06	0.06	0.06
2	0.11	0.11	0.11	0.12	0.12	6.12	0.12	0.12	0.12	0.12	0.12	0.12	0.12	0.12	0.12	0.12
3	0.17	0.17	0.17	0.17	0.17	0.17	0.18	0.18	0.18	0.18	0.18	0.18	0.18	0.18	0.18	0.18
4	0.23	0.23	0.23	0.23	0.23	0.23	0.23	0.24	0.24	0.24	0.24	0.24	0.24	0.24	0.24	0.24
5	0.28	0.29	0.29	0.29	0.29	0.29	0.29	0.29	0.30	0.30	0.30	0.30	0.30	0.30	0.30	0.31
6	0.34	0.34	0.34	0.35	0.35	0.35	0.35	0.35	0.35	0.36	0.36	0.36	0.36	0.36	0.36	0.37
7	0.40	0.40	0.40	0.40	0.41	0.41	0.41	0.41	0.41	0.41	0.42	0.42	0.42	0.42	0.43	0.43
8	0.45	0.46	0.46	0.46	0.46	0.47	0.47	0.47	0.47	0.48	0.48	0.48	0.48	0.48	0.49	0.49
9	0.51	0.51	0.52	0.52	0.52	0.52	0.53	0.53	0.53	0.53	0.54	0.54	0.54	0.55	0.55	0.55
10	0.57	0.57	0.57	0.58	0.58	0.58	0.59	0.59	0.59	0.59	0.60	0.60	0.60	0.61	0.61	0.61
20	1.14	1.14	1.15	1.15	1.16	1.16	1.17	1.18	1.18	1.19	1.19	1.20	1.21	1.21	1.22	1.22
30	1.70	1.71	1.72	1.73	1.74	1.75	1.76	1.76	1.77	1.78	1.79	1.80	1.81	1.82	1.83	1.83
40	2.27	2.28	2.29	2.31	2.32	2.33	2.34	2.35	2.36	2.38	2.39	2.40	2.41	2.42	2.43	2.45
50	2.84	2.85	2.87	2.88	2.90	2.91	2.93	2.94	2.96	2.97	2.99	3.00	3.01	3.03	3.04	3.06
60	3.41	3.42	3.44	3.46	3.48	3.49	3.51	3.53	3.55	3.56	3.58	3.60	3.62	3.63	3.65	3.67
70	3.97	4.00	4.02	4.04	4.06	4.08	4.10	4.12	4.14	4.16	4.18	4.20	4.22	4.24	4.26	4.28
80	4.54	4.57	4.59	4.61	4.64	4.66	4.68	4.71	4.73	4.75	4.78	4.80	4.82	4.85	4.87	4.89
90	5.11	5.14	5.16	5.19	5.22	5.24	5.27	5.29	5.32	5.35	5.37	5.40	5.43	5.45	5.48	5.50
100	5.68	5.71	5.74	5.77	5.80	5.82	5.85	5.88	5.91	5.94	5.97	6.00	6.03	6.06	6.09	6.12
200	11.36	11.42	11.47	11.53	11.59	11.65	11.71	11.77	11.82	11.88	11.94	12.00	12.06	12.12	12.17	12.23
300	17.03	17.12	17.21	17.30	17.39	17.47	17.56	17.65	17.74	17.82	17.91	18.00	18.09	18.17	18.26	18.35
400	22.71	22.83	22.95	23.06	23.18	23.30	23.42	23.58	23.65	23.76	23.88	24.00	24.12	24.23	24.35	24.46
500	28.39	28.54	28.69	28.83	28.98	29.12	29.27	29.42	29.56	29.71	29.85	30.00	30.15	30.29	30.44	30.58
600	34.07	34.25	34.42	34.60	34.77	34.94	35.12	35.30	35.47	35.65	35.82	35.99	36.17	36.35	36.52	36.70
700	39.75	39.96	40.16	40.36	40.57	40.77	40.98	41.18	41.38	41.59	41.79	41.99	42.20	42.41	42.61	42.81
800	45.42	45.66	45.90	46.13	46.36	46.59	46.83	47.06	47.30	47.58	47.76	47.99	48.23	48.46	48.70	48.93
900	51.10	51.37	51.63	51.89	52.16	52.42	52.69	52.95	53.21	53.47	53.73	53.99	54.26	54.52	54.78	55.04
1000	56.78	57.08	57.37	57.66	57.95	58.24	58.54	58.83	59.12	59.41	59.70	59.99	60.29	60.58	60.87	61.16

3 Degrees.

Minutes	45	46	47	48	49	50	51	52	53	54	55	56	57	58	59	60
Dis. in ft.																
1	0.07	0.07	0.07	0.07	0.07	0.07	0.07	0.07	0.07	0.07	0.07	0.07	0.07	0.07	0.07	0.07
2	0.13	0.13	0.13	0.13	0.13	0.13	0.13	0.14	0.14	0.14	0.14	0.14	0.14	0.14	0.14	0.14
3	0.20	0.20	0.20	0.20	0.20	0.20	0.20	0.20	0.20	0.20	0.20	0.21	0.21	0.21	0.21	0.21
4	0.26	0.26	0.26	0.27	0.27	0.27	0.27	0.27	0.27	0.27	0.27	0.27	0.28	0.28	0.28	0.28
5	0.33	0.33	0.33	0.33	0.33	0.34	0.34	0.34	0.34	0.34	0.34	0.34	0.35	0.35	0.35	0.35
6	0.39	0.40	0.40	0.40	0.40	0.40	0.40	0.41	0.41	0.41	0.41	0.41	0.41	0.42	0.42	0.42
7	0.46	0.46	0.46	0.46	0.47	0.47	0.47	0.47	0.48	0.48	0.48	0.48	0.48	0.49	0.49	0.49
8	0.52	0.53	0.53	0.53	0.53	0.54	0.54	0.54	0.54	0.55	0.55	0.55	0.55	0.55	0.56	0.56
9	0.59	0.59	0.60	0.60	0.60	0.60	0.61	0.61	0.61	0.61	0.62	0.62	0.62	0.62	0.63	0.63
10	0.66	0.66	0.66	0.66	0.67	0.67	0.67	0.68	0.68	0.68	0.68	0.69	0.69	0.69	0.70	0.70
20	1.31	1.32	1.32	1.33	1.33	1.34	1.35	1.35	1.36	1.36	1.37	1.38	1.38	1.39	1.39	1.40
30	1.97	1.98	1.98	1.99	2.00	2.01	2.02	2.03	2.04	2.05	2.05	2.06	2.07	2.08	2.09	2.10
40	2.62	2.63	2.65	2.66	2.67	2.68	2.69	2.70	2.72	2.73	2.74	2.75	2.76	2.77	2.79	2.80
50	3.28	3.29	3.31	3.32	3.34	3.35	3.37	3.38	3.39	3.41	3.42	3.44	3.45	3.47	3.48	3.50
60	3.93	3.95	3.97	3.99	4.00	4.02	4.04	4.06	4.07	4.09	4.11	4.13	4.14	4.16	4.18	4.20
70	4.59	4.61	4.63	4.65	4.67	4.69	4.71	4.73	4.75	4.77	4.79	4.81	4.83	4.85	4.87	4.90
80	5.24	5.27	5.29	5.31	5.34	5.36	5.38	5.41	5.43	5.45	5.48	5.50	5.52	5.55	5.57	5.59
90	5.90	5.93	5.95	5.98	6.00	6.03	6.06	6.08	6.11	6.14	6.16	6.19	6.21	6.24	6.27	6.29
100	6.55	6.58	6.61	6.64	6.67	6.70	6.73	6.76	6.79	6.82	6.85	6.88	6.91	6.93	6.96	6.99
200	13.11	13.17	13.23	13.28	13.34	13.40	13.46	13.52	13.58	13.63	13.69	13.75	13.81	13.87	13.93	13.99
300	19.66	19.75	19.84	19.93	20.01	20.10	20.19	20.28	20.36	20.45	20.54	20.63	20.72	20.80	20.89	20.98
400	26.22	26.34	26.45	26.57	26.68	26.80	26.92	27.04	27.15	27.27	27.38	27.50	27.62	27.74	27.85	27.97
500	32.77	32.92	33.07	33.21	33.36	33.50	33.65	33.80	33.94	34.09	34.23	34.38	34.53	34.67	34.82	34.97
600	39.32	39.50	39.68	39.85	40.03	40.20	40.38	40.55	40.73	40.90	41.08	41.26	41.43	41.61	41.78	41.96
700	45.88	46.09	46.29	46.49	46.70	46.90	47.11	47.31	47.52	47.72	47.92	48.13	48.34	48.54	48.74	48.95
800	52.43	52.67	52.90	53.14	53.37	53.60	53.84	54.07	54.30	54.54	54.77	55.01	55.24	55.47	55.70	55.94
900	58.99	59.26	59.52	59.78	60.04	60.30	60.57	60.83	61.09	61.35	61.61	61.88	62.15	62.41	62.67	62.94
1000	65.54	65.84	66.13	66.42	66.71	67.00	67.30	67.59	67.88	68.17	68.46	68.76	69.05	69.34	69.63	69.93

Minutes	0	1	2	3	4	5	6	7	8	9	10	11	12	13	14
Dis. in ft.															
1	0.07	0.07	0.07	0.07	0.07	0.07	0.07	0.07	0.07	0.07	0.07	0.07	0.07	0.07	0.07
2	0.14	0.14	0.14	0.14	0.14	0.14	0.14	0.11	0.14	0.15	0.15	0.15	0.15	0.15	0.15
3	0.21	0.21	0.21	0.21	0.21	0.21	0.22	0.22	0.22	0.22	0.22	0.22	0.22	0.22	0.22
4	0.28	0.28	0.28	0.28	0.28	0.29	0.29	0.29	0.29	0.29	0.29	0.29	0.29	0.29	0.30
5	0.35	0.35	0.35	0.35	0.36	0.36	0.36	0.36	0.36	0.36	0.36	0.36	0.36	0.37	0.37
6	0.42	0.42	0.42	0.42	0.43	0.43	0.43	0.43	0.43	0.44	0.44	0.44	0.44	0.44	0.44
7	0.49	0.49	0.49	0.50	0.50	0.50	0.50	0.50	0.51	0.51	0.51	0.51	0.52	0.52	0.52
8	0.56	0.56	0.56	0.57	0.57	0.57	0.57	0.58	0.58	0.58	0.58	0.58	0.59	0.59	0.59
9	0.63	0.63	0.63	0.64	0.64	0.64	0.65	0.65	0.65	0.65	0.66	0.66	0.66	0.66	0.67
10	0.70	0.70	0.71	0.71	0.71	0.71	0.72	0.72	0.72	0.73	0.73	0.73	0.73	0.74	0.74
20	1.40	1.40	1.41	1.42	1.42	1.43	1.43	1.44	1.45	1.45	1.46	1.46	1.47	1.47	1.48
30	2.10	2.11	2.12	2.12	2.13	2.14	2.15	2.16	2.17	2.18	2.19	2.19	2.20	2.21	2.22
40	2.80	2.81	2.82	2.83	2.84	2.86	2.87	2.88	2.89	2.90	2.91	2.93	2.94	2.95	2.96
50	3.50	3.51	3.53	3.54	3.56	3.57	3.58	3.60	3.61	3.63	3.64	3.66	3.67	3.69	3.70
60	4.20	4.21	4.23	4.25	4.27	4.28	4.30	4.32	4.34	4.35	4.37	4.39	4.41	4.42	4.44
70	4.90	4.92	4.94	4.96	4.98	5.00	5.02	5.04	5.06	5.08	5.10	5.12	5.14	5.16	5.18
80	5.59	5.62	5.64	5.66	5.69	5.71	5.73	5.76	5.78	5.80	5.83	5.85	5.88	5.90	5.92
90	6.29	6.32	6.35	6.37	6.40	6.43	6.45	6.48	6.50	6.53	6.56	6.58	6.61	6.64	6.66
100	6.99	7.02	7.05	7.08	7.11	7.14	7.17	7.20	7.23	7.26	7.29	7.31	7.34	7.37	7.40
200	13.99	14.04	14.10	14.16	14.22	14.28	14.34	14.39	14.45	14.51	14.57	14.63	14.69	14.75	14.80
300	20.98	21.07	21.15	21.24	21.33	21.42	21.50	21.59	21.68	21.77	21.86	21.94	22.03	22.12	22.21
400	27.97	28.09	28.20	28.32	28.44	28.56	28.67	28.78	28.90	29.02	29.14	29.26	29.38	29.49	29.61
500	34.97	35.11	35.26	35.40	35.55	35.70	35.84	35.99	36.13	36.28	36.43	36.58	36.72	36.87	37.01
600	41.96	42.13	42.31	42.48	42.66	42.83	43.01	43.18	43.36	43.54	43.71	43.88	44.06	44.24	44.41
700	48.95	49.15	49.36	49.56	49.77	49.97	50.18	50.38	50.58	50.79	51.00	51.20	51.41	51.61	51.81
800	55.94	56.18	56.41	56.64	56.88	57.11	57.34	57.58	57.81	58.05	58.28	58.51	58.75	58.98	59.22
900	62.94	63.20	63.46	63.72	63.99	64.25	64.51	64.77	65.03	65.30	65.57	65.83	66.10	66.36	66.62
1000	69.93	70.22	70.51	70.80	71.10	71.39	71.68	71.97	72.26	72.56	72.85	73.14	73.44	73.73	74.02

4 Degrees.

Minutes	30	31	32	33	34	35	36	37	38	39	40	41	42	43	44
Dis. in ft.															
1	0.08	0.08	0.08	0.08	0.08	0.08	0.08	0.08	0.08	0.08	0.08	0.08	0.08	0.08	0.08
2	0.16	0.16	0.16	0.16	0.16	0.16	0.16	0.16	0.16	0.16	0.16	0.16	0.16	0.17	0.17
3	0.24	0.24	0.24	0.24	0.24	0.24	0.24	0.24	0.24	0.24	0.24	0.25	0.25	0.25	0.25
4	0.31	0.32	0.32	0.32	0.32	0.32	0.32	0.32	0.32	0.32	0.33	0.33	0.33	0.33	0.33
5	0.39	0.40	0.40	0.40	0.40	0.40	0.40	0.40	0.41	0.41	0.41	0.41	0.41	0.41	0.41
6	0.47	0.47	0.48	0.48	0.48	0.48	0.48	0.48	0.49	0.49	0.49	0.49	0.49	0.50	0.50
7	0.55	0.55	0.56	0.56	0.56	0.56	0.56	0.57	0.57	0.57	0.57	0.57	0.58	0.58	0.58
8	0.63	0.63	0.64	0.64	0.64	0.64	0.64	0.65	0.65	0.65	0.65	0.66	0.66	0.66	0.66
9	0.71	0.71	0.71	0.72	0.72	0.72	0.72	0.73	0.73	0.73	0.73	0.74	0.74	0.74	0.75
10	0.79	0.79	0.79	0.80	0.80	0.80	0.80	0.81	0.81	0.81	0.82	0.82	0.82	0.83	0.83
20	1.57	1.58	1.59	1.60	1.60	1.61	1.62	1.62	1.63	1.63	1.64	1.64	1.65	1.65	1.66
30	2.36	2.37	2.38	2.39	2.40	2.41	2.41	2.42	2.43	2.44	2.45	2.46	2.47	2.48	2.48
40	3.15	3.16	3.17	3.18	3.19	3.21	3.22	3.23	3.24	3.25	3.27	3.28	3.29	3.30	3.31
50	3.94	3.95	3.96	3.98	3.99	4.01	4.02	4.04	4.05	4.07	4.08	4.10	4.11	4.13	4.14
60	4.72	4.74	4.76	4.77	4.79	4.81	4.83	4.85	4.86	4.88	4.90	4.92	4.93	4.95	4.97
70	5.51	5.53	5.55	5.57	5.59	5.61	5.63	5.65	5.67	5.69	5.71	5.73	5.76	5.78	5.80
80	6.30	6.32	6.34	6.37	6.39	6.41	6.44	6.46	6.48	6.51	6.53	6.55	6.58	6.60	6.62
90	7.08	7.11	7.14	7.16	7.19	7.22	7.24	7.27	7.29	7.32	7.35	7.37	7.40	7.43	7.45
100	7.87	7.90	7.93	7.96	7.99	8.02	8.05	8.08	8.10	8.13	8.16	8.19	8.22	8.25	8.28
200	15.74	15.80	15.86	15.92	15.97	16.03	16.09	16.15	16.21	16.27	16.33	16.38	16.44	16.50	16.56
300	23.61	23.70	23.79	23.87	23.96	24.05	24.14	24.23	24.31	24.40	24.49	24.58	24.66	24.75	24.84
400	31.48	31.60	31.72	31.83	31.95	32.07	32.18	32.30	32.42	32.54	32.65	32.77	32.89	33.00	33.12
500	39.35	39.50	39.65	39.79	39.94	40.09	40.23	40.38	40.52	40.67	40.82	40.96	41.11	41.26	41.40
600	47.22	47.40	47.57	47.75	47.92	48.10	48.28	48.45	48.62	48.80	48.98	49.15	49.33	49.51	49.68
700	55.09	55.30	55.50	55.71	55.91	56.12	56.32	56.53	56.73	56.94	57.14	57.34	57.55	57.76	57.96
800	62.96	63.20	63.43	63.66	63.90	64.14	64.37	64.60	64.83	65.07	65.30	65.54	65.77	66.01	66.24
900	70.83	71.10	71.36	71.62	71.88	72.15	72.41	72.68	72.94	73.21	73.47	73.73	73.99	74.26	74.52
1000	78.70	79.00	79.29	79.58	79.87	80.17	80.46	80.75	81.04	81.34	81.63	81.92	82.22	82.51	82.80

4 Degrees.

Minutes	15	16	17	18	19	20	21	22	23	24	25	26	27	28	29	30
Dis. in ft.																
1	0.07	0.07	0.07	0.08	0.08	0.08	0.08	0.08	0.08	0.08	0.08	0.08	0.08	0.08	0.08	0.08
2	0.15	0.15	0.15	0.15	0.15	6.15	0.15	0.15	0.15	0.15	0.15	0.16	0.16	0.16	0.16	0.16
3	0.22	0.22	0.22	0.23	0.23	0.23	0.23	0.23	0.23	0.23	0.23	0.23	0.23	0.23	0.24	0.24
4	0.30	0.30	0.30	0.30	0.30	0.30	0.30	0.31	0.31	0.31	0.31	0.31	0.31	0.31	0.31	0.31
5	0.37	0.37	0.37	0.38	0.38	0.38	0.38	0.38	0.38	0.38	0.39	0.39	0.39	0.39	0.39	0.39
6	0.45	0.45	0.45	0.45	0.45	0.45	0.46	0.46	0.46	0.46	0.46	0.47	0.47	0.47	0.47	0.47
7	0.52	0.52	0.52	0.53	0.53	0.53	0.53	0.53	0.54	0.54	0.54	0.54	0.54	0.55	0.55	0.55
8	0.59	0.60	0.60	0.60	0.60	0.61	0.61	0.61	0.61	0.62	0.62	0.62	0.62	0.62	0.63	0.63
9	0.67	0.67	0.67	0.68	0.68	0.68	0.68	0.69	0.69	0.69	0.70	0.70	0.70	0.70	0.70	0.71
10	0.74	0.75	0.75	0.75	0.75	0.76	0.76	0.76	0.77	0.77	0.77	0.77	0.78	0.78	0.78	0.79
20	1.49	1.49	1.50	1.50	1.51	1.52	1.52	1.53	1.53	1.54	1.54	1.55	1.56	1.56	1.57	1.57
30	2.23	2.24	2.25	2.26	2.26	2.27	2.28	2.29	2.30	2.31	2.32	2.33	2.33	2.34	2.35	2.36
40	2.97	2.98	3.00	3.01	3.02	3.03	3.04	3.05	3.07	3.08	3.09	3.10	3.11	3.12	3.14	3.15
50	3.72	3.73	3.75	3.76	3.77	3.79	3.80	3.82	3.83	3.85	3.86	3.88	3.89	3.91	3.92	3.94
60	4.46	4.48	4.49	4.51	4.53	4.55	4.56	4.58	4.60	4.62	4.63	4.65	4.67	4.69	4.70	4.72
70	5.20	5.22	5.24	5.26	5.28	5.30	5.32	5.35	5.37	5.39	5.41	5.43	5.45	5.47	5.49	5.51
80	5.94	5.97	5.99	6.02	6.04	6.06	6.09	6.11	6.13	6.16	6.18	6.20	6.23	6.25	6.27	6.30
90	6.69	6.71	6.74	6.77	6.79	6.82	6.85	6.87	6.90	6.93	6.95	6.98	7.00	7.03	7.06	7.08
100	7.43	7.46	7.49	7.52	7.55	7.58	7.61	7.64	7.67	7.69	7.72	7.75	7.78	7.81	7.84	7.87
200	14.86	14.92	14.98	15.04	15.10	15.15	15.21	15.27	15.33	15.39	15.45	15.51	15.56	15.62	15.68	15.74
300	22.29	22.38	22.47	22.56	22.64	22.73	22.82	22.91	23.00	23.08	23.17	23.26	23.35	23.44	23.52	23.61
400	29.72	29.84	29.96	30.08	30.19	30.31	30.43	30.54	30.66	30.78	30.90	31.01	31.13	31.25	31.36	31.48
500	37.16	37.30	37.45	37.60	37.74	37.89	38.04	38.18	38.33	38.47	38.62	38.77	38.91	39.06	39.21	39.35
600	44.59	44.76	44.94	45.11	45.29	45.47	45.64	45.82	45.99	46.17	46.34	46.52	46.69	46.87	47.05	47.22
700	52.02	52.22	52.43	52.63	52.84	53.05	53.25	53.45	53.66	53.86	54.07	54.27	54.47	54.69	54.89	55.09
800	59.45	59.68	59.92	60.15	60.38	60.62	60.86	61.09	61.32	61.56	61.79	62.02	62.26	62.50	62.73	62.96
900	66.88	67.14	67.41	67.67	67.93	68.20	68.46	68.72	68.99	69.25	69.52	69.78	70.04	70.31	70.57	70.83
1000	74.31	74.60	74.90	75.19	75.48	75.78	76.07	76.36	76.65	76.95	77.24	77.53	77.82	78.12	78.41	78.70

4 Degrees.

Minutes	45	46	47	48	49	50	51	52	53	54	55	56	57	58	59	60
Dis. in ft.																
1	0.08	0.08	0.08	0.08	0.08	0.08	0.08	0.09	0.09	0.09	0.09	0.09	0.09	0.09	0.09	0.09
2	0.17	0.17	0.17	0.17	0.17	0.17	0.17	0.17	0.17	0.17	0.17	0.17	0.17	0.17	0.17	0.17
3	0.25	0.25	0.25	0.25	0.25	0.25	0.25	0.26	0.26	0.26	0.26	0.26	0.26	0.26	0.26	0.26
4	0.33	0.33	0.33	0.34	0.34	0.34	0.34	0.34	0.34	0.34	0.34	0.35	0.35	0.35	0.35	0.35
5	0.42	0.42	0.42	0.42	0.42	0.42	0.42	0.43	0.43	0.43	0.43	0.43	0.43	0.43	0.44	0.44
6	0.50	0.50	0.50	0.50	0.51	0.51	0.51	0.51	0.51	0.51	0.52	0.52	0.52	0.52	0.52	0.52
7	0.58	0.58	0.59	0.59	0.59	0.59	0.59	0.60	0.60	0.60	0.60	0.60	0.61	0.61	0.61	0.61
8	0.66	0.67	0.67	0.67	0.67	0.68	0.68	0.68	0.68	0.69	0.69	0.69	0.69	0.69	0.70	0.70
9	0.75	0.75	0.75	0.76	0.76	0.76	0.76	0.77	0.77	0.77	0.77	0.78	0.78	0.78	0.78	0.79
10	0.83	0.83	0.84	0.84	0.84	0.85	0.85	0.85	0.85	0.86	0.86	0.86	0.87	0.87	0.87	0.87
20	1.66	1.67	1.67	1.68	1.69	1.69	1.70	1.70	1.71	1.71	1.72	1.73	1.73	1.74	1.74	1.75
30	2.49	2.50	2.51	2.52	2.53	2.54	2.55	2.55	2.56	2.57	2.58	2.59	2.60	2.61	2.62	2.62
40	3.32	3.34	3.35	3.36	3.37	3.38	3.39	3.41	3.42	3.43	3.44	3.45	3.46	3.48	3.49	3.50
50	4.15	4.17	4.18	4.20	4.21	4.23	4.24	4.26	4.27	4.29	4.30	4.32	4.33	4.35	4.36	4.37
60	4.99	5.00	5.02	5.04	5.06	5.07	5.09	5.11	5.13	5.14	5.16	5.18	5.20	5.21	5.23	5.25
70	5.82	5.84	5.86	5.88	5.90	5.92	5.94	5.96	5.98	6.00	6.02	6.04	6.06	6.08	6.10	6.12
80	6.65	6.67	6.69	6.72	6.74	6.76	6.79	6.81	6.84	6.86	6.88	6.91	6.93	6.95	6.98	7.00
90	7.48	7.51	7.53	7.56	7.58	7.61	7.64	7.66	7.69	7.72	7.74	7.77	7.79	7.82	7.85	7.87
100	8.31	8.34	8.37	8.40	8.43	8.46	8.49	8.52	8.54	8.57	8.60	8.63	8.66	8.69	8.72	8.75
200	16.62	16.68	16.74	16.79	16.85	16.91	16.97	17.03	17.09	17.15	17.20	17.26	17.32	17.38	17.44	17.50
300	24.93	25.02	25.10	25.19	25.28	25.37	25.46	25.55	25.63	25.72	25.81	25.90	25.98	26.07	26.16	26.25
400	33.24	33.36	33.47	33.59	33.71	33.82	33.94	34.06	34.18	34.29	34.41	34.53	34.64	34.76	34.88	35.00
500	41.55	41.70	41.84	41.99	42.14	42.28	42.43	42.58	42.72	42.87	43.01	43.16	43.31	43.45	43.60	43.75
600	49.85	50.03	50.21	50.38	50.56	50.74	50.91	51.09	51.26	51.44	51.61	51.79	51.97	52.14	52.31	52.49
700	58.16	58.37	58.58	58.78	58.99	59.19	59.40	59.61	59.81	60.01	60.21	60.42	60.63	60.83	61.03	61.24
800	66.47	66.71	66.94	67.18	67.42	67.65	67.88	68.12	68.35	68.58	68.82	69.06	69.29	69.52	69.75	69.99
900	74.78	75.05	75.31	75.57	75.84	76.10	76.37	76.64	76.90	77.16	77.42	77.69	77.95	78.21	78.47	78.74
1000	83.09	83.39	83.68	83.97	84.27	84.56	84.85	85.15	85.44	85.73	86.02	86.32	86.61	86.90	87.19	87.49

5 Degrees.

Minutes	0	1	2	3	4	5	6	7	8	9	10	11	12	13	14
Dis. in ft.															
1	0.09	0.09	0.09	0.00	0.09	0.09	0.09	0.09	0.09	0.09	0.09	0.09	0.09	0.09	0.09
2	0.17	0.18	0.18	0.18	0.18	0.18	0.18	0.18	0.18	0.18	0.18	0.18	0.18	0.18	0.18
3	0.26	0.26	0.26	0.27	0.27	0.27	0.27	0.27	0.27	0.27	0.27	0.27	0.27	0.27	0.27
4	0.35	0.35	0.35	0.35	0.35	0.36	0.36	0.36	0.36	0.36	0.36	0.36	0.36	0.37	0.37
5	0.44	0.44	0.44	0.44	0.44	0.44	0.45	0.45	0.45	0.45	0.45	0.45	0.46	0.46	0.46
6	0.52	0.53	0.53	0.53	0.53	0.53	0.54	0.54	0.54	0.54	0.54	0.54	0.55	0.55	0.55
7	0.61	0.61	0.61	0.62	0.62	0.62	0.62	0.63	0.63	0.63	0.63	0.63	0.64	0.64	0.64
8	0.70	0.70	0.70	0.71	0.71	0.71	0.71	0.72	0.72	0.72	0.72	0.73	0.73	0.73	0.73
9	0.79	0.79	0.79	0.80	0.80	0.80	0.80	0.81	0.81	0.81	0.81	0.82	0.82	0.82	0.82
10	0.87	0.88	0.88	0.88	0.89	0.89	0.89	0.90	0.90	0.90	0.90	0.91	0.91	0.91	0.92
20	1.75	1.76	1.76	1.77	1.77	1.78	1.79	1.79	1.80	1.80	1.81	1.81	1.82	1.83	1.83
30	2.62	2.63	2.64	2.65	2.66	2.67	2.68	2.69	2.70	2.71	2.72	2.73	2.74	2.75	
40	3.50	3.51	3.52	3.53	3.55	3.56	3.57	3.58	3.59	3.61	3.62	3.63	3.64	3.65	3.66
50	4.37	4.39	4.40	4.42	4.43	4.45	4.46	4.48	4.49	4.51	4.52	4.54	4.55	4.57	4.58
60	5.25	5.27	5.28	5.30	5.32	5.34	5.36	5.37	5.39	5.41	5.43	5.44	5.46	5.48	5.50
70	6.12	6.14	6.16	6.19	6.21	6.23	6.25	6.27	6.29	6.31	6.33	6.35	6.37	6.39	6.41
80	7.00	7.02	7.05	7.07	7.09	7.12	7.14	7.16	7.19	7.21	7.23	7.26	7.28	7.30	7.33
90	7.87	7.90	7.93	7.95	7.98	8.01	8.03	8.06	8.08	8.11	8.14	8.16	8.19	8.22	8.24
100	8.75	8.78	8.81	8.84	8.87	8.90	8.93	8.95	8.98	9.01	9.04	9.07	9.10	9.13	9.16
200	17.50	17.56	17.61	17.67	17.73	17.79	17.85	17.91	17.97	18.03	18.08	18.14	18.20	18.26	18.32
300	26.25	26.33	26.42	26.51	26.60	26.69	26.78	26.86	26.95	27.04	27.13	27.21	27.30	27.39	27.48
400	35.00	35.11	35.23	35.35	35.46	35.58	35.70	35.82	35.93	36.05	36.17	36.28	36.40	36.52	36.64
500	43.75	43.89	44.04	44.19	44.33	44.48	44.63	44.77	44.92	45.07	45.21	45.36	45.51	45.65	45.80
600	52.49	52.67	52.84	53.02	53.20	53.37	53.55	53.72	53.90	54.08	54.25	54.43	54.61	54.78	54.95
700	61.24	61.45	61.65	61.86	62.06	62.27	62.48	62.68	62.88	63.09	63.29	63.50	63.71	63.92	64.11
800	69.99	70.22	70.46	70.70	70.93	71.16	71.40	71.63	71.86	72.10	72.34	72.57	72.81	73.05	73.27
900	78.74	79.00	79.26	79.53	79.79	80.06	80.33	80.59	80.85	81.12	81.38	81.64	81.91	82.18	82.43
1000	87.49	87.78	88.07	88.37	88.66	88.96	89.25	89.54	89.83	90.13	90.42	90.71	91.01	91.30	91.50

5 Degrees.

Minutes	30	31	32	33	34	35	36	37	38	39	40	41	42	43	44
Dis. in ft.															
1	0.10	0.10	0.10	0.10	0.10	0.10	0.10	0.10	0.10	0.10	0.10	0.10	0.10	0.10	0.10
2	0.19	0.19	0.19	0.19	0.19	0.20	0.20	0.20	0.20	0.20	0.20	0.20	0.20	0.20	0.20
3	0.29	0.29	0.29	0.29	0.29	0.29	0.29	0.30	0.30	0.30	0.30	0.30	0.30	0.30	0.30
4	0.39	0.39	0.39	0.39	0.39	0.39	0.39	0.39	0.39	0.40	0.40	0.40	0.40	0.40	0.40
5	0.48	0.48	0.48	0.49	0.49	0.49	0.49	0.49	0.49	0.49	0.50	0.50	0.50	0.50	0.50
6	0.58	0.58	0.58	0.58	0.58	0.59	0.59	0.59	0.59	0.59	0.60	0.60	0.60	0.60	0.60
7	0.67	0.68	0.68	0.68	0.68	0.68	0.69	0.69	0.69	0.69	0.69	0.70	0.70	0.70	0.70
8	0.77	0.77	0.78	0.78	0.78	0.78	0.78	0.79	0.79	0.79	0.79	0.79	0.80	0.80	0.80
9	0.87	0.87	0.87	0.87	0.88	0.88	0.88	0.89	0.89	0.89	0.89	0.90	0.90	0.90	0.90
10	0.96	0.97	0.97	0.97	0.97	0.98	0.98	0.98	0.99	0.99	0.99	1.00	1.00	1.00	1.00
20	1.93	1.93	1.94	1.94	1.95	1.96	1.96	1.97	1.97	1.98	1.98	1.99	2.00	2.00	2.01
30	2.89	2.90	2.91	2.92	2.92	2.93	2.94	2.95	2.96	2.97	2.98	2.99	2.99	3.00	3.01
40	3.85	3.86	3.88	3.89	3.90	3.91	3.92	3.94	3.95	3.96	3.97	3.98	3.99	4.00	4.02
50	4.81	4.83	4.84	4.86	4.87	4.89	4.90	4.92	4.93	4.95	4.96	4.98	4.99	5.01	5.02
60	5.78	5.79	5.81	5.83	5.85	5.87	5.88	5.90	5.92	5.94	5.95	5.97	5.99	6.01	6.02
70	6.74	6.76	6.78	6.80	6.82	6.84	6.86	6.88	6.90	6.93	6.95	6.97	6.99	7.01	7.03
80	7.70	7.73	7.75	7.77	7.80	7.82	7.84	7.87	7.89	7.91	7.94	7.96	7.98	8.01	8.03
90	8.66	8.69	8.72	8.75	8.77	8.80	8.82	8.85	8.88	8.90	8.93	8.96	8.98	9.01	9.04
100	9.63	9.66	9.69	9.72	9.75	9.78	9.81	9.83	9.86	9.89	9.92	9.95	9.98	10.01	10.04
200	19.26	19.32	19.38	19.43	19.49	19.55	19.61	19.67	19.73	19.79	19.85	19.90	19.96	20.02	20.08
300	28.89	28.97	29.06	29.15	29.24	29.33	29.42	29.50	29.59	29.68	29.77	29.86	29.94	30.03	30.12
400	38.52	38.63	38.75	38.87	38.98	39.10	39.22	39.34	39.46	39.57	39.69	39.81	39.92	40.04	40.16
500	48.15	48.29	48.44	48.59	48.73	48.88	49.03	49.17	49.32	49.47	49.61	49.76	49.91	50.06	50.20
600	57.77	57.95	58.13	58.30	58.48	58.66	58.83	59.01	59.18	59.36	59.54	59.71	59.89	60.07	60.24
700	67.40	67.61	67.82	68.02	68.22	68.43	68.64	68.84	69.05	69.25	69.46	69.66	69.87	70.08	70.29
800	77.03	77.26	77.50	77.74	77.97	78.21	78.44	78.68	78.91	79.14	79.38	79.62	79.85	80.09	80.32
900	86.66	86.92	87.19	87.45	87.71	87.98	88.25	88.51	88.78	89.04	89.30	89.57	89.83	90.10	90.36
1000	96.29	96.58	96.88	97.17	97.46	97.76	98.05	98.35	98.64	98.93	99.23	99.52	99.81	100.11	100.40

5 Degrees.

15	16	17	18	19	20	21	22	23	24	25	26	27	28	29	30
0.09	0.09	0.09	0.09	0.09	0.09	0.09	0.09	0.09	0.09	0.09	0.10	0.10	0.10	0.10	0.10
0.18	0.18	0.18	0.19	0.19	6.19	0.19	0.19	0.19	0.19	0.19	0.19	0.19	0.19	0.19	0.19
0.28	0.28	0.28	0.28	0.28	0.28	0.28	0.28	0.28	0.28	0.28	0.29	0.29	0.29	0.29	0.29
0.37	0.37	0.37	0.37	0.37	0.37	0.37	0.38	0.38	0.38	0.38	0.38	0.38	0.38	0.38	0.39
0.46	0.46	0.46	0.46	0.47	0.47	0.47	0.47	0.47	0.47	0.47	0.48	0.48	0.48	0.48	0.48
0.55	0.55	0.55	0.56	0.56	0.56	0.56	0.56	0.57	0.57	0.57	0.57	0.57	0.57	0.58	0.58
0.64	0.65	0.65	0.65	0.65	0.65	0.66	0.66	0.66	0.66	0.66	0.67	0.67	0.67	0.67	0.67
0.74	0.74	0.74	0.74	0.74	0.75	0.75	0.75	0.75	0.76	0.76	0.76	0.76	0.77	0.77	0.77
0.83	0.83	0.83	0.83	0.84	0.84	0.84	0.85	0.85	0.85	0.85	0.86	0.86	0.86	0.86	0.87
0.92	0.92	0.92	0.93	0.93	0.93	0.94	0.94	0.94	0.95	0.95	0.95	0.95	0.96	0.96	0.96
1.84	1.84	1.85	1.86	1.86	1.87	1.87	1.88	1.88	1.89	1.90	1.90	1.91	1.91	1.92	1.93
2.76	2.77	2.77	2.78	2.79	2.80	2.81	2.82	2.83	2.84	2.84	2.85	2.86	2.87	2.88	2.89
3.68	3.69	3.70	3.71	3.72	3.73	3.75	3.76	3.77	3.78	3.79	3.80	3.82	3.83	3.84	3.85
4.59	4.61	4.62	4.64	4.65	4.67	4.68	4.70	4.71	4.73	4.74	4.76	4.77	4.79	4.80	4.81
5.51	5.53	5.55	5.57	5.58	5.60	5.62	5.64	5.65	5.67	5.69	5.71	5.72	5.74	5.76	5.78
6.43	6.45	6.47	6.49	6.51	6.53	6.56	6.58	6.60	6.62	6.64	6.66	6.68	6.70	6.72	6.74
7.35	7.37	7.40	7.42	7.44	7.47	7.49	7.52	7.54	7.56	7.59	7.61	7.63	7.66	7.68	7.70
8.27	8.30	8.32	8.35	8.38	8.40	8.43	8.45	8.48	8.51	8.53	8.56	8.59	8.61	8.64	8.67
9.19	9.22	9.25	9.28	9.31	9.34	9.37	9.40	9.42	9.45	9.48	9.51	9.54	9.57	9.60	9.63
18.38	18.44	18.49	18.55	18.61	18.67	18.73	18.79	18.85	18.91	18.96	19.02	19.08	19.14	19.20	19.26
27.57	27.65	27.74	27.83	27.92	28.01	28.10	28.18	28.27	28.36	28.45	28.53	28.62	28.71	28.80	28.89
36.76	36.87	37.00	37.11	37.22	37.34	37.46	37.58	37.69	37.81	37.93	38.04	38.16	38.28	38.40	38.52
45.95	46.09	46.24	46.39	46.53	46.68	46.83	46.97	47.12	47.27	47.41	47.56	47.71	47.85	48.00	48.15
55.13	55.31	55.48	55.66	55.84	56.01	56.19	56.36	56.54	56.72	56.89	57.07	57.25	57.42	57.60	57.77
64.32	64.53	64.73	64.94	65.14	65.35	65.56	65.76	65.96	66.17	66.37	66.58	66.79	66.99	67.20	67.40
73.51	73.74	73.98	74.22	74.45	74.68	74.92	75.15	75.38	75.62	75.86	76.09	76.33	76.56	76.80	77.03
82.70	82.96	83.22	83.49	83.75	84.02	84.29	84.55	84.81	85.08	85.34	85.60	85.87	86.13	86.40	86.66
91.89	92.18	92.47	92.77	93.06	93.35	93.65	93.94	94.23	94.53	94.82	95.11	95.41	95.70	96.00	96.29

5 Degrees.

45	46	47	48	49	50	51	52	53	54	55	56	57	58	59	60
0.10	0.10	0.10	0.10	0.10	0.10	0.10	0.10	0.10	0.10	0.10	0.10	0.10	0.10	0.10	0.11
0.20	0.20	0.20	0.20	0.20	0.20	0.20	0.21	0.21	0.21	0.21	0.21	0.21	0.21	0.21	0.21
0.30	0.30	0.30	0.30	0.31	0.31	0.31	0.31	0.31	0.31	0.31	0.31	0.31	0.31	0.31	0.32
0.40	0.40	0.41	0.41	0.41	0.41	0.41	0.41	0.41	0.41	0.41	0.42	0.42	0.42	0.42	0.42
0.50	0.50	0.51	0.51	0.51	0.51	0.51	0.51	0.52	0.52	0.52	0.52	0.52	0.52	0.52	0.53
0.60	0.61	0.61	0.61	0.61	0.61	0.61	0.62	0.62	0.62	0.62	0.62	0.63	0.63	0.63	0.63
0.70	0.71	0.71	0.71	0.71	0.72	0.72	0.72	0.72	0.72	0.73	0.73	0.73	0.73	0.73	0.74
0.81	0.81	0.81	0.81	0.81	0.82	0.82	0.82	0.82	0.83	0.83	0.83	0.83	0.84	0.84	0.84
0.91	0.91	0.91	0.91	0.92	0.92	0.92	0.92	0.93	0.93	0.93	0.94	0.94	0.94	0.94	0.95
1.01	1.01	1.01	1.02	1.02	1.02	1.02	1.03	1.03	1.03	1.04	1.04	1.04	1.05	1.05	1.05
2.01	2.02	2.03	2.03	2.04	2.04	2.05	2.06	2.06	2.07	2.07	2.08	2.08	2.09	2.10	2.10
3.02	3.03	3.04	3.05	3.06	3.07	3.07	3.08	3.09	3.10	3.11	3.12	3.13	3.14	3.15	3.15
4.03	4.04	4.05	4.06	4.07	4.09	4.10	4.11	4.12	4.13	4.15	4.16	4.17	4.18	4.19	4.20
5.04	5.05	5.06	5.08	5.09	5.11	5.12	5.14	5.15	5.17	5.18	5.20	5.21	5.23	5.24	5.26
6.04	6.06	6.08	6.09	6.11	6.13	6.15	6.17	6.18	6.20	6.22	6.24	6.25	6.27	6.29	6.31
7.05	7.07	7.09	7.11	7.13	7.15	7.17	7.19	7.21	7.23	7.25	7.28	7.30	7.32	7.34	7.36
8.06	8.08	8.10	8.13	8.15	8.17	8.20	8.22	8.24	8.27	8.29	8.31	8.34	8.36	8.38	8.41
9.06	9.09	9.11	9.14	9.17	9.20	9.22	9.25	9.27	9.30	9.33	9.35	9.38	9.41	9.43	9.46
10.07	10.10	10.13	10.16	10.19	10.22	10.25	10.28	10.31	10.33	10.36	10.39	10.42	10.45	10.48	10.51
20.14	20.20	20.26	20.32	20.37	20.43	20.49	20.55	20.61	20.67	20.73	20.79	20.84	20.90	20.96	21.02
30.21	30.30	30.38	30.47	30.56	30.65	30.74	30.83	30.92	31.00	31.09	31.18	31.27	31.36	31.44	31.53
40.28	40.40	40.51	40.63	40.75	40.87	40.98	41.10	41.22	41.34	41.45	41.57	41.69	41.81	41.92	42.04
50.35	50.50	50.64	50.79	50.94	51.09	51.23	51.38	51.53	51.67	51.82	51.97	52.11	52.26	52.41	52.55
60.42	60.59	60.77	60.95	61.12	61.30	61.48	61.65	61.83	62.00	62.18	62.36	62.53	62.71	62.89	63.06
70.49	70.69	70.90	71.11	71.31	71.52	71.72	71.93	72.14	72.34	72.54	72.75	72.95	73.16	73.37	73.53
80.56	80.79	81.02	81.26	81.50	81.74	81.97	82.20	82.44	82.67	82.90	83.14	83.38	83.62	83.85	84.08
90.63	90.89	91.15	91.42	91.68	91.95	92.21	92.48	92.75	93.01	93.27	93.54	93.80	94.07	94.33	94.59
100.70	100.99	101.28	101.58	101.87	102.17	102.46	102.75	103.05	103.34	103.63	103.93	104.22	104.52	104.81	105.10

13

6 Degrees.

Minutes	0	1	2	3	4	5	6	7	8	9	10	11	12	13	14
Dis. in ft.															
1	0.11	0.11	0.11	0.11	0.11	0.11	0.11	0.10	0.11	0.11	0.11	0.11	0.11	0.11	0.11
2	0.21	0.21	0.21	0.21	0.21	0.21	0.21	0.21	0.21	0.22	0.22	0.22	0.22	0.22	0.22
3	0.32	0.32	0.32	0.32	0.32	0.32	0.32	0.32	0.32	0.32	0.32	0.33	0.33	0.33	0.33
4	0.42	0.42	0.42	0.42	0.43	0.43	0.43	0.43	0.43	0.43	0.43	0.43	0.43	0.44	0.44
5	0.53	0.53	0.53	0.53	0.53	0.53	0.53	0.54	0.54	0.54	0.54	0.54	0.54	0.54	0.55
6	0.63	0.63	0.63	0.64	0.64	0.64	0.64	0.64	0.64	0.65	0.65	0.65	0.65	0.65	0.66
7	0.74	0.74	0.74	0.74	0.74	0.75	0.75	0.75	0.75	0.75	0.76	0.76	0.76	0.76	0.76
8	0.84	0.84	0.85	0.85	0.85	0.85	0.85	0.86	0.86	0.86	0.86	0.87	0.87	0.87	0.87
9	0.95	0.95	0.95	0.95	0.96	0.96	0.96	0.96	0.97	0.97	0.97	0.98	0.98	0.98	0.98
10	1.05	1.05	1.06	1.06	1.06	1.07	1.07	1.07	1.07	1.08	1.08	1.08	1.09	1.09	1.09
20	2.10	2.11	2.11	2.12	2.13	2.13	2.14	2.14	2.15	2.16	2.16	2.17	2.17	2.18	2.18
30	3.15	3.16	3.17	3.18	3.19	3.20	3.21	3.21	3.22	3.23	3.24	3.25	3.26	3.27	3.28
40	4.20	4.22	4.23	4.24	4.25	4.26	4.27	4.29	4.30	4.31	4.32	4.33	4.35	4.36	4.37
50	5.26	5.27	5.28	5.30	5.31	5.33	5.34	5.36	5.37	5.39	5.40	5.42	5.43	5.45	5.46
60	6.31	6.32	6.34	6.36	6.38	6.39	6.41	6.43	6.45	6.47	6.48	6.50	6.52	6.54	6.55
70	7.36	7.38	7.40	7.42	7.44	7.46	7.48	7.50	7.52	7.54	7.56	7.58	7.60	7.63	7.65
80	8.41	8.43	8.46	8.48	8.50	8.53	8.55	8.57	8.60	8.62	8.64	8.67	8.69	8.71	8.74
90	9.46	9.49	9.51	9.54	9.57	9.59	9.62	9.64	9.67	9.70	9.72	9.75	9.78	9.80	9.83
100	10.51	10.54	10.57	10.60	10.63	10.66	10.69	10.72	10.75	10.78	10.81	10.88	10.86	10.89	10.92
200	21.02	21.08	21.14	21.20	21.26	21.32	21.37	21.43	21.49	21.55	21.61	21.67	21.73	21.79	21.85
300	31.53	31.62	31.71	31.80	31.88	31.97	32.06	32.15	32.24	32.33	32.42	32.50	32.59	32.68	32.77
400	42.04	42.16	42.28	42.40	42.51	42.63	42.75	42.86	42.98	43.10	43.22	43.31	43.46	43.57	43.69
500	52.55	52.70	52.85	53.00	53.14	53.29	53.44	53.58	53.73	53.88	54.03	54.17	54.32	54.47	54.62
600	63.06	63.24	63.41	63.59	63.77	63.95	64.12	64.30	64.48	64.65	64.83	65.00	65.18	65.36	65.54
700	73.57	73.78	73.98	74.19	74.40	74.61	74.81	75.01	75.22	75.43	75.64	75.84	76.05	76.25	76.46
800	84.08	84.32	84.55	84.79	85.02	85.26	85.50	85.73	85.97	86.20	86.44	86.67	86.91	87.14	87.38
900	94.59	94.86	95.12	95.39	95.65	95.92	96.18	96.44	96.71	96.98	97.25	97.51	97.78	98.04	98.31
1000	105.10	105.40	105.69	105.99	106.28	106.58	106.87	107.16	107.46	107.75	108.05	108.34	108.64	108.93	109.23

6 Degrees.

Minutes	30	31	32	33	34	35	36	37	38	39	40	41	42	43	44
Dis. in ft.															
1	0.11	0.11	0.11	0.11	0.12	0.12	0.12	0.12	0.12	0.12	0.12	0.12	0.12	0.12	0.12
2	0.23	0.23	0.23	0.23	0.23	0.23	0.23	0.23	0.23	0.23	0.23	0.23	0.23	0.24	0.24
3	0.34	0.34	0.34	0.34	0.35	0.35	0.35	0.35	0.35	0.35	0.35	0.35	0.35	0.35	0.35
4	0.46	0.46	0.46	0.46	0.46	0.46	0.46	0.46	0.47	0.47	0.47	0.47	0.47	0.47	0.47
5	0.57	0.57	0.57	0.57	0.58	0.58	0.58	0.58	0.58	0.58	0.58	0.59	0.59	0.59	0.59
6	0.68	0.69	0.69	0.69	0.69	0.69	0.69	0.70	0.70	0.70	0.70	0.70	0.70	0.71	0.71
7	0.80	0.80	0.80	0.80	0.81	0.81	0.81	0.81	0.81	0.82	0.82	0.82	0.82	0.82	0.83
8	0.91	0.91	0.92	0.92	0.92	0.92	0.93	0.93	0.93	0.93	0.94	0.94	0.94	0.94	0.94
9	1.03	1.03	1.03	1.03	1.04	1.04	1.04	1.04	1.04	1.05	1.05	1.05	1.05	1.06	1.06
10	1.14	1.14	1.15	1.15	1.15	1.15	1.16	1.16	1.16	1.17	1.17	1.17	1.17	1.18	1.18
20	2.28	2.28	2.29	2.30	2.30	2.31	2.31	2.32	2.33	2.33	2.34	2.34	2.35	2.36	2.36
30	3.42	3.43	3.44	3.44	3.45	3.46	3.47	3.48	3.49	3.50	3.51	3.52	3.52	3.53	3.54
40	4.56	4.57	4.58	4.59	4.60	4.62	4.63	4.64	4.65	4.66	4.68	4.69	4.70	4.71	4.72
50	5.70	5.71	5.73	5.74	5.76	5.77	5.79	5.80	5.81	5.83	5.84	5.86	5.87	5.89	5.90
60	6.84	6.85	6.87	6.89	6.91	6.92	6.94	6.96	6.98	7.00	7.01	7.03	7.05	7.07	7.08
70	7.98	8.00	8.02	8.04	8.06	8.08	8.10	8.12	8.14	8.16	8.18	8.20	8.22	8.24	8.26
80	9.12	9.14	9.16	9.19	9.21	9.23	9.26	9.28	9.30	9.33	9.35	9.37	9.40	9.42	9.44
90	10.25	10.28	10.31	10.33	10.36	10.39	10.41	10.44	10.47	10.49	10.52	10.55	10.57	10.60	10.63
100	11.39	11.42	11.45	11.48	11.51	11.54	11.57	11.60	11.63	11.66	11.69	11.72	11.75	11.78	11.81
200	22.79	22.85	22.91	22.96	23.02	23.08	23.14	23.20	23.26	23.32	23.38	23.44	23.49	23.55	23.61
300	34.18	34.27	34.36	34.45	34.53	34.62	34.71	34.80	34.89	34.98	35.06	35.15	35.24	35.33	35.42
400	45.58	45.69	45.81	45.93	46.04	46.16	46.28	46.40	46.52	46.64	46.75	46.87	46.99	47.11	47.22
500	56.97	57.12	57.27	57.41	57.56	57.71	57.85	58.00	58.15	58.30	58.44	58.59	58.74	58.89	59.03
600	68.36	68.54	68.72	68.89	69.07	69.25	69.42	69.60	69.77	69.95	70.13	70.31	70.48	70.66	70.84
700	79.76	79.96	80.17	80.37	80.58	80.79	80.99	81.20	81.40	81.61	81.82	82.03	82.23	82.44	82.64
800	91.15	91.38	91.62	91.86	92.09	92.33	92.56	92.80	93.03	93.27	93.50	93.74	93.98	94.22	94.45
900	102.55	102.81	103.08	103.34	103.60	103.87	104.13	104.40	104.66	104.93	105.19	105.46	105.72	105.99	106.25
1000	113.94	114.23	114.53	114.82	115.11	115.41	115.70	116.00	116.29	116.59	116.88	117.18	117.47	117.77	118.06

14

6 Degrees.

15	16	17	18	19	20	21	22	23	24	25	26	27	28	29	30
0.11	0.11	0.11	0.11	0.11	0.11	0.11	0.11	0.11	0.11	0.11	0.11	0.11	0.11	0.11	0.11
0.22	0.22	0.22	0.22	0.22	6.22	0.22	0.22	0.22	0.22	0.22	0.23	0.23	0.23	0.23	0.23
0.33	0.33	0.33	0.33	0.33	0.33	0.33	0.33	0.34	0.34	0.34	0.34	0.34	0.34	0.34	0.34
0.44	0.44	0.44	0.44	0.44	0.41	0.45	0.45	0.45	0.45	0.45	0.45	0.45	0.45	0.45	0.46
0.55	0.55	0.55	0.55	0.55	0.55	0.56	0.56	0.56	0.56	0.56	0.57	0.57	0.57	0.57	0.57
0.66	0.66	0.66	0.66	0.66	0.67	0.67	0.67	0.67	0.67	0.67	0.68	0.68	0.68	0.68	0.68
0.77	0.77	0.77	0.77	0.77	0.78	0.78	0.78	0.78	0.79	0.79	0.79	0.79	0.79	0.80	0.80
0.88	0.88	0.88	0.88	0.89	0.89	0.89	0.89	0.90	0.90	0.90	0.90	0.90	0.91	0.91	0.91
0.99	0.99	0.99	0.99	1.00	1.00	1.00	1.00	1.01	1.01	1.01	1.01	1.02	1.02	1.02	1.03
1.10	1.10	1.10	1.10	1.11	1.11	1.11	1.12	1.12	1.12	1.12	1.13	1.13	1.13	1.13	1.14
2.19	2.20	2.20	2.20	2.21	2.22	2.23	2.23	2.24	2.24	2.25	2.26	2.26	2.27	2.27	2.28
3.29	3.29	3.30	3.31	3.32	3.33	3.34	3.35	3.36	3.37	3.37	3.38	3.39	3.40	3.41	3.42
4.38	4.39	4.40	4.42	4.43	4.44	4.45	4.46	4.48	4.49	4.50	4.51	4.52	4.53	4.55	4.56
5.48	5.49	5.51	5.52	5.54	5.55	5.56	5.58	5.59	5.61	5.02	5.64	5.65	5.67	5.68	5.70
6.57	6.59	6.61	6.62	6.64	6.66	6.68	6.69	6.71	6.73	6.75	6.77	6.78	6.80	6.82	6.84
7.07	7.09	7.71	7.73	7.75	7.77	7.79	7.81	7.83	7.85	7.87	7.89	7.91	7.93	7.95	7.98
8.76	8.78	8.81	8.83	8.86	8.88	8.90	8.93	8.95	8.97	9.00	9.02	9.04	9.07	9.09	9.12
9.86	9.88	9.91	9.94	9.96	9.99	10.01	10.04	10.07	10.10	10.12	10.15	10.17	10.20	10.23	10.25
10.95	10.98	11.01	11.04	11.07	11.10	11.13	11.16	11.19	11.22	11.25	11.28	11.31	11.34	11.36	11.39
21.90	21.96	22.02	22.08	22.14	22.20	22.26	22.32	22.38	22.43	22.49	22.55	22.61	22.67	22.73	22.79
32.86	32.94	33.03	33.12	33.21	33.30	33.38	33.47	33.56	33.65	33.74	33.83	33.92	34.01	34.09	34.18
43.81	43.92	44.05	44.16	44.28	44.40	44.51	44.63	44.75	44.87	44.98	45.10	45.22	45.34	45.46	45.58
54.76	54.91	55.06	55.20	55.35	55.50	55.64	55.79	55.94	56.09	56.23	56.38	56.53	56.68	56.82	56.97
65.71	65.89	66.07	66.24	66.42	66.59	66.77	66.95	67.13	67.30	67.48	67.66	67.88	68.01	68.18	68.36
76.66	76.87	77.08	77.28	77.49	77.69	77.90	78.11	78.32	78.52	78.72	78.93	79.14	79.35	79.55	79.76
87.62	87.85	88.09	88.32	88.56	88.79	89.02	89.26	89.50	89.74	89.97	90.21	90.44	90.68	90.91	91.15
98.57	98.83	99.10	99.36	99.63	99.89	100.15	100.42	100.69	100.95	101.21	101.48	101.75	102.02	102.28	102.55
109.52	109.81	110.11	110.40	110.70	110.99	111.28	111.58	111.88	112.17	112.46	112.76	113.05	113.35	113.64	113.94

6 Degrees.

45	46	47	48	49	50	51	52	53	54	55	56	57	58	59	60
0.12	0.12	0.12	0.12	0.12	0.12	0.12	0.12	0.12	0.12	0.12	0.12	0.12	0.12	0.12	0.12
0.24	0.24	0.24	0.24	0.24	0.24	0.24	0.24	0.24	0.24	0.24	0.24	0.24	0.24	0.24	0.25
0.36	0.36	0.36	0.36	0.36	0.36	0.36	0.36	0.36	0.36	0.36	0.36	0.37	0.37	0.37	0.37
0.47	0.47	0.48	0.48	0.48	0.48	0.48	0.48	0.48	0.48	0.49	0.49	0.49	0.49	0.49	0.49
0.59	0.59	0.60	0.60	0.60	0.60	0.60	0.60	0.60	0.61	0.61	0.61	0.61	0.61	0.61	0.61
0.71	0.71	0.71	0.72	0.72	0.72	0.72	0.72	0.72	0.73	0.73	0.73	0.73	0.73	0.73	0.74
0.83	0.83	0.83	0.83	0.84	0.84	0.84	0.84	0.84	0.85	0.85	0.85	0.85	0.85	0.86	0.86
0.95	0.95	0.95	0.95	0.96	0.96	0.96	0.96	0.97	0.97	0.97	0.97	0.98	0.98	0.98	0.98
1.07	1.07	1.07	1.07	1.08	1.08	1.08	1.08	1.09	1.09	1.09	1.09	1.10	1.10	1.10	1.11
1.18	1.19	1.19	1.19	1.20	1.20	1.20	1.20	1.21	1.21	1.21	1.22	1.22	1.22	1.22	1.23
2.37	2.37	2.38	2.38	2.39	2.40	2.40	2.41	2.42	2.42	2.43	2.43	2.44	2.44	2.45	2.46
3.55	3.56	3.57	3.58	3.59	3.59	3.60	3.61	3.62	3.63	3.64	3.65	3.66	3.67	3.67	3.68
4.73	4.75	4.76	4.77	4.78	4.79	4.81	4.82	4.83	4.84	4.85	4.86	4.88	4.89	4.90	4.91
5.92	5.93	5.95	5.96	5.98	5.99	6.01	6.02	6.04	6.05	6.07	6.08	6.10	6.11	6.12	6.14
7.10	7.12	7.14	7.15	7.17	7.19	7.21	7.23	7.24	7.26	7.28	7.30	7.31	7.33	7.35	7.37
8.29	8.31	8.33	8.35	8.37	8.39	8.41	8.43	8.45	8.47	8.49	8.51	8.53	8.55	8.57	8.59
9.47	9.49	9.52	9.54	9.56	9.59	9.61	9.63	9.66	9.68	9.70	9.73	9.75	9.78	9.80	9.82
10.65	10.68	10.71	10.73	10.76	10.78	10.81	10.84	10.86	10.89	10.92	10.94	10.97	11.00	11.02	11.05
11.84	11.87	11.90	11.92	11.95	11.98	12.01	12.04	12.07	12.10	12.13	12.16	12.19	12.22	12.25	12.28
23.67	23.73	23.79	23.85	23.91	23.97	24.03	24.08	24.14	24.20	24.26	24.32	24.38	24.44	24.50	24.56
35.51	35.60	35.69	35.77	35.86	35.95	36.04	36.13	36.22	36.30	36.39	36.48	36.57	36.66	36.75	36.83
47.34	47.46	47.58	47.70	47.82	47.93	48.05	48.17	48.29	48.40	48.52	48.64	48.76	48.88	49.00	49.11
59.18	59.33	59.48	59.62	59.77	59.92	60.07	60.21	60.36	60.51	60.66	60.80	60.95	61.10	61.25	61.39
71.02	71.19	71.37	71.54	71.72	71.90	72.08	72.25	72.43	72.61	72.79	72.96	73.14	73.31	73.49	73.67
82.85	83.06	83.27	83.47	83.68	83.88	84.09	84.29	84.50	84.71	84.92	85.12	85.33	85.53	85.74	85.95
94.69	94.92	95.16	95.39	95.63	95.86	96.10	96.34	96.58	96.81	97.05	97.28	97.52	97.75	97.99	98.22
106.52	106.79	107.06	107.32	107.59	107.85	108.12	108.38	108.65	108.91	109.18	109.44	109.71	109.97	110.24	110.50
118.36	118.65	118.95	119.24	119.54	119.83	120.13	120.42	120.72	121.01	121.31	121.60	121.90	122.19	122.49	122.78

7 Degrees.

Minutes	0	1	2	3	4	5	6	7	8	9	10	11	12	13	14
Dis. in ft.															
1	0.12	0.12	0.12	0.12	0.12	0.12	0.12	0.12	0.13	0.13	0.13	0.13	0.13	0.13	0.13
2	0.25	0.25	0.25	0.25	0.25	0.25	0.25	0.25	0.25	0.25	0.25	0.25	0.25	0.25	0.25
3	0.37	0.37	0.37	0.37	0.37	0.37	0.37	0.37	0.38	0.38	0.38	0.38	0.38	0.38	0.38
4	0.49	0.49	0.49	0.49	0.50	0.50	0.50	0.50	0.50	0.50	0.50	0.50	0.51	0.51	0.51
5	0.61	0.62	0.62	0.62	0.62	0.62	0.62	0.62	0.63	0.63	0.63	0.63	0.63	0.63	0.63
6	0.74	0.74	0.74	0.74	0.74	0.75	0.75	0.75	0.75	0.75	0.75	0.76	0.76	0.76	0.76
7	0.86	0.86	0.86	0.87	0.87	0.87	0.87	0.87	0.88	0.88	0.88	0.88	0.88	0.89	0.89
8	0.98	0.98	0.99	0.99	0.99	0.99	1.00	1.00	1.00	1.00	1.01	1.01	1.01	1.01	1.02
9	1.11	1.11	1.11	1.11	1.12	1.12	1.12	1.12	1.13	1.13	1.13	1.13	1.14	1.14	1.14
10	1.23	1.23	1.23	1.24	1.24	1.24	1.25	1.25	1.25	1.25	1.26	1.26	1.26	1.27	1.27
20	2.46	2.46	2.47	2.47	2.48	2.49	2.49	2.50	2.50	2.51	2.51	2 52	2.53	2.53	2.54
30	3.68	3.69	3.70	3.71	3.72	3.73	3.74	3.75	3.75	3.76	3.77	3.78	3.79	3.80	3.81
40	4.91	4.92	4.94	4.95	4 96	4.97	4.98	4.99	5.01	5.02	5.03	5.04	5.05	5.07	5.08
50	6.14	6.15	6.17	6.18	6.20	6.21	6.23	6.24	6.26	6.27	6.29	6.30	6.32	6.33	6.35
60	7.37	7.38	7.40	7.42	7.44	7.46	7.47	7.49	7.51	7.52	7.54	7.56	7.58	7.60	7.62
70	8.59	8.62	8.64	8.66	8.68	8.70	8.72	8.74	8.76	8.78	8.80	8.82	8.84	8.86	8.88
80	9.82	9.85	9.87	9.89	9.92	9.94	9.96	9.99	10.01	10.03	10.06	10.08	10.11	10.13	10.15
90	11.05	11.08	11.10	11.13	11.16	11.18	11.21	11.24	11.26	11.29	11.32	11.34	11.37	11.40	11.42
100	12.28	12.31	12.34	12.37	12.40	12.43	12.46	12.49	12.52	12.54	12.57	12.60	12.63	12.66	12.69
200	24.56	24.62	24.68	24.73	24.79	24.85	24.91	24.97	25.03	25.08	25.15	25.21	25.27	25.33	25.38
300	36.83	36.92	37.01	37.10	37.19	37.28	37.37	37.46	37.55	37.63	37.72	37.81	37.90	37.99	38.08
400	49.11	49.23	49.35	49.47	49.59	49.70	49.82	49.94	50.06	50.18	50.30	50.41	50.53	50.65	50.77
500	61.39	61.54	61.69	61.84	61.99	62.13	62.28	62.43	62.58	62.72	62.87	63.02	63.17	63.32	63.46
600	73.67	73.85	74.03	74.20	74.38	74.56	74.74	74.91	75.09	75.26	75.44	75.62	75.80	75.98	76.15
700	85.95	86.16	86.37	86.57	86.78	86.98	87.19	87.40	87.61	87.81	88.02	88.22	88.43	88.64	88.84
800	98.22	98.46	98.70	98.94	99.18	99.41	99.65	99.88	100.12	100.35	100.59	100.82	101.06	101.30	101.54
900	110.50	110.77	111.04	111.30	111.57	111.83	112.10	112.37	112.64	112.90	113.17	113.43	113.70	113.97	114.23
1000	122.78	123.08	123.38	123.67	123.97	124.26	124.56	124.85	125.15	125.44	125.74	126.03	126.33	126.63	126.92

7 Degrees.

Minutes	30	31	32	33	34	35	36	37	38	39	40	41	42	43	44
Dis. in ft.															
1	0.13	0.13	0.13	0.13	0.13	0.13	0.13	0.13	0.13	0.13	0.13	0.13	0.14	0.14	0.14
2	0.26	0.26	0.26	0.27	0.27	0.27	0.27	0.27	0.27	0.27	0.27	0.27	0.27	0.27	0.27
3	0.39	0.40	0.40	0.40	0.40	0.40	0.40	0.40	0.40	0.40	0.40	0.40	0.41	0.41	0.41
4	0.53	0.53	0.53	0.53	0.53	0.53	0.53	0.53	0.54	0.54	0.54	0.54	0.54	0.54	0.54
5	0.66	0.66	0.66	0.66	0.66	0.67	0.67	0.67	0.67	0.67	0.67	0.67	0.68	0.68	0.68
6	0.79	0.79	0.79	0.80	0.80	0.80	0.80	0.80	0.80	0.81	0.81	0.81	0.81	0.81	0.81
7	0.92	0.92	0.93	0.93	0.93	0.93	0.93	0.94	0.94	0.94	0.94	0.94	0.95	0.95	0.95
8	1.05	1.06	1.06	1.06	1.06	1.07	1.07	1.07	1.07	1.07	1.07	1.08	1.08	1.08	1.09
9	1.18	1.19	1.19	1.19	1.20	1.20	1.20	1.20	1.21	1.21	1.21	1.21	1.22	1.22	1.22
10	1.32	1.32	1.32	1.33	1.33	1.33	1.33	1.34	1.34	1.34	1.35	1.35	1.35	1.36	1.36
20	2.63	2.64	2.65	2.65	2.66	2.66	2.67	2.67	2.68	2.69	2.69	2.70	2.70	2.71	2.72
30	3.95	3.96	3.97	3.98	3.99	3.99	4.00	4.01	4.02	4.03	4.04	4.05	4.06	4.07	4.07
40	5.27	5.28	5.29	5.30	5.31	5.33	5.34	5.35	5.36	5.37	5.38	5.40	5.41	5.42	5.43
50	6.58	6.60	6.61	6.63	6.64	6.66	6.67	6.69	6.70	6.72	6.73	6.75	6.76	6.78	6.79
60	7.90	7.92	7.94	7.95	7.97	7.99	8.01	8.02	8.04	8.06	8.08	8.09	8.11	8.13	8.15
70	9.22	9.24	9.26	9.28	9.30	9.32	9.34	9.36	9.38	9.40	9.42	9.44	9.46	9.49	9.51
80	10.53	10.56	10.58	10.60	10.63	10.65	10.67	10.70	10.72	10.75	10.77	10.79	10.82	10.84	10.86
90	11.85	11.88	11.90	11.93	11.96	11.98	12.01	12.03	12.06	12.09	12.11	12.14	12.17	12.20	12.22
100	13.17	13.20	13.23	13.25	13.28	13.31	13.34	13.37	13.40	13.43	13.46	13.49	13.52	13.55	13.58
200	26.33	26.39	26.45	26.51	26.57	26.63	26.69	26.74	26.80	26.86	26.92	26.98	27.04	27.10	27.16
300	39.50	39.59	39.68	39.76	39.85	39.94	40.03	40.12	40.21	40.30	40.38	40.47	40.56	40.65	40.74
400	52.66	52.78	52.90	53.02	53.14	53.25	53.37	53.49	53.61	53.73	53.84	53.96	54.08	54.20	54.32
500	65.83	65.98	66.13	66.27	66.42	66.57	66.72	66.86	67.01	67.16	67.31	67.46	67.61	67.75	67.90
600	78.99	79.17	79.35	79.52	79.70	79.88	80.06	80.23	80.41	80.59	80.77	80.95	81.13	81.30	81.48
700	92.16	92.37	92.58	92.78	92.99	93.19	93.40	93.60	93.81	94.02	94.23	94.41	94.65	94.85	95.06
800	105.32	105.56	105.80	106.03	106.27	106.50	106.74	106.98	107.22	107.46	107.69	107.93	108.17	108.40	108.64
900	118.49	118.75	119.03	119.29	119.56	119.82	120.09	120.35	120.62	120.89	121.15	121.42	121.69	121.95	122.22
1000	131.65	131.95	132.25	132.54	132.84	133.13	133.42	133.72	134.02	134.32	134.61	134.91	135.21	135.50	135.80

7 Degrees.

15	16	17	18	19	20	21	22	23	24	25	26	27	28	29	30
0.13	0.13	0.13	0.13	0.13	0.13	0.13	0.13	0.13	0.13	0.13	0.13	0.13	0.13	0.13	0.13
0.25	0.26	0.26	0.26	0.26	0.26	0.26	0.26	0.26	0.26	0.26	0.26	0.26	0.26	0.26	0.26
0.38	0.38	0.38	0.38	0.39	0.39	0.39	0.39	0.39	0.39	0.39	0.39	0.39	0.39	0.39	0.39
0.51	0.51	0.51	0.51	0.51	0.51	0.52	0.52	0.52	0.52	0.52	0.52	0.52	0.52	0.53	0.53
0.64	0.64	0.64	0.64	0.64	0.64	0.64	0.65	0.65	0.65	0.65	0.65	0.65	0.66	0.66	0.66
0.76	0.77	0.77	0.77	0.77	0.77	0.77	0.78	0.78	0.78	0.78	0.78	0.78	0.79	0.79	0.79
0.89	0.89	0.89	0.90	0.90	0.90	0.90	0.91	0.91	0.91	0.91	0.91	0.92	0.92	0.92	0.92
1.02	1.02	1.02	1.02	1.03	1.03	1.03	1.03	1.04	1.04	1.04	1.04	1.05	1.05	1.05	1.05
1.14	1.15	1.15	1.15	1.16	1.16	1.16	1.16	1.17	1.17	1.17	1.17	1.18	1.18	1.18	1.18
1.27	1.28	1.28	1.28	1.28	1.29	1.29	1.29	1.30	1.30	1.30	1.30	1.31	1.31	1.31	1.32
2.54	2.55	2.56	2.56	2.57	2.57	2.58	2.59	2.59	2.60	2.60	2.61	2.62	2.62	2.63	2.63
3.82	3.83	3.83	3.84	3.85	3.86	3.87	3.88	3.89	3.90	3.91	3.91	3.92	3.93	3.94	3.95
5.09	5.10	5.11	5.12	5.14	5.15	5.16	5.17	5.18	5.20	5.21	5.22	5.23	5.24	5.25	5.27
6.36	6.38	6.39	6.41	6.42	6.43	6.45	6.46	6.48	6.49	6.51	6.52	6.54	6.55	6.57	6.58
7.63	7.65	7.67	7.69	7.70	7.72	7.74	7.76	7.77	7.79	7.81	7.83	7.85	7.86	7.88	7.90
8.91	8.93	8.95	8.97	8.99	9.01	9.03	9.05	9.07	9.09	9.11	9.13	9.15	9.17	9.20	9.22
10.18	10.20	10.22	10.25	10.27	10.30	10.32	10.34	10.37	10.39	10.41	10.44	10.46	10.48	10.51	10.53
11.45	11.48	11.50	11.53	11.56	11.58	11.61	11.64	11.66	11.69	11.72	11.74	11.77	11.80	11.82	11.85
12.72	12.75	12.78	12.81	12.84	12.87	12.90	12.93	12.96	12.99	13.02	13.05	13.08	13.11	13.14	13.17
25.44	25.50	25.56	25.62	25.68	25.74	25.80	25.86	25.92	25.98	26.03	26.09	26.15	26.21	26.27	26.33
38.17	38.25	38.34	38.43	38.52	38.61	38.69	38.79	38.87	38.96	39.05	39.14	39.23	39.32	39.41	39.50
50.89	51.00	51.12	51.24	51.30	51.48	51.60	51.72	51.83	51.95	52.07	52.19	52.30	52.42	52.54	52.66
63.61	63.76	63.91	64.05	64.20	64.35	64.50	64.65	64.79	64.94	65.09	65.24	65.38	65.53	65.68	65.83
76.33	76.51	76.69	76.86	77.04	77.21	77.39	77.57	77.75	77.93	78.10	78.28	78.46	78.64	78.82	78.99
89.05	89.26	89.47	89.67	89.88	90.08	90.29	90.50	90.71	90.92	91.12	91.33	91.53	91.74	91.95	92.16
101.78	102.01	102.25	102.48	102.72	102.95	103.18	103.43	103.66	103.90	104.14	104.38	104.61	104.85	105.09	105.32
114.50	114.76	115.03	115.29	115.56	115.82	116.08	116.36	116.62	116.88	117.15	117.42	117.68	117.95	118.22	118.49
127.22	127.51	127.81	128.10	128.40	128.69	128.98	129.29	129.58	129.88	130.17	130.47	130.76	131.06	131.36	131.65

7 Degrees.

45	46	47	48	49	50	51	52	53	54	55	56	57	58	59	60
0.14	0.14	0.14	0.14	0.14	0.14	0.14	0.14	0.14	0.14	0.14	0.14	0.14	0.14	0.14	0.14
0.27	0.27	0.27	0.27	0.27	0.28	0.28	0.28	0.28	0.28	0.28	0.28	0.28	0.28	0.28	0.28
0.41	0.41	0.41	0.41	0.41	0.41	0.41	0.41	0.42	0.42	0.42	0.42	0.42	0.42	0.42	0.42
0.54	0.55	0.55	0.55	0.55	0.55	0.55	0.55	0.55	0.56	0.56	0.56	0.56	0.56	0.56	0.56
0.68	0.68	0.68	0.68	0.69	0.69	0.69	0.69	0.69	0.69	0.70	0.70	0.70	0.70	0.70	0.70
0.82	0.82	0.82	0.82	0.82	0.83	0.83	0.83	0.83	0.83	0.83	0.84	0.84	0.84	0.84	0.84
0.95	0.95	0.96	0.96	0.96	0.96	0.97	0.97	0.97	0.97	0.97	0.98	0.98	0.98	0.98	0.98
1.09	1.09	1.09	1.10	1.10	1.10	1.10	1.10	1.11	1.11	1.11	1.11	1.12	1.12	1.12	1.12
1.22	1.23	1.23	1.23	1.24	1.24	1.24	1.24	1.25	1.25	1.25	1.25	1.26	1.26	1.26	1.26
1.36	1.36	1.37	1.37	1.37	1.38	1.38	1.38	1.38	1.39	1.39	1.39	1.40	1.40	1.40	1.41
2.72	2.73	2.73	2.74	2.75	2.75	2.76	2.76	2.77	2.77	2.78	2.78	2.79	2.79	2.80	2.81
4.08	4.09	4.10	4.11	4.12	4.13	4.14	4.15	4.15	4.16	4.17	4.18	4.19	4.20	4.21	4.22
5.44	5.46	5.47	5.48	5.49	5.51	5.53	5.54	5.55	5.56	5.57	5.59	5.60	5.61	5.62	5.63
6.80	6.82	6.83	6.85	6.86	6.88	6.89	6.91	6.92	6.94	6.95	6.97	6.98	7.00	7.01	7.03
8.17	8.18	8.20	8.22	8.24	8.25	8.27	8.29	8.31	8.33	8.34	8.36	8.38	8.40	8.41	8.43
9.53	9.55	9.57	9.59	9.61	9.63	9.65	9.67	9.69	9.71	9.73	9.75	9.78	9.80	9.82	9.84
10.89	10.91	10.94	10.96	10.98	11.01	11.03	11.05	11.08	11.10	11.12	11.15	11.17	11.20	11.22	11.24
12.25	12.28	12.30	12.33	12.36	12.38	12.41	12.44	12.46	12.49	12.52	12.54	12.57	12.60	12.62	12.65
13.61	13.64	13.67	13.70	13.73	13.76	13.79	13.82	13.85	13.88	13.91	13.94	13.97	14.00	14.02	14.05
27.22	27.28	27.34	27.40	27.46	27.52	27.57	27.63	27.69	27.75	27.81	27.87	27.93	27.99	28.05	28.11
40.83	40.92	41.01	41.09	41.18	41.27	41.36	41.45	41.54	41.63	41.72	41.81	41.90	41.99	42.07	42.16
54.44	54.56	54.68	54.79	54.91	55.03	55.15	55.27	55.39	55.50	55.62	55.74	55.86	55.98	56.10	56.22
68.05	68.20	68.35	68.49	68.64	68.79	68.94	69.09	69.24	69.38	69.53	69.68	69.83	69.98	70.12	70.27
81.65	81.83	82.01	82.19	82.37	82.55	82.72	82.90	83.08	83.26	83.44	83.61	83.79	83.97	84.14	84.32
95.26	95.47	95.68	95.89	96.10	96.31	96.51	96.72	96.93	97.13	97.34	97.55	97.76	97.97	98.17	98.38
108.87	109.11	109.35	109.58	109.82	110.06	110.30	110.54	110.78	111.01	111.25	111.48	111.72	111.96	112.19	112.43
122.48	122.75	123.02	123.28	123.55	123.82	124.08	124.35	124.62	124.88	125.15	125.42	125.69	125.96	126.22	126.49
136.09	136.39	136.69	136.98	137.28	137.58	137.87	138.17	138.47	138.76	139.06	139.35	139.65	139.95	140.24	140.54

8 Degrees.

Minutes	0	1	2	3	4	5	6	7	8	9	10	11	12	13	14
Dis. in ft.															
1	0.14	0.14	0.14	0.14	0.14	0.14	0.14	0.14	0.14	0.14	0.14	0.14	0.14	0.14	0.14
2	0.28	0.28	0.28	0.28	0.28	0.28	0.28	0.29	0.29	0.29	0.29	0.29	0.29	0.29	0.29
3	0.42	0.42	0.42	0.42	0.43	0.43	0.43	0.43	0.43	0.43	0.43	0.43	0.43	0.43	0.43
4	0.56	0.56	0.56	0.57	0.57	0.57	0.57	0.57	0.57	0.57	0.57	0.58	0.58	0.58	0.58
5	0.70	0.70	0.71	0.71	0.71	0.71	0.71	0.71	0.71	0.72	0.72	0.72	0.72	0.72	0.72
6	0.84	0.85	0.85	0.85	0.85	0.85	0.85	0.86	0.86	0.86	0.86	0.86	0.86	0.87	0.87
7	0.98	0.99	0.99	0.99	0.99	0.99	1.00	1.00	1.00	1.00	1.00	1.01	1.01	1.01	1.01
8	1.12	1.13	1.13	1.13	1.13	1.14	1.14	1.14	1.14	1.15	1.15	1.15	1.15	1.16	1.16
9	1.26	1.27	1.27	1.27	1.28	1.28	1.28	1.28	1.29	1.29	1.29	1.29	1.30	1.30	1.30
10	1.41	1.41	1.41	1.41	1.42	1.42	1.42	1.43	1.43	1.43	1.44	1.44	1.44	1.44	1.45
20	2.81	2.82	2.82	2.83	2.83	2.84	2.85	2.85	2.86	2.86	2.87	2.88	2.88	2.89	2.89
30	4.22	4.23	4.23	4.24	4.25	4.26	4.27	4.28	4.29	4.30	4.31	4.31	4.32	4.33	4.34
40	5.62	5.63	5.65	5.66	5.67	5.68	5.69	5.70	5.72	5.73	5.74	5.75	5.76	5.78	5.79
50	7.03	7.04	7.06	7.07	7.09	7.10	7.12	7.13	7.15	7.16	7.18	7.19	7.21	7.22	7.24
60	8.43	8.45	8.47	8.49	8.50	8.52	8.54	8.56	8.57	8.59	8.61	8.63	8.65	8.66	8.68
70	9.84	9.86	9.88	9.90	9.92	9.94	9.96	9.98	10.00	10.02	10.05	10.07	10.09	10.11	10.13
80	11.24	11.27	11.29	11.31	11.34	11.36	11.39	11.41	11.43	11.46	11.48	11.50	11.53	11.55	11.58
90	12.65	12.68	12.70	12.73	12.76	12.78	12.81	12.84	12.86	12.89	12.92	12.94	12.97	13.00	13.02
100	14.05	14.08	14.11	14.14	14.17	14.20	14.23	14.26	14.29	14.32	14.35	14.38	14.41	14.44	14.47
200	28.11	28.17	28.23	28.29	28.35	28.40	28.46	28.52	28.58	28.64	28.70	28.76	28.82	28.88	28.94
300	42.16	42.25	42.34	42.43	42.52	42.61	42.70	42.79	42.87	42.96	43.05	43.14	43.23	43.32	43.41
400	56.22	56.34	56.45	56.57	56.69	56.81	56.93	57.05	57.16	57.28	57.40	57.52	57.64	57.76	57.88
500	70.27	70.42	70.57	70.72	70.87	71.01	71.16	71.31	71.46	71.61	71.76	71.90	72.05	72.20	72.35
600	84.32	84.50	84.68	84.86	85.04	85.21	85.39	85.57	85.75	85.93	86.11	86.28	86.46	86.64	86.82
700	98.38	98.59	98.79	99.00	99.21	99.41	99.62	99.83	100.04	100.25	100.46	100.66	100.87	101.08	101.29
800	112.43	112.67	112.90	113.14	113.34	113.62	113.86	114.10	114.33	114.57	114.81	115.04	115.28	115.52	115.76
900	126.49	126.76	127.02	127.29	127.56	127.82	128.09	128.36	128.62	128.89	129.16	129.42	129.69	129.96	130.23
1000	140.54	140.84	141.13	141.43	141.73	142.02	142.32	142.62	142.91	143.21	143.51	143.80	144.10	144.40	144.70

8 Degrees.

Minutes	30	31	32	33	34	35	36	37	38	39	40	41	42	43	44
Dis. in ft.															
1	0.15	0.15	0.15	0.15	0.15	0.15	0.15	0.15	0.15	0.15	0.15	0.15	0.15	0.15	0.15
2	0.30	0.30	0.30	0.30	0.30	0.30	0.30	0.30	0.30	0.30	0.30	0.31	0.31	0.31	0.31
3	0.45	0.45	0.45	0.45	0.45	0.45	0.45	0.45	0.46	0.46	0.46	0.46	0.46	0.46	0.46
4	0.60	0.60	0.60	0.60	0.60	0.60	0.60	0.61	0.61	0.61	0.61	0.61	0.61	0.61	0.61
5	0.75	0.75	0.75	0.75	0.75	0.75	0.76	0.76	0.76	0.76	0.76	0.76	0.77	0.77	0.77
6	0.90	0.90	0.90	0.90	0.90	0.91	0.91	0.91	0.91	0.91	0.91	0.92	0.92	0.92	0.92
7	1.05	1.05	1.05	1.05	1.05	1.06	1.06	1.06	1.06	1.06	1.07	1.07	1.07	1.07	1.08
8	1.20	1.20	1.20	1.20	1.21	1.21	1.21	1.21	1.21	1.22	1.22	1.22	1.22	1.23	1.23
9	1.35	1.35	1.35	1.35	1.36	1.36	1.36	1.36	1.37	1.37	1.37	1.37	1.38	1.38	1.38
10	1.49	1.50	1.50	1.50	1.51	1.51	1.51	1.52	1.52	1.52	1.52	1.53	1.53	1.53	1.54
20	2.99	3.00	3.00	3.01	3.01	3.02	3.02	3.03	3.04	3.04	3.05	3.05	3.06	3.07	3.07
30	4.48	4.49	4.50	4.51	4.52	4.53	4.54	4.55	4.55	4.56	4.57	4.58	4.59	4.60	4.61
40	5.98	5.99	6.00	6.01	6.03	6.04	6.05	6.06	6.07	6.09	6.10	6.11	6.12	6.13	6.14
50	7.47	7.49	7.50	7.52	7.53	7.55	7.56	7.58	7.59	7.61	7.62	7.64	7.65	7.67	7.68
60	8.97	8.99	9.00	9.02	9.04	9.06	9.07	9.09	9.11	9.13	9.15	9.16	9.18	9.20	9.22
70	10.46	10.48	10.50	10.52	10.54	10.57	10.59	10.61	10.63	10.65	10.67	10.69	10.71	10.73	10.75
80	11.96	11.98	12.00	12.03	12.05	12.08	12.10	12.12	12.15	12.17	12.19	12.22	12.24	12.27	12.29
90	13.45	13.48	13.50	13.53	13.56	13.58	13.61	13.64	13.66	13.69	13.72	13.74	13.77	13.80	13.83
100	14.95	14.98	15.01	15.03	15.06	15.09	15.12	15.15	15.18	15.21	15.24	15.27	15.30	15.33	15.36
200	29.89	29.95	30.01	30.07	30.13	30.19	30.25	30.31	30.37	30.43	30.49	30.54	30.60	30.66	30.72
300	44.84	44.93	45.02	45.10	45.19	45.28	45.37	45.46	45.55	45.64	45.73	45.82	45.91	46.00	46.09
400	59.78	59.90	60.02	60.14	60.26	60.38	60.49	60.61	60.73	60.85	60.97	61.09	61.21	61.33	61.45
500	74.73	74.88	75.03	75.17	75.32	75.47	75.62	75.77	75.92	76.07	76.22	76.36	76.51	76.66	76.81
600	89.67	89.85	90.03	90.20	90.38	90.56	90.74	90.92	91.10	91.28	91.46	91.63	91.81	91.99	92.17
700	104.62	104.83	105.04	105.21	105.43	105.66	105.86	106.07	106.28	106.49	106.70	106.90	107.11	107.32	107.53
800	119.56	119.80	120.04	120.27	120.51	120.75	120.98	121.22	121.46	121.70	121.94	122.18	122.42	122.66	122.90
900	134.51	134.78	135.05	135.31	135.58	135.85	136.11	136.38	136.65	136.92	137.19	137.45	137.72	137.99	138.26
1000	149.45	149.75	150.05	150.31	150.64	150.94	151.23	151.53	151.83	152.13	152.43	152.72	153.02	153.32	153.62

8 Degrees.

15	16	17	18	19	20	21	22	23	24	25	26	27	28	29	30
0.14	0.15	0.15	0.15	0.15	0.15	0.15	0.15	0.15	0.15	0.15	0.15	0.15	0.15	0.15	0.15
0.29	0.29	0.29	0.29	0.29	0.29	0.29	0.29	0.29	0.29	0.30	0.30	0.30	0.30	0.30	0.30
0.43	0.44	0.44	0.44	0.44	0.44	0.44	0.44	0.44	0.44	0.44	0.44	0.45	0.45	0.45	0.45
0.58	0.58	0.58	0.58	0.58	0.59	0.59	0.59	0.59	0.59	0.50	0.59	0.59	0.60	0.60	0.60
0.72	0.73	0.73	0.73	0.73	0.73	0.74	0.74	0.74	0.74	0.74	0.74	0.74	0.74	0.75	0.75
0.87	0.87	0.87	0.88	0.88	0.88	0.88	0.88	0.88	0.89	0.89	0.89	0.89	0.89	0.89	0.90
1.01	1.02	1.02	1.02	1.02	1.03	1.03	1.03	1.03	1.03	1.04	1.04	1.04	1.04	1.04	1.05
1.16	1.16	1.16	1.17	1.17	1.17	1.17	1.18	1.18	1.18	1.18	1.19	1.19	1.19	1.19	1.20
1.30	1.31	1.31	1.31	1.32	1.32	1.32	1.32	1 33	1.33	1.33	1.33	1.34	1.34	1.34	1.35
1.45	1.45	1.46	1.46	1.46	1.46	1.47	1.47	1.47	1.48	1.48	1.48	1.49	1.49	1.49	1.49
2.90	2.91	2.91	2.92	2.92	2.93	2.94	2.94	2.95	2.95	2.96	2.97	2.97	2.98	2.98	2.90
4.35	4.36	4.37	4.38	4.39	4.39	4.40	4.41	4.42	4.43	4.44	4.45	4.46	4.47	4.47	4.48
5.80	5.81	5.82	5.85	5.84	5.86	5.87	5.88	5.89	5.91	5.92	5.93	5.94	5.95	5.97	5.98
7.25	7.26	7.28	7.29	7.31	7.32	7.34	7.35	7.37	7.38	7.40	7.41	7.43	7.44	7.46	7.47
8.70	8.72	8.74	8.75	8.77	8.79	8.81	8.82	8.84	8.86	8.88	8.90	8.91	8.93	8.95	8.97
10.15	10.17	10.19	10.21	10.23	10.25	10.27	10.29	10.32	10.34	10.36	10.38	10.40	10.42	10.44	10.46
11.60	11.62	11.65	11.67	11.69	11.72	11.74	11.77	11.79	11.81	11.84	11.86	11.88	11.91	11.93	11.96
13.05	13.08	13.10	13.13	13.16	13.18	13.21	13.24	13.26	13.29	13.32	13.34	13.37	13.40	13.42	13.45
14.50	14.53	14.56	14.59	14.62	14.65	14.68	14.71	14.74	14.77	14.80	14.83	14.86	14.89	14.92	14.95
28.90	29.06	29.12	29.18	29.24	29.30	29.35	29.41	29.47	29.53	29.59	29.65	29.71	29.77	29.83	29.89
43.50	43.59	43.68	43.76	43.85	43.94	44.03	44.12	44.21	44.30	44.39	44 48	44.57	44.66	44.75	44.84
58.00	58.12	58.24	58.35	58.47	58.59	58.71	58.83	58.95	59.07	59.18	59.30	59.42	59.54	59.66	59.78
72.50	72.65	72.80	72.94	73.09	73.24	73.39	73.54	73.69	73.84	73.98	74.13	74.28	74.43	74.58	74.73
86.99	87.17	87.35	87.53	87.71	87.89	88.06	88.24	88.42	88.60	88.78	88.96	89.14	89.32	89.49	89.67
101.49	101.70	101.91	102.12	102.33	102.54	102.74	102.95	103.16	103.37	103.57	103.78	103.99	104.20	104.41	104.62
115.99	116.23	116.47	116.70	116.94	117.18	117.42	117.66	117.90	118.14	118.37	118.61	118.85	119.09	119.32	119.56
130.49	130.76	131.03	131.29	131.56	131.83	132.09	132.36	132.63	132.90	133.16	133.43	133.70	133.97	134.24	134.51
144.99	145.29	145.59	145.88	146.18	146.48	146.77	147.07	147.37	147.67	147.96	148.26	148 56	148.86	149.15	149.45

8 Degrees.

45	46	47	48	49	50	51	52	53	54	55	56	57	58	59	60
0.15	0.15	0.15	0.15	0.16	0.16	0.16	0.16	0.16	0.16	0.16	0.16	0.16	0.16	0.16	0.16
0.31	0.31	0.31	0.31	0.31	0.31	0.31	0.31	0.31	0.31	0.31	0.31	0.31	0.32	0.32	0.32
0.46	0.46	0.46	0.46	0.47	0.47	0.47	0.47	0.47	0.47	0.47	0.47	0.47	0.47	0.47	0.48
0.62	0.62	0.62	0.62	0.62	0.62	0.62	0.62	0.63	0.63	0.63	0.63	0.63	0.63	0.63	0.63
0.77	0.77	0.77	0.77	0.78	0.78	0.78	0.78	0.78	0.78	0.78	0.79	0.79	0.79	0.79	0.79
0.92	0.93	0.93	0.93	0.93	0.93	0.93	0.94	0.94	0.94	0.94	0.94	0.94	0.95	0.95	0.95
1.08	1.08	1.08	1.08	1.09	1.09	1.09	1.09	1.09	1.10	1.10	1.10	1.10	1.10	1.11	1.11
1.23	1.23	1.24	1.24	1.24	1.24	1.25	1.25	1.25	1.25	1.26	1.26	1.26	1.26	1.26	1.27
1.39	1.39	1.39	1.39	1.40	1.40	1.40	1.40	1.41	1.41	1.41	1.41	1.42	1.42	1.42	1.43
1.54	1.54	1.55	1.55	1.55	1.55	1.56	1.56	1.56	1.57	1.57	1.57	1.57	1.58	1.58	1.58
3.08	3.08	3.09	3.10	3.10	3.11	3.11	3.12	3.13	3.13	3.14	3.14	3.15	3.16	3.16	3.17
4.62	4.63	4.64	4.64	4.65	4.66	4.67	4.68	4.69	4.70	4.71	4.72	4.72	4.73	4.74	4.75
6.16	6.17	6.18	6.19	6.20	6.22	6.23	6.24	6.25	6.26	6.28	6.29	6.30	6.31	6.32	6.34
7.70	7.71	7.73	7.74	7.76	7.77	7.79	7.80	7.82	7.83	7.85	7.86	7.87	7.89	7.90	7.92
9.23	9.25	9.27	9.29	9.31	9.32	9.34	9.36	9.38	9.40	9.41	9.43	9.45	9.47	9.49	9.50
10.77	10.79	10.82	10.84	10.86	10.88	10.90	10.92	10.94	10.96	10.98	11.00	11.02	11.05	11.07	11.09
12.31	12.34	12.36	12.38	12.41	12.43	12.46	12.48	12.50	12.53	12.55	12.58	12.60	12.62	12.65	12.67
13.85	13.88	13.91	13.93	13.96	13.99	14.01	14.04	14.07	14.09	14.12	14.15	14.17	14.20	14.23	14.25
15.39	15.42	15.45	15.48	15.51	15.54	15.57	15.60	15.63	15.66	15.69	15.72	15.75	15.78	15.81	15.84
30.78	30.84	30.90	30.96	31.02	31.08	31.14	31.20	31.26	31.32	31.38	31.44	31.50	31.56	31.62	31.68
46.17	46.26	46.35	46.44	46.53	46.62	46.71	46.80	46.89	46.98	47.07	47.16	47.25	47.34	47.43	47.51
61.56	61.68	61.80	61.92	62.04	62.16	62.28	62.40	62.52	62.64	62.76	62.88	63.00	63.12	63.24	63.35
76.96	77.11	77.26	77.41	77.56	77.70	77.85	78.00	78.15	78.30	78.45	78.60	78.75	78.90	79.05	79.19
92.35	92.53	92.71	92.89	93.07	93.24	93.42	93.60	93.78	93.96	94.14	94.31	94.49	94.67	94.85	95.03
107.74	107.95	108.16	108.37	108.58	108.78	108.99	109.20	109.41	109.62	109.83	110.03	110.24	110.45	110.66	110.87
123.13	123.37	123.61	123.85	124.09	124.32	124.56	124.80	125.04	125.28	125.52	125.75	125.99	126.23	126.47	126.70
138.52	138.79	139.06	139.33	139.60	139.86	140.13	140.40	140.67	140.94	141.21	141.47	141.74	142.01	142.28	142.54
153.91	154.21	154.51	154.81	155.11	155.40	155.70	156.00	156.30	156.60	156.90	157.19	157.49	157.79	158.09	158.38

9 Degrees.

Minutes	0	1	2	3	4	5	6	7	8	9	10	11	12	13	14
Dis. in ft.															
1	0.16	0.16	0.16	0.16	0.16	0.16	0.16	0.16	0.16	0.16	0.16	0.16	0.16	0.16	0.16
2	0.32	0.32	0.32	0.32	0.32	0.32	0.32	0.32	0.32	0.32	0.32	0.32	0.32	0.32	0.32
3	0.48	0.48	0.48	0.48	0.48	0.48	0.48	0.48	0.48	0.48	0.49	0.49	0.49	0.49	0.49
4	0.63	0.63	0.64	0.64	0.64	0.64	0.64	0.64	0.64	0.64	0.65	0.65	0.65	0.65	0.65
5	0.79	0.79	0.79	0.80	0.80	0.80	0.80	0.80	0.80	0.81	0.81	0.81	0.81	0.81	0.81
6	0.95	0.95	0.95	0.96	0.96	0.96	0.96	0.96	0.96	0.97	0.97	0.97	0.97	0.97	0.98
7	1.11	1.11	1.11	1.11	1.12	1.12	1.12	1.12	1.13	1.13	1.13	1.13	1.13	1.14	1.14
8	1.27	1.27	1.27	1.27	1.28	1.28	1.28	1.28	1.29	1.29	1.29	1.29	1.30	1.30	1.30
9	1.43	1.43	1.43	1.43	1.44	1.44	1.44	1.44	1.45	1.45	1.45	1.46	1.46	1.46	1.46
10	1.58	1.59	1.59	1.59	1.60	1.60	1.60	1.60	1.61	1.61	1.61	1.62	1.62	1.62	1.63
20	3.17	3.17	3.18	3.19	3.19	3.20	3.20	3.21	3.22	3.22	3.23	3.23	3.24	3.25	3.25
30	4.75	4.76	4.77	4.78	4.79	4.80	4.81	4.82	4.83	4.83	4.84	4.85	4.86	4.87	4.88
40	6.34	6.35	6.36	6.37	6.38	6.39	6.41	6.42	6.43	6.44	6.45	6.47	6.48	6.49	6.50
50	7.92	7.93	7.95	7.96	7.98	7.99	8.01	8.02	8.04	8.05	8.07	8.08	8.10	8.11	8.13
60	9.50	9.52	9.54	9.56	9.57	9.59	9.61	9.63	9.65	9.66	9.68	9.70	9.72	9.74	9.75
70	11.09	11.11	11.13	11.15	11.17	11.19	11.21	11.23	11.25	11.27	11.30	11.32	11.34	11.36	11.38
80	12.67	12.69	12.72	12.74	12.77	12.79	12.81	12.84	12.86	12.89	12.91	12.93	12.96	12.98	13.00
90	14.25	14.28	14.31	14.34	14.36	14.39	14.42	14.44	14.47	14.50	14.52	14.55	14.58	14.60	14.63
100	15.84	15.87	15.90	15.93	15.96	15.99	16.02	16.05	16.08	16.11	16.14	16.17	16.20	16.23	16.26
200	31.68	31.74	31.80	31.86	31.92	31.97	32.03	32.09	32.15	32.21	32.27	32.33	32.39	32.45	32.51
300	47.51	47.60	47.69	47.78	47.87	47.96	48.05	48.14	48.23	48.32	48.41	48.50	48.59	48.68	48.77
400	63.35	63.47	63.59	63.71	63.83	63.95	64.07	64.19	64.31	64.43	64.55	64.67	64.78	64.90	65.02
500	79.19	79.34	79.49	79.64	79.79	79.94	80.09	80.24	80.39	80.54	80.69	80.84	80.98	81.13	81.28
600	95.03	95.21	95.39	95.57	95.75	95.92	96.10	96.28	96.46	96.64	96.82	97.00	97.18	97.36	97.54
700	110.87	111.08	111.29	111.50	111.71	111.91	112.12	112.33	112.54	112.75	112.96	113.17	113.37	113.58	113.79
800	126.70	126.94	127.18	127.42	127.66	127.90	128.14	128.38	128.62	128.86	129.10	129.34	129.57	129.81	130.05
900	142.54	142.81	143.08	143.35	143.62	143.88	144.15	144.42	144.69	144.96	145.23	145.50	145.76	146.03	146.30
1000	158.38	158.68	158.98	159.28	159.58	159.87	160.17	160.47	160.77	161.07	161.37	161.67	161.96	162.26	162.56

9 Degrees.

Minutes	30	31	32	33	34	35	36	37	38	39	40	41	42	43	44
Dis. in ft.															
1	0.17	0.17	0.17	0.17	0.17	0.17	0.17	0.17	0.17	0.17	0.17	0.17	0.17	0 17	0.17
2	0.33	0.34	0.34	0.34	0.34	0.34	0.34	0.34	0.34	0.34	0.34	0.34	0.34	0.34	0.34
3	0.50	0.50	0.50	0.50	0.51	0.51	0.51	0.51	0.51	0.51	0.51	0.51	0.51	0.51	0.51
4	0.67	0.67	0.67	0.67	0.67	0.68	0.68	0.68	0.68	0.68	0.68	0.68	0.68	0.68	0.69
5	0.84	0.84	0.84	0.84	0.84	0.84	0.85	0.85	0.85	0.85	0.85	0.85	0.85	0.86	0.86
6	1.00	1.01	1.01	1.01	1.01	1.01	1.01	1.02	1.02	1.02	1.02	1.02	1.03	1.03	1.03
7	1.17	1.17	1.18	1.18	1.18	1.18	1.18	1.19	1.19	1.19	1.19	1.19	1.20	1.20	1.20
8	1.34	1.34	1.34	1.35	1.35	1.35	1.35	1.36	1.36	1.36	1.36	1.37	1.37	1.37	1.37
9	1.51	1.51	1.51	1.51	1.52	1.52	1.52	1.52	1.53	1.53	1.53	1.54	1.54	1.54	1.54
10	1.67	1.68	1.68	1.68	1.69	1.69	1.69	1.69	1.70	1.70	1.70	1.71	1.71	1.71	1.72
20	3.35	3.35	3.36	3.36	3.37	3.38	3.38	3.39	3.39	3.39	3.40	3.41	3.41	3.42	3.43
30	5.02	5.03	5.04	5.05	5.06	5.07	5.07	5.08	5.09	5.09	5.11	5.12	5.13	5.14	5.15
40	6.69	6.71	6.72	6.73	6.74	6.75	6.77	6.78	6.79	6.80	6.81	6.83	6.84	6.85	6.86
50	8.37	8.38	8.40	8.41	8.43	8.44	8.46	8.47	8.49	8.50	8.52	8.53	8.55	8.56	8.58
60	10.04	10.06	10.08	10.09	10.11	10.13	10.15	10.17	10.18	10.20	10.22	10.24	10.26	10.27	10.29
70	11.71	11.73	11.76	11.78	11.80	11.82	11.84	11.86	11.88	11.90	11.92	11.94	11.97	11.99	12.01
80	13.39	13.41	13.44	13.46	13.48	13.51	13.53	13.56	13.58	13.61	13.63	13.65	13.67	13.70	13.72
90	15.06	15.09	15.11	15.14	15.17	15.20	15.22	15.25	15.28	15.30	15.33	15.36	15.38	15.41	15.44
100	16.73	16.76	16.79	16.82	16.85	16.88	16.91	16.94	16.97	17.00	17.03	17.06	17.09	17.12	17.15
200	33.47	33.53	33.59	33.65	33.71	33.77	33.83	33.89	33.95	34.01	34.07	34.13	34.19	34.25	34.31
300	50.20	50.29	50.38	50.47	50.56	50.65	50.74	50.83	50.92	51.01	51.10	51.19	51.28	51.37	51.46
400	66.94	67.05	67.18	67.30	67.42	67.54	67.66	67.78	67.90	68.02	68.13	68.25	68.37	68.49	68.61
500	83.67	83.82	83.97	84.12	84.27	84.42	84.57	84.72	84.87	85.02	85.17	85.32	85.47	85.62	85.77
600	100.40	100.58	100.76	100.94	101.12	101.30	101.48	101.66	101.84	102.02	102.20	102.38	102.56	102.74	102.92
700	117.14	117.35	117.56	117.77	117.98	118.19	118.40	118.61	118.82	119.03	119.23	119.44	119.65	119.84	120.07
800	133.87	134.11	134.35	134.59	134.83	135.07	135.31	135.55	135.79	136.03	136.26	136.50	136.74	136.98	137.22
900	150.61	150.88	151.15	151.42	151.69	151.96	152.23	152.50	152.77	153.04	153.30	153.57	153.84	154.11	154.38
1000	167.34	167.64	167.94	168.24	168.54	168.84	169.14	169.44	169.74	170.04	170.33	170.63	170.93	171.23	171.53

15	16	17	18	19	20	21	22	23	24	25	26	27	28	29	30
0.16	0.16	0.16	0.16	0.16	0.16	0.16	0.16	0.17	0.17	0.17	0.17	0.17	0.17	0.17	0.17
0.33	0.33	0.33	0.33	0.33	0.33	0.33	0.33	0.33	0.33	0.33	0.33	0.33	0.33	0.33	0.33
0.49	0.49	0.49	0.49	0.49	0.49	0.49	0.49	0.50	0.50	0.50	0.50	0.50	0.50	0.50	0.50
0.65	0.65	0.65	0.66	0.66	0.66	0.66	0.66	0.66	0.66	0.66	0.66	0.67	0.67	0.67	0.67
0.81	0.82	0.82	0.82	0.82	0.82	0.82	0.82	0.83	0.83	0.83	0.83	0.83	0.83	0.84	0.84
0.98	0.98	0.98	0.98	0.98	0.99	0.99	0.99	0.99	0.99	1.00	1.00	1.00	1.00	1.00	1.00
1.14	1.14	1.14	1.15	1.15	1.15	1.15	1.15	1.16	1.16	1.16	1.16	1.17	1.17	1.17	1.17
1.30	1.31	1.31	1.31	1.31	1.31	1.32	1.32	1.32	1.32	1.33	1.33	1.33	1.33	1.34	1.34
1.47	1.47	1.47	1.47	1.48	1.48	1.48	1.48	1.49	1.49	1.49	1.49	1.50	1.50	1.50	1.51
1.63	1.63	1.63	1.64	1.64	1.64	1.65	1.65	1.65	1.66	1.66	1.66	1.66	1.66	1.67	1.67
3.26	3.26	3.27	3.28	3.28	3.29	3.29	3.30	3.31	3.31	3.32	3.32	3.33	3.33	3.34	3.35
4.89	4.89	4.90	4.91	4.92	4.93	4.94	4.95	4.96	4.97	4.98	4.98	4.99	5.00	5.01	5.02
6.51	6.53	6.54	6.55	6.56	6.57	6.59	6.60	6.61	6.62	6.63	6.65	6.66	6.67	6.68	6.69
8.14	8.16	8.17	8.19	8.20	8.22	8.23	8.25	8.26	8.28	8.29	8.31	8.32	8.34	8.35	8.37
9.77	9.79	9.81	9.83	9.84	9.86	9.88	9.90	9.92	9.93	9.95	9.97	9.99	10.00	10.02	10.04
11.40	11.42	11.44	11.46	11.48	11.50	11.53	11.55	11.57	11.59	11.61	11.63	11.65	11.67	11.69	11.71
13.03	13.05	13.08	13.10	13.12	13.15	13.17	13.20	13.22	13.24	13.27	13.29	13.32	13.34	13.36	13.39
14.66	14.68	14.71	14.74	14.77	14.79	14.82	14.85	14.87	14.90	14.92	14.95	14.98	15.01	15.03	15.06
16.29	16.32	16.35	16.38	16.41	16.44	16.47	16.50	16.53	16.56	16.59	16.62	16.64	16.67	16.70	16.73
32.57	32.63	32.69	32.75	32.81	32.87	32.93	32.99	33.05	33.11	33.17	33.23	33.29	33.35	33.41	33.47
48.86	48.95	49.04	49.13	49.22	49.31	49.40	49.49	49.58	49.67	49.76	49.85	49.93	50.02	50.11	50.20
65.14	65.26	65.38	65.50	65.62	65.74	65.86	65.98	66.10	66.22	66.34	66.46	66.58	66.70	66.82	66.94
81.43	81.58	81.73	81.88	82.03	82.18	82.33	82.48	82.62	82.78	82.93	83.08	83.22	83.37	83.52	83.67
97.72	97.90	98.08	98.26	98.44	98.61	98.79	98.97	99.15	99.33	99.51	99.69	99.86	100.04	100.22	100.40
114.00	114.21	114.42	114.63	114.84	115.05	115.26	115.47	115.68	115.89	116.10	116.31	116.51	116.72	116.93	117.14
130.29	130.53	130.77	131.01	131.25	131.48	131.72	131.96	132.20	132.44	132.68	132.92	133.15	133.39	133.63	133.87
146.57	146.84	147.14	147.38	147.65	147.92	148.19	148.46	148.78	149.00	149.27	149.54	149.80	150.07	150.34	150.61
162.86	163.16	163.46	163.76	164.06	164.35	164.65	164.95	165.25	165.55	165.85	166.15	166.44	166.74	167.04	167.34

9 Degrees.

45	46	47	48	49	50	51	52	53	54	55	56	57	58	59	60
0.17	0.17	0.17	0.17	0.17	0.17	0.17	0.17	0.17	0.17	0.17	0.18	0.18	0.18	0.18	0.18
0.34	0.34	0.34	0.35	0.35	0.35	0.35	0.35	0.35	0.35	0.35	0.35	0.35	0.35	0.35	0.35
0.52	0.52	0.52	0.52	0.52	0.52	0.52	0.52	0.52	0.52	0.52	0.53	0.53	0.53	0.53	0.53
0.69	0.69	0.69	0.69	0.69	0.69	0.69	0.70	0.70	0.70	0.70	0.70	0.70	0.70	0.70	0.71
0.86	0.86	0.86	0.86	0.87	0.87	0.87	0.87	0.87	0.87	0.87	0.88	0.88	0.88	0.88	0.88
1.03	1.03	1.03	1.04	1.04	1.04	1.04	1.04	1.05	1.05	1.05	1.05	1.05	1.05	1.06	1.06
1.20	1.20	1.21	1.21	1.21	1.21	1.22	1.22	1.22	1.22	1.22	1.23	1.23	1.23	1.23	1.23
1.37	1.38	1.38	1.38	1.38	1.39	1.39	1.39	1.39	1.40	1.40	1.40	1.40	1.41	1.41	1.41
1.55	1.55	1.55	1.55	1.56	1.56	1.56	1.57	1.57	1.57	1.57	1.58	1.58	1.58	1.58	1.59
1.72	1.72	1.72	1.73	1.73	1.73	1.74	1.74	1.74	1.75	1.75	1.75	1.75	1.76	1.76	1.76
3.44	3.44	3.45	3.45	3.46	3.47	3.47	3.48	3.48	3.49	3.50	3.50	3.51	3.51	3.52	3.53
5.15	5.16	5.17	5.18	5.19	5.20	5.21	5.22	5.23	5.24	5.24	5.25	5.26	5.27	5.28	5.29
6.87	6.89	6.90	6.91	6.92	6.93	6.95	6.96	6.98	6.99	7.01	7.02	7.03	7.04	7.05	
8.59	8.61	8.62	8.64	8.65	8.67	8.68	8.70	8.71	8.73	8.74	8.76	8.77	8.79	8.80	8.82
10.31	10.33	10.35	10.38	10.38	10.40	10.42	10.44	10.45	10.47	10.49	10.51	10.53	10.54	10.56	10.58
12.03	12.05	12.07	12.09	12.11	12.13	12.15	12.18	12.20	12.22	12.24	12.26	12.28	12.30	12.32	12.34
13.75	13.77	13.79	13.82	13.84	13.87	13.89	13.91	13.94	13.96	13.99	14.01	14.03	14.06	14.08	14.11
15.46	15.49	15.52	15.55	15.57	15.60	15.63	15.65	15.68	15.71	15.73	15.76	15.79	15.82	15.84	15.87
17.18	17.21	17.24	17.27	17.30	17.33	17.36	17.39	17.42	17.45	17.48	17.51	17.54	17.57	17.60	17.63
34.37	34.43	34.49	34.55	34.61	34.67	34.73	34.79	34.85	34.91	34.97	35.03	35.09	35.15	35.21	35.27
51.55	51.64	51.73	51.82	51.91	52.00	52.09	52.18	52.27	52.36	52.45	52.54	52.63	52.72	52.81	53.00
68.73	68.85	68.97	69.09	69.21	69.33	69.45	69.57	69.69	69.81	69.93	70.05	70.17	70.29	70.41	70.53
85.92	86.07	86.22	86.37	86.52	86.67	86.82	86.97	87.12	87.27	87.42	87.57	87.72	87.87	88.02	88.17
103.10	103.28	103.46	103.64	103.82	104.00	104.18	104.36	104.54	104.72	104.90	105.08	105.26	105.44	105.62	105.80
120.28	120.49	120.70	120.91	121.12	121.33	121.54	121.75	121.96	122.17	122.38	122.59	122.80	123.01	123.22	123.43
137.46	137.70	137.94	138.18	138.42	138.66	138.90	139.14	139.38	139.62	139.86	140.10	140.34	140.58	140.82	141.06
154.65	154.92	155.19	155.46	155.73	156.00	156.27	156.54	156.81	157.08	157.35	157.62	157.89	158.16	158.43	158.70
171.83	172.13	172.43	172.73	173.03	173.33	173.63	173.93	174.23	174.53	174.83	175.13	175.43	175.73	176.03	176.33

10 Degrees.

Minutes	0	1	2	3	4	5	6	7	8	9	10	11	12	13	14
Dis. in ft.															
1	0.18	0.18	0.18	0.18	0.18	0.18	0.18	0.18	0.18	0.18	0.18	0.18	0.18	0.18	0.18
2	0.35	0.35	0.35	0.35	0.36	0.36	0.36	0.36	0.36	0.36	0.36	0.36	0.36	0.36	0.36
3	0.53	0.53	0.53	0.53	0.53	0.53	0.53	0.54	0.54	0.54	0.54	0.54	0.54	0.54	0.54
4	0.71	0.71	0.71	0.71	0.71	0.71	0.71	0.71	0.72	0.72	0.72	0.72	0.72	0.72	0.72
5	0.88	0.88	0.88	0.89	0.89	0.89	0.89	0.89	0.90	0.90	0.90	0.90	0.90	0.90	0.90
6	1.06	1.06	1.06	1.06	1.07	1.07	1.07	1.07	1.07	1.07	1.07	1.07	1.07	1.07	1.08
7	1.23	1.24	1.24	1.24	1.24	1.24	1.25	1.25	1.25	1.25	1.25	1.25	1.25	1.25	1.26
8	1.41	1.41	1.42	1.42	1.42	1.42	1.43	1.43	1.43	1.43	1.44	1.44	1.44	1.44	1.44
9	1.59	1.59	1.59	1.60	1.60	1.60	1.60	1.61	1.61	1.61	1.61	1.62	1.62	1.62	1.62
10	1.76	1.77	1.77	1.77	1.78	1.78	1.78	1.78	1.79	1.79	1.79	1.80	1.80	1.80	1.80
20	3.53	3.53	3.54	3.54	3.55	3.56	3.56	3.57	3.57	3.58	3.59	3.59	3.60	3.60	3.61
30	5.29	5.30	5.31	5.32	5.33	5.33	5.35	5.35	5.36	5.37	5.38	5.39	5.40	5.41	5.42
40	7.05	7.07	7.08	7.09	7.10	7.11	7.13	7.14	7.15	7.16	7.17	7.19	7.20	7.21	7.22
50	8.82	8.83	8.85	8.86	8.88	8.89	8.91	8.92	8.94	8.95	8.97	8.98	9.00	9.01	9.03
60	10.58	10.60	10.62	10.63	10.65	10.67	10.69	10.71	10.72	10.74	10.76	10.78	10.80	10.81	10.83
70	12.34	12.36	12.39	12.41	12.43	12.45	12.47	12.49	12.51	12.53	12.55	12.57	12.60	12.62	12.64
80	14.11	14.13	14.15	14.18	14.20	14.23	14.25	14.27	14.30	14.32	14.35	14.37	14.39	14.42	14.44
90	15.87	15.90	15.92	15.95	15.98	16.00	16.06	16.06	16.09	16.11	16.14	16.17	16.19	16.22	16.25
100	17.63	17.66	17.69	17.72	17.75	17.78	17.81	17.84	17.87	17.90	17.93	17.96	17.99	18.02	18.05
200	35.27	35.33	35.39	35.45	35.51	35.57	35.63	35.69	35.75	35.81	35.87	35.93	35.99	36.05	36.11
300	52.90	52.99	53.08	53.17	53.26	53.35	53.44	53.53	53.62	53.71	53.80	53.89	53.98	54.07	54.16
400	70.53	70.65	70.77	70.89	71.01	71.13	71.25	71.37	71.49	71.61	71.73	71.85	71.97	72.09	72.21
500	88.17	88.32	88.47	88.62	88.77	88.92	89.07	89.22	89.37	89.52	89.67	89.82	89.97	90.12	90.27
600	105.80	105.98	106.16	106.34	106.52	106.70	106.88	107.06	107.24	107.42	107.60	107.78	107.96	108.14	108.32
700	123.43	123.64	123.85	124.06	124.27	124.48	124.69	124.90	125.11	125.32	125.53	125.74	125.95	126.16	126.37
800	141.06	141.30	141.54	141.78	142.02	142.26	142.50	142.74	142.98	143.22	143.46	143.70	143.94	144.18	144.42
900	158.70	158.97	159.24	159.51	159.78	160.05	160.32	160.59	160.86	161.13	161.40	161.67	161.94	162.21	162.48
1000	176.33	176.63	176.93	177.23	177.53	177.83	178.13	178.43	178.73	179.03	179.33	179.63	179.93	180.23	180.53

10 Degrees.

Minutes	30	31	32	33	34	35	36	37	38	39	40	41	42	43	44
Dis. in ft.															
1	0.19	0.19	0.19	0.19	0.19	0.19	0.19	0.19	0.19	0.19	0.19	0.19	0.19	0.19	0.19
2	0.37	0.37	0.37	0.37	0.37	0.37	0.37	0.37	0.38	0.38	0.38	0.38	0.38	0.38	0.38
3	0.56	0.56	0.56	0.56	0.56	0.56	0.56	0.56	0.56	0.56	0.57	0.57	0.57	0.57	0.57
4	0.74	0.74	0.74	0.74	0.75	0.75	0.75	0.75	0.75	0.75	0.75	0.75	0.76	0.76	0.76
5	0.93	0.93	0.93	0.93	0.93	0.93	0.94	0.94	0.94	0.94	0.94	0.94	0.94	0.95	0.95
6	1.11	1.11	1.12	1.12	1.12	1.12	1.12	1.12	1.13	1.13	1.13	1.13	1.13	1.14	1.14
7	1.30	1.30	1.30	1.30	1.31	1.31	1.31	1.31	1.31	1.32	1.32	1.32	1.32	1.32	1.33
8	1.48	1.49	1.49	1.49	1.49	1.49	1.50	1.50	1.50	1.50	1.51	1.51	1.51	1.51	1.52
9	1.67	1.67	1.67	1.68	1.68	1.68	1.68	1.69	1.69	1.69	1.70	1.70	1.70	1.70	1.71
10	1.85	1.86	1.86	1.86	1.87	1.87	1.87	1.87	1.88	1.88	1.88	1.89	1.89	1.89	1.90
20	3.71	3.71	3.72	3.72	3.73	3.74	3.74	3.75	3.76	3.76	3.77	3.77	3.78	3.79	3.79
30	5.56	5.57	5.58	5.58	5.59	5.61	5.61	5.62	5.63	5.64	5.65	5.66	5.67	5.68	5.69
40	7.41	7.43	7.44	7.45	7.46	7.47	7.49	7.50	7.51	7.52	7.53	7.55	7.56	7.57	7.58
50	9.27	9.28	9.30	9.31	9.33	9.34	9.36	9.37	9.39	9.40	9.42	9.43	9.45	9.46	9.48
60	11.12	11.14	11.16	11.17	11.19	11.21	11.23	11.25	11.27	11.28	11.30	11.32	11.34	11.36	11.37
70	12.97	12.99	13.02	13.04	13.06	13.08	13.10	13.12	13.14	13.16	13.18	13.21	13.23	13.25	13.27
80	14.83	14.85	14.88	14.90	14.92	14.95	14.97	15.00	15.02	15.04	15.07	15.09	15.12	15.14	15.16
90	16.68	16.71	16.73	16.76	16.79	16.82	16.84	16.87	16.90	16.92	16.95	16.98	17.01	17.03	17.06
100	18.53	18.56	18.59	18.62	18.65	18.68	18.72	18.75	18.78	18.81	18.84	18.87	18.90	18.93	18.96
200	37.07	37.13	37.19	37.25	37.31	37.37	37.43	37.49	37.55	37.61	37.67	37.73	37.79	37.85	37.91
300	55.60	55.69	55.78	55.87	55.96	56.05	56.15	56.24	56.33	56.42	56.51	56.60	56.69	56.78	56.87
400	74.14	74.26	74.38	74.50	74.62	74.74	74.86	74.98	75.10	75.22	75.34	75.46	75.58	75.70	75.82
500	92.67	92.82	92.97	93.12	93.27	93.42	93.58	93.73	93.88	94.03	94.18	94.33	94.48	94.63	94.78
600	111.20	111.38	111.56	111.74	111.92	112.10	112.29	112.47	112.65	112.83	113.01	113.19	113.37	113.55	113.73
700	129.74	129.95	130.16	130.37	130.58	130.79	131.01	131.22	131.43	131.64	131.85	132.06	132.27	132.48	132.69
800	148.27	148.51	148.75	148.99	149.23	149.47	149.72	149.96	150.20	150.44	150.68	150.92	151.16	151.40	151.64
900	166.81	167.08	167.35	167.62	167.89	168.16	168.44	168.71	168.98	169.25	169.52	169.79	170.06	170.33	170.60
1000	185.34	185.64	185.94	186.24	186.54	186.84	187.15	187.45	187.75	188.05	188.35	188.65	188.95	189.25	189.55

22

10 Degrees.

15	16	17	18	19	20	21	22	23	24	25	26	27	28	29	30
0.18	0.18	0.18	0.18	0.18	0.18	0.18	0.18	0.18	0.18	0.18	0.18	0.18	0.18	0.19	0.19
0.36	0.36	0.36	0.36	0.36	0.36	0.37	0.37	0.37	0.37	0.37	0.37	0.37	0.37	0.37	0.37
0.54	0.54	0.54	0.54	0.54	0.55	0.55	0.55	0.55	0.55	0.55	0.55	0.55	0.55	0.56	0.56
0.72	0.72	0.73	0.73	0.73	0.73	0.73	0.73	0.73	0.73	0.74	0.74	0.74	0.74	0.74	0.74
0.90	0.91	0.91	0.91	0.91	0.91	0.91	0.91	0.92	0.92	0.92	0.92	0.92	0.92	0.93	0.93
1.08	1.09	1.09	1.09	1.09	1.09	1.10	1.10	1.10	1.10	1.10	1.10	1.11	1.11	1.11	1.11
1.27	1.27	1.27	1.27	1.27	1.28	1.28	1.28	1.28	1.28	1.29	1.29	1.29	1.29	1.30	1.30
1.45	1.45	1.45	1.45	1.46	1.46	1.46	1.46	1 47	1.47	1.47	1.47	1.48	1.48	1.48	1.48
1.63	1.63	1.63	1.64	1.64	1.64	1.64	1.65	1.65	1.65	1.65	1.66	1.66	1.66	1.67	1.67
1.81	1.81	1.81	1.82	1.82	1.82	1.83	1.83	1.83	1.84	1.84	1.84	1.84	1.85	1.85	1.85
3.62	3.62	3.63	3.63	3.64	3.65	3.65	3.66	3.66	3.67	3.68	3.68	3.69	3.69	3.70	3.71
5.42	5.43	5.44	5.45	5.46	5.47	5.48	5.49	5.50	5.51	5.52	5.52	5.53	5.54	5.55	5.56
7.23	7.25	7.26	7.27	7.28	7.29	7.31	7.32	7.33	7.34	7.35	7.37	7.38	7.39	7.40	7.41
9.04	9.06	9.07	9.09	9.10	9.12	9.13	9.15	9.16	9.18	9.19	9.21	9.22	9.24	9 25	9.27
10.85	10.87	10.89	10.90	10.92	10.94	10.96	10.98	10.99	11.01	11.03	11.05	11.07	11.08	11.10	11.12
12.66	12.68	12.70	12.72	12.74	12.76	12.78	12.81	12.83	12.85	12.87	12.89	12.91	12.93	12.95	12.97
14.47	14.49	14.51	14.54	14.56	14.59	14.61	14.63	14.66	14.68	14.71	14.73	14.76	14.78	14.80	14.83
16.27	16.30	16.33	16.36	16.38	16.41	16.44	16.46	16.49	16.52	16.55	16.57	16.60	16.63	16.65	16.68
18.08	18.11	18.14	18.17	18.20	18.23	18.26	18.29	18.32	18.35	18.38	18.41	18.44	18.47	18.50	18.53
36.17	36.23	36.29	36.35	36.41	36.47	36.53	36.59	36.65	36.71	36.77	36.83	36.89	36.95	37.01	37.07
54.25	54.34	54.43	54.52	54.61	54.70	54.79	54.88	54.97	55.06	55.15	55.24	55.33	55.42	55.51	55.60
72.38	72.45	72.57	72.69	72.81	72.93	73.05	73.17	73.29	73.41	73.54	73.66	73.78	73.90	74.02	74.14
90.42	90.57	90.72	90.87	91.02	91.17	91.32	91.47	91.62	91.77	91.92	92.07	92.22	92.37	92.52	92.67
108.50	108.68	108.86	109.04	109.22	109.40	109.58	109.76	109.94	110.12	110.30	110.48	110.66	110.84	111.02	111.20
126.58	126.79	127.00	127.21	127.42	127.63	127.84	128.05	128.26	128.47	128.69	128.90	129.11	129.32	129.53	129.74
144.66	144.90	145.14	145.38	145.62	145.86	146.10	146.34	146.58	146.82	147.07	147.31	147.55	147.79	148.03	148.27
162.75	163.02	163.29	163.56	163.83	164.10	164.37	164.64	164.91	165.18	165.46	165.73	166.00	166.27	166.54	166.81
180.83	181.13	181.43	181.73	182.03	182.33	182.63	182.93	183.23	183.53	183.84	184.14	184.44	184.74	185.04	185.34

10 Degrees.

45	46	47	48	49	50	51	52	53	54	55	56	57	58	59	60
0.19	0.19	0.19	0.19	0.19	0.19	0.19	0.19	0.19	0.19	0.19	0.19	0.19	0.19	0.19	0.19
0.38	0.38	0.38	0.38	0.38	0.38	0.38	0.38	0.38	0.39	0.39	0.39	0.39	0.39	0.39	0.39
0.57	0.57	0.57	0.57	0.57	0.57	0.57	0.58	0.58	0.58	0.58	0.58	0.58	0.58	0.58	0.58
0.76	0.76	0.76	0.76	0.76	0.77	0.77	0.77	0.77	0.77	0.77	0.77	0.77	0.78	0.78	0.78
0.95	0.95	0.95	0.95	0.96	0.96	0.96	0.96	0.96	0.96	0.96	0.97	0.97	0.97	0.97	0.97
1.14	1.14	1.14	1.14	1.15	1.15	1.15	1.15	1.15	1.16	1.16	1.16	1.16	1.16	1.16	1.17
1.33	1.33	1.33	1.34	1.34	1.34	1.34	1.34	1.35	1.35	1.35	1.35	1.35	1.36	1.36	1.36
1.52	1.52	1.52	1.53	1.53	1.53	1.53	1.54	1.54	1.54	1.54	1.55	1.55	1.55	1.55	1.55
1.71	1.71	1.71	1.72	1.72	1.72	1.72	1.73	1.73	1.73	1.74	1.74	1.74	1.74	1.75	1.75
1.90	1.90	1.90	1.91	1.91	1.91	1.92	1.92	1.92	1.93	1.93	1.93	1.93	1.94	1.94	1.94
3.80	3.80	3.81	3.82	3.82	3.83	3.83	3.84	3.85	3.85	3.85	3.86	3.87	3.88	3.88	3.89
5.70	5.70	5.71	5.72	5.73	5.74	5.75	5.76	5.77	5.78	5.79	5.80	5.80	5.81	5.82	5.83
7.59	7.61	7.62	7.63	7.64	7.65	7.67	7.68	7.69	7.70	7.71	7.73	7.74	7.75	7.76	7.77
9.49	9.51	9.52	9.54	9.55	9.57	9.58	9.60	9.61	9.63	9.64	9.66	9.67	9.69	9.70	9.72
11.39	11.41	11.43	11.45	11.46	11.48	11.50	11.52	11.54	11.55	11.57	11.59	11.61	11.63	11.64	11.66
13.29	13.31	13.33	13.35	13.37	13.40	13.42	13.44	13.46	13.48	13.50	13.52	13.54	13.56	13.58	13.61
15.19	15.21	15.24	15.26	15.28	15.31	15.33	15.36	15.38	15.41	15.43	15.45	15.48	15.50	15.53	15.55
17.09	17.11	17.14	17.17	17.20	17.22	17.25	17.28	17.30	17.33	17.36	17.39	17.41	17.44	17.47	17.49
18.99	19.02	19.05	19.08	19.11	19.14	19.17	19.20	19.23	19.26	19.29	19.32	19.35	19.38	19.41	19.44
37.97	38.03	38.09	38.15	38.21	38.27	38.33	38.39	38.45	38.51	38.57	38.63	38.69	38.75	38.81	38.87
56.96	57.05	57.14	57.23	57.32	57.41	57.50	57.59	57.68	57.77	57.86	57.95	58.04	58.13	58.22	58.31
75.94	76.06	76.18	76.30	76.42	76.54	76.66	76.78	76.91	77.03	77.15	77.27	77.39	77.51	77.63	77.75
94.93	95.08	95.23	95.38	95.53	95.68	95.83	95.98	96.14	96.29	96.44	96.59	96.74	96.89	97.04	97.19
113.91	114.10	114.28	114.46	114.64	114.82	115.00	115.18	115.36	115.54	115.72	115.90	116.08	116.26	116.44	116.62
132.90	133.11	133.32	133.53	133.74	133.95	134.16	134.37	134.59	134.80	135.01	135.22	135.43	135.64	135.85	136.06
151.88	152.13	152.37	152.61	152.85	153.09	153.33	153.57	153.82	154.06	154.30	154.54	154.78	155.02	155.26	155.50
170.87	171.14	171.41	171.68	171.95	172.22	172.49	172.76	173.04	173.31	173.58	173.85	174.12	174.39	174.66	174.93
189.85	190.16	190.46	190.76	191.06	191.36	191.66	191.96	192.27	192.57	192.87	193.17	193.47	193.77	194.07	194.37

11 Degrees.

Minutes	0	1	2	3	4	5	6	7	8	9	10	11	12	13	14
Dis. in ft.															
1	0.19	0.19	0.19	0.20	0.20	0.20	0.20	0.20	0.20	0.20	0.20	0.20	0.20	0.20	0.20
2	0.39	0.39	0.39	0.39	0.39	0.39	0.39	0.39	0.39	0.39	0.39	0.40	0.40	0.40	0.40
3	0.58	0.58	0.58	0.59	0.59	0.59	0.59	0.59	0.59	0.59	0.59	0.59	0.59	0.59	0.60
4	0.78	0.78	0.78	0.78	0.78	0.78	0.79	0.79	0.79	0.79	0.79	0.79	0.79	0.79	0.79
5	0.97	0.97	0.97	0.98	0.98	0.98	0.98	0.98	0.98	0.99	0.99	0.99	0.99	0.99	0.99
6	1.17	1.17	1.17	1.17	1.17	1.18	1.18	1.18	1.18	1.18	1.18	1.19	1.19	1.19	1.19
7	1.36	1.36	1.36	1.37	1.37	1.37	1.37	1.38	1.38	1.38	1.38	1.38	1.39	1.39	1.39
8	1.55	1.56	1.56	1.56	1.56	1.57	1.57	1.57	1.57	1.58	1.58	1.58	1.58	1.58	1.59
9	1.75	1.75	1.75	1.76	1.76	1.76	1.77	1.77	1.77	1.77	1.78	1.78	1.78	1.78	1.79
10	1.94	1.95	1.95	1.95	1.96	1.96	1.96	1.96	1.97	1.97	1.97	1.98	1.98	1.98	1.99
20	3.89	3.89	3.90	3.91	3.91	3.92	3.92	3.93	3.94	3.94	3.95	3.95	3.96	3.97	3.97
30	5.83	5.84	5.85	5.86	5.87	5.88	5.89	5.89	5.90	5.91	5.92	5.93	5.94	5.95	5.96
40	7.77	7.79	7.80	7.81	7.82	7.84	7.85	7.86	7.87	7.88	7.90	7.91	7.92	7.93	7.94
50	9.72	9.73	9.75	9.76	9.78	9.79	9.81	9.82	9.84	9.86	9.87	9.89	9.90	9.92	9.93
60	11.66	11.68	11.70	11.72	11.74	11.75	11.77	11.79	11.81	11.83	11.84	11.86	11.88	11.90	11.92
70	13.61	13.63	13.65	13.67	13.69	13.71	13.73	13.75	13.78	13.80	13.82	13.84	13.86	13.88	13.90
80	15.55	15.57	15.60	15.62	15.65	15.67	15.70	15.72	15.74	15.77	15.79	15.82	15.84	15.86	15.89
90	17.49	17.52	17.55	17.58	17.60	17.63	17.66	17.68	17.71	17.74	17.77	17.79	17.82	17.85	17.87
100	19.44	19.47	19.50	19.53	19.56	19.59	19.62	19.65	19.68	19.71	19.74	19.77	19.80	19.83	19.86
200	38.87	38.94	39.00	39.06	39.12	39.18	39.24	39.30	39.36	39.42	39.48	39.54	39.60	39.66	39.72
300	58.31	58.40	58.49	58.59	58.68	58.77	58.86	58.95	59.04	59.13	59.22	59.31	59.40	59.49	59.59
400	77.75	77.87	77.99	78.12	78.24	78.36	78.48	78.60	78.72	78.84	78.96	79.08	79.20	79.32	79.44
500	97.19	97.34	97.49	97.65	97.80	97.95	98.10	98.25	98.40	98.55	98.70	98.85	99.01	99.16	99.31
600	116.62	116.81	116.99	117.17	117.35	117.53	117.71	117.89	118.08	118.26	118.44	118.62	118.81	118.99	119.17
700	136.06	136.28	136.49	136.70	136.91	137.12	137.33	137.54	137.76	137.97	138.18	138.39	138.61	138.82	139.03
800	155.50	155.74	155.98	156.23	156.47	156.71	156.95	157.19	157.44	157.68	157.92	158.16	158.41	158.65	158.89
900	174.93	175.21	175.48	175.76	176.03	176.30	176.57	176.84	177.12	177.39	177.66	177.93	178.21	178.48	178.75
1000	194.37	194.68	194.98	195.29	195.59	195.89	196.19	196.49	196.80	197.10	197.40	197.70	198.01	198.31	198.61

11 Degrees.

Minutes	30	31	32	33	34	35	36	37	38	39	40	41	42	43	44
Dis. in ft.															
1	0.20	0.20	0.20	0.20	0.20	0.20	0.21	0.21	0.21	0.21	0.21	0.21	0.21	0.21	0.21
2	0.41	0.41	0.41	0.41	0.41	0.41	0.41	0.41	0.41	0.41	0.41	0.41	0.41	0.41	0.42
3	0.61	0.61	0.61	0.61	0.61	0.61	0.62	0.62	0.62	0.62	0.62	0.62	0.62	0.62	0.63
4	0.81	0.82	0.82	0.82	0.82	0.82	0.82	0.82	0.82	0.82	0.83	0.83	0.83	0.83	0.83
5	1.02	1.02	1.02	1.02	1.02	1.02	1.03	1.03	1.03	1.03	1.03	1.03	1.04	1.04	1.04
6	1.22	1.22	1.22	1.23	1.23	1.23	1.23	1.23	1.24	1.24	1.24	1.24	1.24	1.24	1.25
7	1.42	1.43	1.43	1.43	1.43	1.43	1.44	1.44	1.44	1.44	1.45	1.45	1.45	1.45	1.45
8	1.63	1.63	1.63	1.63	1.64	1.64	1.64	1.64	1.65	1.65	1.65	1.65	1.66	1.66	1.66
9	1.83	1.83	1.84	1.84	1.84	1.84	1.85	1.85	1.85	1.86	1.86	1.86	1.86	1.87	1.87
10	2.03	2.04	2.04	2.04	2.05	2.05	2.05	2.06	2.06	2.06	2.06	2.07	2.07	2.07	2.08
20	4.07	4.08	4.08	4.09	4.09	4.10	4.11	4.11	4.12	4.12	4.13	4.14	4.14	4.15	4.15
30	6.10	6.11	6.12	6.13	6.14	6.15	6.16	6.17	6.18	6.19	6.19	6.20	6.21	6.22	6.23
40	8.14	8.15	8.16	8.17	8.19	8.20	8.21	8.22	8.24	8.25	8.26	8.27	8.28	8.30	8.31
50	10.17	10.19	10.20	10.22	10.23	10.25	10.26	10.28	10.29	10.31	10.32	10.34	10.35	10.37	10.39
60	12.21	12.23	12.24	12.26	12.28	12.30	12.32	12.33	12.35	12.37	12.39	12.41	12.43	12.44	12.46
70	14.24	14.26	14.28	14.31	14.33	14.35	14.37	14.39	14.41	14.43	14.45	14.48	14.50	14.52	14.54
80	16.28	16.30	16.32	16.35	16.37	16.40	16.42	16.45	16.47	16.49	16.52	16.54	16.57	16.59	16.62
90	18.31	18.34	18.37	18.39	18.42	18.45	18.47	18.50	18.53	18.56	18.58	18.61	18.64	18.67	18.69
100	20.35	20.38	20.41	20.44	20.47	20.50	20.53	20.56	20.59	20.62	20.65	20.68	20.71	20.74	20.77
200	40.69	40.75	40.81	40.87	40.93	40.99	41.05	41.12	41.18	41.24	41.30	41.36	41.42	41.48	41.54
300	61.04	61.13	61.22	61.31	61.40	61.49	61.58	61.67	61.76	61.85	61.95	62.04	62.13	62.22	62.31
400	81.38	81.50	81.62	81.74	81.86	81.99	82.11	82.23	82.35	82.47	82.60	82.72	82.84	82.96	83.08
500	101.73	101.88	102.03	102.18	102.33	102.49	102.64	102.79	102.94	103.09	103.25	103.40	103.55	103.70	103.85
600	122.07	122.25	122.44	122.62	122.80	122.98	123.16	123.35	123.53	123.71	123.89	124.07	124.25	124.43	124.62
700	142.42	142.63	142.84	143.05	143.26	143.48	143.69	143.91	144.12	144.33	144.54	144.75	144.96	145.17	145.39
800	162.76	163.00	163.25	163.49	163.73	163.98	164.22	164.46	164.70	164.94	165.19	165.43	165.67	165.91	166.16
900	183.11	183.38	183.65	183.92	184.19	184.47	184.74	185.02	185.29	185.56	185.84	186.11	186.38	186.65	186.93
1000	203.45	203.75	204.06	204.36	204.66	204.97	205.27	205.58	205.88	206.18	206.49	206.79	207.09	207.39	207.70

11 Degrees.

15	16	17	18	19	20	21	22	23	24	25	26	27	28	29	30
0.20	0.20	0.20	0.20	0.20	0.20	0.20	0.20	0.20	0.20	0.20	0.20	0.20	0.20	0.20	0.20
0.40	0.40	0.40	0.40	0.40	0.40	0.40	0.40	0.40	0.40	0.40	0.40	0.40	0.41	0.41	0.41
0.60	0.60	0.60	0.60	0.60	0.60	0.60	0.60	0.60	0.60	0.60	0.61	0.61	0.61	0.61	0.61
0.80	0.80	0.80	0.80	0.80	0.80	0.80	0.80	0.81	0.81	0.81	0.81	0.81	0.81	0.81	0.81
0.99	1.00	1.00	1.00	1.00	1.00	1.00	1.01	1.01	1.01	1.01	1.01	1.01	1.01	1.02	1.02
1.19	1.20	1.20	1.20	1.20	1.20	1.20	1.21	1.21	1.21	1.21	1.21	1.22	1.22	1.22	1.22
1.39	1.39	1.40	1.40	1.40	1.40	1.41	1.41	1.41	1.41	1.41	1.42	1.42	1.42	1.42	1.42
1.59	1.59	1.60	1.60	1.60	1.60	1.61	1.61	1.61	1.61	1.62	1.62	1.62	1.62	1.63	1.63
1.79	1.79	1.80	1.80	1.80	1.80	1.81	1.81	1.81	1.81	1.82	1.82	1.82	1.83	1.83	1.83
1.99	1.99	2.00	2.00	2.00	2.00	2.01	2.01	2.01	2.02	2.02	2.02	2.03	2.03	2.03	2.03
3.98	3.98	3.99	4.00	4.00	4.01	4.01	4.02	4.03	4.03	4.04	4.04	4.05	4.06	4.06	4.07
5.97	5.98	5.99	5.99	6.00	6.01	6.02	6.03	6.04	6.05	6.06	6.07	6.08	6.09	6.09	6.10
7.96	7.97	7.98	7.99	8.00	8.02	8.03	8.04	8.05	8.07	8.08	8.09	8.10	8.11	8.13	8.14
9.95	9.96	9.98	9.99	10.01	10.02	10.04	10.05	10.07	10.08	10.10	10.11	10.13	10.14	10.16	10.17
11.93	11.95	11.97	11.99	12.01	12.03	12.04	12.06	12.08	12.10	12.12	12.13	12.15	12.17	12.19	12.21
13.92	13.94	13.97	13.99	14.01	14.03	14.05	14.07	14.09	14.11	14.14	14.16	14.18	14.20	14.22	14.24
15.91	15.94	15.96	15.99	16.01	16.03	16.06	16.08	16.11	16.13	16.16	16.18	16.20	16.23	16.25	16.28
17.90	17.93	17.96	17.98	18.01	18.04	18.06	18.09	18.12	18.15	18.17	18.20	18.23	18.26	18.28	18.31
19.89	19.92	19.95	19.98	20.01	20.04	20.07	20.10	20.13	20.16	20.19	20.22	20.25	20.28	20.32	20.35
39.78	39.84	39.90	39.96	40.02	40.08	40.14	40.21	40.27	40.33	40.39	40.45	40.51	40.57	40.63	40.69
59.67	59.76	59.86	59.95	60.04	60.13	60.22	60.31	60.40	60.49	60.58	60.67	60.76	60.85	60.95	61.04
79.56	79.68	79.81	79.93	80.05	80.17	80.29	80.41	80.53	80.65	80.78	80.90	81.02	81.14	81.26	81.38
99.46	99.61	99.76	99.91	100.06	100.21	100.36	100.52	100.67	100.82	100.97	101.12	101.27	101.42	101.58	101.73
119.35	119.53	119.71	119.89	120.07	120.25	120.43	120.62	120.80	120.98	121.16	121.34	121.52	121.70	121.89	122.07
139.24	139.45	139.66	139.87	140.08	140.29	140.50	140.72	140.93	141.14	141.36	141.57	141.78	141.99	142.21	142.42
159.13	159.37	159.62	159.86	160.10	160.34	160.58	160.82	161.06	161.30	161.55	161.79	162.03	162.27	162.52	162.76
179.02	179.29	179.57	179.84	180.11	180.38	180.65	180.93	181.20	181.47	181.75	182.02	182.29	182.56	182.84	183.11
198.91	199.21	199.52	199.82	200.12	200.42	200.72	201.03	201.33	201.63	201.94	202.24	202.54	202.84	203.15	203.45

11 Degrees.

45	46	47	48	49	50	51	52	53	54	55	56	57	58	59	60
0.21	0.21	0.21	0.21	0.21	0.21	0.21	0.21	0.21	0.21	0.21	0.21	0.21	0.21	0.21	0.21
0.42	0.42	0.42	0.42	0.42	0.42	0.42	0.42	0.42	0.42	0.42	0.42	0.42	0.42	0.42	0.43
0.62	0.62	0.63	0.63	0.63	0.63	0.63	0.63	0.63	0.63	0.63	0.63	0.63	0.64	0.64	0.64
0.83	0.83	0.83	0.84	0.84	0.84	0.84	0.84	0.84	0.84	0.84	0.84	0.85	0.85	0.85	0.85
1.04	1.04	1.04	1.04	1.05	1.05	1.05	1.05	1.05	1.05	1.06	1.06	1.06	1.06	1.06	1.06
1.25	1.25	1.25	1.25	1.26	1.26	1.26	1.26	1.26	1.26	1.27	1.27	1.27	1.27	1.27	1.28
1.46	1.46	1.46	1.46	1.46	1.47	1.47	1.47	1.47	1.48	1.48	1.48	1.48	1.48	1.49	1.49
1.66	1.67	1.67	1.67	1.67	1.68	1.68	1.68	1.68	1.69	1.69	1.69	1.69	1.70	1.70	1.70
1.87	1.87	1.88	1.88	1.88	1.89	1.89	1.89	1.89	1.90	1.90	1.90	1.90	1.91	1.91	1.91
2.08	2.08	2.09	2.09	2.09	2.10	2.10	2.10	2.10	2.11	2.11	2.11	2.12	2.12	2.12	2.13
4.16	4.17	4.17	4.18	4.18	4.19	4.20	4.20	4.20	4.21	4.21	4.22	4.23	4.23	4.24	4.25
6.24	6.25	6.26	6.27	6.28	6.29	6.29	6.30	6.31	6.32	6.33	6.34	6.35	6.36	6.37	6.38
8.32	8.33	8.34	8.36	8.37	8.38	8.39	8.40	8.42	8.43	8.44	8.45	8.47	8.48	8.49	8.50
10.40	10.42	10.43	10.45	10.46	10.48	10.49	10.51	10.52	10.54	10.55	10.57	10.58	10.60	10.61	10.63
12.48	12.50	12.52	12.53	12.55	12.57	12.59	12.61	12.63	12.64	12.66	12.68	12.70	12.72	12.74	12.75
14.56	14.58	14.60	14.62	14.64	14.67	14.69	14.71	14.73	14.75	14.77	14.79	14.82	14.84	14.86	14.88
16.64	16.66	16.69	16.71	16.73	16.76	16.79	16.81	16.83	16.86	16.88	16.91	16.93	16.96	16.98	17.00
18.72	18.75	18.77	18.80	18.83	18.86	18.88	18.91	18.94	18.97	18.99	19.02	19.05	19.08	19.10	19.13
20.80	20.83	20.86	20.89	20.92	20.95	20.98	21.01	21.04	21.07	21.10	21.13	21.17	21.20	21.23	21.26
41.60	41.66	41.72	41.78	41.84	41.90	41.96	42.03	42.09	42.15	42.21	42.27	42.33	42.39	42.45	42.51
62.40	62.49	62.58	62.67	62.76	62.86	62.95	63.04	63.13	63.22	63.31	63.40	63.50	63.59	63.68	63.77
83.20	83.32	83.44	83.56	83.68	83.81	83.93	84.05	84.17	84.29	84.42	84.54	84.66	84.78	84.90	85.02
104.00	104.16	104.31	104.46	104.61	104.76	104.91	105.07	105.22	105.37	105.52	105.67	105.83	105.98	106.13	106.28
124.80	124.99	125.17	125.35	125.53	125.71	125.89	126.08	126.26	126.44	126.62	126.80	126.99	127.17	127.35	127.53
145.60	145.82	146.03	146.24	146.45	146.66	146.87	147.09	147.30	147.51	147.73	147.94	148.16	148.37	148.58	148.79
166.40	166.65	166.89	167.13	167.37	167.62	167.86	168.10	168.34	168.58	168.83	169.07	169.32	169.56	169.80	170.04
187.20	187.48	187.75	188.02	188.29	188.57	188.84	189.12	189.39	189.66	189.94	190.21	190.49	190.76	191.03	191.30
208.00	208.31	208.61	208.91	209.21	209.52	209.82	210.13	210.43	210.73	211.04	211.34	211.65	211.95	212.25	212.55

12 Degrees.

Minutes	0	1	2	3	4	5	6	7	8	9	10	11	12	13	14
Dis. in ft.															
1	0.21	0.21	0.21	0.21	0.21	0.21	0.21	0.21	0.21	0.22	0.22	0.22	0.22	0.22	0.22
2	0.43	0.43	0.43	0.43	0.43	0.43	0.43	0.43	0.43	0.43	0.43	0.43	0.43	0.43	0.43
3	0.64	0.64	0.64	0.64	0.64	0.64	0.64	0.64	0.64	0.65	0.65	0.65	0.65	0.65	0.65
4	0.85	0.85	0.85	0.85	0.86	0.86	0.86	0.86	0.86	0.86	0.86	0.86	0.86	0.87	0.87
5	1.06	1.06	1.07	1.07	1.07	1.07	1.07	1.07	1.07	1.08	1.08	1.08	1.08	1.08	1.08
6	1.28	1.28	1.28	1.28	1.28	1.28	1.29	1.29	1.29	1.29	1.29	1.30	1.30	1.30	1.30
7	1.49	1.49	1.49	1.49	1.50	1.50	1.50	1.50	1.50	1.51	1.51	1.51	1.51	1.52	1.52
8	1.70	1.70	1.71	1.71	1.71	1.71	1.72	1.72	1.72	1.72	1.72	1.73	1.73	1.73	1.73
9	1.91	1.92	1.92	1.92	1.92	1.93	1.93	1.93	1.93	1.94	1.94	1.94	1.95	1.95	1.95
10	2.13	2.13	2.13	2.13	2.14	2.14	2.14	2.15	2.15	2.15	2.16	2.16	2.16	2.17	2.17
20	4.25	4.26	4.26	4.27	4.28	4.28	4.29	4.29	4.30	4.31	4.31	4.32	4.32	4.33	4.34
30	6.38	6.39	6.39	6.40	6.41	6.42	6.43	6.44	6.45	6.46	6.47	6.48	6.49	6.50	6.50
40	8.50	8.51	8.53	8.54	8.55	8.56	8.58	8.59	8.60	8.61	8.62	8.64	8.65	8.66	7.67
50	10.63	10.64	10.66	10.67	10.69	10.70	10.72	10.73	10.75	10.76	10.78	10.80	10.81	10.83	10.84
60	12.75	12.77	12.79	12.81	12.83	12.84	12.86	12.88	12.90	12.92	12.94	12.95	12.97	12.99	13.01
70	14.88	14.90	14.92	14.94	14.96	14.99	15.01	15.03	15.05	15.07	15.09	15.11	15.13	15.16	15.18
80	17.00	17.03	17.05	17.08	17.10	17.13	17.15	17.17	17.20	17.22	17.25	17.27	17.30	17.33	17.35
90	19.13	19.16	19.18	19.21	19.24	19.27	19.29	19.32	19.35	19.38	19.40	19.43	19.46	19.49	19.51
100	21.26	21.29	21.32	21.35	21.38	21.41	21.44	21.47	21.50	21.53	21.56	21.59	21.62	21.65	21.68
200	42.51	42.57	42.63	42.69	42.75	42.82	42.88	42.94	43.00	43.06	43.12	43.18	43.24	43.30	43.36
300	63.77	63.86	63.95	64.04	64.13	64.22	64.31	64.40	64.50	64.59	64.68	64.77	64.86	64.95	65.05
400	85.02	85.14	85.26	85.39	85.51	85.63	85.75	85.87	86.00	86.12	86.24	86.36	86.48	86.60	86.73
500	106.28	106.43	106.58	106.74	106.89	107.04	107.19	107.34	107.50	107.65	107.80	107.95	108.11	108.26	108.41
600	127.53	127.72	127.90	128.08	128.26	128.45	128.63	128.81	128.99	129.17	129.36	129.54	129.73	129.91	130.09
700	148.79	149.00	149.21	149.43	149.64	149.86	150.07	150.28	150.49	150.70	150.92	151.13	151.35	151.56	151.77
800	170.04	170.29	170.53	170.78	171.02	171.26	171.50	171.74	171.99	172.23	172.48	172.72	172.97	173.21	173.46
900	191.30	191.57	191.84	192.12	192.39	192.67	192.94	193.21	193.48	193.76	194.04	194.31	194.59	194.86	195.14
1000	212.55	212.86	213.16	213.47	213.77	214.08	214.38	214.68	214.99	215.29	215.60	215.90	216.21	216.51	216.82

12 Degrees.

Minutes	30	31	32	33	34	35	36	37	38	39	40	41	42	43	44
Dis. in ft.															
1	0.22	0.22	0.22	0.22	0.22	0.22	0.22	0.22	0.22	0.22	0.22	0.23	0.23	0.23	0.23
2	0.44	0.44	0.44	0.45	0.45	0.45	0.45	0.45	0.45	0.45	0.45	0.45	0.45	0.45	0.45
3	0.67	0.67	0.67	0.67	0.67	0.67	0.67	0.67	0.67	0.67	0.67	0.68	0.68	0.68	0.68
4	0.89	0.89	0.89	0.89	0.89	0.89	0.89	0.90	0.90	0.90	0.90	0.90	0.90	0.90	0.90
5	1.11	1.11	1.11	1.11	1.11	1.12	1.12	1.12	1.12	1.12	1.12	1.13	1.13	1.13	1.13
6	1.33	1.33	1.33	1.34	1.34	1.34	1.34	1.34	1.34	1.34	1.35	1.35	1.35	1.35	1.36
7	1.55	1.55	1.56	1.56	1.56	1.56	1.56	1.57	1.57	1.57	1.57	1.58	1.58	1.58	1.58
8	1.77	1.78	1.78	1.78	1.78	1.79	1.79	1.79	1.79	1.80	1.80	1.80	1.80	1.81	1.81
9	2.00	2.00	2.00	2.00	2.01	2.01	2.01	2.01	2.01	2.02	2.02	2.02	2.03	2.03	2.03
10	2.22	2.22	2.22	2.23	2.23	2.23	2.24	2.24	2.24	2.24	2.25	2.25	2.25	2.26	2.26
20	4.43	4.44	4.45	4.45	4.46	4.46	4.47	4.48	4.48	4.49	4.50	4.50	4.51	4.51	4.52
30	6.65	6.66	6.67	6.68	6.69	6.70	6.71	6.71	6.72	6.73	6.74	6.75	6.76	6.77	6.78
40	8.87	8.88	8.89	8.90	8.92	8.93	8.94	8.95	8.97	8.98	8.99	9.00	9.01	9.03	9.04
50	11.09	11.10	11.12	11.13	11.15	11.16	11.18	11.19	11.21	11.22	11.24	11.25	11.27	11.28	11.30
60	13.30	13.32	13.34	13.36	13.38	13.39	13.41	13.43	13.45	13.47	13.49	13.50	13.52	13.54	13.56
70	15.52	15.54	15.56	15.58	15.60	15.63	15.65	15.67	15.69	15.71	15.73	15.75	15.78	15.80	15.82
80	17.74	17.76	17.78	17.81	17.83	17.86	17.88	17.91	17.93	17.96	17.98	18.00	18.03	18.05	18.08
90	19.95	19.98	20.01	20.03	20.06	20.09	20.12	20.14	20.17	20.20	20.23	20.26	20.28	20.31	20.34
100	22.17	22.20	22.23	22.26	22.29	22.32	22.35	22.38	22.41	22.45	22.48	22.51	22.54	22.57	22.60
200	44.34	44.40	44.46	44.52	44.58	44.64	44.71	44.77	44.83	44.89	44.95	45.01	45.07	45.13	45.19
300	66.51	66.60	66.69	66.78	66.88	66.97	67.06	67.15	67.24	67.34	67.43	67.52	67.61	67.70	67.79
400	88.68	88.80	88.92	89.04	89.17	89.29	89.41	89.53	89.66	89.78	89.90	90.02	90.14	90.27	90.39
500	110.85	111.00	111.16	111.31	111.46	111.61	111.77	111.92	112.07	112.23	112.38	112.53	112.68	112.84	112.99
600	133.02	133.20	133.39	133.57	133.75	133.93	134.12	134.30	134.48	134.67	134.85	135.04	135.22	135.40	135.58
700	155.19	155.40	155.62	155.83	156.04	156.25	156.47	156.68	156.90	157.12	157.33	157.54	157.75	157.97	158.18
800	177.36	177.60	177.85	178.09	178.34	178.58	178.82	179.06	179.31	179.56	179.80	180.05	180.29	180.54	180.78
900	199.53	199.80	200.08	200.35	200.63	200.90	201.18	201.45	201.73	202.01	202.28	202.55	202.82	203.10	203.37
1000	221.70	222.00	222.31	222.61	222.92	223.22	223.53	223.83	224.14	224.45	224.75	225.06	225.36	225.67	225.97

12 Degrees.

15	16	17	18	19	20	21	22	23	24	25	26	27	28	29	30
0.22	0.22	0.22	0.22	0.22	0.22	0.22	0.22	0.22	0.22	0.22	0.22	0.22	0.22	0.22	0.22
0.43	0.43	0.44	0.44	0.44	0.44	0.44	0.44	0.44	0.44	0.44	0.44	0.44	0.44	0.44	0.44
0.65	0.65	0.65	0.65	0.66	0.66	0.66	0.66	0.66	0.66	0.66	0.66	0.66	0.66	0.66	0.67
0.87	0.87	0.87	0.87	0.87	0.87	0.88	0.88	0.88	0.88	0.88	0.88	0.88	0.88	0.89	0.89
1.09	1.09	1.09	1.09	1.09	1.09	1.09	1.10	1.10	1.10	1.10	1.10	1.10	1.11	1.11	1.11
1.30	1.30	1.31	1.31	1.31	1.31	1.31	1.32	1.32	1.32	1.32	1.32	1.32	1.33	1.33	1.33
1.52	1.52	1.52	1.53	1.53	1.53	1.53	1.53	1 54	1.54	1.54	1.54	1.55	1.55	1.55	1.55
1.74	1.74	1.74	1.74	1.75	1.75	1.75	1.75	1.76	1.76	1.76	1.76	1.77	1.77	1.77	1.77
1.95	1.96	1.96	1.96	1.97	1.97	1.97	1.97	1.98	1.98	1.98	1.98	1.99	1.99	1.99	2.00
2.17	2.17	2.18	2.18	2.18	2.19	2.19	2.19	2.20	2.20	2.20	2.20	2.21	2.21	2.21	2.22
4.34	4.35	4.35	4.36	4.37	4.37	4.38	4.39	4.39	4.40	4.40	4.41	4.42	4.42	4.43	4.43
6.51	6.52	6.53	6.54	6.55	6.56	6.57	6.58	6.59	6.60	6.61	6.61	6.62	6.63	6.64	6.65
8.68	8.70	8.71	8.72	8.73	8.75	8.76	8.77	8.78	8.79	8.81	8.82	8.83	8.84	8.86	8.87
10.86	10.87	10.89	10.90	10.92	10.93	10.95	10.96	10.98	10.99	11.01	11.02	11.04	11.05	11.07	11.09
13.03	13.05	13.06	13.08	13.10	13.12	13.14	13.16	13.17	13.19	13.21	13.23	13.25	13.26	13.28	13.30
15.20	15.22	15.24	15.26	15.28	15.31	15.33	15.35	15.37	15.39	15.41	15.43	15.45	15.48	15.50	15.52
17.37	17.39	17.42	17.44	17.47	17.49	17.52	17.54	17.56	17.59	17.61	17.64	17.66	17.69	17.71	17.74
19.54	19.57	19.60	19.62	19.65	19.68	19.71	19.73	19.76	19.79	19.82	19.84	19.87	19.90	19.93	19.95
21.71	21.74	21.77	21.80	21.83	21.87	21.90	21.93	21.96	21.99	22.02	22.05	22.08	22.11	22.14	22.17
43.42	43.49	43.55	43.61	43.67	43.73	43.79	43.85	43.91	43.97	44.03	44.09	44.16	44.22	44.28	44.34
65.14	65.23	65.32	65.41	65.50	65.60	65.69	65.78	65.87	65.96	66.05	66.14	66.23	66.32	66.42	66.51
86.85	86.97	87.09	87.22	87.34	87.46	87.58	87.70	87.82	87.94	88.07	88.19	88.31	88.43	88.56	88.68
108.56	108.72	108.87	109.02	109.17	109.33	109.48	109.63	109.78	109.93	110.09	110.24	110.39	110.54	110.70	110.85
130.27	130.46	130.64	130.82	131.00	131.19	131.37	131.56	121.74	131.92	132.10	132.28	132.47	132.65	132.83	133.02
151.98	152.20	152.41	152.63	152.84	153.06	153.27	153.48	153.69	153.90	154.12	154.33	154.55	154.76	154.97	155.19
173.70	173.94	174.18	174.43	174.67	174.92	175.16	175.41	175.65	175.89	176.14	176.38	176.62	176.86	177.11	177.36
195.41	195.69	195.96	196.24	196.51	196.79	197.06	197.33	197.60	197.87	198.15	198.42	198.70	198.97	199.25	199.53
217.12	217.43	217.73	218.04	218.34	218.65	218.95	219.26	219.56	219.86	220.17	220.47	220.78	221.08	221.39	221.70

12 Degrees.

45	46	47	48	49	50	51	52	53	54	55	56	57	58	59	60
0.23	0.23	0.23	0.23	0.23	0.23	0.23	0.23	0.23	0.23	0.23	0.23	0.23	0.23	0.23	0.23
0.45	0.45	0.45	0.45	0.46	0.46	0.46	0.46	0.46	0.46	0.46	0.46	0.46	0.46	0.46	0.46
0.68	0.68	0.68	0.68	0.68	0.68	0.68	0.69	0.69	0.69	0.69	0.69	0.69	0.69	0.69	0.69
0.91	0.91	0.91	0.91	0.91	0.91	0.91	0.91	0.91	0.92	0.92	0.92	0.92	0.92	0.92	0.92
1.13	1.13	1.13	1.14	1.14	1.14	1.14	1.14	1.14	1.15	1.15	1.15	1.15	1.15	1.15	1.15
1.36	1.36	1.36	1.36	1.37	1.37	1.37	1.37	1.37	1.37	1.38	1.38	1.38	1.38	1.38	1.39
1.58	1.59	1.59	1.59	1.59	1.59	1.60	1.60	1.60	1.60	1.61	1.61	1.61	1.61	1.61	1.62
1.81	1.81	1.82	1.82	1.82	1.82	1.82	1.83	1.83	1.83	1.83	1.84	1.84	1.84	1.84	1.85
2.04	2.04	2.04	2.04	2.05	2.05	2.05	2.06	2.06	2.06	2.06	2.07	2.07	2.07	2.08	2.08
2.26	2.27	2.27	2.27	2.28	2.28	2.28	2.28	2.29	2.29	2.29	2.30	2.30	2.30	2.31	2.31
4.53	4.53	4.54	4.54	4.55	4.56	4.56	4.57	4.57	4.58	4.59	4.59	4.60	4.61	4.61	4.62
6.79	6.80	6.81	6.82	6.83	6.83	6.84	6.85	6.86	6.87	6.88	6.89	6.90	6.91	6.92	6.93
9.05	9.06	9.08	9.09	9.10	9.11	9.12	9.14	9.15	9.16	9.17	9.19	9.20	9.21	9.22	9.23
11.31	11.33	11.34	11.36	11.38	11.39	11.41	11.42	11.44	11.45	11.47	11.48	11.50	11.51	11.53	11.54
13.58	13.59	13.61	13.63	13.65	13.67	13.69	13.71	13.72	13.74	13.76	13.78	13.80	13.82	13.83	13.85
15.84	15.86	15.88	15.90	15.93	15.95	15.97	15.99	16.01	16.03	16.05	16.07	16.10	16.12	16.14	16.16
18.10	18.13	18 15	18.18	18.20	18.22	18.25	18.27	18.30	18.32	18.35	18.37	18.40	18.42	18.44	18.47
20.37	20.39	20.42	20.45	20.48	20.50	20.53	20.56	20.58	20.61	20.64	20.67	20.70	20.72	20.75	20.78
22.63	22.66	22.69	22.72	22.75	22.78	22.81	22.84	22.87	22.90	22.93	22.96	23.00	23.03	23.06	23.09
45.26	45.32	45.38	45.44	45.50	45.56	45.62	45.68	45.74	45.81	45.87	45.93	45.99	46.05	46.11	46.17
67.88	67.97	68.07	68.16	68.25	68.34	68.43	68.53	68.62	68.71	68.80	68.89	68.99	69.08	69.17	69.26
90.51	90.63	90.76	90.88	91.00	91.12	91.24	91.37	91.49	91.61	91.73	91.86	91.98	92.10	92.22	92.35
113.14	113.29	113.45	113.60	113.75	113.91	114.06	114.21	114.36	114.52	114.67	114.82	114.98	115.13	115.28	115.44
135.77	135.95	136.13	136.32	136.50	136.69	136.87	137.05	137.23	137.42	137.60	137.78	137.97	138.16	138.34	138.52
158.40	158.61	158.82	159.04	159.25	159.47	159.68	159.89	160.10	160.32	160.53	160.75	160.97	161.18	161.39	161.61
181.02	181.26	181.51	181.76	182.00	182.25	182.49	182.74	182.98	183.22	183.46	183.71	183.96	184.21	184.45	184.70
203.65	203.92	204.20	204.48	204.75	205.03	205.30	205.58	205.85	206.13	206.40	206.68	206.96	207.23	207.50	207.78
226.28	226.58	226.89	227.20	227.50	227.81	228.11	228.42	228.72	229.03	229.33	229.64	229.95	230.26	230.56	230.87

13 Degrees.

Minutes	0	1	2	3	4	5	6	7	8	9	10	11	12	13	14
Dis. in ft.															
1	0.23	0.23	0.23	0.23	0.23	0.23	0.23	0.23	0.23	0.23	0.23	0.23	0.23	0.23	0.24
2	0.46	0.46	0.46	0.46	0.46	0.46	0.17	0.47	0.47	0.47	0.47	0.47	0.47	0.47	0.47
3	0.69	0.69	0.69	0.70	0.70	0.70	0.70	0.70	0.70	0.70	0.70	0.70	0.70	0.70	0.71
4	0.92	0.92	0.93	0.93	0.93	0.93	0.93	0.93	0.93	0.93	0.94	0.94	0.94	0.94	0.94
5	1.15	1.16	1.16	1.16	1.16	1.16	1.16	1.17	1.17	1.17	1.17	1.17	1.17	1.17	1.18
6	1.39	1.39	1.39	1.39	1.39	1.39	1.40	1.40	1.40	1.40	1.40	1.41	1.41	1.41	1.41
7	1.62	1.62	1.62	1.62	1.62	1.63	1.63	1.63	1.63	1.64	1.64	1.64	1.64	1.64	1.65
8	1.85	1.85	1.85	1.85	1.86	1.86	1.86	1.86	1.87	1.87	1.87	1.87	1.88	1.88	1.88
9	2.08	2.08	2.08	2.09	2.09	2.09	2.09	2.10	2.10	2.10	2.10	2.11	2.11	2.11	2.12
10	2.31	2.31	2.31	2.32	2.32	2.32	2.33	2.33	2.33	2.34	2.34	2.34	2.35	2.35	2.35
20	4.62	4.62	4.63	4.64	4.64	4.65	4.65	4.66	4.67	4.67	4.68	4.68	4.69	4.70	4.70
30	6.93	6.94	6.94	6.95	6.96	6.97	6.98	6.99	7.00	7.01	7.02	7.03	7.04	7.05	7.05
40	9.23	9.25	9.26	9.27	9.28	9.30	9.31	9.32	9.33	9.35	9.36	9.37	9.38	9.39	9.41
50	11.54	11.56	11.57	11.59	11.60	11.62	11.64	11.65	11.67	11.68	11.70	11.71	11.73	11.74	11.76
60	13.85	13.87	13.89	13.91	13.93	13.94	13.96	13.98	14.00	14.02	14.04	14.05	14.07	14.09	14.11
70	16.16	16.18	16.20	16.23	16.25	16.27	16.29	16.31	16.33	16.35	16.38	16.40	16.42	16.44	16.46
80	18.47	18.49	18.52	18.54	18.57	18.59	18.62	18.64	18.67	18.69	18.71	18.74	18.76	18.79	18.81
90	20.78	20.81	20.83	20.86	20.89	20.92	20.94	20.97	21.00	21.03	21.05	21.08	21.11	21.14	21.16
100	23.09	23.12	23.15	23.18	23.21	23.24	23.27	23.30	23.33	23.36	23.39	23.43	23.46	23.49	23.52
200	46.17	46.23	46.30	46.36	46.42	46.48	46.54	46.60	46.66	46.73	46.79	46.85	46.91	46.97	47.03
300	69.26	69.35	69.44	69.54	69.63	69.72	69.81	69.90	70.00	70.09	70.18	70.27	70.37	70.46	70.55
400	92.35	92.47	92.59	92.72	92.84	92.96	93.08	93.20	93.33	93.45	93.57	93.70	93.82	93.94	94.06
500	115.44	115.59	115.74	115.90	116.05	116.20	116.36	116.51	116.66	116.82	116.97	117.12	117.28	117.43	117.58
600	138.52	138.70	138.89	139.07	139.25	139.44	139.63	139.81	139.99	140.18	140.36	140.54	140.73	140.92	141.10
700	161.61	161.82	162.04	162.25	162.46	162.68	162.90	163.11	163.32	163.54	163.75	163.97	164.19	164.40	164.61
800	184.70	184.94	185.18	185.43	185.67	185.92	186.17	186.41	186.66	186.90	187.14	187.39	187.64	187.89	188.13
900	207.78	208.05	208.33	208.61	208.88	209.16	209.44	209.71	209.99	210.27	210.54	210.82	211.10	211.37	211.64
1000	230.87	231.17	231.48	231.79	232.09	232.40	232.71	233.01	233.32	233.63	233.93	234.24	234.55	234.86	235.16

13 Degrees.

Minutes	30	31	32	33	34	35	36	37	38	39	40	41	42	43	44
Dis. in ft.															
1	0.24	0.24	0.24	0.24	0.24	0.24	0.24	0.24	0.24	0.24	0.24	0.24	0.24	0.24	0.24
2	0.48	0.48	0.48	0.48	0.48	0.48	0.48	0.48	0.49	0.49	0.49	0.49	0.49	0.49	0.49
3	0.72	0.72	0.72	0.72	0.72	0.72	0.73	0.73	0.73	0.73	0.73	0.73	0.73	0.73	0.73
4	0.96	0.96	0.96	0.96	0.97	0.97	0.97	0.97	0.97	0.97	0.97	0.97	0.98	0.98	0.98
5	1.20	1.20	1.20	1.21	1.21	1.21	1.21	1.21	1.21	1.21	1.22	1.22	1.22	1.22	1.22
6	1.44	1.44	1.44	1.45	1.45	1.45	1.45	1.45	1.46	1.46	1.46	1.46	1.46	1.46	1.47
7	1.68	1.68	1.69	1.69	1.69	1.69	1.69	1.70	1.70	1.70	1.70	1.70	1.71	1.71	1.71
8	1.92	1.92	1.93	1.93	1.93	1.93	1.94	1.94	1.94	1.94	1.95	1.95	1.95	1.95	1.96
9	2.16	2.16	2.17	2.17	2.17	2.17	2.18	2.18	2.18	2.19	2.19	2.19	2.19	2.20	2.20
10	2.40	2.40	2.41	2.41	2.41	2.42	2.42	2.42	2.43	2.43	2.43	2.43	2.44	2.44	2.44
20	4.80	4.81	4.81	4.82	4.83	4.83	4.84	4.84	4.85	4.86	4.86	4.87	4.88	4.88	4.89
30	7.20	7.21	7.22	7.23	7.24	7.25	7.26	7.27	7.28	7.29	7.29	7.30	7.31	7.32	7.33
40	9.60	9.62	9.63	9.64	9.65	9.66	9.68	9.69	9.70	9.71	9.73	9.74	9.75	9.76	9.78
50	12.00	12.02	12.04	12.05	12.07	12.08	12.10	12.11	12.13	12.14	12.16	12.17	12.19	12.20	12.22
60	14.40	14.42	14.44	14.46	14.48	14.50	14.52	14.53	14.55	14.57	14.59	14.61	14.63	14.64	14.66
70	16.81	16.83	16.85	16.87	16.89	16.91	16.93	16.96	16.98	17.00	17.02	17.04	17.06	17.09	17.11
80	19.21	19.23	19.25	19.28	19.30	19.33	19.35	19.38	19.40	19.43	19.45	19.48	19.50	19.53	19.55
90	21.61	21.64	21.66	21.69	21.72	21.75	21.77	21.80	21.83	21.86	21.88	21.91	21.94	21.97	22.00
100	24.01	24.04	24.07	24.10	24.13	24.16	24.19	24.22	24.25	24.29	24.32	24.35	24.38	24.41	24.44
200	48.02	48.08	48.14	48.20	48.26	48.32	48.38	48.45	48.51	48.57	48.63	48.69	48.76	48.82	48.88
300	72.02	72.12	72.21	72.30	72.39	72.49	72.58	72.67	72.76	72.86	72.95	73.04	73.13	73.22	73.32
400	96.03	96.16	96.28	96.40	96.52	96.65	96.77	96.89	97.02	97.14	97.26	97.39	97.51	97.63	97.76
500	120.04	120.20	120.35	120.50	120.66	120.81	120.96	121.12	121.27	121.43	121.58	121.74	121.89	122.04	122.20
600	144.05	144.23	144.42	144.60	144.79	144.97	145.15	145.34	145.52	145.71	145.90	146.08	146.27	146.45	146.63
700	168.06	168.27	168.49	168.70	168.92	169.13	169.34	169.56	169.78	170.00	170.21	170.43	170.65	170.86	171.07
800	192.06	192.31	192.56	192.80	193.05	193.30	193.54	193.78	194.03	194.28	194.53	194.78	195.02	195.26	195.51
900	216.07	216.35	216.63	216.90	217.18	217.46	217.73	218.01	218.29	218.57	218.84	219.12	219.40	219.67	219.95
1000	240.08	240.39	240.70	241.00	241.31	241.62	241.92	242.23	242.54	242.85	243.16	243.47	243.78	244.08	244.39

13 Degrees.

15	16	17	18	19	20	21	22	23	24	25	26	27	28	29	30
0.24	0.24	0.24	0.24	0.24	0.24	0.24	0.24	0.24	0.24	0.24	0.24	0.24	0.24	0.24	0.24
0.47	0.47	0.47	0.47	0.47	0.47	0.47	0.48	0.48	0.48	0.48	0.48	0.48	0.48	0.48	0.48
0.71	0.71	0.71	0.71	0.71	0.71	0.71	0.71	0.71	0.71	0.72	0.72	0.72	0.72	0.72	0.72
0.94	0.94	0.94	0.95	0.95	0.95	0.95	0.95	0.95	0.95	0.95	0.96	0.96	0.96	0.96	0.96
1.18	1.18	1.18	1.18	1.18	1.19	1.19	1.19	1.19	1.19	1.19	1.20	1.20	1.20	1.20	1.20
1.41	1.41	1.42	1.42	1.42	1.42	1.42	1.43	1.43	1.43	1.43	1.43	1.43	1.44	1.44	1.44
1.65	1.65	1.65	1.65	1.66	1.66	1.66	1.66	1 67	1.67	1.67	1.67	1.67	1.68	1.68	1.68
1.88	1.89	1.89	1.89	1.89	1.90	1.90	1.90	1.90	1.91	1.91	1.91	1.91	1.92	1.92	1.92
2.12	2.12	2.12	2.13	2.13	2.13	2.14	2.14	2.14	2.14	2.15	2.15	2.15	2.16	2.16	2.16
2.35	2.36	2.36	2.36	2.37	2.37	2.37	2.38	2.38	2.38	2.39	2.39	2.39	2.39	2.40	2.40
4.71	4.72	4.72	4.73	4.73	4.74	4.75	4.75	4.76	4.76	4.77	4.78	4.78	4.79	4.80	4.80
7.06	7.07	7.08	7.09	7.10	7.11	7.12	7.13	7.14	7.15	7.16	7.17	7.17	7.18	7.19	7.20
9.42	9.43	9.44	9.46	9.47	9.48	9.49	9.50	9.52	9.53	9.54	9.55	9.57	9.58	9.59	9.60
11.77	11.79	11.80	11.82	11.84	11.85	11.87	11.88	11.90	11.91	11.93	11.94	11.96	11.97	11.99	12.00
14.13	14.15	14.16	14.18	14.20	14.22	14.24	14.26	14.28	14.29	14.31	14.33	14.35	14.37	14.39	14.40
16.48	16.50	16.53	16.55	16.57	16.59	16.61	16.63	16.66	16.68	16.70	16.72	16.74	16.76	16.78	16.81
18.84	18.86	18.89	18.91	18.94	18.96	18.98	19.01	19.03	19.06	19.08	19.11	19.13	19.16	19.18	19.21
21.19	21.22	21 25	21.28	21.30	21.33	21.36	21.39	21.41	21.44	21.47	21.50	21.52	21.55	21.58	21.61
23.55	23.58	23.61	23.64	23.67	23.70	23.73	23.76	23.79	23.82	23.85	23.89	23.92	23.95	23.98	24.01
47.09	47.16	47.22	47.28	47.34	47.40	47.46	47.52	47.59	47.65	47.71	47.77	47.83	47.89	47.95	48.02
70.64	70.73	70.82	70.92	71.01	71.10	71.19	71.29	71.38	71.47	71.56	71.66	71.75	71.84	71.93	72.02
94.19	94.31	94.43	94.56	94.68	94.80	94.92	95.05	95.17	95.29	95.42	95.54	95.66	95.78	95.91	96.03
117.74	117.89	118.04	118.20	118.35	118.51	118.66	118.81	118.97	119.12	119.27	119.43	119.58	119.73	119.89	120.04
141.28	141.47	141.65	141.83	142.02	142.21	142.39	142.57	142.76	142.94	143.12	143.31	143.49	143.68	143.86	144.05
164.83	165.05	165.26	165.47	165.69	165.91	166.12	166.33	166.55	166.76	166.98	167.20	167.41	167.62	167.84	168.06
188.38	188.62	188.86	189.11	189.36	189.61	189.85	190.10	190.34	190.58	190.83	191.08	191.33	191.57	191.82	192.06
211.92	212.20	212.47	212.75	213.03	213.31	213.58	213.86	214.14	214.41	214.69	214.97	215.24	215.51	215.79	216.07
235.47	235.78	236.08	236.39	236.70	237.01	237.31	237.62	237.93	238.23	238.54	238.85	239.16	239.46	239.77	240.08

13 Degrees.

45	46	47	48	49	50	51	52	53	54	55	56	57	58	59	60
0.24	0.25	0.25	0.25	0.25	0.25	0.25	0.25	0.25	0.25	0.25	0.25	0.25	0.25	0.25	0.25
0.49	0.49	0.49	0.49	0.49	0.49	0.49	0.49	0.49	0.49	0.49	0.50	0.50	0.50	0.50	0.50
0.73	0.74	0.74	0.74	0.74	0.74	0.74	0.74	0.74	0.74	0.74	0.74	0.75	0.75	0.75	0.75
0.98	0.98	0.98	0.98	0.98	0.98	0.99	0.99	0.99	0.99	0.99	0.99	0.99	0.99	1.00	1.00
1.22	1.23	1.23	1.23	1.23	1.23	1.23	1.23	1.24	1.24	1.24	1.24	1.24	1.24	1.25	1.25
1.47	1.47	1.47	1.47	1.48	1.48	1.48	1.48	1.48	1.48	1.49	1.49	1.49	1.49	1.49	1.50
1.71	1.72	1.72	1.72	1.72	1.72	1.73	1.73	1.73	1.73	1.73	1.73	1.74	1.74	1.74	1.75
1.96	1.96	1.96	1.96	1.97	1.97	1.97	1.97	1.98	1.98	1.98	1.98	1.99	1.99	1.99	1.99
2.20	2.21	2.21	2.21	2.21	2.22	2.22	2.22	2.22	2.23	2.23	2.23	2.24	2.24	2.24	2.24
2.45	2.45	2.45	2.46	2.46	2.46	2.47	2.47	2.47	2.47	2.48	2.48	2.48	2.49	2.49	2.49
4.89	4.90	4.91	4.91	4.92	4.92	4.93	4.94	4.94	4.95	4.96	4.96	4.97	4.97	4.98	4.99
7.34	7.35	7.36	7.37	7.38	7.39	7.40	7.41	7.42	7.42	7.43	7.44	7.45	7.46	7.47	7.48
9.79	9.80	9.81	9.82	9.84	9.85	9.86	9.87	9.89	9.90	9.91	9.92	9.94	9.95	9.96	9.97
12.24	12.25	12.27	12.28	12.30	12.31	12.33	12.34	12.36	12.37	12.39	12.40	12.42	12.44	12.45	12.47
14.68	14.70	14.72	14.74	14.76	14.77	14.79	14.81	14.83	14.85	14.87	14.89	14.90	14.92	14.94	14.96
17.13	17.15	17.17	17.19	17.22	17.24	17.26	17.28	17.30	17.32	17.34	17.37	17.39	17.41	17.43	17.45
19.58	19.60	19.62	19.65	19.67	19.70	19.72	19.75	19.77	19.80	19.82	19.85	19.87	19.90	19.92	19.95
22.02	22.05	22.08	22.11	22.13	22.16	22.19	22.22	22.25	22.27	22.30	22.33	22.36	22.38	22.41	22.44
24.47	24.50	24.53	24.56	24.59	24.62	24.66	24.69	24.72	24.75	24.78	24.81	24.84	24.87	24.90	24.93
48.94	49.00	49.06	49.12	49.19	49.25	49.31	49.37	49.43	49.49	49.56	49.62	49.68	49.74	49.80	49.87
73.41	73.50	73.59	73.69	73.78	73.87	73.97	74.06	74.15	74.24	74.33	74.43	74.52	74.61	74.71	74.80
97.88	98.00	98.12	98.25	98.37	98.50	98.62	98.74	98.87	98.99	99.11	99.24	99.36	99.48	99.61	99.73
122.35	122.51	122.66	122.81	122.97	123.12	123.28	123.43	123.59	123.74	123.89	124.05	124.20	124.36	124.51	124.67
146.82	147.01	147.19	147.37	147.56	147.74	147.93	148.12	148.30	148.48	148.67	148.85	149.04	149.23	149.41	149.60
171.29	171.51	171.72	171.93	172.15	172.37	172.59	172.80	173.02	173.23	173.45	173.66	173.88	174.10	174.31	174.53
195.76	196.01	196.25	196.50	196.74	196.99	197.24	197.49	197.74	197.98	198.22	198.47	198.72	198.97	199.22	199.46
220.23	220.51	220.78	221.06	221.34	221.62	221.90	222.17	222.45	222.72	223.00	223.28	223.56	223.84	224.12	224.40
244.70	245.01	245.31	245.62	245.93	246.24	246.55	246.86	247.17	247.47	247.78	248.09	248.40	248.71	249.02	249.33

14 Degrees.

Minutes	0	1	2	3	4	5	6	7	8	9	10	11	12	13	14
Dis. in ft.															
1	0.25	0.25	0.25	0.25	0.25	0.25	0.25	0.25	0.25	0.25	0.25	0.25	0.25	0.25	0.25
2	0.50	0.50	0.50	0.50	0.50	0.50	0.50	0.50	0.50	0.50	0.50	0.51	0.51	0.51	0.51
3	0.75	0.75	0.75	0.75	0.75	0.75	0.75	0.75	0.76	0.76	0.76	0.76	0.76	0.76	0.76
4	1.00	1.00	1.00	1.00	1.00	1.00	1.00	1.01	1.01	1.01	1.01	1.01	1.01	1.01	1.01
5	1.25	1.25	1.25	1.25	1.25	1.25	1.26	1.26	1.26	1.26	1.26	1.26	1.27	1.27	1.27
6	1.50	1.50	1.50	1.50	1.50	1.50	1.51	1.51	1.51	1.51	1.51	1.51	1.52	1.52	1.52
7	1.75	1.75	1.75	1.75	1.75	1.76	1.76	1.76	1.76	1.76	1.77	1.77	1.77	1.77	1.78
8	1.99	2.00	2.00	2.00	2.00	2.01	2.01	2.01	2.01	2.02	2.02	2.02	2.02	2.03	2.03
9	2.24	2.25	2.25	2.25	2.26	2.26	2.26	2.26	2.27	2.27	2.27	2.27	2.28	2.28	2.28
10	2.49	2.50	2.50	2.50	2.51	2.51	2.51	2.51	2.52	2.52	2.52	2.53	2.53	2.53	2.54
20	4.99	4.99	5.00	5.01	5.01	5.02	5.02	5.03	5.03	5.04	5.05	5.05	5.05	5.07	5.07
30	7.48	7.49	7.50	7.51	7.52	7.53	7.54	7.54	7.55	7.56	7.57	7.58	7.59	7.60	7.61
40	9.97	9.99	10.00	10.01	10.02	10.03	10.05	10.06	10.07	10.08	10.10	10.11	10.12	10.13	10.15
50	12.47	12.48	12.50	12.51	12.53	12.54	12.56	12.57	12.59	12.61	12.62	12.64	12.65	12.67	12.68
60	14.96	14.98	15.00	15.02	15.03	15.05	15.07	15.09	15.11	15.13	15.15	15.16	15.18	15.20	15.22
70	17.45	17.47	17.50	17.52	17.54	17.56	17.58	17.60	17.63	17.65	17.67	17.69	17.71	17.73	17.76
80	19.95	19.97	20.00	20.02	20.04	20.07	20.09	20.12	20.14	20.17	20.19	20.22	20.24	20.27	20.29
90	22.44	22.47	22.50	22.52	22.55	22.58	22.61	22.63	22.66	22.69	22.72	22.75	22.77	22.80	22.83
100	24.93	24.96	25.00	25.03	25.06	25.09	25.12	25.15	25.18	25.21	25.24	25.27	25.30	25.34	25.37
200	49.87	49.93	49.99	50.05	50.11	50.17	50.24	50.30	50.36	50.42	50.48	50.55	50.61	50.67	50.73
300	74.80	74.89	74.99	75.08	75.17	75.26	75.35	75.45	75.54	75.63	75.73	75.82	75.91	76.01	76.10
400	99.73	99.86	99.98	100.10	100.22	100.35	100.47	100.60	100.72	100.84	100.97	101.09	101.22	101.34	101.46
500	124.67	124.82	124.98	125.13	125.28	125.44	125.59	125.75	125.90	126.06	126.21	126.37	126.52	126.68	126.83
600	149.60	149.78	149.97	150.15	150.34	150.52	150.71	150.89	151.08	151.27	151.45	151.64	151.82	152.01	152.20
700	174.53	174.75	174.97	175.18	175.39	175.61	175.83	176.04	176.26	176.48	176.69	176.91	177.13	177.35	177.56
800	199.46	199.71	199.96	200.20	200.45	200.70	200.94	201.19	201.44	201.69	201.94	202.18	202.43	202.68	202.93
900	224.40	224.68	224.96	225.23	225.50	225.78	226.06	226.34	226.62	226.90	227.18	227.46	227.74	228.02	228.29
1000	249.33	249.64	249.95	250.25	250.56	250.87	251.18	251.49	251.80	252.11	252.42	252.73	253.04	253.35	253.66

14 Degrees.

Minutes	30	31	32	33	34	35	36	37	38	39	40	41	42	43	44
Dis. in ft.															
1	0.26	0.26	0.26	0.26	0.26	0.26	0.26	0.26	0.26	0.26	0.26	0.26	0.26	0.26	0.26
2	0.52	0.52	0.52	0.52	0.52	0.52	0.52	0.52	0.52	0.52	0.52	0.52	0.52	0.53	0.53
3	0.78	0.78	0.78	0.78	0.78	0.78	0.78	0.78	0.78	0.78	0.79	0.79	0.79	0.79	0.79
4	1.03	1.04	1.04	1.04	1.04	1.04	1.04	1.04	1.04	1.05	1.05	1.05	1.05	1.05	1.05
5	1.29	1.29	1.30	1.30	1.30	1.30	1.30	1.30	1.31	1.31	1.31	1.31	1.31	1.31	1.31
6	1.55	1.55	1.56	1.56	1.56	1.56	1.56	1.56	1.57	1.57	1.57	1.57	1.57	1.58	1.58
7	1.81	1.81	1.81	1.82	1.82	1.82	1.82	1.83	1.83	1.83	1.83	1.83	1.84	1.84	1.84
8	2.07	2.07	2.07	2.08	2.08	2.08	2.08	2.09	2.09	2.09	2.09	2.10	2.10	2.10	2.10
9	2.33	2.33	2.33	2.34	2.34	2.34	2.34	2.35	2.35	2.35	2.36	2.36	2.36	2.36	2.37
10	2.59	2.59	2.59	2.60	2.60	2.60	2.60	2.61	2.61	2.61	2.62	2.62	2.62	2.63	2.63
20	5.17	5.18	5.18	5.19	5.20	5.20	5.21	5.22	5.22	5.23	5.23	5.24	5.25	5.25	5.26
30	7.76	7.77	7.78	7.79	7.80	7.81	7.81	7.82	7.83	7.84	7.85	7.86	7.87	7.88	7.89
40	10.34	10.36	10.37	10.38	10.39	10.41	10.42	10.43	10.44	10.46	10.47	10.48	10.49	10.51	10.52
50	12.93	12.95	12.96	12.98	13.00	13.02	13.04	13.06	13.07	13.09	13.10	13.12	13.13	13.14	13.15
60	15.52	15.54	15.55	15.57	15.59	15.61	15.63	15.65	15.67	15.68	15.70	15.72	15.74	15.76	15.78
70	18.10	18.13	18.15	18.17	18.19	18.21	18.23	18.26	18.28	18.30	18.32	18.34	18.36	18.39	18.41
80	20.69	20.71	20.74	20.76	20.79	20.81	20.84	20.86	20.89	20.91	20.94	20.96	20.99	21.01	21.04
90	23.28	23.30	23.33	23.36	23.39	23.42	23.44	23.47	23.50	23.53	23.55	23.58	23.61	23.64	23.67
100	25.86	25.89	25.92	25.96	25.99	26.02	26.05	26.08	26.11	26.14	26.17	26.20	26.24	26.27	26.30
200	51.72	51.79	51.85	51.91	51.97	52.03	52.10	52.16	52.22	52.28	52.34	52.41	52.47	52.53	52.59
300	77.59	77.68	77.77	77.87	77.96	78.05	78.14	78.24	78.33	78.42	78.52	78.61	78.71	78.80	78.89
400	103.45	103.57	103.70	103.82	103.94	104.07	104.19	104.32	104.44	104.56	104.69	104.82	104.94	105.06	105.19
500	129.31	129.47	129.62	129.78	129.93	130.09	130.24	130.40	130.55	130.71	130.86	131.02	131.18	131.33	131.49
600	155.17	155.36	155.54	155.73	155.92	156.10	156.29	156.47	156.66	156.85	157.03	157.22	157.41	157.60	157.78
700	181.03	181.25	181.47	181.69	181.90	182.12	182.34	182.55	182.77	182.99	183.20	183.45	183.65	183.86	184.08
800	206.90	207.14	207.39	207.61	207.89	208.14	208.38	208.63	208.88	209.13	209.38	209.63	209.88	210.13	210.38
900	232.76	233.04	233.32	233.60	233.87	234.15	234.43	234.71	234.99	235.27	235.55	235.84	236.12	236.39	236.67
1000	258.62	258.93	259.24	259.55	259.86	260.17	260.48	260.79	261.10	261.41	261.72	262.04	262.35	262.66	262.97

15	16	17	18	19	20	21	22	23	24	25	26	27	28	29	30
0.25	0.25	0.25	0.25	0.26	0.26	0.26	0.26	0.26	0.26	0.26	0.26	0.26	0.26	0.26	0.26
0.51	0.51	0.51	0.51	0.51	0.51	0.51	0.51	0.51	0.51	0.51	0.51	0.51	0.52	0.52	0.52
0.76	0.76	0.76	0.76	0.77	0.77	0.77	0.77	0.77	0.77	0.77	0.77	0.77	0.77	0.77	0.78
1.02	1.02	1.02	1.02	1.02	1.02	1.02	1.02	1.03	1.03	1.03	1.03	1.03	1.03	1.03	1.03
1.27	1.27	1.27	1.27	1.28	1.28	1.28	1.28	1.28	1.28	1.29	1.29	1.29	1.29	1.29	1.29
1.52	1.53	1.53	1.53	1.53	1.53	1.53	1.54	1.54	1.54	1.54	1.55	1.55	1.55	1.55	1.55
1.78	1.78	1.78	1.78	1.79	1.79	1.79	1.79	1.80	1.80	1.80	1.80	1.80	1.81	1.81	1.81
2.03	2.03	2.04	2.04	2.04	2.04	2.05	2.05	2.05	2.05	2.06	2.06	2.06	2.06	2.07	2.07
2.29	2.29	2.29	2.29	2.30	2.30	2.30	2.31	2.31	2.31	2.31	2.32	2.32	2.32	2.32	2.33
2.54	2.54	2.55	2.55	2.55	2.56	2.56	2.56	2.56	2.57	2.57	2.57	2.58	2.58	2.58	2.59
5.08	5.09	5.09	5.10	5.10	5.11	5.12	5.12	5.13	5.14	5.14	5.15	5.15	5.16	5.17	5.17
7.62	7.63	7.64	7.65	7.66	7.67	7.67	7.68	7.69	7.70	7.71	7.72	7.73	7.74	7.75	7.76
10.16	10.17	10.18	10.20	10.21	10.22	10.23	10.25	10.26	10.27	10.28	10.30	10.31	10.32	10.33	10.34
12.70	12.71	12.73	12.75	12.76	12.78	12.79	12.81	12.82	12.84	12.85	12.87	12.88	12.90	12.92	12.93
15.24	15.26	15.28	15.29	15.31	15.33	15.35	15.37	15.39	15.41	15.42	15.44	15.46	15.48	15.50	15.52
17.78	17.80	17.82	17.84	17.86	17.89	17.91	17.93	17.95	17.97	17.99	18.02	18.04	18.06	18.08	18.10
20.32	20.34	20.37	20.39	20.42	20.44	20.47	20.49	20.52	20.54	20.57	20.59	20.62	20.64	20.66	20.69
22.86	22.89	22.91	22.94	22.97	23.00	23.02	23.05	23.08	23.11	23.14	23.17	23.19	23.22	23.25	23.28
25.40	25.43	25.46	25.49	25.52	25.55	25.61	25.61	25.65	25.68	25.71	25.74	25.77	25.80	25.83	25.86
50.79	50.86	50.92	50.98	51.04	51.10	51.17	51.23	51.29	51.35	51.41	51.48	51.54	51.60	51.66	51.72
76.19	76.28	76.38	76.47	76.56	76.66	76.75	76.84	76.94	77.03	77.12	77.22	77.31	77.40	77.49	77.59
101.59	101.71	101.84	101.96	102.08	102.21	102.33	102.46	102.58	102.70	102.83	102.96	103.08	103.20	103.32	103.45
126.99	127.14	127.30	127.45	127.61	127.76	127.92	128.07	128.23	128.38	128.54	128.69	128.85	129.00	129.16	129.31
152.38	152.57	152.76	152.94	153.13	153.31	153.50	153.68	153.87	154.06	154.24	154.43	154.61	154.80	154.99	155.17
177.78	178.00	178.21	178.43	178.65	178.86	179.08	179.30	179.52	179.73	179.95	180.17	180.38	180.60	180.82	181.03
203.18	203.42	203.67	203.92	204.17	204.42	204.66	204.91	205.16	205.41	205.66	205.91	206.15	206.40	206.65	206.90
228.57	228.85	229.13	229.41	229.69	229.97	230.25	230.53	230.81	231.08	231.36	231.65	231.92	232.20	232.48	232.76
253.97	254.28	254.59	254.90	255.21	255.52	255.83	256.14	256.45	256.76	257.07	257.39	257.69	258.00	258.31	258.62

14 Degrees.

45	46	47	48	49	50	51	52	53	54	55	56	57	58	59	60
0.26	0.26	0.26	0.26	0.26	0.26	0.27	0.27	0.27	0.27	0.27	0.27	0.27	0.27	0.27	0.27
0.53	0.53	0.53	0.53	0.53	0.53	0.53	0.53	0.53	0.53	0.53	0.53	0.53	0.53	0.54	0.54
0.79	0.79	0.79	0.79	0.79	0.79	0.80	0.80	0.80	0.80	0.80	0.80	0.80	0.80	0.80	0.80
1.05	1.05	1.06	1.06	1.06	1.06	1.06	1.06	1.06	1.06	1.07	1.07	1.07	1.07	1.07	1.07
1.32	1.32	1.32	1.32	1.32	1.32	1.33	1.33	1.33	1.33	1.33	1.34	1.34	1.34	1.34	1.34
1.58	1.58	1.58	1.59	1.59	1.59	1.59	1.59	1.59	1.60	1.60	1.60	1.60	1.60	1.61	1.61
1.84	1.85	1.85	1.85	1.85	1.85	1.86	1.86	1.86	1.86	1.86	1.87	1.87	1.87	1.87	1.88
2.11	2.11	2.11	2.11	2.12	2.12	2.12	2.12	2.13	2.13	2.13	2.13	2.14	2.14	2.14	2.14
2.37	2.37	2.38	2.38	2.38	2.38	2.39	2.39	2.39	2.39	2.40	2.40	2.40	2.41	2.41	2.41
2.63	2.64	2.64	2.64	2.65	2.65	2.65	2.65	2.66	2.66	2.66	2.67	2.67	2.67	2.68	2.68
5.27	5.28	5.28	5.28	5.29	5.30	5.30	5.31	5.32	5.32	5.33	5.33	5.34	5.35	5.35	5.36
7.90	7.91	7.92	7.93	7.94	7.94	7.95	7.96	7.97	7.98	7.99	8.00	8.01	8.02	8.03	8.04
10.53	10.54	10.56	10.57	10.58	10.59	10.61	10.62	10.63	10.64	10.66	10.67	10.68	10.69	10.71	10.72
13.16	13.18	13.20	13.21	13.23	13.24	13.26	13.27	13.29	13.30	13.32	13.34	13.35	13.37	13.38	13.40
15.80	15.82	15.83	15.85	15.87	15.89	15.91	15.93	15.95	15.96	15.98	16.00	16.02	16.04	16.06	16.08
18.43	18.45	18.47	18.49	18.52	18.54	18.56	18.58	18.60	18.63	18.65	18.67	18.69	18.71	18.73	18.76
21.06	21.09	21.11	21.14	21.16	21.19	21.21	21.24	21.26	21.29	21.31	21.34	21.36	21.39	21.41	21.44
23.70	23.72	23.75	23.78	23.81	23.83	23.86	23.89	23.92	23.95	23.98	24.00	24.03	24.06	24.09	24.12
26.33	26.36	26.39	26.42	26.45	26.48	26.51	26.55	26.58	26.61	26.64	26.67	26.70	26.73	26.76	26.80
52.66	52.72	52.78	52.84	52.90	52.97	53.03	53.09	53.15	53.22	53.28	53.34	53.40	53.47	53.53	53.59
78.98	79.08	79.17	79.26	79.36	79.45	79.54	79.64	79.73	79.82	79.92	80.01	80.10	80.20	80.29	80.39
105.31	105.44	105.56	105.68	105.81	105.93	106.06	106.18	106.31	106.43	106.56	106.68	106.80	106.93	107.06	107.18
131.64	131.80	131.95	132.11	132.26	132.42	132.57	132.73	132.89	133.04	133.20	133.35	133.51	133.67	133.82	133.98
157.97	158.15	158.34	158.53	158.71	158.90	159.08	159.27	159.46	159.65	159.83	160.02	160.21	160.40	160.60	160.77
184.30	184.51	184.73	184.95	185.16	185.38	185.60	185.82	186.04	186.26	186.47	186.69	186.91	187.13	187.35	187.57
210.62	210.87	211.12	211.37	211.62	211.86	212.11	212.36	212.62	212.86	213.11	213.36	213.61	213.86	214.11	214.36
236.95	237.23	237.51	237.79	238.07	238.35	238.63	238.91	239.19	239.47	239.75	240.03	240.31	240.60	240.88	241.16
263.28	263.59	263.90	264.21	264.52	264.83	265.14	265.45	265.77	266.08	266.39	266.70	267.01	267.33	267.64	267.95

15 Degrees.

Minutes	0	1	2	3	4	5	6	7	8	9	10	11	12	13	14
Dis. in ft.															
1	0.27	0.27	0.27	0.27	0.27	0.27	0.27	0.27	0.27	0.27	0.27	0.27	0.27	0.27	0.27
2	0.54	0.54	0.54	0.54	0.54	0.54	0.54	0.54	0.54	0.54	0.54	0.54	0.54	0.54	0.54
3	0.80	0.80	0.81	0.81	0.81	0.81	0.81	0.81	0.81	0.81	0.81	0.81	0.82	0.82	0.82
4	1.07	1.07	1.07	1.08	1.08	1.08	1.08	1.08	1.08	1.08	1.08	1.09	1.09	1.09	1.09
5	1.34	1.34	1.54	1.34	1.35	1.35	1.35	1.35	1.35	1.35	1.36	1.36	1.36	1.36	1.36
6	1.61	1.61	1.61	1.61	1.62	1.62	1.62	1.62	1.62	1.62	1.63	1.63	1.63	1.63	1.63
7	1.88	1.88	1.88	1.88	1.88	1.89	1.89	1.89	1.89	1.90	1.90	1.90	1.90	1.90	1.91
8	2.14	2.15	2.15	2.15	2.15	2.16	2.16	2.16	2.16	2.17	2.17	2.17	2.17	2.18	2.18
9	2.41	2.41	2.42	2.42	2.42	2.43	2.43	2.43	2.43	2.43	2.44	2.44	2.44	2.45	2.45
10	2.68	2.68	2.69	2.69	2.69	2.70	2.70	2.70	2.70	2.71	2.71	2.71	2.72	2.72	2.72
20	5.36	5.37	5.37	5.38	5.38	5.39	5.40	5.40	5.41	5.42	5.42	5.43	5.43	5.44	5.45
30	8.04	8.05	8.06	8.07	8.08	8.09	8.09	8.10	8.11	8.12	8.13	8.14	8.15	8.16	8.17
40	10.72	10.73	10.74	10.76	10.77	10.78	10.79	10.81	10.82	10.83	10.84	10.86	10.87	10.88	10.89
50	13.40	13.41	13.43	13.44	13.46	13.48	13.49	13.51	13.52	13.54	13.55	13.57	13.58	13.60	13.62
60	16.08	16.10	16.11	16.13	16.15	16.17	16.19	16.21	16.23	16.25	16.26	16.28	16.30	16.32	16.34
70	18.76	18.78	18.80	18.82	18.84	18.87	18.89	18.91	18.93	18.95	18.97	19.00	19.02	19.04	19.06
80	21.44	21.46	21.49	21.51	21.54	21.56	21.59	21.61	21.64	21.66	21.69	21.71	21.74	21.76	21.79
90	24.12	24.14	24.17	24.20	24.23	24.26	24.28	24.31	24.34	24.37	24.40	24.42	24.45	24.48	24.51
100	26.80	26.83	26.86	26.89	26.92	26.95	26.98	27.01	27.05	27.08	27.11	27.14	27.17	27.20	27.23
200	53.59	53.65	53.71	53.78	53.84	53.90	53.96	54.03	54.09	54.15	54.21	54.28	54.34	54.40	54.46
300	80.39	80.48	80.57	80.67	80.76	80.85	80.95	81.04	81.14	81.23	81.32	81.41	81.51	81.60	81.70
400	107.18	107.30	107.43	107.56	107.68	107.80	107.93	108.05	108.18	108.30	108.43	108.55	108.68	108.80	108.93
500	133.98	134.13	134.29	134.45	134.60	134.76	135.07	135.23	135.38	135.54	135.69	135.85	136.01	136.16	
600	160.77	160.96	161.14	161.33	161.52	161.71	161.89	162.08	162.27	162.46	162.64	162.83	163.01	163.21	163.39
700	187.57	187.78	188.00	188.22	188.44	188.66	188.87	189.09	189.32	189.53	189.75	189.97	190.18	190.41	190.62
800	214.36	214.61	214.86	215.11	215.36	215.61	215.86	216.10	216.36	216.61	216.86	217.10	217.35	217.61	217.86
900	241.16	241.43	241.71	242.00	242.28	242.56	242.84	243.12	243.41	243.68	243.96	244.24	244.52	244.81	245.09
1000	267.95	268.26	268.57	268.89	269.20	269.51	269.82	270.13	270.45	270.76	271.07	271.38	271.69	272.01	272.32

15 Degrees.

Minutes	30	31	32	33	34	35	36	37	38	39	40	41	42	43	44
Dis. in ft.															
1	0.28	0.28	0.28	0.28	0.28	0.28	0.28	0.28	0.28	0.28	0.28	0.28	0.28	0.28	0.28
2	0.55	0.56	0.56	0.56	0.56	0.56	0.56	0.56	0.56	0.56	0.56	0.56	0.56	0.56	0.56
3	0.83	0.83	0.83	0.83	0.84	0.84	0.84	0.84	0.84	0.84	0.84	0.84	0.84	0.84	0.85
4	1.11	1.11	1.11	1.11	1.11	1.12	1.12	1.12	1.12	1.12	1.12	1.12	1.12	1.13	1.13
5	1.39	1.39	1.39	1.39	1.39	1.39	1.40	1.40	1.40	1.40	1.40	1.40	1.41	1.41	1.41
6	1.66	1.67	1.67	1.67	1.67	1.67	1.68	1.68	1.68	1.68	1.68	1.68	1.69	1.69	1.69
7	1.94	1.94	1.95	1.95	1.95	1.95	1.95	1.96	1.96	1.96	1.96	1.97	1.97	1.97	1.97
8	2.22	2.22	2.22	2.23	2.23	2.23	2.23	2.24	2.24	2.24	2.24	2.25	2.25	2.25	2.25
9	2.50	2.50	2.50	2.50	2.51	2.51	2.51	2.52	2.52	2.52	2.52	2.53	2.53	2.53	2.54
10	2.77	2.78	2.78	2.78	2.79	2.79	2.79	2.80	2.80	2.80	2.80	2.81	2.81	2.81	2.82
20	5.55	5.55	5.56	5.57	5.57	5.58	5.58	5.59	5.60	5.60	5.61	5.62	5.62	5.63	5.63
30	8.32	8.33	8.34	8.35	8.36	8.37	8.38	8.39	8.39	8.40	8.41	8.42	8.43	8.44	8.45
40	11.09	11.11	11.12	11.13	11.14	11.16	11.17	11.18	11.19	11.21	11.22	11.23	11.24	11.26	11.27
50	13.87	13.88	13.90	13.91	13.93	13.94	13.96	13.98	13.99	14.01	14.02	14.04	14.05	14.07	14.09
60	16.64	16.66	16.68	16.70	16.71	16.73	16.75	16.77	16.79	16.81	16.83	16.85	16.86	16.88	16.90
70	19.41	19.43	19.46	19.48	19.50	19.52	19.54	19.57	19.59	19.61	19.63	19.65	19.68	19.70	19.72
80	22.19	22.21	22.24	22.26	22.29	22.31	22.34	22.36	22.39	22.41	22.44	22.46	22.49	22.51	22.54
90	24.96	24.99	25.02	25.04	25.07	25.10	25.13	25.16	25.18	25.21	25.24	25.27	25.30	25.33	25.35
100	27.73	27.76	27.80	27.83	27.86	27.89	27.92	27.95	27.98	28.01	28.05	28.08	28.11	28.14	28.17
200	55.47	55.53	55.59	55.65	55.72	55.78	55.84	55.90	55.97	56.03	56.09	56.15	56.22	56.28	56.34
300	83.20	83.29	83.39	83.48	83.57	83.67	83.76	83.86	83.95	84.04	84.14	84.23	84.32	84.42	84.51
400	110.93	111.06	111.18	111.31	111.43	111.56	111.68	111.81	111.93	112.06	112.18	112.31	112.43	112.56	112.68
500	138.67	138.82	138.98	139.14	139.29	139.45	139.60	139.76	139.92	140.07	140.23	140.39	140.54	140.70	140.86
600	166.40	166.58	166.77	166.96	167.15	167.33	167.52	167.71	167.90	168.08	168.28	168.46	168.65	168.84	169.03
700	194.13	194.35	194.57	194.79	195.01	195.22	195.44	195.66	195.88	196.10	196.32	196.54	196.76	196.98	197.20
800	221.86	222.11	222.36	222.62	222.86	223.11	223.36	223.62	223.86	224.11	224.37	224.62	224.86	225.12	225.37
900	249.60	249.88	250.16	250.44	250.72	251.00	251.28	251.57	251.85	252.13	252.41	252.69	252.97	253.26	253.54
1000	277.33	277.64	277.95	278.27	278.58	278.89	279.20	279.52	279.83	280.14	280.46	280.77	281.08	281.40	281.71

15 Degrees.

15	16	17	18	19	20	21	22	23	24	25	26	27	28	29	30
0.27	0.27	0.27	0.27	0.27	0.27	0.27	0.27	0.28	0.28	0.28	0.28	0.28	0.28	0.28	0.28
0.55	0.55	0.55	0.55	0.55	0.55	0.55	0.55	0.55	0.55	0.55	0.55	0.55	0.55	0.55	0.55
0.82	0.82	0.82	0.82	0.82	0.82	0.82	0.82	0.83	0.83	0.83	0.83	0.83	0.83	0.83	0.83
1.09	1.09	1.09	1.09	1.10	1.10	1.10	1.10	1.10	1.10	1.10	1.10	1.11	1.11	1.11	1.11
1.36	1.36	1.37	1.37	1.37	1.37	1.37	1.37	1.38	1.38	1.38	1.38	1.38	1.38	1.39	1.39
1.64	1.64	1.64	1.64	1.64	1.65	1.65	1.65	1.65	1.65	1.65	1.66	1.66	1.66	1.66	1.66
1.91	1.91	1.91	1.91	1.92	1.92	1.92	1.92	1.93	1.93	1.93	1.93	1.93	1.94	1.94	1.94
2.18	2.18	2.19	2.19	2.19	2.19	2.20	2.20	2.20	2.20	2.21	2.21	2.21	2.21	2.22	2.22
2.45	2.46	2.46	2.46	2.46	2.47	2.47	2.47	2.48	2.48	2.48	2.48	2.49	2.49	2.49	2.50
2.73	2.73	2.73	2.74	2.74	2.74	2.75	2.75	2.75	2.75	2.76	2.76	2.76	2.77	2.77	2.77
5.45	5.46	5.47	5.47	5.48	5.48	5.49	5.50	5.50	5.51	5.52	5.52	5.53	2.53	5.54	5.55
8.18	8.19	8.20	8.21	8.22	8.23	8.24	8.24	8.25	8.26	8.27	8.28	8.29	8.30	8.31	8.32
10.91	10.92	10.93	10.94	10.96	10.97	10.98	10.99	11.01	11.02	11.03	11.04	11.06	11.07	11.08	11.09
13.63	13.65	13.66	13.68	13.69	13.71	13.73	13.74	13.76	13.77	13.79	13.80	13.82	13.84	13.85	13.87
16.36	16.38	16.40	16.41	16.43	16.45	16.47	16.49	16.51	16.53	16.55	16.56	16.58	16.60	16.62	16.64
19.08	19.11	19.13	19.15	19.17	19.19	19.22	19.24	19.26	19.28	19.30	19.32	19.35	19.37	19.39	19.41
21.81	21.84	21.86	21.88	21.91	21.94	21.96	21.99	22.01	22.04	22.06	22.09	22.11	22.14	22.16	22.19
24.54	24.57	24.59	24.62	24.65	24.68	24.71	24.76	24.76	24.79	24.82	24.85	24.87	24.90	24.93	24.96
27.26	27.29	27.33	27.36	27.39	27.42	27.45	27.48	27.51	27.55	27.58	27.61	27.64	27.67	27.70	27.73
54.53	54.59	54.65	54.71	54.78	54.84	54.90	54.96	55.03	55.09	55.15	55.21	55.28	55.34	55.40	55.47
81.79	81.88	81.96	82.07	82.16	82.26	82.35	82.45	82.54	82.64	82.73	82.82	82.91	83.01	83.10	83.20
109.05	109.18	109.30	109.42	109.55	109.68	109.80	109.93	110.05	110.18	110.30	110.43	110.55	110.68	110.80	110.93
136.32	136.47	136.63	136.78	136.94	137.10	137.25	137.41	137.57	137.73	137.88	138.04	138.19	138.35	138.51	138.67
163.58	163.76	163.95	164.14	164.33	164.51	164.70	164.89	165.08	165.27	165.46	165.64	165.83	166.02	166.21	166.40
190.84	191.06	191.28	191.49	191.72	191.93	192.15	192.37	192.59	192.82	193.03	193.25	193.47	193.69	193.91	194.13
218.10	218.35	218.60	218.85	219.10	219.35	219.60	219.86	220.10	220.36	220.61	220.86	221.10	221.36	221.61	221.86
245.37	245.64	245.93	246.20	246.49	246.77	247.05	247.34	247.62	247.91	248.18	248.46	248.74	249.03	249.31	249.60
272.63	272.94	273.25	273.56	273.88	274.19	274.50	274.82	275.13	275.45	275.76	276.07	276.38	276.70	277.01	277.33

15 Degrees.

45	46	47	48	49	50	51	52	53	54	55	56	57	58	59	60
0.28	0.28	0.28	0.28	0.28	0.28	0.28	0.28	0.28	0.28	0.29	0.29	0.29	0.29	0.29	0.29
0.56	0.56	0.57	0.57	0.57	0.57	0.57	0.57	0.57	0.57	0.57	0.57	0.57	0.57	0.57	0.57
0.85	0.85	0.85	0.85	0.85	0.85	0.85	0.85	0.85	0.85	0.86	0.86	0.86	0.86	0.86	0.86
1.13	1.13	1.13	1.13	1.13	1.13	1.14	1.14	1.14	1.14	1.14	1.14	1.14	1.14	1.15	1.15
1.41	1.41	1.41	1.41	1.42	1.42	1.42	1.42	1.42	1.42	1.43	1.43	1.43	1.43	1.43	1.43
1.69	1.69	1.70	1.70	1.70	1.70	1.70	1.71	1.71	1.71	1.71	1.71	1.72	1.72	1.72	1.72
1.97	1.98	1.98	1.98	1.98	1.99	1.99	1.99	1.99	1.99	2.00	2.00	2.00	2.00	2.01	2.01
2.26	2.26	2.26	2.26	2.27	2.27	2.27	2.27	2.28	2.28	2.28	2.28	2.29	2.29	2.29	2.29
2.54	2.54	2.54	2.55	2.55	2.55	2.56	2.56	2.56	2.56	2.57	2.57	2.57	2.57	2.58	2.58
2.82	2.82	2.83	2.83	2.83	2.84	2.84	2.84	2.85	2.85	2.85	2.85	2.86	2.86	2.86	2.87
5.64	5.65	5.65	5.66	5.67	5.67	5.68	5.68	5.69	5.70	5.70	5.71	5.72	5.72	5.73	5.74
8.46	8.47	8.48	8.49	8.50	8.51	8.52	8.53	8.54	8.55	8.56	8.56	8.57	8.58	8.59	8.60
11.28	11.29	11.31	11.32	11.33	11.34	11.36	11.37	11.39	11.41	11.41	11.42	11.43	11.43	11.46	11.47
14.10	14.12	14.13	14.15	14.16	14.18	14.20	14.21	14.23	14.24	14.26	14.27	14.29	14.31	14.32	14.34
16.92	16.94	16.96	16.98	17.00	17.02	17.04	17.05	17.07	17.09	17.11	17.13	17.15	17.17	17.19	17.21
19.74	19.76	19.79	19.81	19.83	19.85	19.87	19.90	19.92	19.94	19.96	19.98	20.01	20.03	20.05	20.07
22.56	22.59	22.61	22.64	22.66	22.69	22.71	22.74	22.76	22.79	22.81	22.84	22.86	22.89	22.91	22.94
25.38	25.41	25.44	25.47	25.50	25.52	25.55	25.58	25.61	25.64	25.67	25.69	25.72	25.75	25.78	25.81
28.20	28.23	28.27	28.30	28.33	28.36	28.39	28.42	28.45	28.49	28.52	28.55	28.58	28.61	28.64	28.68
56.41	56.47	56.53	56.59	56.66	56.72	56.78	56.85	56.91	56.97	57.03	57.10	57.16	57.22	57.29	57.35
84.61	84.70	84.74	84.89	84.98	85.08	85.18	85.27	85.36	85.46	85.55	85.65	85.74	85.83	85.93	86.03
112.81	112.94	113.06	113.19	113.31	113.44	113.57	113.69	113.82	113.94	114.07	114.20	114.32	114.44	114.57	114.70
141.02	141.17	141.33	141.49	141.64	141.80	141.96	142.12	142.27	142.43	142.59	142.75	142.90	143.06	143.22	143.38
169.22	169.40	169.60	169.78	169.97	170.16	170.35	170.54	170.72	170.92	171.10	171.29	171.48	171.67	171.86	172.05
197.42	197.64	197.86	198.08	198.30	198.52	198.74	198.96	199.18	199.40	199.62	199.84	200.01	200.28	200.50	200.73
225.62	225.87	226.13	226.38	226.62	226.88	227.14	227.38	227.63	227.89	228.14	228.39	228.64	228.89	229.14	229.40
253.83	254.11	254.39	254.67	254.95	255.24	255.53	255.81	256.09	256.37	256.65	256.94	257.22	257.50	257.79	258.08
282.03	282.34	282.65	282.97	283.28	283.60	283.92	284.23	284.54	284.86	285.17	285.49	285.80	286.11	286.43	286.75

16 Degrees.

Minutes	0	1	2	3	4	5	6	7	8	9	10	11	12	13	14
Dis. in ft.															
1	0.29	0.29	0.29	0.29	0.29	0.29	0.29	0.29	0.29	0.29	0.29	0.29	0.29	0.29	0.29
2	0.57	0.57	0.57	0.58	0.58	0.58	0.58	0.58	0.58	0.58	0.58	0.58	0.58	0.58	0.58
3	0.86	0.86	0.86	0.86	0.86	0.86	0.87	0.87	0.87	0.87	0.87	0.87	0.87	0.87	0.87
4	1.15	1.15	1.15	1.15	1.15	1.15	1.15	1.16	1.16	1.16	1.16	1.16	1.16	1.16	1.16
5	1.43	1.44	1.44	1.44	1.44	1.44	1.44	1.44	1.45	1.45	1.45	1.45	1.45	1.45	1.46
6	1.72	1.72	1.72	1.73	1.73	1.73	1.73	1.73	1.74	1.74	1.74	1.74	1.74	1.75	1.75
7	2.01	2.01	2.01	2.01	2.02	2.02	2.02	2.02	2.02	2.03	2.03	2.03	2.03	2.04	2.04
8	2.29	2.30	2.30	2.30	2.30	2.31	2.31	2.31	2.31	2.32	2.32	2.32	2.32	2.33	2.33
9	2.58	2.58	2.59	2.59	2.59	2.59	2.60	2.60	2.60	2.61	2.61	2.61	2.61	2.62	2.62
10	2.87	2.87	2.87	2.88	2.88	2.88	2.89	2.89	2.89	2.90	2.90	2.90	2.91	2.91	2.91
20	5.74	5.74	5.75	5.75	5.76	5.77	5.77	5.78	5.79	5.79	5.80	5.80	5.81	5.82	5.82
30	8.60	8.61	8.62	8.63	8.64	8.65	8.65	8.66	8.67	8.68	8.69	8.70	8.71	8.72	8.73
40	11.47	11.48	11.50	11.51	11.52	11.53	11.55	11.56	11.57	11.58	11.60	11.61	11.62	11.63	11.65
50	14.34	14.35	14.37	14.38	14.40	14.42	14.43	14.45	14.46	14.48	14.49	14.51	14.53	14.54	14.56
60	17.21	17.22	10.24	17.26	17.28	17.30	17.32	17.34	17.36	17.37	17.39	17.41	17.43	17.45	17.47
70	20.07	20.09	20.12	20.14	20.16	20.18	20.20	20.23	20.25	20.27	20.29	20.31	20.34	20.36	20.38
80	22.94	22.96	22.99	23.02	23.04	23.07	23.09	23.12	23.14	23.17	23.19	23.22	23.24	23.27	23.29
90	25.81	25.84	25.86	25.89	25.92	25.95	25.98	26.01	26.03	26.06	26.09	26.12	26.15	26.18	26.20
100	28.68	28.71	28.74	28.77	28.80	28.83	28.86	28.90	28.93	28.96	28.99	29.02	29.05	29.08	29.12
200	57.35	57.41	57.48	57.54	57.60	57.66	57.73	57.79	57.85	57.92	57.98	58.04	58.10	58.17	58.23
300	86.03	86.12	86.21	86.31	86.40	86.50	86.59	86.69	86.78	86.87	86.97	87.06	87.16	87.25	87.35
400	114.70	114.82	114.95	115.08	115.20	115.33	115.45	115.58	115.70	115.83	115.96	116.08	116.21	116.34	116.46
500	143.38	143.53	143.69	143.85	144.00	144.16	141.32	144.48	144.63	144.79	144.95	145.11	145.26	145.42	145.58
600	172.05	172.24	172.43	172.61	172.80	172.99	173.18	173.37	173.56	173.75	173.93	174.13	174.31	174.50	174.69
700	200.73	200.94	201.17	201.38	201.60	201.82	202.04	202.27	202.48	202.71	202.92	203.15	203.36	203.59	203.81
800	229.40	229.65	229.90	230.15	230.40	230.66	230.91	231.16	231.41	231.66	231.91	232.17	232.42	232.67	232.92
900	258.08	258.35	258.64	258.92	259.20	259.49	259.77	260.06	260.33	260.62	260.90	261.19	261.47	261.76	262.04
1000	286.75	287.06	287.38	287.69	288.00	288.32	288.63	288.95	289.26	289.58	289.89	290.21	290.52	290.84	291.15

16 Degrees.

Minutes	30	31	32	33	34	35	36	37	38	39	40	41	42	43	44
Dis. in ft.															
1	0.30	0.30	0.30	0.30	0.30	0.30	0.30	0.30	0.30	0.30	0.30	0.30	0.30	0.30	0.30
2	0.59	0.59	0.59	0.59	0.59	0.60	0.60	0.60	0.60	0.60	0.60	0.60	0.60	0.60	0.60
3	0.89	0.89	0.89	0.89	0.89	0.89	0.89	0.90	0.90	0.90	0.90	0.90	0.90	0.90	0.90
4	1.18	1.19	1.19	1.19	1.19	1.19	1.19	1.19	1.19	1.20	1.20	1.20	1.20	1.20	1.20
5	1.48	1.48	1.48	1.49	1.49	1.49	1.49	1.49	1.49	1.50	1.50	1.50	1.50	1.50	1.50
6	1.78	1.78	1.78	1.78	1.78	1.79	1.79	1.79	1.79	1.79	1.80	1.80	1.80	1.80	1.80
7	2.07	2.08	2.08	2.08	2.08	2.08	2.09	2.09	2.09	2.09	2.09	2.10	2.10	2.10	2.10
8	2.37	2.37	2.37	2.38	2.38	2.38	2.38	2.39	2.39	2.39	2.40	2.40	2.40	2.40	2.41
9	2.67	2.67	2.67	2.67	2.68	2.68	2.68	2.68	2.69	2.69	2.69	2.69	2.70	2.70	2.71
10	2.96	2.97	2.97	2.97	2.97	2.98	2.98	2.98	2.99	2.99	2.99	3.00	3.00	3.00	3.01
20	5.92	5.93	5.94	5.94	5.95	5.96	5.96	5.97	5.97	5.98	5.99	5.99	6.00	6.01	6.01
30	8.89	8.90	8.91	8.91	8.92	8.93	8.94	8.95	8.96	8.97	8.98	8.99	9.00	9.01	9.02
40	11.85	11.86	11.87	11.89	11.90	11.91	11.92	11.94	11.95	11.96	11.98	11.99	12.00	12.01	12.03
50	14.81	14.83	14.84	14.86	14.87	14.89	14.91	14.92	14.94	14.95	14.97	14.99	15.00	15.02	15.03
60	17.77	17.79	17.81	17.83	17.85	17.87	17.89	17.91	17.92	17.94	17.96	17.98	18.00	18.02	18.04
70	20.73	20.76	20.78	20.80	20.82	20.85	20.87	20.89	20.91	20.93	20.96	20.98	21.00	21.02	21.05
80	23.70	23.72	23.75	23.77	23.80	23.82	23.85	23.88	23.90	23.92	23.95	23.98	24.00	24.03	24.05
90	26.66	26.69	26.72	26.74	26.77	26.80	26.83	26.86	26.89	26.92	26.94	26.97	27.00	27.03	27.06
100	29.62	29.65	29.69	29.72	29.75	29.78	29.81	29.84	29.87	29.91	29.94	29.97	30.00	30.03	30.07
200	59.24	59.31	59.37	59.43	59.50	59.56	59.62	59.69	59.75	59.81	59.88	59.94	60.00	60.07	60.13
300	88.86	88.96	89.06	89.15	89.24	89.34	89.43	89.53	89.62	89.72	89.81	89.91	90.00	90.10	90.20
400	118.48	118.61	118.74	118.86	118.99	119.12	119.24	119.37	119.50	119.62	119.75	119.88	120.00	120.13	120.26
500	148.11	148.27	148.43	148.58	148.74	148.90	149.06	149.22	149.37	149.53	149.69	149.85	150.01	150.17	150.33
600	177.73	177.92	178.11	178.30	178.49	178.68	178.87	179.06	179.24	179.44	179.63	179.82	180.01	180.20	180.39
700	207.35	207.57	207.80	208.01	208.24	208.46	208.68	208.90	209.12	209.34	209.57	209.79	210.01	210.23	210.46
800	236.97	237.22	237.48	237.73	237.98	238.24	238.49	238.74	238.99	239.25	239.50	239.76	240.01	240.26	240.52
900	266.59	266.88	267.17	267.44	267.73	268.02	268.30	268.59	268.87	269.15	269.44	269.73	270.01	270.30	270.59
1000	296.21	296.53	296.85	297.16	297.48	297.80	298.11	298.43	298.74	299.06	299.38	299.70	300.01	300.33	300.65

16 Degrees.

15	16	17	18	19	20	21	22	23	24	25	26	27	28	29	30
0.29	0.29	0.29	0.29	0.29	0.29	0.29	0.29	0.29	0.29	0.29	0.29	0.30	0.30	0.30	0.30
0.58	0.58	0.58	0.58	0.59	0.59	0.59	0.59	0.59	0.59	0.59	0.59	0.59	0.59	0.59	0.59
0.87	0.88	0.88	0.88	0.88	0.88	0.88	0.88	0.88	0.88	0.88	0.83	0.89	0.89	0.89	0.89
1.17	1.17	1.17	1.17	1.18	1.17	1.17	1.17	1.18	1.18	1.18	1.18	1.18	1.18	1.18	1.18
1.46	1.46	1.46	1.46	1.46	1.47	1.47	1.47	1.47	1.47	1.47	1.48	1.48	1.48	1.48	1.48
1.75	1.75	1.75	1.75	1.76	1.76	1.76	1.76	1.76	1.77	1.77	1.77	1.77	1.78	1.78	1.78
2.04	2.04	2.04	2.05	2.05	2.05	2.05	2.06	2.06	2.06	2.06	2.07	2.07	2.07	2.07	2.07
2.33	2.33	2.34	2.34	2.34	2.34	2.35	2.35	2.35	2.35	2.36	2.36	2.36	2.36	2.37	2.37
2.62	2.63	2.63	2.63	2.63	2.64	2.64	2.64	2.65	2.65	2.65	2.65	2.66	2.66	2.66	2.67
2.01	2.92	2.92	2.92	2.93	2.93	2.93	2.94	2.94	2.94	2.95	2.95	2.95	2.96	2.96	2.96
5.83	5.84	5.84	5.85	5.85	5.86	5.87	5.87	5.88	5.89	5.89	5.90	5.91	5.91	5.92	5.92
8.74	8.75	8.76	8.77	8.78	8.79	8.80	8.81	8.82	8.83	8.84	8.85	8.86	8.87	8.88	8.89
11.66	11.67	11.68	11.70	11.71	11.72	11.73	11.75	11.76	11.77	11.79	11.80	11.81	11.82	11.84	11.85
14.57	14.59	14.61	14.62	14.64	14.65	14.67	14.68	14.70	14.72	14.73	14.75	14.76	14.78	14.80	14.81
17.49	17.51	17.53	17.55	17.56	17.58	17.60	17.62	17.64	17.66	17.68	17.70	17.72	17.73	17.75	17.77
20.40	20.43	20.45	20.47	20.49	20.51	20.54	20.56	20.58	20.60	20.62	20.65	20.67	20.69	20.71	20.73
23.32	23.34	23.37	23.39	23.42	23.44	23.47	23.49	23.52	23.54	23.57	23.60	23.62	23.65	23.67	23.70
26.23	26.26	26.29	26.32	26.35	26.37	26.40	26.43	26.46	26.49	26.52	26.55	26.57	26.60	26.60	26.66
29.15	29.18	29.21	29.24	29.27	29.31	29.34	29.37	29.40	29.43	29.46	29.50	29.53	29.56	29.59	29.62
58.29	58.36	58.42	58.48	58.55	58.61	58.67	58.74	58.80	58.86	58.93	58.99	59.05	59.12	59.18	59.24
87.44	87.54	87.63	87.73	87.82	87.92	88.01	88.10	88.20	88.29	88.39	88.49	88.58	88.67	88.77	88.86
116.59	116.72	116.84	116.97	117.10	117.22	117.35	117.47	117.60	117.72	117.85	117.98	118.10	118.23	118.36	118.48
145.74	145.90	146.06	146.21	146.37	146.53	146.69	146.84	147.00	147.16	147.32	147.48	147.63	147.79	147.95	148.11
174.88	175.27	175.45	175.64	175.88	176.02	176.21	176.21	176.59	176.59	176.97	177.10	177.17	177.54	177.54	177.73
204.03	204.25	204.48	204.69	204.92	205.14	205.36	205.58	205.80	206.02	206.24	206.47	206.68	206.91	207.13	207.35
233.18	233.43	233.69	233.94	234.19	234.44	234.70	234.94	235.45	235.70	235.96	236.21	236.46	236.72	236.72	236.97
262.32	262.61	262.90	263.18	263.47	263.75	264.04	264.33	264.60	264.88	265.17	265.46	265.73	266.02	266.31	266.59
291.47	291.70	292.11	292.42	292.74	293.05	293.37	293.68	294.00	294.31	294.63	294.95	295.26	295.58	295.90	296.21

16 Degrees.

45	46	47	48	49	50	51	52	53	54	55	56	57	58	59	60
0.30	0.30	0.30	0.30	0.30	0.30	0.30	0.30	0.30	0.30	0.30	0.30	0.30	0.31	0.31	0.31
0.60	0.60	0.60	0.60	0.60	0.60	0.61	0.61	0.61	0.61	0.61	0.61	0.61	0.61	0.61	0.61
0.90	0.90	0.90	0.91	0.91	0.91	0.91	0.91	0.91	0.91	0.91	0.91	0.92	0.92	0.92	0.92
1.20	1.21	1.21	1.21	1.21	1.21	1.21	1.21	1.21	1.22	1.22	1.22	1.22	1.22	1.22	1.22
1.50	1.51	1.51	1.51	1.51	1.51	1.51	1.52	1.52	1.52	1.52	1.52	1.53	1.53	1.53	1.53
1.81	1.81	1.81	1.81	1.81	1.82	1.82	1.82	1.82	1.82	1.83	1.83	1.83	1.83	1.83	1.88
2.11	2.11	2.11	2.11	2.12	2.12	2.12	2.12	2.12	2.13	2.13	2.13	2.14	2.14	2.14	2.14
2.41	2.41	2.41	2.42	2.42	2.42	2.42	2.43	2.43	2.43	2.43	2.44	2.44	2.44	2.44	2.45
2.71	2.71	2.71	2.72	2.72	2.72	2.73	2.73	2.73	2.73	2.74	2.74	2.74	2.75	2.75	2.75
3.01	3.01	3.02	3.02	3.02	3.03	3.03	3.03	3.04	3.04	3.04	3.04	3.05	3.05	3.05	3.06
6.02	6.03	6.03	6.04	6.04	6.05	6.06	6.06	6.07	6.08	6.08	6.09	6.10	6.10	6.11	6.11
9.03	9.04	9.05	9.06	9.07	9.08	9.09	9.10	9.11	9.11	9.12	9.13	9.14	9.15	9.16	9.17
12.04	12.05	12.06	12.08	12.10	12.11	12.11	12.13	12.14	12.15	12.17	12.18	12.19	12.20	12.22	12.23
15.05	15.06	15.08	15.10	15.11	15.13	15.14	15.16	15.18	15.19	15.21	15.22	15.24	15.25	15.27	15.29
18.06	18.08	18.10	18.12	18.15	18.17	18.19	18.21	18.21	18.29	18.25	18.27	18.29	18.31	18.32	18.34
21.07	21.09	21.11	21.13	21.16	21.18	21.20	21.22	21.25	21.27	21.29	21.31	21.33	21.36	21.38	21.40
24.08	24.10	24.13	24.15	24.18	24.20	24.23	24.26	24.28	24.31	24.33	24.36	24.38	24.41	24.43	24.46
27.09	27.12	27.14	27.17	27.20	27.23	27.26	27.29	27.32	27.34	27.37	27.40	27.43	27.46	27.49	27.52
30.10	30.13	30.16	30.19	30.22	30.26	30.29	30.32	30.35	30.38	30.41	30.45	30.48	30.51	30.54	30.57
60.19	60.26	60.32	60.38	60.45	60.51	60.57	60.64	60.70	60.76	60.83	60.89	60.96	61.02	61.08	61.15
90.29	90.38	90.48	90.58	90.67	90.77	90.86	90.96	91.05	91.15	91.24	91.34	91.43	91.53	91.62	91.72
120.39	120.51	120.64	120.77	120.90	121.02	121.15	121.28	121.40	121.53	121.66	121.78	121.91	122.04	122.16	122.29
150.49	150.64	150.80	150.96	151.12	151.28	151.44	151.60	151.76	151.91	152.07	152.23	152.39	152.55	152.71	152.87
180.58	180.77	180.96	181.15	181.34	181.53	181.72	181.91	182.11	182.29	182.48	182.68	182.87	183.05	183.25	183.44
210.68	210.90	211.12	211.34	211.57	211.79	212.01	212.23	212.46	212.67	212.90	213.12	213.35	213.56	213.79	214.01
240.78	241.02	241.28	241.54	241.79	242.04	242.30	242.55	242.81	243.06	243.31	243.57	243.82	244.07	244.33	244.58
270.87	271.15	271.44	271.73	272.02	272.30	272.58	272.87	273.16	273.43	273.73	274.01	274.30	274.58	274.87	275.16
300.97	301.28	301.60	301.92	302.24	302.55	302.87	303.19	303.51	303.82	304.14	304.46	304.78	305.09	305.41	305.73

17 Degrees.

Minutes	0	1	2	3	4	5	6	7	8	9	10	11	12	13	14
Dis. in ft.															
1	0.31	0.31	0.31	0.31	0.31	0.31	0.31	0.31	0.31	0.31	0.31	0.31	0.31	0.31	0.31
2	0.61	0.61	0.61	0.61	0.61	0.61	0.62	0.62	0.62	0.62	0.62	0.62	0.62	0.62	0.62
3	0.92	0.92	0.92	0.92	0.92	0.92	0.92	0.92	0.92	0.93	0.93	0.93	0.93	0.93	0.93
4	1.22	1.22	1.23	1.23	1.23	1.23	1.23	1.23	1.23	1.23	1.24	1.24	1.24	1.24	1.24
5	1.53	1.53	1.53	1.53	1.54	1.54	1.54	1.54	1.54	1.54	1.54	1.55	1.55	1.55	1.55
6	1.83	1.84	1.84	1.84	1.84	1.84	1.85	1.85	1.85	1.85	1.85	1.85	1.86	1.86	1.86
7	2.14	2.14	2.14	2.15	2.15	2.15	2.15	2.16	2.16	2.16	2.16	2.16	2.17	2.17	2.17
8	2.45	2.45	2.45	2.45	2.46	2.46	2.46	2.46	2.47	2.47	2.47	2.47	2.48	2.48	2.48
9	2.75	2.75	2.76	2.76	2.76	2.77	2.77	2.77	2.77	2.78	2.78	2.78	2.79	2.79	2.79
10	3.06	3.06	3.06	3.07	3.07	3.07	3.08	3.08	3.08	3.09	3.09	3.09	3.09	3.10	3.10
20	6.11	6.12	6.13	6.13	6.14	6.15	6.15	6.16	6.17	6.17	6.18	6.18	6.19	6.20	6.20
30	9.17	9.18	9.19	9.20	9.21	9.22	9.23	9.24	9.25	9.26	9.27	9.28	9.29	9.30	9.31
40	12.23	12.24	12.25	12.27	12.28	12.29	12.31	12.32	12.33	12.34	12.36	12.37	12.38	12.39	12.41
50	15.29	15.30	15.32	15.33	15.35	15.37	15.38	15.40	15.41	15.43	15.45	15.46	15.48	15.49	15.51
60	18.34	18.36	18.38	18.40	18.42	18.44	18.46	18.48	18.50	18.52	18.54	18.55	18.57	18.59	18.61
70	21.40	21.42	21.45	21.47	21.49	21.51	21.53	21.56	21.58	21.60	21.62	21.65	21.67	21.69	21.71
80	24.46	24.48	24.51	24.54	24.56	24.59	24.61	24.64	24.66	24.69	24.71	24.74	24.76	24.79	24.82
90	27.52	27.54	27.57	27.60	27.63	27.66	27.69	27.72	27.75	27.77	27.80	27.83	27.86	27.89	27.92
100	30.57	30.61	30.64	30.67	30.70	30.73	30.76	30.80	30.83	30.86	30.89	30.92	30.96	30.99	31.02
200	61.15	61.21	61.27	61.34	61.40	61.46	61.53	61.59	61.66	61.72	61.78	61.85	61.91	61.97	62.04
300	91.72	91.82	91.91	92.01	92.10	92.20	92.29	92.39	92.48	92.58	92.68	92.77	92.87	92.96	93.06
400	122.29	122.42	122.55	122.68	122.80	122.93	123.06	123.18	123.31	123.44	123.57	123.70	123.82	123.95	124.08
500	152.87	153.03	153.19	153.35	153.50	153.66	153.82	153.98	154.14	154.30	154.46	154.62	154.77	154.94	155.10
600	183.44	183.63	183.82	184.01	184.20	184.39	184.58	184.78	184.97	185.16	185.35	185.54	185.73	185.92	186.11
700	214.01	214.24	214.46	214.68	214.90	215.12	215.35	215.57	215.80	216.02	216.24	216.47	216.69	216.91	217.13
800	244.58	244.84	245.10	245.35	245.60	245.86	246.11	246.37	246.62	246.88	247.14	247.39	247.64	247.90	248.15
900	275.16	275.45	275.73	276.02	276.30	276.59	276.88	277.16	277.45	277.74	278.03	278.32	278.60	278.88	279.17
1000	305.73	306.05	306.37	306.69	307.00	307.32	307.64	307.96	308.28	308.60	308.92	309.24	309.55	309.87	310.19

17 Degrees.

Minutes	30	31	32	33	34	35	36	37	38	39	40	41	42	43	44
Dis. in ft.															
1	0.32	0.32	0.32	0.32	0.32	0.32	0.32	0.32	0.32	0.32	0.32	0.32	0.32	0.32	0.32
2	0.63	0.63	0.63	0.63	0.63	0.63	0.63	0.64	0.64	0.64	0.64	0.64	0.64	0.64	0.64
3	0.95	0.95	0.95	0.95	0.95	0.95	0.95	0.95	0.95	0.95	0.96	0.96	0.96	0.96	0.96
4	1.26	1.26	1.26	1.27	1.27	1.27	1.27	1.27	1.27	1.27	1.27	1.28	1.28	1.28	1.28
5	1.58	1.58	1.58	1.58	1.58	1.58	1.59	1.59	1.59	1.59	1.59	1.59	1.60	1.60	1.60
6	1.89	1.89	1.90	1.90	1.90	1.90	1.91	1.91	1.91	1.91	1.91	1.91	1.91	1.92	1.92
7	2.21	2.21	2.21	2.21	2.22	2.22	2.22	2.22	2.23	2.23	2.23	2.23	2.23	2.24	2.24
8	2.52	2.52	2.53	2.53	2.53	2.54	2.54	2.54	2.54	2.55	2.55	2.55	2.55	2.56	2.56
9	2.84	2.84	2.84	2.85	2.85	2.85	2.85	2.86	2.86	2.86	2.87	2.87	2.87	2.88	2.88
10	3.15	3.16	3.16	3.16	3.17	3.17	3.17	3.18	3.18	3.18	3.19	3.19	3.19	3.19	3.20
20	6.31	6.31	6.32	6.33	6.33	6.34	6.34	6.35	6.36	6.36	6.37	6.38	6.38	6.39	6.40
30	9.46	9.47	9.48	9.49	9.50	9.51	9.52	9.53	9.54	9.55	9.56	9.56	9.57	9.58	9.59
40	12.61	12.62	12.64	12.65	12.66	12.68	12.69	12.70	12.71	12.73	12.74	12.75	12.77	12.78	12.79
50	15.77	15.78	15.80	15.81	15.83	15.85	15.86	15.88	15.89	15.91	15.93	15.94	15.96	15.97	15.99
60	18.92	18.94	18.96	18.98	18.99	19.01	19.03	19.05	19.07	19.09	19.11	19.13	19.15	19.17	19.19
70	22.07	22.09	22.12	22.14	22.16	22.18	22.21	22.23	22.25	22.27	22.30	22.32	22.34	22.36	22.38
80	25.22	25.25	25.28	25.30	25.33	25.35	25.38	25.40	25.43	25.45	25.48	25.51	25.53	25.56	25.58
90	28.38	28.41	28.43	28.46	28.49	28.52	28.55	28.58	28.61	28.64	28.67	28.69	28.72	28.75	28.78
100	31.53	31.56	31.59	31.63	31.66	31.69	31.72	31.75	31.79	31.82	31.85	31.88	31.91	31.95	31.98
200	63.06	63.12	63.19	63.25	63.32	63.38	63.44	63.51	63.57	63.64	63.70	63.76	63.83	63.89	63.96
300	94.59	94.69	94.78	94.88	94.97	95.07	95.17	95.26	95.36	95.45	95.55	95.65	95.74	95.84	95.93
400	126.12	126.25	126.38	126.50	126.63	126.76	126.89	127.02	127.14	127.27	127.40	127.53	127.66	127.78	127.91
500	157.65	157.81	157.97	158.13	158.29	158.45	158.61	158.77	158.93	159.09	159.25	159.41	159.57	159.73	159.89
600	189.18	189.37	189.56	189.76	189.95	190.14	190.33	190.52	190.72	190.91	191.10	191.29	191.48	191.68	191.87
700	220.71	220.93	221.16	221.38	221.61	221.83	222.05	222.28	222.50	222.73	222.95	223.17	223.40	223.62	223.85
800	252.24	252.50	252.75	253.01	253.26	253.52	253.78	254.03	254.29	254.54	254.80	255.06	255.31	255.57	255.82
900	283.77	284.06	284.35	284.63	284.92	285.21	285.50	285.79	286.07	286.36	286.65	286.94	287.23	287.51	287.80
1000	315.30	315.62	315.94	316.26	316.58	316.90	317.22	317.54	317.86	318.18	318.50	318.82	319.14	319.46	319.78

17 Degrees.

15	16	17	18	19	20	21	22	23	24	25	26	27	28	29	30
0.31	0.31	0.31	0.31	0.31	0.31	0.31	0.31	0.31	0.31	0.31	0.31	0.31	0.31	0.31	0.32
0.62	0.62	0.62	0.62	0.62	0.62	0.63	0.63	0.63	0.63	0.63	0.63	0.63	0.63	0.63	0.63
0.93	0.93	0.93	0.93	0.94	0.94	0.94	0.94	0.94	0.94	0.94	0.94	0.94	0.94	0.94	0.95
1.24	1.24	1.24	1.25	1.25	1.25	1.25	1.25	1.25	1.25	1.25	1.26	1.26	1.26	1.26	1.26
1.55	1.55	1.56	1.56	1.56	1.56	1.56	1.56	1.57	1.57	1.57	1.57	1.57	1.57	1.57	1.58
1.86	1.87	1.87	1.87	1.87	1.87	1.87	1.88	1.88	1.88	1.88	1.88	1.89	1.89	1.89	1.89
2.17	2.18	2.18	2.18	2.18	2.18	2.19	2.19	2.19	2.19	2.20	2.20	2.20	2.20	2.20	2.21
2.48	2.49	2.49	2.49	2.49	2.50	2.50	2.50	2.50	2.51	2.51	2.51	2.51	2.52	2.52	2.52
2.79	2.80	2.80	2.80	2.81	2 81	2.81	2.81	2.82	2.82	2.82	2.83	2.83	2.83	2.83	2.84
3.11	3.11	3.11	3.11	3.12	3.12	3.12	3.13	3.13	3.13	3.14	3.14	3.14	3.15	3.15	3.15
6.21	6.22	6.22	6.23	6.24	6.24	6.25	6.25	6.26	6.27	6.27	6.28	6.29	6.29	6.30	6.31
9.32	9.32	9.33	9.34	9.35	9.36	9.37	9.38	9.39	9.40	9.41	9.42	9.43	9.44	9.45	9.46
12.42	12.43	12.45	12.46	12.47	12.48	12.50	12.51	12.52	12.54	12.55	12.56	12.57	12.59	12.60	12.61
15.53	15.54	15.56	15.57	15.59	15.61	15.62	15.64	15.65	15.67	15.69	15.70	15.72	15.73	15.75	15.77
18.63	18.65	18.67	18.69	18.71	18.73	18.75	18.76	18.78	18.80	18.82	18.84	18.86	18.88	18.90	18.92
21.74	21.76	21.78	21.80	21.83	21.85	21.87	21.89	21.91	21.94	21.96	21.98	22.00	22.03	22.05	22.07
24.84	24.87	24.89	24.92	24.94	24.97	24.99	25.02	25.05	25.07	25.10	25.12	25.15	25.17	25.20	25.22
27.95	27.97	28.00	28.03	28.06	28.09	28.12	28.15	28.18	28.20	28.23	28.26	28.29	28.32	28.35	28.38
31.05	31.08	31.11	31.15	31.18	31.21	31.24	31.27	31.31	31.34	31.37	31.40	31.43	31.47	31.50	31.53
62.10	62.17	62.23	62.29	62.36	62.42	62.48	62.55	62.61	62.68	62.74	62.80	62.87	62.93	63.00	63.06
93.15	93.25	93.34	93.44	93.53	93.63	93.73	93.82	93.92	94.01	94.11	94.21	94.30	94.40	94.49	94.59
124.20	124.33	124.46	124.58	124.71	124.84	124.97	125.10	125.22	125.35	125.48	125.61	125.74	125.86	125.99	126.12
155.26	155.42	155.57	155.73	155.89	156.05	156.21	156.37	156.53	156.69	156.85	157.01	157.17	157.33	157.49	157.65
186.31	186.50	186.68	186.87	187.07	187.26	187.45	187.64	187.84	188.03	188.22	188.41	188.60	188.80	188.99	189.18
217.36	217.58	217.80	218.02	218.25	218.47	218.69	218.92	219.14	219.37	219.59	219.81	220.04	220.26	220.48	220.71
248.41	248.66	248.91	249.17	249.42	249.68	249.04	250.19	250.45	250.70	250.96	251.22	251.47	251.73	251.98	252.24
279.46	279.75	280.03	280.31	280.60	280.89	281.18	281.47	281.75	282.04	282.33	282.62	282.91	283.19	283.48	283.77
310.51	310.83	311.14	311.46	311.78	312.10	312.42	312.74	313.06	313.38	313.70	314.02	314.34	314.66	314.98	315.30

17 Degrees.

45	46	47	48	49	50	51	52	53	54	55	56	57	58	59	60
0.32	0.32	0.32	0.32	0.32	0.32	0.32	0.32	0.32	0.32	0.32	0.32	0.32	0.32	0.32	0.32
0.64	0.64	0.64	0.64	0.64	0.64	0.64	0.64	0.65	0.65	0.65	0.65	0.65	0.65	0.65	0.65
0.96	0.96	0.96	0.96	0.96	0.97	0.97	0.97	0.97	0.97	0.97	0.97	0.97	0.97	0.97	0.97
1.28	1.28	1.28	1.28	1.29	1.29	1.29	1.29	1.29	1.29	1.29	1.29	1.30	1.30	1.30	1.30
1.60	1.60	1.60	1.61	1.61	1.61	1.61	1.61	1.61	1.61	1.62	1.62	1.62	1.62	1.62	1.62
1.92	1.92	1.92	1.93	1.93	1.93	1.93	1.93	1.94	1.94	1.94	1.94	1.94	1.95	1.95	1.95
2.24	2.24	2.25	2.25	2.25	2.25	2.26	2.26	2.26	2.26	2.26	2.27	2.27	2.27	2.27	2.27
2.56	2.56	2.57	2.57	2.57	2.57	2.58	2.58	2.58	2.58	2.59	2.59	2.59	2.59	2.60	2.60
2.88	2.88	2.89	2.89	2.89	2.90	2.90	2.90	2.90	2.91	2.91	2.91	2.92	2.92	2.92	2.92
3.20	3.20	3.21	3.21	3.21	3.22	3.22	3.22	3.23	3.23	3.23	3.24	3.24	3.24	3.25	3.25
6.40	6.41	6.41	6.42	6.43	6.43	6.44	6.45	6.45	6.46	6.47	6.47	6.48	6.49	6.49	6.50
9.60	9.61	9.62	9.63	9.64	9.65	9.66	9.67	9.68	9.69	9.70	9.71	9.72	9.73	9.74	9.75
12.80	12.82	12.83	12.84	12.86	12.87	12.88	12.89	12.91	12.92	12.93	12.95	12.96	12.97	12.98	13.00
16.01	16.02	16.04	16.05	16.07	16.09	16.10	16.12	16.13	16.15	16.17	16.18	16.20	16.21	16.23	16.25
19.21	19.23	19.24	19.27	19.28	19.30	19.32	19.34	19.36	19.38	19.40	19.42	19.44	19.46	19.48	19.50
22.41	22.43	22.45	22.47	22.50	22.52	22.56	22.59	22.61	22.63	22.65	22.68	22.70	22.72	22.74	22.74
25.61	25.63	25.66	25.68	25.71	25.74	25.76	25.79	25.81	25.84	25.86	25.89	25.92	25.94	25.97	25.99
28.81	28.84	28.87	28.90	28.93	28.95	28.98	29.01	29.04	29.07	29.10	29.13	29.16	29.19	29.21	29.24
32.01	32.04	32.07	32.11	32.14	32.17	32.20	32.24	32.27	32.30	32.33	32.36	32.40	32.43	32.46	32.49
64.02	64.08	64.15	64.21	64.28	64.34	64.41	64.47	64.53	64.60	64.66	64.73	64.79	64.86	64.92	64.98
96.08	96.13	96.22	96.32	96.42	96.51	96.61	96.71	96.80	96.90	96.99	97.09	97.19	97.28	97.38	97.48
128.04	128.17	128.30	128.42	128.56	128.68	128.81	128.94	129.07	129.20	129.32	129.45	129.58	129.71	129.84	129.97
160.05	160.21	160.37	160.53	160.70	160.86	161.02	161.18	161.34	161.50	161.66	161.82	161.98	162.14	162.30	162.46
192.06	192.25	192.44	192.64	192.83	193.03	193.22	193.41	193.60	193.79	193.99	194.18	194.37	194.57	194.76	194.95
224.07	224.29	224.52	224.74	224.97	225.20	225.42	225.65	225.87	226.10	226.32	226.54	226.77	227.00	227.22	227.44
256.08	256.34	256.59	256.85	257.11	257.37	257.62	257.88	258.14	258.39	258.65	258.90	259.16	259.42	259.68	259.94
288.09	288.38	288.67	288.95	289.25	289.54	289.83	290.12	290.40	290.69	290.98	291.27	291.56	291.85	292.14	292.43
320.10	320.42	320.74	321.06	321.39	321.71	322.03	322.35	322.67	322.99	323.31	323.63	323.95	324.28	324.60	324.92

18 Degrees.

Minutes	0	1	2	3	4	5	6	7	8	9	10	11	12	13	14
Dia. in ft.															
1	0.32	0.33	0.33	0.33	0.33	0.33	0.33	0.33	0.33	0.33	0.33	0.33	0.33	0.33	0.33
2	0.65	0.65	0.65	0.65	0.65	0.65	0.65	0.65	0.65	0.66	0.66	0.66	0.66	0.66	0.66
3	0.97	0.98	0.98	0.98	0.98	0.98	0.98	0.98	0.98	0.98	0.98	0.99	0.99	0.99	0.99
4	1.30	1.30	1.30	1.30	1.30	1.31	1.31	1.31	1.31	1.31	1.31	1.31	1.32	1.32	1.32
5	1.62	1.63	1.63	1.63	1.63	1.63	1.63	1.64	1.64	1.64	1.64	1.64	1.64	1.65	1.65
6	1.95	1.95	1.95	1.96	1.96	1.96	1.96	1.96	1.96	1.97	1.97	1.97	1.97	1.97	1.98
7	2.27	2.28	2.28	2.28	2.28	2.29	2.29	2.29	2.29	2.29	2.30	2.30	2.30	2.30	2.31
8	2.60	2.60	2.60	2.61	2.61	2.61	2.61	2.62	2.62	2.62	2.63	2.63	2.63	2.63	2.64
9	2.92	2.93	2.93	2.93	2.94	2.94	2.94	2.94	2.95	2.95	2.95	2.96	2.96	2.96	2.96
10	3.25	3.25	3.26	3.26	3.26	3.27	3.27	3.27	3.27	3.28	3.28	3.28	3.29	3.29	3.29
20	6.50	6.50	6.51	6.52	6.52	6.53	6.54	6.54	6.55	6.56	6.56	6.57	6.58	6.58	6.59
30	9.75	9.76	9.77	9.78	9.79	9.80	9.81	9.82	9.82	9.83	9.84	9.85	9.86	9.87	9.88
40	13.00	13.01	13.02	13.04	13.05	13.06	13.07	13.09	13.10	13.11	13.13	13.14	13.15	13.16	13.18
50	16.25	16.26	16.28	16.29	16.31	16.33	16.34	16.36	16.37	16.39	16.41	16.42	16.44	16.46	16.47
60	19.50	19.51	19.53	19.55	19.57	19.59	19.61	19.63	19.65	19.67	19.69	19.71	19.73	19.75	19.77
70	22.74	22.77	22.79	22.81	22.83	22.86	22.88	22.90	22.92	22.95	22.97	22.99	23.01	23.04	23.06
80	25.99	26.02	26.04	26.07	26.10	26.12	26.15	26.17	26.20	26.23	26.25	26.28	26.30	26.33	26.35
90	29.24	29.27	29.30	29.33	29.36	29.39	29.42	29.45	29.48	29.50	29.53	29.56	29.59	29.62	29.65
100	32.49	32.52	32.56	32.59	32.62	32.65	32.69	32.72	32.75	32.78	32.81	32.85	32.89	32.91	32.94
200	64.98	65.05	65.11	65.18	65.24	65.31	65.37	65.43	65.50	65.56	65.63	65.69	65.76	65.82	65.89
300	97.48	97.57	97.67	97.76	97.86	97.96	98.06	98.15	98.25	98.35	98.44	98.54	98.63	98.73	98.83
400	129.97	130.10	130.22	130.35	130.48	130.61	130.74	130.87	131.00	131.13	131.26	131.38	131.51	131.64	131.77
500	162.46	162.62	162.78	162.94	163.10	163.27	163.43	163.59	163.75	163.91	164.07	164.23	164.39	164.56	164.72
600	194.95	195.14	195.34	195.53	195.72	195.92	196.11	196.30	196.49	196.69	196.88	197.08	197.27	197.47	197.66
700	227.44	227.67	227.89	228.12	228.34	228.57	228.80	229.02	229.24	229.47	229.70	229.92	230.15	230.38	230.60
800	259.91	260.19	260.45	260.70	260.96	261.22	261.48	261.74	261.99	262.26	262.51	262.77	263.02	263.29	263.54
900	292.43	292.72	293.00	293.29	293.58	293.88	294.17	294.45	294.74	295.04	295.33	295.61	295.90	296.20	296.49
1000	324.92	325.24	325.56	325.88	326.20	326.53	326.85	327.17	327.49	327.82	328.14	328.46	328.78	329.11	329.43

18 Degrees.

Minutes	30	31	32	33	34	35	36	37	38	39	40	41	42	43	44
Dia. in ft.															
1	0.33	0.33	0.34	0.34	0.34	0.34	0.34	0.34	0.34	0.34	0.34	0.34	0.34	0.34	0.34
2	0.67	0.67	0.67	0.67	0.67	0.67	0.67	0.67	0.67	0.68	0.68	0.68	0.68	0.68	0.68
3	1.00	1.00	1.01	1.01	1.01	1.01	1.01	1.01	1.01	1.01	1.01	1.01	1.02	1.02	1.02
4	1.34	1.34	1.34	1.34	1.34	1.34	1.35	1.35	1.35	1.35	1.35	1.35	1.35	1.36	1.36
5	1.67	1.67	1.68	1.68	1.68	1.68	1.68	1.68	1.69	1.69	1.69	1.69	1.69	1.69	1.70
6	2.01	2.01	2.01	2.01	2.02	2.02	2.02	2.02	2.02	2.03	2.03	2.03	2.03	2.03	2.03
7	2.34	2.34	2.35	2.35	2.35	2.35	2.36	2.36	2.36	2.36	2.36	2.37	2.37	2.37	2.37
8	2.68	2.68	2.68	2.68	2.69	2.69	2.69	2.69	2.70	2.70	2.70	2.71	2.71	2.71	2.71
9	3.01	3.01	3.02	3.02	3.02	3.03	3.03	3.03	3.03	3.04	3.04	3.04	3.05	3.05	3.05
10	3.35	3.35	3.35	3.36	3.36	3.36	3.37	3.37	3.37	3.38	3.38	3.38	3.39	3.39	3.39
20	6.69	6.70	6.70	6.71	6.72	6.72	6.73	6.74	6.74	6.75	6.76	6.76	6.77	6.78	6.78
30	10.04	10.05	10.06	10.07	10.08	10.09	10.10	10.11	10.12	10.13	10.14	10.15	10.16	10.17	10.18
40	13.38	13.40	13.41	13.42	13.44	13.45	13.46	13.47	13.49	13.50	13.51	13.53	13.54	13.55	13.57
50	16.73	16.75	16.76	16.78	16.79	16.81	16.83	16.84	16.86	16.88	16.89	16.91	16.92	16.94	16.96
60	20.08	20.10	20.11	20.13	20.15	20.17	20.19	20.21	20.23	20.25	20.27	20.29	20.31	20.33	20.35
70	23.42	23.44	23.47	23.49	23.51	23.53	23.56	23.58	23.60	23.63	23.65	23.67	23.69	23.72	23.74
80	26.77	26.79	26.82	26.85	26.87	26.90	26.92	26.95	26.97	27.00	27.03	27.05	27.08	27.10	27.13
90	30.11	30.14	30.17	30.20	30.23	30.26	30.29	30.32	30.35	30.38	30.41	30.43	30.46	30.49	30.52
100	33.46	33.49	33.52	33.56	33.59	33.62	33.65	33.69	33.72	33.75	33.78	33.82	33.85	33.88	33.91
200	66.92	66.98	67.05	67.11	67.18	67.24	67.31	67.37	67.44	67.50	67.57	67.63	67.69	67.76	67.83
300	100.38	100.48	100.57	100.67	100.77	100.86	100.96	101.05	101.15	101.25	101.35	101.45	101.54	101.64	101.74
400	133.84	133.97	134.10	134.23	134.36	134.48	134.62	134.74	134.87	135.00	135.13	135.26	135.39	135.52	135.65
500	167.30	167.46	167.62	167.79	167.95	168.11	168.27	168.43	168.59	168.76	168.92	169.08	169.24	169.40	169.57
600	200.76	200.95	201.14	201.31	201.53	201.73	201.92	202.12	202.31	202.51	202.70	202.89	203.08	203.28	203.48
700	234.22	234.44	234.67	234.90	235.12	235.35	235.58	235.80	236.03	236.26	236.48	236.71	236.93	237.16	237.39
800	267.68	267.94	268.19	268.46	268.71	268.97	269.23	269.49	269.74	270.00	270.26	270.52	270.79	271.01	271.30
900	301.14	301.43	301.72	302.01	302.30	302.59	302.89	303.17	303.46	303.76	304.05	304.34	304.62	304.92	305.22
1000	334.60	334.92	335.24	335.56	335.89	336.21	336.54	336.86	337.18	337.50	337.83	338.15	338.47	338.80	339.13

18 Degrees.

15	16	17	18	19	20	21	22	23	24	25	26	27	28	29	30
0.33	0.33	0.33	0.33	0.33	0.33	0.33	0.33	0.33	0.33	0.33	0.33	0.33	0.33	0.33	0.33
0.66	0.66	0.66	0.66	0.66	0.66	0.66	0.66	0.66	0.66	0.67	0.67	0.67	0.67	0.67	0.67
0.99	0.99	0.99	0.99	0.99	0.99	1.00	1.00	1.00	1.00	1.00	1.00	1.00	1.00	1.00	1.00
1.32	1.32	1.32	1.32	1.32	1.33	1.33	1.33	1.33	1.33	1.33	1.33	1.33	1.34	1.34	1.34
1.65	1.65	1.65	1.65	1.66	1.66	1.66	1.66	1.66	1.66	1.66	1.67	1.67	1.67	1.67	1.67
1.98	1.98	1.98	1.98	1.99	1.99	1.99	1.99	1.99	2.00	2.00	2.00	2.00	2.00	2.01	2.01
2.31	2.31	2.31	2.32	2.32	2.32	2.32	2.32	2.33	2.33	2.33	2.33	2.34	2.34	2.34	2.34
2.64	2.64	2.64	2.65	2.65	2.65	2.65	2.66	2.66	2.66	2.66	2.67	2.67	2.67	2.67	2.68
2.97	2.97	2.97	2.98	2.98	2.98	2.99	2.99	2.99	2.99	3.00	3.00	3.00	3.01	3.01	3.01
3.30	3.30	3.30	3.31	3.31	3.31	3.32	3.32	3.32	3.33	3.33	3.33	3.34	3.34	3.34	3.35
6.60	6.60	6.61	6.61	6.62	6.63	6.63	6.64	6.65	6.65	6.66	6.67	6.67	6.68	6.69	6.69
9.89	9.90	9.91	9.92	9.93	9.94	9.95	9.96	9.97	9.98	9.99	10.00	10.01	10.02	10.03	10.04
13.19	13.20	13.22	13.23	13.24	13.25	13.27	13.28	13.29	13.31	13.32	13.33	13.35	13.36	13.37	13.38
16.49	16.50	16.52	16.54	16.55	16.57	16.58	16.60	16.62	16.63	16.65	16.67	16.68	16.70	16.71	16.73
19.79	19.80	19.82	19.84	19.86	19.88	19.90	19.92	19.94	19.96	19.98	20.00	20.02	20.04	20.06	20.08
23.08	23.10	23.13	23.15	23.17	23.20	23.22	23.24	23.26	23.29	23.31	23.33	23.35	23.38	23.40	23.42
26.38	26.41	26.43	26.46	26.48	26.51	26.54	26.56	26.59	26.61	26.64	26.66	26.69	26.72	26.74	26.76
29.68	29.71	29.74	29.76	29.79	29.82	29.85	29.88	29.91	29.94	29.97	30.00	30.03	30.06	30.08	30.11
32.98	33.01	33.04	33.07	33.10	33.14	33.17	33.20	33.23	33.27	33.30	33.33	33.36	33.40	33.43	33.46
65.95	66.01	66.08	66.14	66.21	66.27	66.34	66.40	66.47	66.53	66.60	66.67	66.73	66.79	66.85	66.92
98.93	99.02	99.12	99.22	99.31	99.41	99.51	99.60	99.70	99.80	99.89	100.00	100.09	100.18	100.28	100.88
131.90	132.03	132.16	132.29	132.42	132.55	132.68	132.80	132.93	133.06	133.19	133.32	133.45	133.58	133.71	133.84
164.88	165.04	165.20	165.36	165.52	165.69	165.85	166.01	166.17	166.33	166.49	166.65	166.82	166.98	167.14	167.30
197.85	198.04	198.23	198.43	198.62	198.82	199.01	199.21	199.40	199.60	199.79	200.00	200.18	200.37	200.56	200.76
230.83	231.05	231.27	231.50	231.73	231.96	232.18	232.41	232.63	232.86	233.09	233.31	233.54	233.77	233.99	234.22
263.80	264.06	264.31	264.58	264.83	265.10	265.35	265.61	265.86	266.13	266.38	266.64	266.90	267.15	267.42	267.68
296.78	297.06	297.35	297.65	297.94	298.23	298.52	298.81	299.10	299.89	299.68	300.00	300.27	300.56	300.84	301.14
329.75	330.07	330.89	330.72	331.04	331.37	331.69	332.01	332.33	332.66	332.98	333.30	333.63	333.95	334.27	334.60

18 Degrees.

18 Degrees.

45	46	47	48	49	50	51	52	53	54	55	56	57	58	59	60
0.34	0.34	0.34	0.34	0.34	0.34	0.34	0.34	0.34	0.34	0.34	0.34	0.34	0.34	0.34	0.34
0.68	0.68	0.68	0.68	0.68	0.68	0.68	0.68	0.68	0.68	0.69	0.9	0.69	0.69	0.69	0.69
1.02	1.02	1.02	1.02	1.02	1.02	1.02	1.03	1.03	1.03	1.03	1.03	1.03	1.03	1.03	1.03
1.36	1.36	1.36	1.36	1.36	1.36	1.37	1.37	1.37	1.37	1.37	1.37	1.37	1.37	1.38	1.38
1.70	1.70	1.70	1.70	1.70	1.71	1.71	1.71	1.71	1.71	1.71	1.72	1.72	1.72	1.72	1.72
2.04	2.04	2.04	2.04	2.04	2.05	2.05	2.05	2.05	2.05	2.06	2.06	2.06	2.06	2.06	2.07
2.38	2.38	2.38	2.38	2.39	2.39	2.39	2.39	2.39	2.40	2.40	2.40	2.40	2.41	2.41	2.41
2.72	2.72	2.72	2.72	2.73	2.73	2.73	2.73	2.74	2.74	2.74	2.74	2.75	2.75	2.75	2.75
3.06	3.06	3.06	3.06	3.07	3.07	3.07	3.08	3.08	3.08	3.08	3.09	3.09	3.09	3.10	3.10
3.39	3.40	3.40	3.40	3.41	3.41	3.41	3.42	3.42	3.42	3.43	3.43	3.43	3.44	3.44	3.44
6.79	6.80	6.80	6.81	6.82	6.82	6.83	6.83	6.84	6.85	6.85	6.86	6.87	6.87	6.88	6.89
10.18	10.19	10.20	10.21	10.22	10.23	10.24	10.25	10.26	10.27	10.28	10.29	10.30	10.31	10.32	10.33
13.58	13.59	13.61	13.62	13.63	13.64	13.66	13.67	13.68	13.69	13.71	13.72	13.73	13.75	13.76	13.77
16.97	16.99	17.01	17.02	17.04	17.05	17.07	17.09	17.10	17.12	17.14	17.15	17.17	17.18	17.20	17.22
20.37	20.39	20.41	20.43	20.45	20.46	20.48	20.50	20.52	20.54	20.56	20.58	20.60	20.62	20.64	20.66
23.76	23.78	23.81	23.83	23.85	23.88	23.90	23.92	23.94	23.97	23.99	24.01	24.03	24.06	24.08	24.10
27.16	27.18	27.21	27.23	27.26	27.29	27.31	27.34	27.36	27.39	27.42	27.44	27.47	27.49	27.52	27.55
30.55	30.58	30.61	30.64	30.67	30.70	30.73	30.76	30.78	30.81	30.84	30.87	30.90	30.98	30.96	30.99
33.95	33.98	34.01	34.04	34.08	34.11	34.14	34.17	34.21	34.24	34.27	34.30	34.34	34.37	34.40	34.48
67.89	67.95	68.02	68.08	68.15	68.22	68.28	68.35	68.41	68.47	68.54	68.61	68.67	68.74	68.80	68.87
101.84	101.93	102.03	102.13	102.23	102.32	102.42	102.52	102.62	102.71	102.81	102.91	103.01	103.10	103.20	103.30
135.78	135.91	136.04	136.17	136.80	136.43	136.56	136.69	136.82	136.95	137.08	137.21	137.34	137.47	137.60	137.73
169.73	169.89	170.05	170.21	170.38	170.54	170.71	170.87	171.03	171.19	171.35	171.52	171.68	171.84	172.00	172.17
203.67	203.86	204.06	204.25	204.45	204.65	204.85	205.04	205.23	205.42	205.62	205.82	206.01	206.21	206.40	206.60
237.62	237.84	238.07	238.29	238.53	238.76	238.99	239.21	239.44	239.66	239.89	240.12	240.35	240.58	240.80	241.03
271.56	271.82	272.08	272.34	272.60	272.86	273.13	273.38	273.64	273.90	274.16	274.42	274.68	274.94	275.20	275.46
305.51	305.79	306.09	306.38	306.68	306.97	307.27	307.56	307.85	308.13	308.43	308.73	309.02	309.31	309.60	309.90
339.45	339.77	340.10	340.42	340.75	341.08	341.41	341.73	342.05	342.37	342.70	343.08	343.35	343.68	344.00	344.33

19 Degrees.

Minutes	0	1	2	3	4	5	6	7	8	9	10	11	12	13	14
Dis. in ft.															
1	0.34	0.34	0.34	0.35	0.35	0.35	0.35	0.35	0.35	0.35	0.35	0.35	0.35	0.35	0.35
2	0.69	0.69	0.69	0.69	0.69	0.69	0.69	0.69	0.69	0.69	0.70	0.70	0.70	0.70	0.70
3	1.03	1.03	1.03	1.04	1.04	1.04	1.04	1.04	1.04	1.04	1.04	1.04	1.04	1.05	1.05
4	1.38	1.38	1.38	1.38	1.38	1.38	1.39	1.39	1.39	1.39	1.39	1.39	1.39	1.39	1.40
5	1.72	1.72	1.72	1.73	1.73	1.73	1.73	1.73	1.73	1.74	1.74	1.74	1.74	1.74	1.74
6	2.07	2.07	2.07	2.07	2.07	2.08	2.08	2.08	2.08	2.08	2.09	2.09	2.09	2.09	2.09
7	2.41	2.41	2.41	2.42	2.42	2.42	2.42	2.43	2.43	2.43	2.43	2.44	2.44	2.44	2.44
8	2.75	2.76	2.76	2.76	2.77	2.77	2.77	2.77	2.78	2.78	2.78	2.78	2.79	2.79	2.79
9	3.10	3.10	3.10	3.11	3.11	3.11	3.12	3.12	3.12	3.13	3.13	3.13	3.13	3.14	3.14
10	3.44	3.45	3.45	3.45	3.46	3.46	3.46	3.47	3.47	3.47	3.48	3.48	3.48	3.49	3.49
20	6.89	6.89	6.90	6.91	6.91	6.92	6.93	6.93	6.94	6.95	6.95	6.96	6.96	6.97	6.98
30	10.33	10.34	10.35	10.36	10.37	10.38	10.39	10.40	10.41	10.42	10.43	10.44	10.45	10.46	10.47
40	13.77	13.79	13.80	13.81	13.83	13.84	13.85	13.86	13.88	13.89	13.90	13.92	13.93	13.94	13.96
50	17.22	17.23	17.25	17.27	17.28	17.30	17.31	17.33	17.35	17.36	17.38	17.40	17.41	17.43	17.44
60	20.66	20.68	20.70	20.72	20.74	20.76	20.78	20.80	20.82	20.84	20.85	20.87	20.89	20.91	20.93
70	24.10	24.13	24.15	24.17	24.19	24.22	24.24	24.26	24.29	24.31	24.33	24.35	24.38	24.40	24.42
80	27.55	27.57	27.60	27.62	27.65	27.68	27.70	27.73	27.76	27.78	27.81	27.83	27.86	27.88	27.91
90	30.99	31.02	31.05	31.08	31.11	31.14	31.17	31.19	31.22	31.25	31.28	31.31	31.34	31.37	31.40
100	34.43	34.47	34.50	34.53	34.56	34.60	34.63	34.66	34.69	34.73	34.76	34.79	34.82	34.86	34.89
200	68.87	68.93	69.00	69.06	69.13	69.19	69.26	69.32	69.39	69.45	69.52	69.58	69.65	69.71	69.78
300	103.30	103.40	103.49	103.59	103.69	103.79	103.88	103.98	104.08	104.18	104.27	104.37	104.47	104.57	104.67
400	137.73	137.86	137.99	138.12	138.25	138.38	138.51	138.64	138.78	138.90	139.03	139.16	139.29	139.42	139.56
500	172.17	172.33	172.49	172.65	172.82	172.98	173.14	173.31	173.47	173.63	173.79	173.96	174.12	174.28	174.45
600	206.60	206.79	206.99	207.18	207.38	207.58	207.77	207.97	208.16	208.36	208.55	208.75	208.94	209.14	209.33
700	241.03	241.26	241.49	241.71	241.94	242.17	242.40	242.63	242.86	243.08	243.31	243.54	243.76	243.99	244.22
800	275.46	275.72	275.98	276.24	276.50	276.77	277.02	277.29	277.55	277.81	278.06	278.33	278.58	278.85	279.11
900	309.90	310.19	310.48	310.77	311.07	311.36	311.65	311.95	312.25	312.53	312.82	313.19	313.41	313.70	314.00
1000	344.33	344.65	344.98	345.30	345.63	345.96	346.28	346.61	346.94	347.26	347.58	347.91	348.23	348.56	348.89

19 Degrees.

Minutes	30	31	32	33	34	35	36	37	38	39	40	41	42	43	44
Dis. in ft.															
1	0.35	0.35	0.35	0.36	0.36	0.36	0.36	0.36	0.36	0.36	0.36	0.36	0.36	0.36	0.36
2	0.71	0.71	0.71	0.71	0.71	0.71	0.71	0.71	0.71	0.71	0.71	0.72	0.72	0.72	0.72
3	1.06	1.06	1.07	1.07	1.07	1.07	1.07	1.07	1.07	1.07	1.07	1.07	1.07	1.08	1.08
4	1.42	1.42	1.42	1.42	1.42	1.42	1.42	1.43	1.43	1.43	1.43	1.43	1.43	1.43	1.43
5	1.77	1.77	1.77	1.78	1.78	1.78	1.78	1.78	1.78	1.79	1.79	1.79	1.79	1.79	1.79
6	2.12	2.13	2.13	2.13	2.13	2.13	2.14	2.14	2.14	2.14	2.14	2.15	2.15	2.15	2.15
7	2.48	2.48	2.48	2.49	2.49	2.49	2.49	2.49	2.50	2.50	2.50	2.50	2.51	2.51	2.51
8	2.83	2.84	2.84	2.84	2.84	2.85	2.85	2.85	2.85	2.86	2.86	2.86	2.86	2.87	2.87
9	3.19	3.19	3.19	3.20	3.20	3.20	3.20	3.21	3.21	3.21	3.21	3.22	3.22	3.22	3.23
10	3.54	3.54	3.55	3.55	3.55	3.56	3.56	3.56	3.57	3.57	3.57	3.58	3.58	3.58	3.59
20	7.08	7.09	7.10	7.10	7.11	7.12	7.12	7.13	7.13	7.14	7.15	7.15	7.16	7.17	7.17
30	10.62	10.63	10.64	10.65	10.66	10.67	10.68	10.69	10.70	10.71	10.72	10.73	10.74	10.75	10.76
40	14.16	14.18	14.19	14.20	14.22	14.23	14.24	14.26	14.27	14.28	14.30	14.31	14.32	14.34	14.35
50	17.71	17.72	17.74	17.76	17.77	17.79	17.80	17.82	17.84	17.85	17.87	17.89	17.90	17.92	17.94
60	21.25	21.27	21.29	21.31	21.33	21.35	21.36	21.38	21.40	21.42	21.44	21.46	21.48	21.50	21.52
70	24.79	24.81	24.83	24.86	24.88	24.90	24.93	24.95	24.97	24.99	25.02	25.04	25.06	25.09	25.11
80	28.33	28.36	28.38	28.41	28.43	28.46	28.49	28.51	28.54	28.57	28.59	28.62	28.64	28.67	28.70
90	31.87	31.90	31.93	31.96	31.99	32.02	32.05	32.08	32.11	32.14	32.17	32.20	32.23	32.25	32.28
100	35.41	35.45	35.48	35.51	35.54	35.58	35.61	35.64	35.67	35.71	35.74	35.77	35.81	35.84	35.87
200	70.82	70.89	70.95	71.02	71.09	71.15	71.22	71.28	71.35	71.41	71.48	71.55	71.61	71.68	71.74
300	106.24	106.34	106.43	106.53	106.63	106.73	106.82	106.92	107.02	107.12	107.22	107.32	107.42	107.51	107.61
400	141.65	141.78	141.91	142.04	142.17	142.30	142.43	142.56	142.70	142.83	142.96	143.09	143.22	143.35	143.48
500	177.06	177.23	177.39	177.55	177.72	177.88	178.04	178.21	178.37	178.54	178.70	178.87	179.03	179.19	179.36
600	212.47	212.67	212.86	213.06	213.26	213.45	213.65	213.85	214.04	214.24	214.44	214.64	214.84	215.03	215.23
700	247.88	248.12	248.34	248.57	248.80	249.03	249.26	249.49	249.72	249.95	250.18	250.41	250.64	250.87	251.10
800	283.30	283.56	283.82	284.08	284.34	284.60	284.86	285.13	285.39	285.65	285.92	286.18	286.45	286.70	286.97
900	318.71	319.01	319.29	319.59	319.89	320.18	320.47	320.77	321.07	321.36	321.66	321.96	322.25	322.54	322.84
1000	354.12	354.45	354.77	355.10	355.43	355.75	356.08	356.41	356.74	357.07	357.40	357.73	358.06	358.38	358.71

19 Degrees.

15	16	17	18	19	20	21	22	23	24	25	26	27	28	29	30
0.35	0.35	0.35	0.35	0.35	0.35	0.35	0.35	0.35	0.35	0.35	0.35	0.35	0.35	0.35	0.35
0.70	0.70	0.70	0.70	0.70	0.70	0.70	0.70	0.70	0.70	0.70	0.71	0.71	0.71	0.71	0.71
1.05	1.05	1.05	1.05	1.05	1.05	1.05	1.05	1.06	1.06	1.06	1.06	1.06	1.06	1.06	1.06
1.40	1.40	1.40	1.40	1.40	1.40	1.40	1.41	1.41	1.41	1.41	1.41	1.41	1.41	1.42	1.42
1.75	1.75	1.75	1.75	1.75	1.75	1.76	1.76	1.76	1.76	1.76	1.76	1.77	1.77	1.77	1.77
2.10	2.10	2.10	2.10	2.10	2.11	2.11	2.11	2.11	2.11	2.11	2.12	2.12	2.12	2.12	2.12
2.44	2.45	2.45	2.45	2.45	2.46	2.46	2.46	2.46	2.47	2.47	2.47	2.47	2.47	2.48	2.48
2.79	2.80	2.80	2.80	2.80	2.81	2.81	2.81	2.81	2.82	2.82	2.82	2.83	2.83	2.83	2.83
3.14	3.15	3.15	3.15	3.15	3.16	3.16	3.16	3.17	3.17	3.17	3.18	3.18	3.18	3.18	3.19
3.49	3.50	3.50	3.50	3.51	3.51	3.51	3.52	3.52	3.52	3.52	3.53	3.53	3.53	3.54	3.54
6.98	6.99	7.00	7.00	7.01	7.02	7.02	7.03	7.04	7.04	7.05	7.06	7.06	7.07	7.08	7.08
10.48	10.49	10.50	10.51	10.52	10.53	10.54	10.55	10.55	10.56	10.57	10.58	10.59	10.60	10.61	10.62
13.97	13.98	13.99	14.01	14.02	14.03	14.05	14.06	14.07	14.09	14.10	14.11	14.13	14.14	14.15	14.16
17.46	17.48	17.49	17.51	17.53	17.54	17.56	17.58	17.59	17.61	17.62	17.64	17.66	17.67	17.69	17.71
20.95	20.97	20.99	21.01	21.03	21.05	21.07	21.09	21.11	21.13	21.15	21.17	21.19	21.21	21.23	21.25
24.44	24.47	24.49	24.51	24.54	24.56	24.58	24.61	24.63	24.65	24.67	24.70	24.72	24.74	24.77	24.79
27.94	27.96	27.99	28.02	28.04	28.07	28.09	28.12	28.15	28.17	28.20	28.22	28.25	28.28	28.30	28.33
31.43	31.46	31.48	31.52	31.55	31.58	31.61	31.64	31.66	31.69	31.72	31.75	31.78	31.81	31.84	31.87
34.92	34.95	34.99	35.02	35.05	35.09	35.12	35.15	35.18	35.22	35.25	35.28	35.31	35.35	35.38	35.41
69.84	69.91	69.97	70.04	70.10	70.17	70.23	70.30	70.37	70.43	70.50	70.56	70.63	70.69	70.76	70.82
104.76	104.86	104.96	105.06	105.16	105.26	105.35	105.45	105.55	105.65	105.74	105.84	105.94	106.04	106.14	106.24
139.68	139.82	139.95	140.09	140.21	140.34	140.47	140.60	140.73	140.86	140.99	141.12	141.25	141.38	141.52	141.65
174.61	174.77	174.94	175.10	175.26	175.43	175.59	175.75	175.92	176.08	176.24	176.41	176.57	176.73	176.90	177.06
209.53	209.72	209.92	210.12	210.31	210.51	210.70	210.90	211.10	211.29	211.49	211.69	211.89	212.08	212.27	212.47
244.45	244.68	244.91	245.14	245.36	245.60	245.82	246.05	246.28	246.51	246.74	246.97	247.19	247.42	247.65	247.88
279.37	279.63	279.90	280.16	280.42	280.68	280.94	281.20	281.46	281.72	281.98	282.25	282.50	282.77	283.03	283.30
314.29	314.59	314.88	315.18	315.47	315.77	316.05	316.35	316.65	316.94	317.23	317.53	317.82	318.11	318.41	318.71
349.21	349.54	349.87	350.20	350.52	350.85	351.17	351.50	351.83	352.15	352.48	352.81	353.13	353.46	353.79	354.12

19 Degrees.

45	46	47	48	49	50	51	52	53	54	55	56	57	58	59	60
0.36	0.36	0.36	0.36	0.36	0.36	0.36	0.36	0.36	0.36	0.36	0.36	0.36	0.36	0.36	0.36
0.72	0.72	0.72	0.72	0.72	0.72	0.72	0.72	0.72	0.72	0.72	0.72	0.73	0.73	0.73	0.73
1.08	1.08	1.08	1.08	1.08	1.08	1.08	1.08	1.09	1.09	1.09	1.09	1.09	1.09	1.09	1.09
1.44	1.44	1.44	1.44	1.44	1.44	1.44	1.45	1.45	1.45	1.45	1.45	1.45	1.45	1.45	1.46
1.80	1.80	1.80	1.80	1.80	1.80	1.81	1.81	1.81	1.81	1.81	1.81	1.81	1.82	1.82	1.82
2.15	2.16	2.16	2.16	2.16	2.16	2.17	2.17	2.17	2.17	2.17	2.18	2.18	2.18	2.18	2.18
2.51	2.52	2.52	2.52	2.52	2.52	2.53	2.53	2.53	2.53	2.54	2.54	2.54	2.54	2.55	2.55
2.87	2.87	2.88	2.88	2.88	2.89	2.89	2.89	2.89	2.90	2.90	2.90	2.90	2.91	2.91	2.91
3.23	3.23	3.24	3.24	3.24	3.25	3.25	3.25	3.26	3.26	3.26	3.26	3.27	3.27	3.27	3.28
3.59	3.59	3.60	3.60	3.60	3.61	3.61	3.61	3.62	3.62	3.62	3.62	3.63	3.63	3.64	3.64
7.18	7.19	7.20	7.20	7.21	7.21	7.22	7.23	7.23	7.24	7.24	7.25	7.26	7.27	7.27	7.28
10.77	10.78	10.79	10.80	10.81	10.82	10.83	10.84	10.85	10.86	10.87	10.88	10.89	10.90	10.91	10.92
14.36	14.37	14.39	14.40	14.41	14.43	14.44	14.45	14.47	14.48	14.49	14.51	14.52	14.53	14.55	14.56
17.95	17.97	17.98	18.00	18.02	18.03	18.05	18.07	18.08	18.10	18.12	18.13	18.15	18.17	18.18	18.20
21.54	21.56	21.58	21.60	21.62	21.64	21.66	21.68	21.70	21.72	21.74	21.76	21.78	21.80	21.82	21.84
25.13	25.16	25.18	25.20	25.22	25.25	25.27	25.29	25.32	25.34	25.36	25.39	25.41	25.43	25.45	25.48
28.72	28.75	28.78	28.80	28.83	28.85	28.88	28.91	28.93	28.96	28.99	29.01	29.04	29.07	29.09	29.12
32.31	32.34	32.37	32.40	32.43	32.46	32.49	32.52	32.55	32.58	32.61	32.64	32.67	32.70	32.73	32.76
35.90	35.94	35.97	36.00	36.04	36.07	36.10	36.13	36.17	36.20	36.23	36.27	36.30	36.33	36.36	36.40
71.81	71.87	71.94	72.00	72.07	72.14	72.20	72.27	72.33	72.40	72.46	72.53	72.60	72.66	72.73	72.79
107.71	107.81	107.91	108.01	108.11	108.20	108.30	108.40	108.50	108.60	108.70	108.80	108.90	109.00	109.09	109.19
143.62	143.75	143.88	144.01	144.14	144.27	144.40	144.54	144.67	144.80	144.93	145.06	145.20	145.33	145.46	145.59
179.52	179.69	179.85	180.01	180.18	180.34	180.51	180.67	180.84	181.00	181.16	181.33	181.50	181.66	181.82	181.99
215.42	215.62	215.81	216.01	216.21	216.41	216.61	216.80	217.00	217.19	217.39	217.59	217.79	217.99	218.18	218.38
251.33	251.56	251.78	252.01	252.25	252.48	252.71	252.94	253.17	253.39	253.62	253.86	254.09	254.32	254.55	254.78
287.23	287.50	287.75	288.02	288.28	288.54	288.81	289.07	289.34	289.59	289.86	290.12	290.39	290.66	290.91	291.18
323.14	323.43	323.72	324.02	324.32	324.61	324.91	325.21	325.50	325.79	326.09	326.39	326.69	326.99	327.28	327.57
359.04	359.37	359.69	360.02	360.35	360.68	361.01	361.34	361.67	361.99	362.32	362.65	362.99	363.32	363.64	363.97

20 Degrees.

Minutes	0	1	2	3	4	5	6	7	8	9	10	11	12	13	14
Dis. in ft.															
1	0.36	0.36	0.36	0.36	0.37	0.37	0.37	0.37	0.37	0.37	0.37	0.37	0.37	0.37	0.37
2	0.73	0.73	0.73	0.73	0.73	0.73	0.73	0.73	0.73	0.73	0.74	0.74	0.74	0.74	0.74
3	1.09	1.09	1.09	1.09	1.10	1.10	1.10	1.10	1.10	1.10	1.10	1.10	1.10	1.10	1.11
4	1.46	1.46	1.46	1.46	1.46	1.46	1.47	1.47	1.47	1.47	1.47	1.47	1.47	1.47	1.47
5	1.82	1.82	1.82	1.82	1.83	1.83	1.83	1.83	1.83	1.83	1.84	1.84	1.84	1.84	1.84
6	2.18	2.19	2.19	2.19	2.19	2.19	2.20	2.20	2.20	2.20	2.20	2.21	2.21	2.21	2.21
7	2.55	2.55	2.55	2.55	2.56	2.56	2.56	2.56	2.57	2.57	2.57	2.57	2.58	2.58	2.58
8	2.91	2.91	2.92	2.92	2.92	2.92	2.93	2.93	2.93	2.94	2.94	2.94	2.94	2.95	2.95
9	3.28	3.28	3.28	3.28	3.29	3.29	3.29	3.30	3.30	3.30	3.31	3.31	3.31	3.31	3.32
10	3.64	3.64	3.65	3.65	3.65	3.66	3.66	3.66	3.67	3.67	3.67	3.68	3.68	3.68	3.69
20	7.28	7.29	7.29	7.30	7.31	7.31	7.32	7.33	7.33	7.34	7.35	7.85	7.36	7.37	7.37
30	10.92	10.93	10.94	10.95	10.96	10.97	10.98	10.99	11.00	11.01	11.02	11.03	11.04	11.05	11.06
40	14.56	14.57	14.59	14.60	14.61	14.62	14.64	14.65	14.66	14.68	14.69	14.70	14.72	14.73	14.74
50	18.20	18.22	18.23	18.25	18.26	18.28	18.30	18.31	18.33	18.35	18.36	18.38	18.40	18.41	18.43
60	21.84	21.86	21.88	21.90	21.92	21.94	21.96	21.98	22.00	22.02	22.04	22.06	22.08	22.10	22.12
70	25.48	25.50	25.52	25.55	25.57	25.59	25.62	25.64	25.66	25.69	25.71	25.73	25.76	25.78	25.80
80	29.12	29.14	29.17	29.20	29.22	29.25	29.28	29.30	29.33	29.36	29.38	29.41	29.43	29.46	29.49
90	32.76	32.79	32.82	32.85	32.88	32.91	32.94	32.97	33.00	33.02	33.05	33.08	33.11	33.14	33.17
100	36.40	36.43	36.46	36.50	36.53	36.56	36.60	36.63	36.66	36.69	36.73	36.76	36.79	36.83	36.86
200	72.79	72.86	72.93	72.99	73.06	73.12	73.19	73.26	73.32	73.39	73.45	73.52	73.59	73.65	73.72
300	109.19	109.29	109.39	109.49	109.59	109.69	109.79	109.88	109.98	110.08	110.18	110.28	110.38	110.48	110.58
400	145.59	145.72	145.85	145.98	146.12	146.25	146.38	146.51	146.64	146.78	146.91	147.04	147.17	147.30	147.44
500	181.99	182.15	182.32	182.48	182.65	182.81	182.98	183.14	183.30	183.47	183.64	183.80	183.97	184.13	184.30
600	218.38	218.58	218.78	218.98	219.17	219.37	219.57	219.77	219.97	220.16	220.36	220.56	220.76	220.96	221.15
700	254.78	255.01	255.24	255.47	255.70	255.93	256.17	256.40	256.63	256.86	257.09	257.32	257.55	257.78	258.01
800	291.18	291.44	291.70	291.97	292.23	292.50	292.76	293.02	293.29	293.55	293.82	294.08	294.34	294.61	294.87
900	327.57	327.87	328.17	328.46	328.76	329.06	329.36	329.65	329.95	330.25	330.54	330.84	331.14	331.43	331.73
1000	363.97	364.30	364.63	364.96	365.29	365.62	365.95	366.28	366.61	366.94	367.27	367.60	367.93	368.26	368.59

20 Degrees.

Minutes	30	31	32	33	34	35	36	37	38	39	40	41	42	43	44
Dis. in ft.															
1	0.37	0.37	0.37	0.37	0.37	0.38	0.38	0.38	0.38	0.38	0.38	0.38	0.38	0.38	0.38
2	0.75	0.75	0.75	0.75	0.75	0.75	0.75	0.75	0.75	0.75	0.75	0.76	0.76	0.76	0.76
3	1.12	1.12	1.12	1.12	1.13	1.13	1.13	1.13	1.13	1.13	1.13	1.13	1.13	1.13	1.14
4	1.50	1.50	1.50	1.50	1.50	1.50	1.50	1.50	1.51	1.51	1.51	1.51	1.51	1.51	1.51
5	1.87	1.87	1.87	1.87	1.88	1.88	1.88	1.88	1.88	1.88	1.89	1.89	1.89	1.89	1.89
6	2.24	2.25	2.25	2.25	2.25	2.26	2.26	2.26	2.26	2.26	2.26	2.27	2.27	2.27	2.27
7	2.62	2.62	2.62	2.62	2.63	2.63	2.63	2.63	2.64	2.64	2.64	2.64	2.65	2.65	2.65
8	2.99	2.99	3.00	3.00	3.00	3.00	3.01	3.01	3.01	3.01	3.02	3.02	3.02	3.03	3.03
9	3.37	3.37	3.37	3.37	3.38	3.38	3.38	3.38	3.39	3.39	3.39	3.40	3.40	3.40	3.41
10	3.74	3.71	3.75	3.75	3.75	3.75	3.76	3.76	3.77	3.77	3.77	3.78	3.78	3.78	3.79
20	7.48	7.48	7.49	7.50	7.50	7.51	7.52	7.52	7.53	7.54	7.54	7.55	7.56	7.56	7.57
30	11.22	11.23	11.24	11.25	11.26	11.27	11.28	11.29	11.30	11.31	11.31	11.32	11.33	11.34	11.35
40	14.96	14.97	14.98	15.00	15.01	15.02	15.03	15.05	15.06	15.07	15.09	15.10	15.11	15.13	15.14
50	18.69	18.71	18.73	18.74	18.76	18.78	18.79	18.81	18.83	18.84	18.86	18.88	18.89	18.91	18.93
60	22.43	22.45	22.47	22.49	22.51	22.53	22.55	22.57	22.59	22.61	22.63	22.65	22.67	22.69	22.71
70	26.17	26.20	26.22	26.24	26.26	26.29	26.31	26.33	26.36	26.38	26.40	26.43	26.45	26.47	26.50
80	29.91	29.94	29.96	29.99	30.02	30.04	30.07	30.10	30.12	30.15	30.18	30.20	30.23	30.26	30.28
90	33.65	33.68	33.71	33.74	33.77	33.80	33.83	33.86	33.89	33.92	33.95	33.98	34.01	34.04	34.07
100	37.39	37.42	37.46	37.49	37.52	37.55	37.59	37.62	37.65	37.69	37.72	37.75	37.79	37.82	37.85
200	74.78	74.81	74.91	74.98	75.04	75.11	75.17	75.24	75.31	75.37	75.44	75.51	75.57	75.64	75.71
300	112.17	112.27	112.37	112.46	112.56	112.66	112.76	112.86	112.96	113.06	113.16	113.26	113.36	113.46	113.56
400	149.56	149.69	149.82	149.95	150.08	150.22	150.35	150.48	150.62	150.75	150.88	151.02	151.15	151.28	151.41
500	186.95	187.11	187.28	187.44	187.61	187.77	187.94	188.11	188.27	188.44	188.61	188.77	188.94	189.10	189.27
600	221.33	224.53	224.73	224.98	225.13	225.32	225.52	225.73	225.92	226.12	226.33	226.52	226.72	226.92	227.12
700	261.72	261.95	262.19	262.42	262.65	262.88	263.11	263.35	263.58	263.81	264.05	264.28	264.51	264.74	264.97
800	299.11	299.38	299.64	299.90	300.17	300.43	300.70	300.97	301.23	301.50	301.77	302.03	302.30	302.56	302.82
900	336.50	336.80	337.10	337.39	337.69	337.99	338.28	338.59	338.80	339.18	339.49	339.79	340.08	340.38	340.68
1000	373.89	374.22	374.55	374.88	375.21	375.54	375.87	376.21	376.54	376.87	377.21	377.54	377.87	378.20	378.53

20 Degrees.

15	16	17	18	19	20	21	22	23	24	25	26	27	28	29	30
0.37	0.37	0.37	0.37	0.37	0.37	0.37	0.37	0.37	0.37	0.37	0.37	0.37	0.37	0.37	0.37
0.74	0.74	0.74	0.74	0.74	0.74	0.74	0.74	0.74	0.74	0.74	0.74	0.75	0.75	0.75	0.75
1.11	1.11	1.11	1.11	1.11	1.11	1.11	1.11	1.11	1.12	1.12	1.12	1.12	1.12	1.12	1.12
1.48	1.48	1.48	1.48	1.48	1.48	1.48	1.48	1.49	1.49	1.49	1.49	1.49	1.49	1.49	1.50
1.84	1.85	1.85	1.85	1.85	1.85	1.85	1.86	1.86	1.86	1.86	1.86	1.86	1.87	1.87	1.87
2.21	2.22	2.22	2.22	2.22	2.22	2.23	2.23	2.23	2.23	2.23	2.24	2.24	2.24	2.24	2.24
2.58	2.58	2.59	2.59	2.59	2.59	2.60	2.60	2.60	2.60	2.61	2.61	2.61	2.61	2.61	2.62
2.95	2.95	2.96	2.96	2.96	2.96	2.97	2.97	2.97	2.98	2.98	2.98	2.98	2.99	2.99	2.99
3.32	3.32	3.33	3.33	3.33	3.34	3.34	3.34	3.34	3.35	3.35	3.35	3.35	3.36	3.36	3.37
3.69	3.69	3.70	3.70	3.70	3.71	3.71	3.71	3.72	3.72	3.72	3.72	3.72	3.73	3.73	3.74
7.38	7.39	7.39	7.40	7.40	7.41	7.42	7.42	7.43	7.44	7.44	7.45	7.46	7.46	7.47	7.48
11.07	11.08	11.09	11.10	11.11	11.12	11.13	11.14	11.15	11.16	11.17	11.18	11.19	11.20	11.21	11.22
14.76	14.77	14.78	14.80	14.81	14.82	14.84	14.85	14.86	14.88	14.89	14.90	14.92	14.93	14.94	14.96
18.45	18.46	18.48	18.50	18.51	18.53	18.55	18.56	18.58	18.60	18.61	18.63	18.64	18.66	18.67	18.69
22.14	22.16	22.17	22.19	22.21	22.23	22.25	22.27	22.29	22.31	22.33	22.35	22.37	22.39	22.41	22.43
25.82	25.85	25.87	25.89	25.92	25.94	25.96	25.99	26.01	26.03	26.06	26.08	26.10	26.13	26.15	26.17
29.51	29.54	29.57	29.59	29.62	29.65	29.67	29.70	29.73	29.75	29.78	29.80	29.83	29.86	29.88	29.91
33.20	33.23	33.26	33.29	33.32	33.35	33.38	33.41	33.44	33.47	33.50	33.53	33.56	33.59	33.62	33.65
36.89	36.93	36.96	36.99	37.02	37.06	37.09	37.12	37.16	37.19	37.22	37.26	37.29	37.32	37.36	37.39
73.78	73.85	73.92	73.98	74.05	74.11	74.18	74.25	74.31	74.38	74.45	74.51	74.58	74.64	74.71	74.78
110.68	110.78	110.87	110.97	111.07	111.17	111.27	111.37	111.47	111.57	111.67	111.77	111.87	111.97	112.07	112.17
147.57	147.70	147.83	147.96	148.10	148.23	148.36	148.50	148.63	148.76	148.89	149.03	149.16	149.29	149.42	149.56
184.46	184.63	184.79	184.96	185.12	185.29	185.45	185.62	185.79	185.95	186.12	186.28	186.45	186.61	186.78	186.95
221.35	221.55	221.75	221.95	222.14	222.34	222.54	222.74	222.94	223.14	223.34	223.54	223.73	223.93	224.13	224.33
258.24	258.48	258.71	258.94	259.17	259.40	259.63	259.87	260.10	260.33	260.56	260.79	261.02	261.25	261.49	261.72
295.14	295.40	295.66	295.92	296.19	296.46	296.72	296.99	297.26	297.52	297.78	298.05	298.31	298.58	298.84	299.11
332.03	332.33	332.62	332.92	333.22	333.51	333.81	334.11	334.41	334.71	335.01	335.30	335.60	335.90	336.20	336.50
368.92	369.25	369.58	369.91	370.24	370.57	370.90	371.24	371.57	371.90	372.23	372.56	372.89	373.22	373.55	373.89

20 Degrees.

45	46	47	48	49	50	51	52	53	54	55	56	57	58	59	60
0.38	0.38	0.38	0.38	0.38	0.38	0.38	0.38	0.38	0.38	0.38	0.38	0.38	0.38	0.38	0.38
0.76	0.76	0.76	0.76	0.76	0.76	0.76	0.76	0.76	0.76	0.76	0.77	0.77	0.77	0.77	0.77
1.14	1.14	1.14	1.14	1.14	1.14	1.14	1.14	1.14	1.15	1.15	1.15	1.15	1.15	1.15	1.15
1.51	1.52	1.52	1.52	1.52	1.52	1.52	1.52	1.53	1.53	1.53	1.53	1.53	1.53	1.53	1.54
1.89	1.90	1.90	1.90	1.90	1.90	1.90	1.91	1.91	1.91	1.91	1.91	1.91	1.92	1.92	1.92
2.27	2.28	2.28	2.28	2.28	2.28	2.29	2.29	2.29	2.29	2.29	2.29	2.30	2.30	2.30	2.30
2.65	2.65	2.66	2.66	2.66	2.66	2.67	2.67	2.67	2.67	2.68	2.68	2.68	2.68	2.68	2.69
3.03	3.03	3.04	3.04	3.04	3.04	3.05	3.05	3.05	3.05	3.06	3.06	3.06	3.07	3.07	3.07
3.41	3.41	3.42	3.42	3.42	3.42	3.43	3.43	3.43	3.44	3.44	3.44	3.45	3.45	3.45	3.45
3.79	3.79	3.80	3.80	3.80	3.81	3.81	3.81	3.82	3.82	3.82	3.83	3.83	3.83	3.84	3.84
7.58	7.58	7.59	7.60	7.60	7.61	7.61	7.62	7.62	7.63	7.64	7.65	7.66	7.66	7.67	7.68
11.37	11.38	11.39	11.40	11.41	11.42	11.43	11.44	11.45	11.46	11.47	11.48	11.49	11.50	11.51	11.52
15.15	15.17	15.18	15.19	15.21	15.22	15.24	15.25	15.26	15.27	15.29	15.30	15.31	15.33	15.34	15.35
18.94	18.96	18.98	18.99	19.01	19.03	19.04	19.06	19.08	19.09	19.11	19.13	19.14	19.16	19.18	19.19
22.73	22.75	22.77	22.79	22.81	22.83	22.85	22.87	22.89	22.91	22.93	22.95	22.97	22.99	23.01	23.03
26.52	26.54	26.57	26.59	26.61	26.64	26.66	26.68	26.71	26.73	26.75	26.78	26.80	26.82	26.85	26.87
30.31	30.34	30.36	30.39	30.42	30.44	30.47	30.50	30.52	30.55	30.58	30.60	30.63	30.66	30.68	30.71
34.10	34.13	34.16	34.19	34.22	34.25	34.28	34.31	34.34	34.37	34.40	34.43	34.46	34.49	34.52	34.55
37.89	37.92	37.95	37.99	38.02	38.05	38.09	38.12	38.15	38.19	38.22	38.25	38.29	38.32	38.35	38.39
75.77	75.84	75.91	75.97	76.04	76.11	76.17	76.24	76.31	76.37	76.44	76.51	76.57	76.64	76.71	76.77
113.66	113.76	113.86	113.96	114.06	114.16	114.26	114.36	114.46	114.56	114.66	114.76	114.86	114.96	115.06	115.16
151.55	151.68	151.81	151.95	152.08	152.21	152.34	152.48	152.61	152.75	152.88	153.01	153.14	153.28	153.41	153.55
189.44	189.60	189.77	189.94	190.10	190.27	190.43	190.60	190.77	190.94	191.10	191.27	191.41	191.60	191.77	191.94
227.33	227.52	227.72	227.92	228.12	228.32	228.52	228.72	228.92	229.12	229.32	229.52	229.72	229.92	230.12	230.32
265.21	265.44	265.67	265.91	266.14	266.37	266.60	266.84	267.07	267.31	267.54	267.77	268.00	268.24	268.47	268.71
303.10	303.36	303.62	303.90	304.16	304.42	304.69	304.96	305.22	305.50	305.76	306.02	306.29	306.56	306.82	307.10
340.98	341.28	341.58	341.88	342.18	342.48	342.77	343.08	343.38	343.68	343.98	344.28	344.57	344.88	345.18	345.48
378.87	379.20	379.53	379.87	380.20	380.53	380.86	381.20	381.53	381.87	382.20	382.53	382.86	383.20	383.53	383.87

21 Degrees.

Minutes	0	1	2	3	4	5	6	7	8	9	10	11	12	13	14
Dis. in ft.															
1	0.38	0.38	0.38	0.38	0.38	0.38	0.39	0.39	0.39	0.39	0.39	0.39	0.39	0.39	0.39
2	0.77	0.77	0.77	0.77	0.77	0.77	0.77	0.77	0.77	0.77	0.77	0.78	0.78	0.78	0.78
3	1.15	1.15	1.15	1.15	1.16	1.16	1.16	1.16	1.16	1.16	1.16	1.16	1.16	1.16	1.17
4	1.54	1.54	1.54	1.54	1.54	1.54	1.54	1.54	1.55	1.55	1.55	1.55	1.55	1.55	1.55
5	1.92	1.92	1.92	1.92	1.93	1.93	1.93	1.93	1.93	1.93	1.94	1.94	1.94	1.94	1.94
6	2.30	2.31	2.31	2.31	2.31	2.31	2.32	2.32	2.32	2.32	2.32	2.33	2.33	2.33	2.33
7	2.69	2.69	2.69	2.69	2.70	2.70	2.70	2.70	2.71	2.71	2.71	2.71	2.72	2.72	2.72
8	3.07	3.07	3.08	3.08	3.08	3.08	3.09	3.09	3.09	3.09	3.10	3.10	3.10	3.11	3.11
9	3.45	3.46	3.46	3.46	3.47	3.47	3.47	3.48	3.48	3.48	3.48	3.49	3.49	3.49	3.50
10	3.84	3.84	3.85	3.85	3.85	3.86	3.86	3.86	3.87	3.87	3.87	3.88	3.88	3.88	3.89
20	7.68	7.68	7.69	7.70	7.70	7.71	7.72	7.72	7.73	7.74	7.74	7.75	7.76	7.76	7.77
30	11.52	11.53	11.54	11.55	11.56	11.57	11.58	11.59	11.60	11.61	11.62	11.63	11.64	11.65	11.66
40	15.35	15.37	15.38	15.39	15.41	15.42	15.43	15.45	15.46	15.47	15.47	15.49	15.50	15.51	15.54
50	19.19	19.21	19.23	19.24	19.26	19.28	19.29	19.31	19.33	19.34	19.36	19.38	19.39	19.41	19.43
60	23.03	23.05	23.07	23.09	23.11	23.13	23.15	23.17	23.19	23.21	23.23	23.25	23.27	23.29	23.31
70	26.87	26.89	26.92	26.94	26.96	26.99	27.01	27.03	27.06	27.08	27.10	27.13	27.15	27.17	27.20
80	30.71	30.74	30.76	30.79	30.82	30.84	30.87	30.90	30.92	30.95	30.98	31.00	31.03	31.06	31.08
90	34.55	34.58	34.61	34.64	34.67	34.70	34.73	34.76	34.79	34.82	34.85	34.88	34.91	34.94	34.97
100	38.39	38.42	38.45	38.49	38.52	38.55	38.59	38.62	38.65	38.69	38.72	38.75	38.79	38.82	38.85
200	76.77	76.84	76.91	76.97	77.04	77.11	77.17	77.24	77.31	77.37	77.44	77.51	77.57	77.64	77.71
300	115.16	115.26	115.36	115.46	115.56	115.66	115.76	115.86	115.96	116.06	116.16	116.26	116.36	116.46	116.56
400	153.55	153.68	153.81	153.95	154.08	154.21	154.35	154.48	154.61	154.75	154.88	155.02	155.15	155.28	155.42
500	191.94	192.10	192.27	192.44	192.60	192.77	192.94	193.10	193.27	193.44	193.60	193.77	193.94	194.11	194.27
600	230.32	230.52	230.72	230.92	231.12	231.32	231.52	231.72	231.92	232.12	232.32	232.52	232.72	232.93	233.12
700	268.71	268.94	269.17	269.41	269.64	269.87	270.10	270.34	270.57	270.81	271.04	271.28	271.51	271.75	271.98
800	307.10	307.36	307.62	307.90	308.16	308.42	308.70	308.96	309.22	309.50	309.76	310.03	310.30	310.57	310.83
900	345.48	345.78	346.08	346.38	346.68	346.98	347.28	347.58	347.88	348.18	348.48	348.79	349.09	349.39	349.69
1000	383.87	384.20	384.53	384.87	385.20	385.53	385.87	386.20	386.53	386.87	387.20	387.54	387.87	388.21	388.54

21 Degrees.

Minutes	30	31	32	33	34	35	36	37	38	39	40	41	42	43	44
Dis. in ft.															
1	0.39	0.39	0.39	0.39	0.40	0.40	0.40	0.40	0.40	0.40	0.40	0.40	0.40	0.40	0.40
2	0.79	0.79	0.79	0.79	0.79	0.79	0.79	0.79	0.79	0.79	0.79	0.80	0.80	0.80	0.80
3	1.18	1.18	1.18	1.18	1.19	1.19	1.19	1.19	1.19	1.19	1.19	1.19	1.19	1.19	1.20
4	1.58	1.58	1.58	1.58	1.58	1.58	1.58	1.59	1.59	1.59	1.59	1.59	1.59	1.59	1.59
5	1.97	1.97	1.97	1.97	1.98	1.98	1.98	1.98	1.98	1.98	1.99	1.99	1.99	1.99	1.99
6	2.36	2.37	2.37	2.37	2.37	2.37	2.38	2.38	2.38	2.38	2.38	2.39	2.39	2.39	2.39
7	2.76	2.76	2.76	2.76	2.77	2.77	2.77	2.77	2.78	2.78	2.78	2.78	2.79	2.79	2.79
8	3.15	3.15	3.16	3.16	3.16	3.16	3.17	3.17	3.17	3.18	3.18	3.18	3.18	3.19	3.19
9	3.55	3.55	3.55	3.55	3.56	3.56	3.56	3.56	3.57	3.57	3.57	3.58	3.58	3.58	3.59
10	3.94	3.94	3.95	3.95	3.95	3.96	3.96	3.96	3.97	3.97	3.97	3.98	3.98	3.98	3.99
20	7.88	7.89	7.89	7.90	7.91	7.91	7.92	7.93	7.93	7.94	7.95	7.95	7.96	7.97	7.97
30	11.82	11.83	11.84	11.85	11.86	11.87	11.89	11.89	11.90	11.91	11.92	11.93	11.94	11.95	11.96
40	15.76	15.77	15.78	15.80	15.81	15.82	15.84	15.85	15.86	15.88	15.89	15.90	15.92	15.93	15.94
50	19.70	19.71	19.73	19.74	19.76	19.78	19.80	19.81	19.83	19.85	19.86	19.88	19.90	19.91	19.93
60	23.63	23.66	23.67	23.70	23.72	23.74	23.76	23.78	23.80	23.82	23.84	23.86	23.88	23.90	23.92
70	27.57	27.60	27.62	27.64	27.67	27.69	27.72	27.74	27.76	27.79	27.81	27.83	27.86	27.88	27.90
80	31.51	31.54	31.57	31.59	31.62	31.65	31.67	31.70	31.73	31.76	31.78	31.81	31.84	31.86	31.89
90	35.45	35.48	35.51	35.54	35.57	35.60	35.63	35.66	35.69	35.72	35.75	35.78	35.82	35.85	35.88
100	39.39	39.43	39.46	39.49	39.53	39.56	39.59	39.63	39.66	39.69	39.73	39.76	39.80	39.83	39.86
200	78.78	78.85	78.92	78.98	79.05	79.12	79.19	79.25	79.32	79.39	79.45	79.52	79.59	79.66	79.72
300	118.17	118.28	118.37	118.48	118.58	118.68	118.78	118.88	118.98	119.08	119.18	119.28	119.39	119.49	119.59
400	157.56	157.70	157.83	157.97	158.10	158.24	158.37	158.51	158.64	158.78	158.91	159.04	159.18	159.32	159.45
500	196.96	197.13	197.29	197.46	197.63	197.80	197.97	198.14	198.30	198.47	198.64	198.81	198.98	199.15	199.31
600	236.35	236.55	236.75	236.95	237.15	237.35	237.56	237.76	237.96	238.16	238.36	238.57	238.77	238.97	239.17
700	275.74	275.98	276.21	276.44	276.68	276.91	277.15	277.39	277.62	277.86	278.09	278.33	278.57	278.80	279.03
800	315.13	315.40	315.66	315.91	316.20	316.47	316.74	317.02	317.28	317.55	317.82	318.09	318.36	318.63	318.90
900	354.52	354.83	355.12	355.43	355.73	356.03	356.34	356.64	356.94	357.25	357.54	357.85	358.16	358.46	358.76
1000	393.91	394.25	394.58	394.92	395.25	395.59	395.93	396.27	396.60	396.94	397.27	397.61	397.95	398.29	398.62

21 Degrees.

15	16	17	18	19	20	21	22	23	24	25	26	27	28	29	30
0.39	0.39	0.39	0.39	0.39	0.39	0.39	0.39	0.39	0.39	0.39	0.39	0.39	0.39	0.39	0.39
0.78	0.78	0.78	0.78	0.78	0.78	0.78	0.78	0.78	0.78	0.78	0.78	0.79	0.79	0.79	0.79
1.17	1.17	1.17	1.17	1.17	1.17	1.17	1.17	1.17	1.18	1.18	1.18	1.18	1.18	1.18	1.18
1.56	1.56	1.56	1.56	1.56	1.56	1.56	1.56	1.57	1.57	1.57	1.57	1.57	1.57	1.57	1.58
1.94	1.95	1.95	1.95	1.95	1.95	1.95	1.96	1.96	1.96	1.96	1.96	1.96	1.97	1.97	1.97
2.33	2.34	2.34	2.34	2.34	2.34	2.35	2.35	2.35	2.35	2.35	2.36	2.36	2.36	2.36	2.36
2.72	2.72	2.73	2.73	2.73	2.73	2.74	2.74	2.74	2.74	2.75	2.75	2.75	2.75	2.75	2.76
3.11	3.11	3.12	3.12	3.12	3.12	3.13	3.13	3.13	3.14	3.14	3.14	3.14	3.15	3.15	3.15
3.50	3.50	3.51	3.51	3.51	3.52	3.52	3.52	3.52	3.53	3.53	3.53	3.53	3.54	3.54	3.55
3.89	3.89	3.90	3.90	3.90	3.91	3.91	3.91	3.92	3.92	3.92	3.93	3.93	3.93	3.94	3.94
7.78	7.78	7.79	7.80	7.80	7.81	7.82	7.82	7.83	7.84	7.84	7.85	7.86	7.86	7.87	7.88
11.67	11.68	11.69	11.70	11.71	11.72	11.73	11.74	11.75	11.76	11.77	11.78	11.79	11.80	11.81	11.82
15.56	15.57	15.58	15.60	15.61	15.62	15.64	15.65	15.66	15.68	15.69	15.70	15.72	15.73	15.74	15.76
19.44	19.46	19.48	19.49	19.51	19.53	19.55	19.56	19.58	19.60	19.61	19.63	19.65	19.66	19.68	19.70
23.33	23.35	23.37	23.39	23.41	23.43	23.45	23.47	23.49	23.51	23.53	23.55	23.57	23.59	23.61	23.63
27.22	27.25	27.27	27.29	27.32	27.34	27.36	27.39	27.41	27.43	27.46	27.48	27.50	27.53	27.55	27.57
31.11	31.14	31.16	31.19	31.22	31.24	31.27	31.30	31.33	31.35	31.38	31.41	31.43	31.46	31.49	31.51
35.00	35.03	35.06	35.09	35.12	35.15	35.18	35.21	35.24	35.27	35.30	35.33	35.36	35.39	35.42	35.45
38.89	38.92	38.96	38.99	39.02	39.06	39.09	39.12	39.16	39.19	39.22	39.26	39.29	39.32	39.36	39.39
77.78	77.84	77.91	77.98	78.04	78.11	78.18	78.25	78.31	78.38	78.45	78.51	78.58	78.65	78.71	78.78
116.66	116.77	116.87	116.97	117.07	117.17	117.27	117.37	117.47	117.57	117.67	117.77	117.87	117.97	118.07	118.17
155.55	155.69	155.82	155.96	156.09	156.22	156.36	156.49	156.63	156.76	156.89	157.03	157.16	157.30	157.43	157.56
194.44	194.61	194.78	194.95	195.11	195.28	195.45	195.62	195.79	195.95	196.12	196.29	196.45	196.62	196.79	196.96
233.33	233.53	233.74	233.93	234.14	234.34	234.54	234.74	234.94	235.14	235.34	235.54	235.74	235.93	236.14	236.35
272.22	272.45	272.69	272.92	273.15	273.39	273.63	273.86	274.10	274.33	274.56	274.80	275.03	275.27	275.50	275.74
311.10	311.38	311.65	311.91	312.18	312.45	312.72	312.99	313.26	313.52	313.78	314.06	314.32	314.59	314.86	315.13
349.99	350.30	350.60	350.90	351.20	351.50	351.81	352.11	352.41	352.71	353.01	353.31	353.61	353.92	354.21	354.52
388.88	389.22	389.56	389.89	390.22	390.56	390.90	391.23	391.57	391.90	392.23	392.57	392.90	393.24	393.57	393.91

21 Degrees.

45	46	47	48	49	50	51	52	53	54	55	56	57	58	59	60
0.40	0.40	0.40	0.40	0.40	0.40	0.40	0.40	0.40	0.40	0.40	0.40	0.40	0.40	0.40	0.40
0.80	0.80	0.80	0.80	0.80	0.80	0.80	0.80	0.80	0.80	0.80	0.80	0.81	0.81	0.81	0.81
1.20	1.20	1.20	1.20	1.20	1.20	1.20	1.20	1.20	1.21	1.21	1.21	1.21	1.21	1.21	1.21
1.60	1.60	1.60	1.60	1.60	1.60	1.60	1.61	1.61	1.61	1.61	1.61	1.61	1.61	1.61	1.62
1.99	2.00	2.00	2.00	2.00	2.00	2.00	2.01	2.01	2.01	2.01	2.01	2.02	2.02	2.02	2.02
2.39	2.40	2.40	2.40	2.40	2.40	2.41	2.41	2.41	2.41	2.41	2.42	2.42	2.42	2.42	2.42
2.79	2.80	2.80	2.80	2.80	2.80	2.81	2.81	2.81	2.81	2.81	2.82	2.82	2.82	2.83	2.83
3.19	3.19	3.20	3.20	3.20	3.21	3.21	3.21	3.21	3.22	3.22	3.22	3.22	3.23	3.23	3.23
3.59	3.59	3.60	3.60	3.60	3.61	3.61	3.61	3.61	3.62	3.62	3.62	3.63	3.63	3.63	3.64
3.99	3.99	4.00	4.00	4.00	4.01	4.01	4.01	4.02	4.02	4.02	4.03	4.03	4.03	4.04	4.04
7.98	7.99	8.00	8.00	8.00	8.01	8.02	8.03	8.03	8.04	8.05	8.05	8.06	8.07	8.07	8.08
11.97	11.98	11.99	12.00	12.01	12.02	12.03	12.04	12.05	12.06	12.07	12.08	12.09	12.10	12.11	12.12
15.96	15.97	15.99	16.00	16.01	16.03	16.04	16.05	16.07	16.08	16.09	16.11	16.12	16.13	16.15	16.16
19.95	19.97	19.98	20.00	20.02	20.03	20.05	20.07	20.08	20.10	20.12	20.13	20.15	20.17	20.18	20.20
23.94	23.96	23.98	24.00	24.02	24.04	24.06	24.08	24.10	24.12	24.14	24.16	24.18	24.20	24.22	24.24
27.93	27.95	27.97	28.00	28.02	28.05	28.07	28.09	28.12	28.14	28.16	28.19	28.21	28.23	28.26	28.28
31.92	31.94	31.97	32.00	32.02	32.05	32.08	32.11	32.13	32.16	32.19	32.21	32.24	32.27	32.30	32.32
35.91	35.94	35.97	36.00	36.03	36.06	36.09	36.12	36.15	36.18	36.21	36.24	36.27	36.30	36.33	36.36
39.90	39.93	39.96	40.00	40.03	40.07	40.10	40.13	40.17	40.20	40.23	40.27	40.30	40.34	40.37	40.40
79.79	79.86	79.93	79.99	80.06	80.13	80.20	80.26	80.33	80.40	80.47	80.53	80.60	80.67	80.74	80.81
119.69	119.79	119.89	119.99	120.09	120.20	120.30	120.40	120.50	120.60	120.70	120.80	120.90	121.01	121.11	121.21
159.58	159.72	159.85	159.99	160.12	160.26	160.40	160.53	160.66	160.80	160.93	161.07	161.20	161.34	161.48	161.61
199.48	199.65	199.82	199.99	200.16	200.33	200.50	200.66	200.83	201.00	201.17	201.34	201.51	201.68	201.85	202.02
239.38	239.58	239.78	239.98	240.19	240.40	240.59	240.79	241.00	241.20	241.40	241.61	241.81	242.01	242.21	242.42
279.27	279.51	279.74	279.98	280.22	280.46	280.69	280.92	281.16	281.40	281.63	281.87	282.11	282.35	282.58	282.82
319.17	319.44	319.70	319.98	320.25	320.52	320.79	321.06	321.33	321.60	321.86	322.14	322.41	322.68	322.95	323.22
359.06	359.37	359.67	359.97	360.28	360.59	360.89	361.19	361.49	361.80	362.10	362.40	362.71	363.02	363.32	363.63
398.96	399.30	399.63	399.97	400.31	400.65	400.99	401.32	401.66	402.00	402.33	402.67	403.01	403.35	403.69	404.03

22 Degrees.

Minutes	0	1	2	3	4	5	6	7	8	9	10	11	12	13	14
Dist. in ft.															
1	0.40	0.40	0.40	0.41	0.41	0.41	0.41	0.41	0.41	0.41	0.41	0.41	0.41	0.41	0.41
2	0.81	0.81	0.81	0.81	0.81	0.81	0.81	0.81	0.81	0.81	0.81	0.82	0.82	0.82	0.82
3	1.21	1.21	1.21	1.22	1.22	1.22	1.22	1.22	1.22	1.22	1.22	1.22	1.22	1.23	1.23
4	1.62	1.62	1.62	1.62	1.62	1.62	1.62	1.63	1.63	1.63	1.63	1.63	1.63	1.63	1.63
5	2.02	2.02	2.02	2.03	2.03	2.03	2.03	2.03	2.03	2.04	2.04	2.04	2.04	2.04	2.04
6	2.42	2.43	2.43	2.43	2.43	2.44	2.44	2.44	2.44	2.44	2.45	2.45	2.45	2.45	2.45
7	2.83	2.83	2.83	2.84	2.84	2.84	2.84	2.84	2.85	2.85	2.85	2.85	2.86	2.86	2.86
8	3.23	3.23	3.24	3.24	3.24	3.25	3.25	3.25	3.25	3.26	3.26	3.26	3.26	3.27	3.27
9	3.64	3.64	3.64	3.65	3.65	3.65	3.65	3.66	3.66	3.66	3.67	3.67	3.67	3.68	3.68
10	4.04	4.04	4.04	4.05	4.05	4.05	4.06	4.06	4.07	4.07	4.07	4.08	4.08	4.08	4.08
20	8.08	8.09	8.09	8.10	8.11	8.11	8.12	8.13	8.13	8.14	8.15	8.16	8.16	8.17	8.18
30	12.12	12.13	12.14	12.15	12.16	12.17	12.18	12.19	12.20	12.21	12.22	12.23	12.24	12.25	12.26
40	16.16	16.17	16.19	16.20	16.22	16.23	16.24	16.26	16.27	16.28	16.30	16.31	16.32	16.34	16.35
50	20.20	20.22	20.24	20.25	20.27	20.29	20.30	20.32	20.34	20.35	20.37	20.39	20.40	20.42	20.44
60	24.24	24.26	24.28	24.30	24.32	24.34	24.36	24.38	24.40	24.42	24.44	24.47	24.49	24.51	24.53
70	28.28	28.31	28.33	28.35	28.38	28.40	28.42	28.45	28.47	28.49	28.52	28.54	28.57	28.59	28.61
80	32.32	32.35	32.38	32.40	32.43	32.46	32.48	32.51	32.54	32.57	32.59	32.62	32.65	32.67	32.70
90	36.36	36.39	36.42	36.45	36.48	36.51	36.55	36.58	36.61	36.64	36.67	36.70	36.73	36.76	36.79
100	40.40	40.44	40.47	40.50	40.54	40.57	40.61	40.64	40.67	40.71	40.74	40.78	40.81	40.84	40.88
200	80.81	80.87	80.94	81.01	81.08	81.14	81.21	81.28	81.35	81.41	81.48	81.55	81.62	81.69	81.75
300	121.21	121.31	121.41	121.51	121.61	121.72	121.82	121.92	122.02	122.12	122.22	122.33	122.43	122.53	122.63
400	161.61	161.75	161.88	162.02	162.15	162.29	162.42	162.56	162.69	162.83	162.96	163.10	163.24	163.37	163.51
500	202.02	202.19	202.35	202.52	202.69	202.86	203.03	203.20	203.37	203.54	203.71	203.88	204.05	204.22	204.39
600	242.42	242.62	242.82	243.02	243.23	243.43	243.63	243.84	244.04	244.24	244.45	244.65	244.85	245.06	245.26
700	282.82	283.06	283.29	283.53	283.77	284.00	284.24	284.48	284.71	284.95	285.19	285.43	285.66	285.90	286.14
800	323.22	323.50	323.76	324.03	324.30	324.58	324.85	325.12	325.38	325.66	325.93	326.20	326.47	326.74	327.02
900	363.43	363.98	364.23	364.54	364.84	365.15	365.45	365.76	366.06	366.36	366.66	366.98	367.28	367.59	367.90
1000	404.03	404.37	404.70	405.04	405.38	405.72	406.06	406.40	406.73	407.07	407.41	407.75	408.09	408.43	408.77

22 Degrees.

15	16	17	18	19	20	21	22	23	24	25	26	27	28	29	30
0.41	0.41	0.41	0.41	0.41	0.41	0.41	0.41	0.41	0.41	0.41	0.41	0.41	0.41	0.41	0.41
0.82	0.82	0.82	0.82	0.82	0.82	0.82	0.82	0.82	0.82	0.83	0.83	0.83	0.83	0.83	0.83
1.23	1.23	1.23	1.23	1.23	1.23	1.23	1.23	1.24	1.24	1.24	1.24	1.24	1.24	1.24	1.24
1.64	1.64	1.64	1.64	1.64	1.64	1.64	1.65	1.65	1.65	1.65	1.65	1.65	1.65	1.66	1.66
2.05	2.05	2.05	2.05	2.05	2.05	2.06	2.06	2.06	2.06	2.06	2.06	2.07	2.07	2.07	2.07
2.45	2.46	2.46	2.46	2.46	2.46	2.47	2.47	2.47	2.47	2.48	2.48	2.48	2.48	2.48	2.49
2.86	2.87	2.87	2.87	2.87	2.88	2.88	2.88	2.88	2.89	2.89	2.89	2.89	2.89	2.90	2.90
3.27	3.28	3.28	3.28	3.28	3.29	3.29	3.29	3.29	3.30	3.30	3.30	3.31	3.31	3.31	3.31
3.68	3.69	3.69	3.69	3.69	3.70	3.70	3.70	3.71	3.71	3.71	3.71	3.72	3.72	3.72	3.73
4.09	4.09	4.10	4.10	4.10	4.11	4.11	4.11	4.12	4.12	4.13	4.13	4.13	4.14	4.14	4.14
8.18	8.19	8.20	8.20	8.21	8.22	8.22	8.23	8.24	8.24	8.25	8.26	8.26	8.27	8.28	8.28
12.27	12.28	12.29	12.30	12.31	12.32	12.33	12.34	12.35	12.37	12.38	12.39	12.40	12.41	12.42	12.43
16.36	16.38	16.39	16.41	16.42	16.43	16.45	16.46	16.47	16.49	16.50	16.51	16.53	16.54	16.55	16.57
20.46	20.47	20.49	20.51	20.52	20.54	20.56	20.57	20.59	20.61	20.63	20.64	20.66	20.68	20.69	20.71
24.55	24.57	24.59	24.61	24.63	24.65	24.67	24.69	24.71	24.73	24.75	24.77	24.79	24.81	24.83	24.85
28.64	28.66	28.69	28.71	28.73	28.76	28.78	28.80	28.83	28.85	28.88	28.90	28.92	28.95	28.97	28.99
32.73	32.76	32.78	32.81	32.83	32.86	32.89	32.92	32.95	32.97	33.00	33.03	33.06	33.08	33.11	33.14
36.82	36.85	36.88	36.91	36.94	36.97	37.00	37.03	37.06	37.10	37.13	37.16	37.19	37.22	37.25	37.28
40.91	40.95	40.98	41.01	41.05	41.08	41.12	41.15	41.18	41.22	41.25	41.29	41.32	41.35	41.39	41.42
81.82	81.89	81.96	82.03	82.09	82.16	82.23	82.30	82.37	82.43	82.50	82.57	82.64	82.71	82.77	82.84
122.73	122.84	122.94	123.04	123.14	123.24	123.35	123.45	123.55	123.65	123.75	123.86	123.96	124.06	124.16	124.26
163.64	163.78	163.92	164.05	164.19	164.32	164.46	164.60	164.73	164.87	165.00	165.14	165.28	165.41	165.55	165.68
204.56	204.73	204.90	205.07	205.24	205.41	205.58	205.75	205.92	206.09	206.26	206.43	206.60	206.77	206.94	207.11
245.47	245.67	245.87	246.08	246.28	246.49	246.69	246.89	247.10	247.30	247.51	247.71	247.91	248.12	248.32	248.53
286.38	286.62	286.85	287.09	287.33	287.57	287.81	288.04	288.28	288.52	288.76	289.00	289.23	289.47	289.71	289.95
327.29	327.56	327.88	328.10	328.38	328.65	328.92	329.19	329.46	329.74	330.01	330.28	330.55	330.82	331.10	331.37
368.20	368.51	368.81	369.12	369.42	369.73	370.04	370.34	370.65	370.95	371.26	371.57	371.87	372.18	372.48	372.79
409.11	409.45	409.79	410.13	410.47	410.81	411.15	411.49	411.83	412.17	412.51	412.85	413.19	413.53	413.87	414.21